I have enjoyed all ⟨
to Save may be the de
- Katy C.

MW00627444

Reading a new book by Carol Moncado is like getting together again with a bunch of old friends to find out what's new in their lives. Her newest release, Grace to Save, fits right in there...Get ready for a good read as you find out more about old friends. Now I need to get back to the housework I neglected to finish reading, Travis, Cassie, & Abi's story!
- Margaret N.

I love a good romance and this one is good with a whole lot more...I loved the story and how the author weaves Serenity Landing into all her stories. Her characters are old friends who pop in for a visit now and then. We see God's redemption and love throughout the book.
- Linda R.

What a read! Moncado brought a lot of emotions into Grace to Save...trauma of 9/11, bad decisions, inability to forgive, abandonment, romance, and then soooo many consequences. I sooooo love the way that this author is so great at weaving Serenity Landing and the people that we know and love from other stories into each of her books!
- R. H.

Discovering Home

Serenity Landing Second Chances 1

Carol Moncado

USA Today Bestselling Author

This is a work of fiction set in a fictionalized southwest Missouri and a redrawn, fictionalized Europe. Any resemblance to real events or to actual persons, living or dead, is coincidental. Any reference to historical figures, places, or events, whether fictional or actual, is a fictional representation.

Scripture taken from the Holy Bible, King James Version.

Cover photos:
People: goodluz/depositphotos.com
Yarn pops(courtesy of Show Me Yarn): CANDID Publications, 2016
Author photo: Captivating by Keli, 2010

First edition, CANDID Publications, 2016

ISBN-10: 1-944408-94-0
ISBN-13: 978-1-944408-94-7

Chapter One

Movement in the woods to the left of the gate caught Jonathan Langley-Cranston's eye.

Seeing a wild animal there wasn't unusual. He lived in the country. It went with the territory.

But something about this shadow was different.

He moved the gearstick out of first into neutral and set the parking brake.

Moving slowly, he tried to avoid the mud puddles. The shadow skittered to another tree, drawing him further in. He swore under his breath as his foot, in a brand new Bruno Magli shoe, slipped into a puddle just big enough to soak it all.

A few more steps and he found the shadow huddled against a tree. Reaching down, he tried to pick up the animal, but the pile of fur seemed to shrink back even further. Jonathan used his foot to sort of trap the little thing against the tree, blocking its means of escape and finally managing to get his hands on the trembling ball of hair.

He half expected a bark or growl, but instead heard only whimpering. Caring less about his suit than his shoes, he pulled the small dog closer.

"Hey, little fella," he crooned. "It's okay. I've got you." The black fur was so shaggy Jonathan couldn't see the dog's eyes. "Let's get you inside. It's too wet and cold for you to be out here."

July in the Missouri Ozarks was a study in contrasts. One year hot enough to be mistaken for the Sahara. The next comparatively frigid. This was a frigid year. Though nothing like it would be in a few months, the night before had been jeans and sweatshirt cool.

He wasn't nearly as careful going back to his car. His shoes were already ruined, but the suit could be cleaned. Climbing into the low-slung 2017 Ford Mustang, he gently settled the dog onto the passenger seat, but for all his fear, the animal scampered back over onto Jonathan's lap. He snuggled close even as he practically vibrated in fear.

Pressing the button on his visor, Jonathan put the car back in gear and eased through the gate as it opened. The winding drive didn't take long, and in just a couple minutes, he pulled into the garage. Holding the shaking mass of wet fur close, Jonathan went into the house and set him on a towel on the kitchen counter.

Now what?

"Is there something you need to tell me, sir?"

Jonathan turned to see George, his butler and all-around-right-hand-man, walking into the kitchen. "He was outside the gate."

"He, sir?"

The quivering mass of fur whimpered again. "I guess it could be a she. I haven't looked yet."

"Probably covered in fleas and ticks."

He hadn't thought about that, but it made sense. "Most

likely." Options flooded through his mind. "Would you watch him or her for a minute while I change? Then we'll get him a bath and take a picture or two to put online in case someone's missing him."

The look on George's face told Jonathan what he thought the chances of that were. About the same Jonathan did. Someone had dumped this poor dog in the woods near Serenity Lake. Jonathan toed off his shoes and kicked them into the mud room before stripping his socks off and holding them with one finger and his thumb. "Weigh him on the kitchen scale for me?" Jonathan called as he headed for the stairs. "Can't imagine he'll break it."

George muttered a response, but Jonathan couldn't hear it clearly. He could figure out the gist though. There would be no weighing on the kitchen scale.

It only took a couple minutes to change into an old pair of jeans and a t-shirt that had seen better days. When he made it back downstairs with a giant fluffy towel in his hand, the two hadn't moved at all, though George held his phone.

"You would do well to wash him in Dawn dish detergent, sir. Let it soak for about fifteen minutes to kill the fleas. It may or may not help with the ticks, too."

"And you decided not to do it yourself?" Jonathan kept his chuckle to himself, more or less.

"I didn't want to deprive you of the privilege."

Jonathan scooped the dog up carefully and set him in the deep sink before pulling the dish soap from underneath. Once the water warmed up to a reasonable level, he used the wand to rinse as much of the dirt and mud off as he could. After working the dish soap into the fur, Jonathan wrapped the whole bubbly mess in the towel and held him - definitely a him - close to his chest.

"It's all right, bud. We'll get you taken care of." Jonathan wasn't up on guesstimating weights, but if he had to bet, he'd say this dog weighed maybe four pounds, five tops, and half of that was probably fur. For fifteen minutes, he tried to comfort the little thing before putting him back in the sink and rinsing him again with warm water.

Fleas and ticks both swirled down the drain, along with more dirt, mud, and suds. Jonathan washed him twice more like that before the water seemed to run mostly clear. With the dog wrapped up in a dry towel, Jonathan went into the living room to figure out his plan.

"You are *not* sitting on my couches like that, sir." George appeared out of nowhere.

Jonathan rolled his eyes and headed for the stairs. The dog was clean enough to put on the floor in his room for a few minutes while he changed again.

He texted a couple of friends to see if they could recommend a vet. In just a couple minutes, he heard back from one of them who used one of the top vets in the area - and who happened to be open late. Armed with directions, he took off, this time in his Toyota Tundra. It could handle the dirt better than his Mustang.

He didn't call ahead, just prayed that they would take pity on this poor dog. And him. He didn't know what else to do.

The clinic was across the street from two of the Serenity Landing elementary schools. Only two other cars were in the lot, and when he walked in, he could tell they were wrapping things up.

"Can I help you, sir?"

He held the small guy a little closer. "I found this dog in the woods a couple hours ago. I didn't know you were open, or I would have come straight here. I know I don't have an appointment, but I'd appreciate some help."

The front desk gal came around and reached for the dog. "Come here, sweetheart," she crooned. "Did someone lose you?"

"I don't think so. I've already given him like three baths with Dawn dish soap." He pulled out his phone and showed her a picture. "I know he doesn't look a ton better, but he's cleaner at least. I didn't see him until today, but I'd guess he's been out there a while."

"Probably," she said, using an almost baby voice. "Let's get the vet to take a look at you."

Nearly an hour later, well after closing time, Jonathan left with the still-scared dog in his arms. He also had varied medicines, the knowledge that he didn't have a microchip, and a shopping list. After deliberating on the ninety second drive to Walmart, he decided to look like a dork and carry a blanket in with him. No one would notice the dog inside it. Not something he'd normally do, but desperate times and all.

Once the dog and blanket were snuggled in the seat of the cart, he bee-lined for the back of the store and the pet area. Dry dog food. Wet dog food. A dog bed. A crate. Collar. Leash.

"Hey! I know you!"

Jonathan turned at the sound of a little girl's voice. No more than four or five, the girl practically bounced on her toes. He smiled but didn't say anything.

"You danced with me!"

"Lorelai," her mother reprimanded. "Leave the nice man alone."

"But he danced with me! And let me see at Mrs. Ginger's wedding."

Jonathan glanced up at the mother and remembered. He definitely remembered her, though he'd never known her name. "That's right." He knelt down. "You sat with me for the whole wedding, didn't you? And you let me have your first dance." He winked at her. "I remember it very well."

He also remembered the dance with her mother.

The girl's attention turned to the cart, her eyes wide. "Do you have a doggy in your cart?" she whispered. "Doggies aren't supposed to be in the store."

Jonathan looked over to see the blanket wiggling. "I know. But I found this dog out in the woods a little while ago, and we just left the vet. He's super scared so I didn't want to leave him alone in the truck."

"Can I pet him?"

He winced. "Not right now. He's sick, and I wouldn't want you to catch it. Besides, he doesn't think he looks very handsome at the moment. He needs a haircut but can't get one until he's all better."

"I think he's handsome." Only his nose was showing.

"Lorelai, it's time to go." Her mother pushed the cart toward the food section of the store.

"Are you gonna get him clothes?"

"Should I?" He had never thought to dress a dog. That was a froo-froo girl thing to do. But he wouldn't turn this little girl down.

She reached for an outfit hanging there. "He needs this one." Camouflaged with hunter orange trim. Perfect.

"Let's find his size, then." They looked through until they found an extra-small. "He only weighs about four pounds you know."

Lorelai's eyes went wide. "That's little. I weighed six pounds when I was born."

"That's pretty little, too." Wasn't it? What did he know?

"Six and a half," her mother interjected. "And it's time to go."

"You better listen to your mother." He pulled his wallet out and handed over one of his business cards. "If your mom will email me, I'll send you some pictures after he gets all cleaned up, okay?"

Lorelai took it and nodded eagerly. "Does he have a name yet?"

"Nope."

She cocked her head, blond hair falling over one shoulder. "Mr. Benny Hercules."

"Mr. Benny Hercules?" Not Fido? Rex? And Hercules? Really?

"Yep."

He chuckled. "All right. Mr. Benny Hercules it is."

She held the card in both hands. "Please email him, Mommy?"

Her mom sighed and nodded. "Fine."

Here was his chance. "Can I know your name so I know whose email to expect?"

"Kenzie Ann!" Lorelai practically shouted. "Unless she's in trouble with Papaw. Then he uses her whole name."

Jonathan met Kenzie's gorgeous hazel eyes. "A pleasure to meet you, Kenzie Ann."

"Just Kenzie is fine." She looked at the card in Lorelai's hand. "Jon."

He winced and held out a hand. "Jonathan. My mother was very insistent about that. I should probably get over it, but I haven't yet."

When she didn't take it, he let his arm drop back to his side. "I'll email you later, Jonathan." She looked down at her daughter. "We've got to get going, Lorelai."

The two walked off, but Lorelai turned back and waved. "Bye, Mr. Jonathan! I can't wait for pictures of Mr. Benny Hercules!"

He watched them walk off, then picked up a couple other things he thought he might need and headed home.

If MacKenzie Annette Davidson heard one more word about Mr. Jonathan and Mr. Benny Hercules, she'd snap.

"Lorelai, honey, I think it's time to talk about something else." Anything else. Any*one* else.

Because when her daughter mentioned Jonathan William Langley-Cranston IV, all Kenzie could do was remember the breathless feeling of dancing in his arms. She'd known who he was even then and couldn't help but refer to him by his full name like the media tended to do. She'd nearly choked calling him Jon.

"But you'll email him, right?"

"Yes." She had no choice. Her daughter wouldn't leave her alone if she didn't.

Rain pelted her windshield, but no matter how fast the wipers went, they couldn't quite keep up. Not when they desperately needed replacing. She'd hoped to beat the rain home, but no such luck. Her weak high beams barely sliced through the darkness of the back country road that led to home. She took the last turn, still half a mile from her little house and screamed as the wheels lost contact with the pavement. The whole thing couldn't have lasted more than a few seconds, but to Kenzie, it seemed an eternity before the car came to a stop slanted sideways.

In the ditch.

"Are you okay?" Her first movement was to turn on the overhead light and check on her daughter.

Wide eyes met hers as Lorelai nodded.

"Thank you, Jesus," Kenzie whispered. "Okay, stay put, all right, sweetheart?"

Lorelai nodded again. After a few more deep breaths, Kenzie dug her umbrella out of the pocket in the door and opened it, but the water sloshed inside the car as the virtual river ran off the road. She changed her mind and closed the door again.

"Okay, God," she whispered. "Now what?" It was her own

fault, because she'd forgotten how the water built up and ran through this particular corner. A list of people who might be able to help sped through her head. She dismissed them all. Her parents were out of town. Friends had cars worse than hers or small kids of their own.

"Mama, could Mr. Jonathan help us?"

"How could he help?"

"He has a truck."

He had said that, hadn't he? "I don't know how to get a hold of him." Could the two of them walk home? It wasn't far, but it was dark and pouring rain.

"His card."

Right. "I don't think it had his phone number on it." She hadn't looked at it that closely.

"It has numbers," Lorelai insisted, as stubborn as her mother.

She pulled her phone out of her purse as Lorelai handed the card to her. Sure enough. A phone number. But did she dare call him? There were so many reasons not to, not the least of which was that she barely knew him.

"Please, Mama."

Kenzie turned to see tears filling her daughter's eyes, fear had to be creeping into her daughter's heart.

"Remember 2 Timothy 1:7?" They'd memorized it. "What shouldn't we have?"

Lorelai took a deep breath, and Kenzie could see her attitude change. "Fear. God's angels are protecting us."

"That's right." And it made her decision for her. Carefully, she punched in the numbers and waited for someone to answer, unsure of what to pray for. An answer or not.

"Hello?" She could hear the puzzle in his voice.

"Can I speak to Jonathan, please?"

"This is him."

"This is Kenzie. My daughter, Lorelai, and I ran into you at the store a little while ago."

"I remember." His voice warmed. "What's up?"

A tear streaked down her cheek. "I need help, and I don't know where else to turn."

"Okay." Caution. Given his identity and the money that went with it, he likely got hit up for "help" all the time.

"My car skidded off the road, and we're stuck in a ditch." She rushed through her explanation. "Home isn't far, but I could really use some help getting there."

"Let me get a few things together, and I'll leave in like three minutes. Where are you?"

She gave him directions.

"I know where that is. It'll probably take me about twenty minutes. Are you safe?"

"I think so. There's not much past this point in the road except our house."

"What about flash flooding?"

"I've never seen the road as bad as it is now." Surely it wouldn't get any worse until he got there, right?

"Okay. I'm calling a friend who may be able to get there more quickly, but I'll be there as soon as I can."

"Thanks." He hung up before she could say anything else. "He's on his way."

"I like Mr. Jonathan."

"I know you do." Probably too much, especially given the little they knew about him.

For the next twenty minutes, they sang songs and did everything she could think of to keep her daughter's mind off the fact that they were stuck in a ditch. Bright lights cut through the darkness as a black SUV drove very slowly through the water, careful to avoid splashing the car. Flashers turned on as he came to a stop a few feet further down the road.

A small, powerful flashlight shown into the car. "Are you all right?" Jonathan called.

Kenzie nodded.

"Do you want to help me get Lorelai out first?" he asked.

She nodded again. The way the car was situated, the back door was higher out of the water.

"Get your stuff together, anything you want to take, just in case, and we'll get it in my car."

He reached for Lorelai and tucked her close as he took a couple large steps up the embankment and settled her in his SUV. It took several more trips to get everything out - paperwork in the glove box, a book of CDs, Lorelai's organizer that fit over the back of Kenzie's seat and held a myriad of indispensable items, and Lorelai's booster seat.

Then, before Kenzie could get out on her own, Jonathan was there, again, holding out a hand to help her. His strong hand gripped her forearm as she held onto his for dear life.

She had underestimated the strength of the current, and therefore, his strength, because he acted like it was nothing. In a minute, they were both in the front seat of his vehicle. Despite the summer month, he had the heat blasting, and she was grateful.

"Now, where to?"

She directed him to their house, but when she turned to tell Lorelai to get ready to run for it, the little girl was already asleep.

"I'll get her. You head on inside." Jonathan's quiet voice reassured her.

"Thank you." What would she have done if he hadn't come to her rescue?

The front door locks stuck worse than usual, and she had to force the door open. Something stopped her in her tracks, even before she turned the light on.

"What is it?"

She glanced back to see Jonathan holding a trash bag of things from her car. He'd thought ahead and brought some bags to keep stuff dry.

"I'm not sure." Kenzie took a step inside, and her heart sank.

Squish.

Another step.

Squish.

She wanted to remain in denial, but she couldn't. Not for much longer. Dread filled her as she pulled her phone out. It took three tries to get the flashlight turned on. The couch looked normal, though she wished Jonathan wasn't about to see their ever-so-humble abode. Or that they slept on bunk beds in the single bedroom. She moved the light, taking a deep breath, and then looked at the floor.

As she suspected, the area around the door was soaking wet, but why?

She looked at the ceiling.

And there it was.

Bubbles full of water, dripping down in several places all over the living area.

Steeling herself, she looked at the floor more closely.

Over an inch of water stood on the other end of the slightly sloping floor.

They wouldn't be able to stay here.

And they had nowhere else to go.

Chapter Two

Jonathan looked around the living room with only Kenzie's flashlight to help him see. What he could see didn't look good.

Deep inside, he knew she needed someone to help. "Okay. First things first, we don't turn on the lights. Good call waiting a minute." He didn't give her a chance to reply. "Second, we fill up my SUV with everything we can. Get all the important stuff like computers or pictures, favorite blankets and stuffed animals, anything irreplaceable. Then we fill it to the brim with everything else we can. Is all the furniture yours or did it come furnished?" Hadn't she said she was renting?

"It came furnished." He could hear the shock in her voice.

"Okay. Then is there any furniture that's yours that you want to get out of here?"

She pointed toward a door. "The rocking chair in the bedroom was my great-grandmother's."

His first stop was to put the bag back in the SUV and grab

the roll of trash bags. He handed it to her. "Start filling these with clothes or whatever else you want to take. Use the clothes to wrap up anything breakable like picture frames." She took them and seemed to do what he asked while he went to get the rocking chair.

Bunk beds? Was this the only bedroom? And had he thought through what he was going to do once they left?

He pulled his phone out and called his nearest neighbor again. Josh Wilson hadn't answered earlier but did this time. He would send a couple of people over to help - along with a couple more vehicles. Sure enough, in less than five minutes, three of his employees and three SUVs would be on their way. The rocking chair went into his, though.

"Who were you talking to?" Kenzie came into the bedroom with a trash bag already open.

"A friend of mine. He's sending some people to help us and some vehicles to make sure there's plenty of room to load everything."

"I don't have anywhere to take it all."

"You're coming to my place." She started to protest, but he held up a hand. "Don't. I have plenty of room for both of you and all your stuff. In fact, I'll have Josh's employees and a couple of mine working tonight to make sure there's as little residual water damage as possible to any of it. There are three dryers in my house, I don't know why, since my cousin and I are the only ones living in the house, and she just moved in, but there are."

With his flashlight, he could see tears finally coming down her cheeks. "I can't let you do that. Just take us to the hotel in town."

Jonathan let it drop for the moment, but he would do his best to get her to take him up on his offer. They wouldn't let her take all this stuff into the hotel anyway.

By the time the other vehicles arrived, everything she wanted to take had been loaded into black trash bags. In fact, it almost all fit into the back of his SUV after all.

"Okay, let these guys know what your priorities are as far as anything else that goes, and I'll get you and Lorelai somewhere warm and dry."

Using one of his mini-flashlights this time, Kenzie gave a few directions to CJ, one of Josh's employees. If he had to bet, Jonathan imagined all the furniture would be loaded up and moved out, too. There were two trailers brought along, likely for just such a purpose.

Once back in his SUV, he drove carefully along the road until after they passed her car. He didn't ask, but headed for his house.

"I told you the hotel would be fine."

"It would," he conceded. "But my place is free, and there's no issue with a bunch of trash bags full of stuff that needs drying." He came to a stop at the sign for State Highway ZZ. "I have a ton of room. You two can have your own suite tonight, and tomorrow, I'll have someone clean the guest apartment and you two can live there until you figure something else out. It has an entrance from the house you can use, but I won't. Not without knocking and you letting me in. I'd let you stay there tonight, but the water's turned off right now for some renovations. I think they're almost done." They weren't nearly done, but last he'd checked, they were doing it piece by piece and would never be more than a day or two from a good stopping point.

He stayed at the stop sign until she finally gave a nod. "Fine."

"Plus, you're going to have to deal with insurance for your car, and you'll need something to drive. I have a bunch of options, so you don't have to worry about that either."

She just stared out the window as he turned south toward Serenity Lake. Ten minutes later, he pressed the buttons to open first the gate and then the garage.

"What do you need tonight?"

Kenzie held up a bag. "I put everything we needed in here since I wasn't sure I'd be able to get to it anywhere else."

Jonathan opened the back door and reached in to unbuckle Lorelai.

"Mr. Jonathan?" Her sleepy voice betrayed her confusion.

"I've got you, sweetheart." He picked her up and settled her across his body. "You're going to sleep at my house tonight, okay?"

"'Kay."

She was already drifting back to sleep. When he turned he saw Kenzie just sort of staring at the doors to the house.

"That one." He nodded toward the closest one. "That goes to the kitchen."

He followed her through and motioned toward the stairs.

Whimpering and whining greeted him, but he'd worry about the dog in a minute. "I'll show you where you two can sleep tonight."

His first inclination was to give them the suite across the hall from his, but he sensed that might not be the best way to win Kenzie's trust. Instead, he pointed out his room as they walked past, just so she'd know where it was, and then continued further to another suite. He laid Lorelai on the bed, over Kenzie's protests that she was a mess.

"It's fine. She'll be fine," he assured her in a whisper. "Now, let's get you something warm to drink." He started for the kitchen. "Coffee or hot chocolate?"

Overwhelmed, Kenzie couldn't do anything but follow Jonathan back down the hallway and into the kitchen. "Um, hot chocolate is fine."

He opened a cabinet and pulled out an individual K-cup to put into the Keurig. Fancy. In just a few seconds, it was gurgling and spitting out chocolate. In a couple more minutes, she took the offered whipped cream, mini-marshmallows, and chocolate syrup. As she doctored it, using far more than she normally would because it had been just that kind of night, Jonathan started for the stairs again.

"I'll be right back." Before she could say anything, he was gone.

Great.

Once she had her mug fixed just the way she wanted it, Kenzie wasn't sure what she was supposed to do. Finally, she decided wandering around would be okay. In the living room, she found a bunch of pictures on the wall and looked through them. Family photos, including photos with assorted famous people. There was definitely an age progression. More recent pictures showed people she recognized but couldn't place.

"Please tell me you didn't see the pictures when I was little."

Kenzie turned to see him standing there with that little dog tucked in his arms. She shrugged. "I guess." She pointed to a picture of him with a beautiful woman. "Who's that? She looks familiar."

He came to stand next to her. "That is Queen Adeline of Montevaro."

She blinked. Twice. "A queen?"

"Yep. She attended Serenity Landing University. We had a bunch of classes together. Even dated for a while, though we both knew she wasn't in love with me. She was in love with a guy her father and Parliament didn't think was good enough for her. He saved her life, his parents found an ancient treasure, and suddenly Parliament was okay with him. We'd already ended things officially by then though."

"So you dated a queen?" She didn't even begin to know what to do with that information.

"She wasn't a queen yet," he protested.

"Close enough." She tilted her head to look closer. "Wasn't her father in an accident or something with the President?" Hadn't she seen that on the news?

"The First Family was skiing with her parents when he had a skiing accident. It was all over the news for a couple weeks. Then she married a guy from Serenity Landing. In fact, his cousin, who grew up here, married her brother."

"Wow. Did you date the cousin, too?" Sarcasm seeped out. And where did that question come from?

"I didn't...date...her."

Kenzie glanced over. "You don't sound too sure."

"We went to dinner and stuff a couple times, but never real dates. I was her plus one to the wedding where you and I first met." He winced. "I did kiss her once, though."

"Right." Because she was a princess now. "So you dated a girl before she was a princess and a princess before she became queen. Any other royalty?"

He didn't answer, and she turned to look at him, pain visible on his face this time. With one hand, he scratched the dog's head. "I dated Addie's sister. Princess Anastasia of Montevaro."

"I take it she wasn't in love with some guy?" *Please don't have been in love with her!* The thought surprised Kenzie. So did her breathless anticipation of the answer.

Jonathan didn't answer for a moment. "I thought I loved her. I think we could have had a successful relationship, even though she was in love with someone else at the time. I know how odd that sounds, but he didn't value what she brought to the table the same way I did. I think she could have fallen for me, that we could have been good together, if he hadn't come around. She was there for me when I needed someone most, in a way no one else was."

"I see."

He sighed. "Not really. I've not ever talked to anyone about my relationship with Ana. Not really."

"Are you still in love with her?"

Jonathan shook his head. "She's married. They adopted a little girl, and when I talked to her the other day, she hinted they might be having another child soon."

"That doesn't answer the question. 'Are you still in love with her' has nothing to do with her relationship status."

"I know." He stared at the picture. "I don't think I am. I haven't seen her in ages, though we do talk occasionally about some charity work we're both involved in. She asks for updates about my brother, but there never are any. I haven't really dated anyone since she dumped me, though. Not seriously."

Kenzie didn't know what to do with most of that information. His brother? She felt like she should know what he was talking about.

She heard him take a deep breath and blow it out. "So that's my dating history in the last few years. I dated a bunch of girls who were in love with other guys. I haven't been brave enough to put myself out there since. Not really. A couple of blind dates to get some friends off my back, but that's it." There was something about how he said "friends" that made her wonder about what kind of friends those were.

"I'm sorry." She didn't know what else to say. What else could she say? Except no if he ever asked her out. Not that he would.

"I checked on Lorelai when I was upstairs. She's still out."

Kenzietook a long sip of her drink. "Thank you for your help tonight. I don't know what I would have done if you hadn't answered your phone."

"I have no doubt you would have figured something out. I have a feeling you're incredibly resourceful."

"I try to be." But she wouldn't have been able to go anywhere else if he hadn't answered. They would have made it to the house then been stuck with all that water.

"You're raising a little girl by yourself. You can't help but be strong." He tilted his head toward the seating area. "Have a seat."

She sat in one of the big chairs while he sat on the sofa. He didn't look at her when he spoke again. "We need to talk."

Chapter Three

*J*onathan hadn't opened up to anyone before about his dating history with the Montevarian royal family. Not really. He'd talked to his cousin and her boyfriend some, but he didn't know what compelled him to tell Kenzie as much as he had.

"What do we need to talk about?"

He didn't want to tell her this. "A couple of things. Your car is probably totaled." Probably not a surprise.

She took a deep breath then another sip of her hot chocolate. "Okay." Resigned was probably the right word.

"The guys we left at the house have taken everything to Josh's house. He's got a big garage to set everything out in. Some of the furniture is probably shot and the house is likely uninhabitable for the foreseeable future."

"Not too much of a shock I suppose. Not with that much water in it."

"You'll probably want to call your landlord. You might even

try him now so that he can get on it, or so you can at least say you tried to contact him immediately."

He watched her pull her phone out of her pocket and make a call. She left a message. "Guess I did my part."

"How long have you two lived there?"

She shrugged. "A few years. A friend of mine from high school grew up in the other house on the property. She knew I needed somewhere to live with Lorelai, so they rented it to me pretty cheap. They sold the property but made sure I'd be able to keep renting. He raised the rent a lot last year, though."

"And hasn't been taking care of it?"

"I didn't know that." She moved to a more defensive stance. "He said he had someone come out and fix the roof after the straight line wind damage a couple months ago."

"Hey!" He held up his hands in mock surrender. "I'm not blaming you. I do think you might have a case against him depending on how he responds to all of this. But in the meantime, you can stay here as long as you want."

She started to protest.

"Seriously. It's just me and my cousin in this house. I can show you the apartment if you'd like."

Kenzie hesitated then stood. "Sure. Why not?"

He didn't believe she really planned to stay, but was humoring him. He wanted to help her, if she'd just let him.

"And if you need a car for a bit, you're welcome to borrow any of the ones here."

"Sure." She stood. "Can we see this place?"

He led her up the stairs and to the door leading to the apartment. "I'm sure it's a mess right now, but it should be livable in a couple days." Jonathan opened the door and flipped on the light.

The sight that met them shocked him as much as it must have

Kenzie.

Studs were exposed in several walls. Visible subflooring appeared throughout the living area - and what was usually the kitchen, but appeared to be a collection of partially discolored walls, now lacking cabinets.

"Um..." He did a 360 degree turn to take it all in.

"This will be livable in a couple days?"

"I thought it would be." He ran a hand through his hair. "I don't know what happened. They were supposed to be doing relatively minor, cosmetic updates before my cousin moved in. New carpet, paint, stuff like that, not a remodel."

"Your cousin?"

"Yeah. She'd planned to move in here, but she wouldn't mind letting you for a while. She's probably getting married before too long anyway."

He heard her blow out a breath. "Okay. No big deal. I can find another place."

"No!" Jonathan turned to face her. "Seriously. I have so much room here, just for me and my cousin and, now, Mr. Benny Hercules. Even George doesn't live in the house. I'll find out what's going on in here and get it done as quickly as possible. Even with all this, if I tell them to get on it, it shouldn't be too long."

Kenzie hesitated, and he could see her pride warring with her more practical side. Finally, she nodded. "For now."

He flipped the light back off, and they went back into the main part of the house.

Kenzie stopped at the door that led to Lorelai's room. "I think I'm going to take a shower and turn in, if that's okay."

"Of course. There should be shampoo and stuff in the bathroom if you need it."

"Thanks." She looked like she wanted to say something more,

but instead, turned and went into the room, closing the door. He could hear the lock click.

Jonathan scratched Mr. Benny Hercules's head. How could he convince her to let him help as long as needed? Not just because he was fascinated with her and her daughter, but because something in them appealed to his sense of...was it his humanity? Something inside him really just wanted to help them. They struggled in ways he never had. If she'd take money, he'd give that to her. Enough to get her on her feet in a real way, where she didn't have to worry about first and last months' rent to get a new place or a car payment.

She wouldn't let him though. He knew that.

Hopefully, she'd be okay with "borrowing" a couple of bedrooms in his house and a car when she needed one.

He took Mr. Benny Hercules to his room and shut the door. "All right, bud. It's bedtime." He headed to the area where he'd set up the crate, complete with dog bed and the snuggly blanket recommended by Lorelai inside. Mr. Benny Hercules went in and turned around, soulful eyes staring up at Jonathan as he closed the door.

By the time he stepped in the shower a moment later, Mr. Benny Hercules's whining had already picked up in volume. Poor thing. Probably didn't like being left alone. Jonathan hurried through his shower, pulling on a pair of pajama pants before going back into his room. He opened the crate and let the dog out.

The mangy mutt skittered out of the crate and bolted to the other side of the room and under the bed. Great. Jonathan lowered himself to the floor and saw what he'd feared. The dog, huddled against the wall right in the middle, would be impossible to get out.

Food maybe? Water?

"Do you want some water, Mr. Benny Hercules?" Was it his imagination or did the dog's ears perk up a bit at the mention of water?

Worth a shot. The little guy hadn't had anything to eat or drink since Jonathan found him. He found the bowls and filled them, setting them in a spot where Mr. Benny Hercules could see them. Jonathan moved to a chair on the far side of the room and listened carefully. Noises that could be shuffling toward the edge of the bed came from underneath. After a minute, a black nose poked out from under the long hanging spread. It moved slowly forward until the whole nose, and then the whole head popped out. Moving a bit faster, he headed for the bowls, and soon his long pink tongue lapped up the water. Every few seconds, he'd stop and stare at Jonathan, his look a combination of scared and suspicious.

It didn't take long for the water to disappear. Jonathan cautiously moved toward the dog, who seemed to get more and more frightened but didn't back away. Snuggling the dog close, he put him back in the crate and headed for his own bed. The pathetic whimpering was too much and soon Mr. Benny Hercules was curled into a ball on one corner of the bed while Jonathan snapped the light off and settled into sleep himself. He had a funny feeling he was going to have a fight on his hands in the morning, and he needed to be ready.

<hr>

"Mama?"

The voice woke Kenzie up from a deep sleep. It always did.

"Mama?" Lorelai's tone turned more frantic.

"In here, baby girl," she called, swinging her legs over the side of the bed. "I'm coming." She trotted through the bathroom that joined the two rooms.

"Where are we?"

Kenzie sat on the edge of the bed. "The ceiling at our house was leaking so Mr. Jonathan took us to his house." His very big, very empty house.

Lorelai visibly relaxed. "Oh. That's nice of him."

"Very nice." She brushed the hair off her daughter's forehead. "Do you think you can go back to sleep now?"

The little girl nodded. "Night, Mommy."

Kenzie kissed Lorelai's nose. "I'm right through the bathroom if you need me, okay? I'll leave a light on so you can see."

Lorelai nodded, but her eyes were already drifting shut.

Kenzie stared in the direction of the ceiling as thoughts tumbled over and over in her mind. It was a good thing her grandmother wouldn't know she was spending the night in a man's house. She'd try to force them to get married.

Kenzie had no desire to be married again.

Ever.

But, she could admit to herself, at times like this when no one else was around, not waking up alone held a certain appeal.

At least now she wasn't on a top bunk.

It took a while, but Kenzie eventually dozed off, her sleep filled with dreams of a dark-haired man sweeping her off her feet.

When she woke, it took a second or two for her to realize where she was and another to realize just how late in the morning it had to be. Lorelai's room was empty with the door to the hallway standing wide open. Without bothering to do more than empty her bladder, she headed downstairs, where little girl giggles directed her to the kitchen.

"What's going on in here?" she asked, leaning against the wall with her arms crossed over her chest.

Lorelai looked up from where she stood next to the griddle. "Mr. Jonathan is teaching me to make pancakes!"

"How nice of him." Kenzie walked toward the island, perching on the edge of one of the bar stools when she reached them. "That means you can make me breakfast now."

"I will someday, Mama." Lorelai was so earnest. So serious most of the time. At times like this, when she was reminded, Kenzie missed the giggly happy-go-lucky girl Lorelai should be.

The three of them ate their pancakes at the bar, small talk flowing easily between Jonathan and Lorelai. Just as Kenzie was about to offer to clean up, a beeping sound caught Jonathan's attention, and he pulled out his phone.

"Excuse me," he said wiping his mouth on his napkin. "I'll be right back." He left without giving her time to answer.

With a shrug, she began to clean up anyway with Lorelai helping.

The front door opened, and Jonathan's voice drifted toward her. "I wish you'd told me you were coming."

Who?

"Nonsense, darling." There was a clicking of heels to go with the woman's voice. "We can come anytime we want."

"Of course you can, but..."

Before Jonathan could finish his sentence, an older woman rounded the corner. "Well, well, well." There was a snide, almost sinister, tone to her voice. "What have we here? Holding out on us, Jonathan?"

Jonathan brushed past his mother. "No, Mother. These are some friends of mine. Kenzie and her daughter, Lorelai. They were displaced by the storm last night. They're staying upstairs until the apartment is done, or they can find their own place." He looked at them. "Kenzie, Lorelai, these are my parents and my nana."

Sure enough a man and an elderly woman had followed him and his mother into the kitchen.

Nana tilted her head, her eyes narrowing as she looked at Kenzie.

"So when's the wedding?" Mrs. Cranston set her purse on the island.

"Mother." Jonathan's voice held a warning tone Kenzie hadn't heard from anyone in a long time.

And wedding? What was she talking about?

"We made ourselves very clear, did we not?"

"You did," Jonathan acknowledged, though he didn't say about what.

"So when is the wedding?"

She couldn't take it any longer. "What are you talking about?"

Mrs. Cranston turned to her. "We made it quite clear to our son when he moved in that he was to have no...female companions spending the night. If he did, we expected the wedding to be announced post-haste."

Kenzie rolled her eyes. "Oh, please. My house had an inch or more of water standing in it. Jonathan was kind enough to offer my daughter and me a place to sleep. I've not seen the inside of your son's room nor has he been in the one he offered me. I am *not* his companion. I'm his friend."

"Dr. Who has 'panions!" The little voice piped up behind Kenzie.

Kenzie closed her eyes and breathed a prayer. "Yes, sweetheart. Dr. Who's friends are called his companions." How did her daughter get sucked into the BBC show again? Right. Kenzie loved it, and she didn't let Lorelai watch *all* of the episodes.

"The point remains the same," Mrs. Cranston interjected. "We had a deal, Jonathan."

"And if the house still belonged to you, you might have a

point." He looked stressed. "The house and the trust fund became mine when I turned twenty-five."

Wouldn't that be nice? The only thing Kenzie would get when she turned twenty-five was a hug from her daughter and a homemade card she wouldn't trade for the world.

"Pastor will be here in half an hour." His father walked back in from the other room.

"Why?" Jonathan sounded suspicious. "You can't think we're actually getting married because of something you said years ago and has no bearing on what didn't happen here last night."

"Of course, you aren't." Nana surprised Kenzie, and Jonathan, too, if the look on his face was any indication. "Don't be ridiculous. They'll get married when the time's right and not because you two tell them, too."

"Thank you, Nana." Jonathan kissed his grandmother on the cheek as his father sighed and took out his phone.

"You're welcome, child." She looked straight at Kenzie as she said it. There was a gleam in her eyes Kenzie didn't understand.

She had a feeling this wasn't the end of it.

Chapter Four

Jonathan let his head drop as he leaned his outstretched arm on the counter. What was that all about?

"We'll be leaving."

He looked up to see Kenzie standing there. "What?"

"I sent Lorelai upstairs to pack her things. I don't want to cause problems between you and your parents."

"You won't," he promised. "This is my house, my land, not theirs anymore. They can't kick you out, and they certainly can't make us get married."

She snorted. "Don't worry about that. I wouldn't dream of tying you down because someone tried to make you."

He struggled to comprehend. "Because there's no way I'd want to marry you? Is that what you're saying?"

Kenzie shrugged. "If the shoe fits... The last thing you'd want is to get tied down to a single mom with the additional burden of a little girl."

There had to be more to what she was saying. Something he

wasn't understanding. "If my parents did, somehow, end up forcing us to get married, I wouldn't consider marrying you tying me down. I wouldn't consider Lorelai a burden. Whoever you end up marrying someday is going to be an incredibly lucky guy." He pointed at her. "*You* are one in a million, and Lorelai is fantastic."

Something still seemed to roil behind her eyes, but he couldn't figure out what it might be. "If you say so."

Jonathan walked to her side. "What is it, Kenz?" Did the nickname work for her? Her eyes registered surprise. "Did you want me to let them force us into a marriage neither one of us wants or is ready for?"

Her eyes left his and seemed to focus somewhere in the middle of his chest. "No."

He took another step toward her. "Then what is it?"

"Not having to worry about money ever again would be nice," she finally whispered.

"I have more than my fair share of problems," he pointed out. "You're right that money isn't one of them, but money doesn't buy happiness. It doesn't buy health. It doesn't buy family."

"But it can give you a stable roof over your head. Consistent food on the table. Never going hungry so your child can eat."

Jonathan reached up and ran a finger down the side of her cheek. "Is that what it's been like for you, Kenzie? Struggling to make it on your own?"

"Not recently, but sometimes," she admitted.

He crooked his finger under her chin and tilted her head up until her eyes met his again. "I want you to promise me something, MacKenzie Ann."

"What?"

"Whatever happens with us, if nothing ever happens with us, if you walk out that door in ten minutes, and I never see you again, I need you to promise me something."

She didn't say anything though her eyes seemed to see into his very soul.

"Promise me," he encouraged gently. "If you ever find yourself in a position where you feel forced to choose between eating and feeding your daughter, you'll call me. I'll send you money, no questions asked. No repayment needed. You should never be in that position, and I want you to promise me you'll let me help if you ever find yourself there again."

"Jonathan…" She was going to refuse. He knew it.

Before she could, he did what he'd wanted to do since that first dance two years earlier.

He kissed her.

His fingers threaded into her hair as she leaned into him, and he felt her hands grasping his t-shirt. She responded, matching his intensity with a fervor of her own that surprised him. Her hands slid up his chest and around his neck holding him closer until he wrapped his arms around her.

Jonathan released her lips and trailed kisses along the line of her jaw. "Kenz," he whispered.

"I know," she whispered back.

"Just know that physical attraction wouldn't be an issue after the wedding." He came back for one more searing, toe-curling kiss, before gentling the contact and letting her go.

"I knew you two were a thing."

Jonathan rested his forehead against Kenzie's and closed his eyes. "What do you need, Nana?"

She chuckled. "Nothing. Just coming in for a drink. But if you don't want your parents to think there's more going on than there is, I'd make two suggestions."

He brushed a kiss against Kenzie's forehead before moving away from her. "What's that?"

"First, don't kiss the poor girl in the middle of the kitchen like you're a dying man in the middle of the desert, and she's a drink of water." There was a twinkle in her eyes. "Second, Ms. Kenzie might not want to wander around in her pajamas."

Jonathan glanced over in time to see Kenzie turn a most becoming shade of pink and, for the first time, he noticed her attire. Soft gray cotton with puffy clouds and sheep all over.

Kenzie ducked her head, her face growing pinker. "I'm gonna go now." She hurried up the stairs.

"You like her." It wasn't a question.

"I do," Jonathan confirmed. "I barely know her, though. We met at a wedding a couple years ago then again at the store last night." Had it really only been the night before? "Lorelai was quite taken with my dog. Kenzie had no one else to call when her car got stuck in a ditch."

"Dog?"

The door to the garage opened and barks could be heard even before the click of nails on the tile. Jonathan looked over to see Mr. Benny Hercules, freshly shaved, running into the kitchen.

"The groomer tried to do it for free," George informed him. "I wouldn't let her, but she felt sorry for the poor thing."

Jonathan knelt down and held his hand out toward the little dog. "You look much more handsome," he crooned.

"She cut his hair shorter than she usually would have," George went on. "It was a mess."

"He'd been out in the woods for days," he explained to his grandmother. "I found him yesterday afternoon."

"I think he looks quite handsome in his bandanna."

Mr. Benny Hercules finally got close enough Jonathan could pick him up. Tucking the dog close to his chest, he walked toward Nana. "This is Mr. Benny Hercules, so named by Miss Lorelai."

Nana held out a hand for Mr. Benny Hercules to sniff. After

a few investigatory sniffs, his little pink tongue licked her finger.

"I think he likes you."

"Who would dump this sweet thing in the woods?"

"I have no idea." Jonathan tilted his head as something occurred to him. "Where are your dogs, Nana?" She always took her Yorkies with her everywhere.

"This was a last minute trip, and I decided not to bring them." She ran a hand over Mr. Benny Hercules's head. "I'm glad I did. This little guy needs to get used to this place before they take over everything."

"I don't know that I'm keeping him," Jonathan warned her. "I haven't decided."

Nana just smiled.

"I don't!" he protested.

"Keep telling yourself that, my boy." She turned toward the living room and motioned for him to follow her. "Now, when are you going to marry that girl?""

<hr />

Kenzie's cheeks still flamed, but she wasn't sure if it was from the kiss or from Jonathan's grandmother pointing out she was still in her jammies.

"Are we really leaving, Mama?" Lorelai had her few things in a pile on the bed she'd slept in.

"I don't know, sweetheart." She didn't want to. Things hadn't been too tough lately, not with her yarn selling well enough to give a bit of a cushion, but they'd had their share of tough times, and a few bills too many. Some weren't getting paid, ever, but she couldn't do anything about it. The bills weren't even truly hers, though the collectors didn't seem to care. Not worrying about where to live for a while would be nice. She checked her phone. A missed call from her landlord.

She went into her room to listen to the message and knew she had no choice. They would have to stay here as long as Jonathan would let them. Her landlord didn't know when the house would be ready, implied the whole thing was her fault, made sure she knew he still expected her rent on time, and that she'd need to pay for the furniture if it was ruined or not returned.

It couldn't be legal for him to do all that, but she didn't have the energy or means to fight him on it. Jonathan's words came back to her. *Promise me.* But she wasn't choosing food for herself or her daughter. This was different. But it did mean she would have to take him up on his offer to live here for a while, whether she wanted to or not. Maybe he really would have that apartment ready soon. At least then she could pretend it wasn't the same house.

"Mama!" Lorelai's voice called from downstairs. "Come see Mr. Benny Hercules!"

"I'll be down in a minute!" She changed into a pair of shorts and a t-shirt before heading out.

"There you are, darling."

Kenzie turned to see Jonathan's mother walking down the hall. "Hello, Mrs. Cranston. How are you?" *Be polite!*

"Fine. How are you?"

"Fine," Kenzie answered cautiously. "How was your trip?"

Mrs. Cranston waved a hand. "It was fine. I want to know more about you." Before Kenzie could say anything, she went on. "And to let you know that, despite our earlier comments, we have no intention of allowing our son to marry someone like you."

The words knifed through her heart, but through sheer determination alone, she kept her face neutral. "Don't worry, Mrs. Cranston. I have no intention of marrying your son."

"That's good. I would hate for you to get your hopes up only to have them dashed when he marries someone with more...social standing." The woman didn't actually look down her nose at Kenzie, but she may as well have.

Kenzie couldn't help but laugh. "I'm quite certain social standing is not one of Jonathan's top criteria for his wife."

"You can think that all you want."

"If that was his top priority, don't you think he would have pushed harder to marry the crown princess?"

The only evidence of her shock was the rapid eye blinking. Finally, Mrs. Cranston asked, "Pardon?"

They didn't know? Kenzie kept her face carefully nonchalant. "You'd have to ask him." Did his family not know he'd dated Queen Adeline? Or Princess Ana? If they were so concerned with social status, those women would have been their top choices.

Without waiting for an answer, Mrs. Cranston started for the stairs. Kenzie trailed behind. "Jonathan, dear. I have a question for you." She wasn't even in the same room with him.

"What's up, Mother?"

"You declined to marry Adeline before her coronation?" That wasn't exactly what Kenzie had said.

Jonathan looked confused, his gaze shifting between his mother, his grandmother, and her.

Sorry, she mouthed.

"What about Addie?" he asked.

"Did you or did you not decline to marry her before her coronation?"

He closed his eyes and seemed to breathe a prayer. "Addie and I dated. We even talked about marriage a couple of times, but she was in love with Charlie long before our first date. She didn't think her father or Parliament would let them get married. We were never in love, and I certainly never proposed. For the record,

I wasn't in love with Ellie or Ana either."

"You dated Princess Anastasia?" His mother's voice neared a screech. "You told us she was your friend."

"She is a friend."

Mrs. Cranston looked around and headed for the kitchen. "I need a drink."

"There's no alcohol here, Mother," Jonathan called after her.

"I'll send George for some."

"I pay George, and he won't get you any. This is a dry house, and you know that."

Kenzie hadn't. She enjoyed the occasional glass of wine for a special occasion with friends, but never would have noticed if Jonathan hadn't said something. What was that about?

"Why ever not?" Mrs. Cranston nearly flopped onto a chaise lounge.

"Because I don't drink, and I don't keep alcohol in my house. Period." Kenzie sensed a story there. "If you feel the need to have a drink, perhaps you could stay at the resort."

"Nonsense. I'm not staying at a resort when we have a house at our disposal." She closed her eyes as her head fell back. "The mention of that princess, though, reminds me of Philip."

"I know, Mom." Jonathan's voice softened. "That's one reason I don't mention Ana." He looked over at Kenzie, his expression exasperated. "Besides, she's happily married with an adopted daughter. I think I heard she's expecting a child, too. I haven't talked to any of them in a while."

"You spent so much time with royalty. Why couldn't you have married one of them?"

"Because I wasn't in love with any of them. Yvette's too young and was engaged to Nicklaus from the time she was a baby. Christiana and Alexander are made for each other. So are Addie and Charlie. And Ana and Jonah." From what he'd said the night before, that one had to hurt the most. "I spent time with several members of royal families a couple years ago. I keep in contact with them. But I was never in a relationship with any of them where we were in love and talking marriage."

Crafty. How he avoided mentioning he'd been in love with Princess Anastasia.

"Very well." She opened one eye. "What is that thing you're holding?"

"This is Mr. Benny Hercules. My new dog."

"You have a dog? What breed?"

"The vet thinks he's a shorkie. Part Shih-tzu, part Yorkie."

"No papers?" And that encapsulated Mrs. Cranston and who she thought her son should end up with, both as a pet and a spouse.

"No, Mother, but I don't care." And that encapsulated Jonathan's thoughts on the matter.

Maybe.

The memory of his lips on hers screamed into the forefront of her mind. Yes, there was chemistry, but a relationship took so much more than that. She took a kiss like that to mean something serious, but did Jonathan? And if he did, and something more were to come of this thing, would he stand up to his mother to marry down to someone like her?

Why was she even thinking these things? There was no point. Despite the kiss to end all kisses, she and Jonathan had no future.

Nana's voice broke through her thoughts. "It doesn't matter, Nadine. Jonathan didn't marry any of those other girls. He's going to marry Kenzie here, so you better get used to the idea."

Kenzie blinked.

Twice.

What?

Chapter Five

Jonathan knew better than to take his grandmother seriously. He seldom did when she started making plans for his future. Kenzie didn't appear to know that. And she'd somehow let it slip to his mother that he and Addie had discussed marriage at some point. His family had never known he'd seriously dated the now-queen. As far as they'd known, he'd escorted her to a few functions while he was overseas working on schoolwork with her.

They didn't know he'd kissed her.

They didn't know he'd told her some of his deepest, darkest secrets.

And they really didn't know he'd been in love with her younger sister six months later.

At least Kenzie hadn't let that slip, too.

"Nana," he chided gently. "Don't say such things. Who I marry and when is up to me and the lady in question. You're not to interfere. Be nice to Kenzie."

"I like Kenzie, dear. I would be quite happy with Kenzie as

your wife." She winked at Lorelai. "That would make this lovely girl my great-granddaughter. I can think of nothing I'd like better."

"Marrying royalty would have been nice. What other royalty do we know?" His mother tapped on her phone.

"Jonathan doesn't need to marry royalty, dear," Nana chided. "I know members of several other ruling families, including some with eligible daughters." Her voice grew thoughtful. "In fact, one of them will be visiting the States soon enough, but who Jonathan marries is up to him. He has more than enough social status for both of them. He's related to presidents. He's related to the Queen of England. He doesn't need anyone else's social standing."

"He's related to the queen through my side of the family and the connection is tenuous at best. Marrying a queen would have been better."

"Oh, I know the connection."

Jonathan stepped in. "Nana, you and Grandmamahave been comparing family trees my entire lifetime. It's time to stop. If I marry someone, when I marry someone, it will be because I want to. Nothing else will matter."

"Of course." But a smile remained on her face.

Jonathan turned to Kenzie. "Is there anywhere you need to be today?"

She shook her head. "No. The first place we have to be is church tomorrow."

"Have you heard from your landlord?"

He could sense her hesitation. "Nothing I can't handle, but he's not sure when we can move back in the house."

"Oh, George?" his mother called. "Can you please come here?"

George entered from the kitchen. "Yes, ma'am?"

"Could you please take this..." She waved her hand in the

general direction of Lorelai. "...little girl to do something? The grown-ups have something to discuss."

"Of course, ma'am. We couldn't have her sensitive ears hearing things they're not supposed to." He held out a hand. "Come along, Miss Lorelai. Perhaps we can go feed the horses a snack."

Lorelai had looked hesitant, but at the mention of horses, she bounded up. "Can I, Mama?"

Kenzie nodded. "You may go, but listen to Mr. George, and be good."

"Yay!" The little girl bounded toward George. "Let's go!"

Kenzie, Jonathan, and Nana laughed, but Jonathan noticed his parents didn't join in. Once they'd walked out the door with a bag of carrots, Jonathan turned to his mother. "What exactly do we have to discuss?"

"The cockamamie plan we heard about from your aunt and uncle. That's why we're here."

He managed to hide his wince. "What about it?"

"Are you really planning to adopt that girl's baby?" His mother tilted her head. "You would never find a wife of good-breeding if you adopted an illegitimate child. I won't allow you to do it."

Jonathan glanced at Kenzie, who was studying her hands. "I'm not sure you have much say in my life, Mother. I'm an adult with a job and a home of my own and more money than you can shake a stick at. If you cut me off from my inheritance, I'll barely feel it. You can threaten all you want, but this is my life, and you don't control it."

"I think it's fantastic." Everyone turned to Nana, who had a smug grin on her face. "You adopt that dear baby, but you will never be able to do it all on your own. You'll need help. You could hire a nanny, of course, but it would be much better if you just married this young lady here. After all, you've already spent the night together, and I saw that kiss. There was enough heat to melt an iceberg. There's clearly something going on between you. Kenzie Ann is more than qualified to help you raise that child, and Lorelai needs a father."

Jonathan looked over at Kenzie to see her inability to hide her wide-eyed reaction. "Nana..."

Before he could go on, his mother interrupted. "A kiss like that? In front of your grandmother? Really, Jonathan. If you're sowing more wild oats with this woman, that's one thing, but that better be all it is."

He felt himself getting more irate as she spoke. Finally, he stood. "Mother, Father, Nana, it's none of your business. If I choose to adopt the baby, that's my business, and I'll figure it out. If I choose to pursue a relationship with Kenzie, that's my business, not any of yours. But I guarantee you, whatever is or is not going on with her, she is *not* a 'wild oat.' I finished sowing them a long time ago. I learned my lessons, some of them the hard way, but I don't need to learn them again, and I certainly don't think you have any room to talk. Or should we bring 2002 into the picture?"

His father wouldn't look at him. His mother glared. His grandmother looked amused.

"It's irrelevant," his father finally told him.

"Not if you're telling me how to run my life, it's not."

"Personally, I think Jonathan adopting that baby is a splendid idea. He and Kenzie will be fabulous parents." Nana just smiled at him.

He felt his jaw clench. "Nana, there is no me and Kenzie. We are not an item, and we are not getting married."

Nana was the picture of innocence. "If you want her business to succeed you will."

Kenzie's heart stopped. She looked at Jonathan, who simply looked puzzled.

"Don't threaten her," Jonathan told his grandmother.

"I'm not."

Kenzie couldn't follow all of the discussion. "Pardon me," she finally interrupted. "But this involves my life and my daughter. Jonathan knows me the best out of all of you, but we've spent a grand total of half an hour together in our entire lives. None of you know whether Lorelai already has a fabulous father." She didn't. "Or how successful my business is." Not very. "Or have the right to tell me how to run my life." Not that she was doing a very good job at it.

"I didn't even know she owned a business," Jonathan pointed out.

"I do. A very small one. It's not even my main job. It's not really earning money yet." She needed it to and soon. There had been rumors of layoffs at work, and she had no idea what she'd do if it happened and her business wasn't built up yet.

"What do you do?" Jonathan seemed genuinely interested. His mother and father looked condescending. Nana was clearly amused.

"I own a yarn dyeing business. I have a friend who helps me, and I pay her a commission on whatever I sell that she helped me with, but I do most of it myself."

"Yarn dyeing?" Jonathan's brows pulled together. "You mean like the stuff at Walmart?"

Kenzie wrinkled her nose. "Not like the stuff at Walmart. That's the Walmart version of yarn. What I get is higher quality. It's not quite white, but a bit more cream colored. I dye it, using my own recipe and process. Then I sell it online or at trade shows."

"Trade shows?" His mother practically looked down her nose at Kenzie. "How...quaint."

And then Kenzie turned to Jonathan. "I have to go. Can I borrow a car?"

An understandably puzzled look crossed his face. "What's up?"

"All of my stuff is in the workshop behind the house. Everything. If I don't get it out of there soon, he might seize it."

"Who?"

"My landlord." She hadn't planned to get into all of this with him, especially with his family right there. "He basically said the whole thing is my fault, and he still expects his rent paid on time, 'or else.'"

"I fail to see how that is legal, dear." Nana tilted her head. "Besides, I'm quite certain Jonathan will help you in any legal matters."

"Of course I will."

Kenzie shook her head. "First, no. I'll handle my own legal issues. Second, it's not just the yarn. It's the dyes. They're not cheap. My recipes. My notes. My processes. It's all written down in there, and it's all proprietary. If he claims it's all his because I broke my lease, he can sell it. I don't make much money yet, but I make some of the best yarn in the business. I design my own colors, and they're different than everyone else's. I doubt he'd realize what he could make by selling it, but if he destroys it, it's almost just as bad."

Jonathan took his phone out of his pocket. In seconds he was talking to CJ, one of the guys from the night before. "All taken care of. CJ still has the keys. He and another of Josh's employees will head over and load everything up. They'll bring it back here."

A wave of relief washed over her. "Thank you."

"You're doing quite a bit for someone you don't care about."

His mother's biting tone cut.

"I never said I didn't care about her." Jonathan's voice held a surprising amount of defeat. "Mother, can you please butt out?"

"One of my sons disappeared. Another wants nothing to do with me. Before you know it, all of my children will have turned against me."

"Oh, please, Mother."

Kenzie's phone buzzed at her. She pulled it out to check the message. Another voicemail from her landlord. "Excuse me."

She walked out of the room, dreading listening to the message, but glad to get away from Jonathan's family. The vile words left a sick feeling in the pit of her stomach.

"What is it?" Jonathan's gentle words offset some of the feeling.

"My landlord." She held out the phone. "The last two messages are from him."

Jonathan took it and listened to both of them. "He can't do any of that. He can bluster and threaten and hope you fall in line, but he can't do any of that."

"Are you sure?"

"Pretty sure." He handed the phone back and pulled out his. A couple minutes later, he was talking again. "Hey, Daniel. Jonathan Cranston. I need a favor. A friend of mine is living in a rental house. Last night, the roof leaked like crazy. When we left, there was over an inch of standing water in some places. Josh sent over some guys to empty the house." He stopped. "It's a small place. Most of the furniture came with it, but we figured if we left it there it would all be ruined." Another hesitation. "Right. So a little bit ago, I sent some guys over to get some stuff out of another building on the property, a workshop of some kind, all things that belong to my friend as part of a business she runs."

This time the hesitation lasted nearly a minute. "Exactly. The original lease was signed with another landlord who later sold the property, but included in the condition that my friend be allowed to rent for at least the next three years and couldn't raise the rent more than a certain amount. He maxed out that amount as soon as he could."

Kenzie wasn't sure how she felt about Jonathan talking to some random guy about her life. She knew she didn't like it, but beyond that, she made herself be grateful God had seen fit to have them run into each other the night before.

Speaking of the night before, where was Mr. Benny Hercules? Hadn't he darted into the kitchen at one point?

She left Jonathan in the kitchen and started looking around. In the mud room, under the bench designed for taking your boots off and on, a gray bundle of fur quivered.

"Hey, Mr. Benny Hercules." Kenzie knelt next to the bench and held out her hand to let him sniff. "Why are you way back there? Do they scare you, too?"

He took a tentative shuffle toward her, crawling on his paws. As soon as he was close enough, she picked him up and cradled him close. She could see why he looked gray. The groomer had shaved him very close to the skin. The skin itself was scratched and sores were scabbing over. "You poor puppy," she crooned, scratching him lightly on the other side of his head. "Mr. Jonathan will take good care of you."

"I hope you and Lorelai will help me."

She looked up to see Jonathan leaning against the door frame. "While we're here, we'll be happy to."

He walked into the room and held out a hand. "Come on."

Kenzie hesitated but took it and in just a couple minutes, they were in a Jeep Wrangler, headed toward a field on his property. It didn't take long, but they reached a spot where they'd crested a hill. Below them, the woods spread out and just beyond that, a dock on Serenity Lake beckoned. "You have some fantastic views."

"I do."

She continued to cuddle Mr. Benny Hercules close as he shivered.

"There's something we need to talk about."

Kenzie's stomach dropped. Those words were never followed by anything good.

Jonathan wasn't sure how to tell her the news, but decided it was like a Band-Aid. "There's no easy way to say this, but your landlord is a jerk. Josh's men are loading up your stuff right now, but he could decide to come after you, saying anything left behind becomes his property when you broke your lease by removing all of the furniture."

"When I did what now?"

"Don't worry. It won't hold up in court. If you'd moved and taken it all, it would be one thing, but under the circumstances, it'd be seen as protecting the property, and no judge would go for it. That said, *if* you had broken your lease and left stuff behind, it automatically becomes his, and retrieving it is stealing."

He saw Kenzie close her eyes, and her grip tightened on the little dog. "Then tell them to leave it all."

"No. It won't hold up in court. And I don't think he really wants to take you to court. He just wants you off the property, probably so he can sell it to a developer."

"I still can't afford to fight him if he does sue me."

"Don't worry about that. I have lawyers who owe me favors. A couple of phone calls will call his bluff, and he'll go away."

Jonathan shrugged. "Unless I decide to buy his company and fire him."

"Please don't do that."

He turned his head to see a tear running down her cheek. "Okay. I won't. Not right now, anyway. But at least let me have some people make some phone calls. No overt intimidation or anything, just 'hey, I'm Kenzie's lawyer, so deal with me from now on.' If he's smart, he'll listen." Jonathan wasn't holding out much hope this guy was smart enough to back off.

She nodded. "Okay. If you don't mind, and they don't mind, and it's not actually costing you any money. Then okay."

"It won't cost me any money." Something like this could be done as a favor, but he had enough lawyers on retainer to get it done anyway.

"Then thank you."

"You know you're more than welcome to stay with me as long as you need to. I'm sorry I forgot my cousin is supposed to be moving into the apartment. I promise, she won't mind staying in the basement suite for now, though. I expect to hear she's engaged sometime soon." Gwendolyn and Adam seemed to be the real deal. She wouldn't mind, not to help take care of someone else for a short period. "The apartment won't be ready for a bit anyway, even if I can get them to rush it."

"Thank you."

"And pick a car, any car. You can pick a different one each day or choose one to be yours for the time being. Either way. Doesn't matter to me."

"I don't want to be in your debt." She continued to stare out toward the lake.

"You're not. I'm a nice guy trying to do a nice thing for a friend, that's it."

She continued to scratch the side of Mr. Benny Hercules's

head, and he seemed to have finally relaxed against her. "What about this baby adoption thing?"

Jonathan sighed and put his left foot up on the dash. "My cousin is pregnant. A one night stand with an ex-boyfriend or something. I'm not sure of the details, and they don't matter. She's dating a fantastic guy now, but her parents and my other grandmother showed up a few days ago trying to convince her to marry the ex. She said she might put the baby up for adoption. Grandmama said 'who's good enough to raise a Cranston?' and I said, 'how about a Langley-Cranston?' Mostly I was trying to get them off her back. I don't even know for sure that she's putting the baby up for adoption, much less that I'm going to be the one adopting him. I guess my aunt called my parents though."

"Would you?"

A loaded question if there ever was one. "I don't know. I'm at a different place in my life. I want a family." He ran a hand through his hair. "I figured I'd go the old-fashioned route. Fall in love, get married, have a few kids. But my love life has been pretty non-existent since Ana told me she was going to marry Jonah. I never really wanted to be a father before, at least not in any immediate sense, just someday. But, something's changed."

"You'd do the single dad thing? Voluntarily?"

He turned that over in his head. "Maybe. I'd definitely give it a lot of careful consideration. I think, in general, it's *best* for kids to be raised in a house with a mom and a dad who love each other and the kids. That doesn't mean there aren't an awful lot of single parents doing fantastic jobs, but I think that's the ideal."

"Me, too." Her answer surprised him.

"What happened to Lorelai's dad?" The question surprised both of them.

She didn't answer immediately. He was about to tell her he'd mind his own business when she spoke. "I'd rather not talk about it. Not now."

"That's fine." His phone vibrated in his pocket. The text message made him smile. "Your landlord won't bother you anymore."

She turned to him and blinked. "What?"

"I told my lawyer where the house was. He has had dealings with your landlord before that never turned out well for the landlord. He called. Said he represented you, and that should be the end of that." The text also said the guy hadn't believed him at first. Hopefully, he wouldn't push it.

"I can't pay you anything," she blurted out.

"For what?" His genuine confusion came through.

"For the extra utilities or even the gas in the car, most likely. A lot of our stuff is going to need to be replaced. I work down in Branson, but my job could be eliminated soon, and I need to save every penny. I'm going to have to put Lorelai back in preschool soon, and that's not cheap."

An idea occurred to him, and he chuckled.

"What?"

"It just hit me. If we did get married, you wouldn't have to worry about any of that, and you could grow your business as fast or as slow as you wanted."

Kenzie didn't look amused. She seemed to be searching his face for something, though he didn't know what. "Are you asking me to marry you? Because right now, I just might say yes."

Chapter Six

If she'd expected Jonathan to startle or recoil at the idea of proposing to her, Kenzie was surprised. He just continued to stare out toward the lake.

It took a minute before he spoke. "If I thought you really meant it, we could talk about the possibility, but I don't think you do."

One part of her - the part of her that was so tired of trying to do it all herself, of shouldering the burden all on her own - wanted to be serious about it. The fiercely independent side breathed a sigh of relief that he wasn't.

Jonathan put his foot down and restarted the engine. "We should get back before George and Lorelai get back from feeding the horses."

As they neared the house, they found Lorelai skipping along holding George's hand. "Mama!" she called as soon as she saw them. Jonathan stopped the Jeep. "I gotta feed a horse!"

"That's awesome, honey." Kenzie set Mr. Benny Hercules at

her side then held out her arms, and Lorelai climbed up onto her lap. Jonathan drove slowly back to put the Jeep in the garage. Lorelai thought it was great fun to sit in the front and not a booster seat.

"Can I drive, Mr. Jonathan?"

Kenzie looked over at Jonathan who shrugged. "We can drive just right around the circle here." He reached for her. "Come here, kiddo."

Lorelai scrambled over Kenzie and onto Jonathan's lap. "Yay!"

"Now, I'll do the pedals for you, okay? But you'll have to tell me what to do, and you can steer." He spent a couple of minutes showing her what all the wands and buttons did, but Lorelai was impatient.

"Let's go!"

Jonathan chuckled. "Okay."

Kenzie noticed he kept his hands on the bottom of the steering wheel, and the Jeep didn't move very fast at all. In fact, she was pretty sure he never did more than tap the gas to get it going.

The look on Lorelai's face was one of pure joy. It made Kenzie smile, too. Her little girl didn't always have much reason to grin like that.

After a few minutes, they put the Jeep in park, and Kenzie took Lorelai inside. She'd decided, sometime in the last hour or so, that until they had the apartment to live in, they'd spend as much time in their suite of rooms as possible, especially while Jonathan's family was there.

They watched a movie, cuddled up in a chair.

"Mama?" Lorelai asked.

"Yes?"

"Are we goin' to the pool today?"

"We don't have a car today, sugar. You'll be there Monday for swim team practice." Her little girl had taken to the water like a fish. Kenzie had missed the first two swim meets, made an evening one, then missed the last one. Their championship, the biggest meet of the year, was coming up. Fortunately, Lorelai and Alyssa Wilson had gotten to be best friends. Alyssa's parents had very kindly taken care of getting Lorelai to and from practice in the mornings and to practice in the evenings because she wasn't home in time most nights. They'd been lifesavers.

"But I wanna swim." Lorelai crossed her arms in front of her chest and gave her best pout.

"Not today." Kenzie remained firm. She wouldn't ask for help. Not if she didn't have to. It was bad enough they were going to have to stay here indefinitely.

Lorelai accepted the answer, but Kenzie knew she wasn't happy about it. They spent the rest of the day in Kenzie's room, watching movies and playing a couple rounds of Candy Land. George had brought the game when he told them they were expected to dress for dinner and that clothes would be laid out in Lorelai's room for both of them, unless Kenzie had something else for them to wear.

She wanted to skip dressing up for dinner, just to annoy Jonathan's mother, but that wasn't a very nice thing to do, and she didn't want to make things harder for Jonathan than they already were.

So Lorelai ended up in a "twirly" dress, complete with crinoline underneath it. Kenzie found a green silk sheath dress waiting for her, and a text from Jonathan apologizing for its necessity.

They made it down to the dining room to find something out of a movie or the set of the grandparents' house on *Gilmore Girls*. Hopefully, Lorelai would cooperate and not break anything.

She found herself sitting next to Jonathan and across from her daughter. At least Jonathan's grandmother was seated next to Lorelai. She seemed to be the kindest of the three guests.

"When is your cousin going to be back?" his mother asked about halfway through the meal. "I'd like to settle this nonsense about you adopting her baby once and for all."

Jonathan swallowed his bite of food. "Gwendolyn went to Adam's parents' hometown for the weekend to meet his extended family. They'll be back sometime tomorrow."

Kenzie nearly choked on her bite of roast. "Gwendolyn is your cousin?"

Jonathan looked over at her. "You know her?"

"Of course. She helps the Wilsons with carpooling Alyssa and Lorelai to swim team." She took a sip of her water. "I didn't know anyone knew, though. I only guessed the other day."

"I don't think she's told very many people yet."

"Miss Gwennie's havin' a baby?" Lorelai piped in.

"Yes, Lorelai, but it's a surprise so we can't tell anyone else, okay?" Kenzie gave her best mom look.

Lorelai shrugged. "'Kay." She went back to eating her carrots, the one vegetable she really liked.

Kenzie prayed she'd remember it was a secret when talking to Alyssa in a couple of days or that she'd forget about it all together.

Jonathan's mother started in. "I, for one, am glad she's giving the baby up for adoption. Not to you, of course, but it's far better for her to give that child to a couple worthy of raising a Cranston. Single mothers aren't the heroes they're made out to be in the media, you know."

Kenzie stared at her food, knowing the slight was meant for her as much as the absent Gwendolyn.

"Mother." Jonathan's voice was low and full of warning.

"Oh, please. I shouldn't have to worry about offending strangers in my own home."

"This isn't your home," Jonathan reminded all of them. "This home was bought by my trust fund and owned, in whole, by me after my twenty-fifth birthday. It never has been your home for more than a few days at a time."

"Regardless…"

"No, Mother. This is my home, and you will not insult my guests."

"You wouldn't kick me out," his mother scoffed.

"No, I wouldn't, but I would excuse myself and my guests from your presence as often as possible, which is pretty much all the time."

Kenzie reached over and rested her hand on Jonathan's leg. A bit more forward than she'd normally be, but she didn't want him getting too worked up on her behalf. She'd dealt with people like his mother off and on for years.

As she'd hoped, Jonathan let it drop. The rest of dinner passed in near complete silence, except for Lorelai's chattering with Jonathan's grandmother about every topic under the sun.

Finally, she had Lorelai tucked into bed and met Jonathan on the back porch. Had it really only been twelve hours since that toe-curling kiss in the kitchen?

"Thanks for meeting me out here." Jonathan leaned back against the railing. "There's something I need to tell you."

"What's that?" Kenzie crossed her arms against the cool breeze coming from the direction of the lake. How many times had he said something like that in the last two days? And it had never been anything good.

"All of your yarn and everything is in the workshop, but I don't know if that's good news."

Kenzie swallowed hard. If her yarn was ruined, she was sunk.

Jonathan watched as Kenzie's shoulders slumped. "How bad is it?"

"I have no idea, honestly. I do know there was some water damage."

Kenzie's head fell forward. "That's bad. That's very bad. What exactly got wet?"

"I don't know. The roof was leaking in the other building, too."

"The dyes are all powders that should be sealed. Even if the little bit that's already mixed up got ruined, it wouldn't be too bad." She ran a hand down her face. "It's the yarn that's the big deal. It was all in Rubbermaid tubs, but if it wasn't completely set, the dye could run from one skein to another. Any skein that picks up dye from another is ruined. I mean, I could still sell it, but it would have to be at a steep discount because it's 'imperfect.' And that's far less likely than some of it being moldy."

"How do you sell it?"

"I sell some online, but most of it I sell at trade shows. There's a big one coming up in a couple weeks. I've already paid for the booth. Most of my yarn is already dyed. I've been working toward this show for months. My friend who usually helps me hasn't been able to because she's pregnant. So even if I had the plain yarn to use to replace the damaged yarn, I don't have the time to get it all done. But I don't have the plain yarn anyway. Almost all of it has already been dyed."

Jonathan didn't understand half of what she said, but held out his hand. "Let's not borrow trouble then. Let's go see what we can see."

Kenzie's hand fit perfectly in his. Jonathan squeezed it lightly as he led her down the stairs toward the workshop behind the detached garage. "What kind of equipment do you need to dye?"

"If they brought it, most of it should be here. I have a couple of microwaves and a good scale, then some pots and crockpots. I have one hot plate, but a stove would be handy. The stove in the workroom is mine, but they probably wouldn't have brought it."

Fortunately, Kenzie held his right hand. With his left, he dug the keys out of his pocket and opened the door. He stepped back to let her go in first. "The light switch is on the right, there."

She flipped it, only to hear a loud popping sound. "Light bulb's out," she commented. "Just the way my luck goes this weekend."

Jonathan dropped her hand and pulled his phone out of his other pocket. "Want to look this way?" He swiped until the flashlight came on.

He saw Kenzie's shadow shake its head. "No. I'd rather wait until I can actually see it all."

They went outside, and he locked the door back. "But you're going to obsess about it all night, won't you?"

There was a slight hesitation before she answered. "Probably."

"Then why don't I keep your mind off it?" He took her hand again. "Why don't we sit and talk on the porch until you're good and tired?"

She nodded. "I guess. I probably won't be able to sleep for a while."

They reached the deck, and he led her to the swing. She let him put his arm around her shoulders and gently tugged on her arm, until she rested against him.

Jonathan tipped his head until his cheek rested against her hair. "Thank you for letting me help, Kenz. I know it can't be easy for you."

"How can you know that? How can you know how hard it is to accept help?"

He pushed his foot against the deck to swing them back and forth. "You think because of who I am, the family I come from, that I've never had problems?"

Kenzie shrugged, but didn't say anything.

"I know you know that's not true. Nearly two years ago, my brother disappeared not five miles from here. Without a trace. To this day, we have no idea what happened to him."

"Philip?"

"Yeah. He wasn't in good shape to start with. Drugs and alcohol and all kinds of problems, but he was my brother." He rubbed his thumb up and down her arm. "I keep dreaming that someday, he'll stroll right up to the door, ring the doorbell, and then waltz in and start talking like nothing happened." Jonathan pulled in a deep breath and let it out slowly. "I know the likelihood of that ever happening is about the same as you marrying me after two days." He tried to insert a bit of a chuckle, so she'd know he wasn't serious. "But that doesn't keep a guy from dreaming."

"I guess money doesn't keep you from having problems. I *do* think it would be nice to not have those problems include things like putting food on the table."

Their conversation from before came back to him. "You already promised me you'd call if you ever got to that point again."

"I know, but still..."

"You're right. I don't know that kind of hardship, but everyone has troubles of different kinds." Other, different, pain from his past tried to push its way to the forefront, but he didn't let it. No. It was best to keep those things buried.

The swing moved gently back and forth as Jonathan's eyes began to droop.

"I think I may have to go to work tomorrow. Could Lorelai stay here with you? I don't normally have to work Sundays, but there's a meeting tomorrow. I've tried getting out of it, but I haven't heard yet if I can."

"Of course. I love having her around."

"She can be a handful."

Jonathan chuckled again. "But I'm not Mom. She's like most kids, I'd imagine. Behaves a lot better for others than for Mom or Dad."

"True. She does seem to do that."

Kenzie's words were slowing down, just as Jonathan's mental acuity seemed to be. But sitting here with her was too comfortable. They fit together too well.

Jonathan closed his eyes and let his mind drift. What would it be like to spend time like this with Kenzie all the time?

He was pretty sure it was as close to heaven as he'd find on earth.

Chapter Seven

Sunday was a very long day for Kenzie. She and Lorelai rode with Jonathan to Grace Community Chapel. They attended there most of the time, when they went. With her schedule, it wasn't always possible. Lorelai usually went to Kenzie's parents' church when they were babysitting. It was good for Kenzie, but everything was hanging over her head, threatening to fall and suffocate her.

Starting with her yarn and ending with waking up next to Jonathan on the porch swing the next morning being glared at by his mother. She threatened to make them get married again.

This time, Kenzie knew there was no way Mrs. Cranston would actually encourage her son to marry her. As soon as they returned from church, Kenzie received a text saying she did have to be at the work meeting. Admonishing Lorelai to behave for Mr. Jonathan, she drove the forty-five minutes in a borrowed car to Branson, sat through a five hour meeting, and took her pittance of a severance pay check when she left.

By the time she got back to Jonathan's house, her tears of frustration were long spent, and she was just in time to tuck Lorelai in to bed. She went back downstairs to find Jonathan sitting in the living room with a tablet.

"How'd your meeting go?" he asked, looking up.

She shrugged. "About like I expected." Did she want to tell him the whole truth? He'd know in the morning. "I got laid off. I knew it was coming, but that doesn't make it any easier." She hesitated. "Can I have another hot chocolate?"

Jonathan set his tablet down and walked toward her. "Kenzie, this is your home, at least for now. You're welcome to anything in it."

She tried to remember where everything she needed could be found. In just a minute, the brew was bubbling out of the Keurig.

"Are you going to be okay?"

Kenzie stared at the hot liquid as it streamed into the cup. "I don't have any choice but to be okay. I have a little girl who depends on me. I'll find another day job." She didn't know how or where, but she would.

"And your yarn?"

"It's self-sustaining. That's about it, right now. So far, I've kept some to make life a little easier, but put most of what I make back into the business. I was hoping to be able to support myself on it in the next couple of years, but I don't know what I'll do if that yarn is ruined. I didn't get to go look at it today, so unless the light bulb is replaced..."

She glanced over in time to see Jonathan wince. "Sorry. I forgot about it. Lorelai and I were having so much fun. She begged me to take her to her swim team practice in the morning."

"You don't need to do that. I'm sure you have plenty of other things to do."

Jonathan shook his head. "Nope. I'm taking tomorrow off. I'll take her to swim team practice if you want, you can sleep in, then together we'll go look at the yarn and see what kind of shape it's in."

"I'd like to take her in the morning, if you don't mind." She hadn't made it to very many of the practices for more than a few minutes in the evenings.

"If I don't mind? She's your daughter." The chuckle in his voice warmed her insides.

"I know, but if she asked you, she wants you to go." Kenzie shook her head. "She won't want me there."

"I find that hard to believe."

Time to change the subject. "Where's the dog?"

"Mr. Benny Hercules?" Jonathan turned back to the living room. "Last I saw, he was under the couch, as far back as he could get."

"How come?"

"Because he's scared of his own shadow."

"And you're sure someone dumped him? He seems so sweet."

"I think he likes you better than me. But we haven't had any nibbles on the posts online. No one says he's been missed."

Kenzie finished doctoring her hot chocolate with all the good stuff she normally didn't allow herself to indulge in. Carefully carrying it into the living room, she set it on the end table then knelt down to see if she could get the dog to come to her. It took the light on her phone to see him under there, and even then she could only see the red of his eyes.

"He won't come to you, either?"

"No." She laid down on the floor and reached as far back as she could. It took a bit extra stretching, but she was able to get her finger hooked under Mr. Benny Hercules's collar and pull him out gently. He huddled as far into his own skin as he could, but Kenzie was determined to get him to trust her. She snuggled him close as she sank into one of the chairs.

"That's one way to do it." Jonathan sat across from her. "What can I do to help, Kenz?"

She scritched the side of Mr. Benny Hercules's neck. "You're already doing it. Just letting us live here, letting me borrow a car, that's plenty. More than I could begin to hope for. If we hadn't run into you the other night, I don't know what I would have done."

Kenzie lowered her head until she wasn't looking Jonathan in the eye. "I didn't want to call you. It was Lorelai's idea. I didn't even remember I had your card until she insisted on calling you."

"Then I'm doubly glad I saw Mr. Benny Hercules that night. I was able to take care of him, but even more importantly, it meant you called me when you needed help." He didn't say anything for a minute. "What will you do if your yarn is ruined?"

She'd been trying desperately to avoid thinking that very thing. "I don't know what I'll do. I may have to just stop doing business until I can get a job and get back on my feet all together. I don't have enough money to do both."

"You're welcome here indefinitely, you know that, right? Don't worry about 'getting back on your feet,' just worry about doing what you need to do."

Kenzie just nodded. She didn't like it, but she was grateful.

They talked for a few more minutes, then Jonathan excused himself to take a phone call. Without really thinking about what she was doing, she snuggled Mr. Benny Hercules close and headed to her room. She set him on her bed and got ready for bed herself. As she did, Kenzie realized she didn't even know if Jonathan's parents and grandmother had left while she was gone.

She curled up in the warmest, softest bed she'd ever slept in and slept the most peaceful sleep she had in a long time.

Jonathan laughed as Lorelai gave him a wet hug. "You did great, munchkin."

She turned to her mother. "Did I, Mama?"

Kenzie smiled from her perch on one of the lounge chairs. "You did fantastic."

"Livs said I did great."

Jonathan had met Alivia several times but hadn't realized she was in charge of the swim team at the Serenity Landing Aquatic Center. She was engaged to CJ, and both worked for Josh Wilson. CJ was one of the guys who'd helped load everything up from Kenzie's house on Friday.

Lorelai went back to the pool to practice her dive again.

"She only has to not drown from one end to the other," Kenzie told him. "In her age group, they don't really disqualify them unless they touch the side or bottom or hang off the ropes."

Jonathan scooted back until he was stretched out on the blue nylon fabric. "She doesn't seem to be doing much better than that, does she?" He watched the others. "None of them do."

"They're little," Kenzie offered by way of explanation.

Practice wrapped up about nine, and Lorelai begged to continue her regular routine of spending the day with her friend, Alyssa Wilson. Jonathan didn't encourage Kenzie one way or the other, but Kenzie decided to let her after clearing it with Stephanie, Alyssa's step-mom.

Gwendolyn had driven into town early that morning with Adam, but she'd been busy before Jonathan had a chance to talk to her. He hadn't texted her about the new living arrangements, preferring to talk to her in person and hoping no one else spilled it before he had the chance to. Before leaving, he made a sign for her to call him. She nodded before going back to helping someone sign up for a party.

Kenzie's pensive look worried him as she stared out at the workshop. "I guess it's time to face the music and see what kind of shape all that yarn's in."

"I asked George to make sure that light got changed first thing this morning." He pulled the truck straight to the workshop. "Let's see what we can figure out." He was afraid of what they would find. She had to be nearly petrified. As he understood it, this was pretty much Kenzie's life savings.

He unlocked the door and stepped aside to let Kenzie go ahead of him.

She sucked in a breath and let it out. "Okay. Let's take a look at this."

Kenzie went to the first Rubbermaid tub and opened it. Her closed eyes and relaxed shoulders told Jonathan it wasn't all bad.

"This yarn is okay, but it's what I had left that wasn't dyed or sorted. It doesn't even look wet."

After she put the lid back on, he moved the tub for her. "That's good. No problem there."

"There's not much there, though. Almost everything was already dyed or sorted to be dyed over the weekend, which clearly didn't get done." She opened the next tub. This time her shoulders didn't relax. They slumped.

"Not good?" he asked when she didn't say anything.

"No. I don't remember how I'd left everything, but I don't think I would have left it like this. I'm guessing whoever packed it up just put it all in tubs, not knowing that's not the best plan. Either that or I put them all in together, which I could have done, and the lid wasn't on so everything got wet."

Jonathan moved to her side. "What happened?"

"Some of them ran. Mostly one of the red ones I couldn't remember if I had cooked them to set or not. The purples are probably okay, but the reds, oranges, yellows, all of them are ruined."

He started to reach in, to pull one of the skeins out, but she stopped him.

"Hold on." Kenzie dug around in one of the other buckets and handed him a pair of doctor's type gloves. "Put these on or your hands will turn colors."

Jonathan put them on, and pulled a red skein out. Sure enough, it had purple dye on it as well. "You can't sell these as unique or something?"

"No. I can sell them as damaged, but for something that would take a whole skein, it's ruined." She let the skeins she was holding drop back into the bucket, then moved the whole thing aside. He tossed the skein into the bucket he'd taken it from while she opened another one.

"How's that one?"

"Ruined." He could hear the tears and frustration in her voice. She held up a bundle that, for all he could tell, was a mishmash of colors anyway. "This is self-striping. And the colors have bled all over the place."

Jonathan rubbed his head with one knuckle. "Self-striping?"

"If you use it for certain things, like socks or a scarf, it should end up striped on it's own. You don't need to change skeins or anything to make it striped."

He tilted his head and looked at it a bit more carefully. "Cool. That's a smart idea."

She shrugged. "It wasn't my idea, though I figured out how to do it a couple different ways. Thick stripes, thin stripes, whatever. But these are ruined anyway."

They went through several more buckets to find that all of

them were completely or partially ruined, except for the one with her samples of finished work. Her whispered, "Thank you, God," told Jonathan how big a deal this really was. The Walmart bags of undyed yarn she'd apparently sorted the night before the storm were drenched and could easily have mold setting in them even if it wasn't yet visible. That made her think the rest of the now-imperfect and damp yarn could too.

By the time she finished going through them, Kenzie was the picture of defeat. She sank to the ground, back against the wall, and snapped off her gloves.

Jonathan sat next to her, close enough their shoulders were nearly touching. "How bad is it? Really?" he asked, taking off his own gloves.

"There's very little I can sell for full price. I don't have enough yarn to redo everything, even if I had the time." She leaned her head back. "Actually, I probably do have the time, if I had the yarn. I'm not working, after all. I could dry out the wet yarn, dye it starting tomorrow or Wednesday. I could probably even get more yarn by then, but..."

"But what?"

"The problem is the money. I don't have the cash to replace all of this. Even if I put it on a credit card, which I don't have, *and* I sold everything new and old, next weekend, I don't know that I'd break even overall."

Jonathan wasn't quite sure how to ask her what he wanted to ask. "Would you let me help?"

Kenzie leaned her head back against the wall behind her. She knew what Jonathan was asking her. He wanted to give her the money to make up for all of it.

She couldn't accept that.

Could she?

No. She'd never taken money from anyone. She wouldn't start now.

No one had ever offered before, but that was beside the point. She wouldn't have taken it if they had.

"I won't take your money, Jonathan," she finally told him, her voice low.

"I'm not offering to *give* you money."

She looked sideways up at him. He wasn't looking at her. "Then what are you offering?"

"I'm offering to buy all that yarn off of you."

Not the answer she expected. "And what would you do with thousands of yards of yarn?"

"Doesn't matter. I'm offering to pay you fair market value for all of the damaged yarn."

Her eyes narrowed. "Fair market value for *damaged* yarn or what I would have sold it for before the damage?"

He shrugged. "Will you let me do the second?"

It cut against every grain she had, but she did consider it.

For about three seconds, then she shook her head. "No. I can't let you do that."

"You have to stand on your own two feet?"

"For better or worse."

He snapped off one of his gloves. "Those sound like marrying words."

"Maybe." Was that thought really crossing her mind? The one where she hitched her metaphorical wagon to the high class coach of the Langley-Cranston family?

"You'd consider marrying me rather than letting me buy your yarn out?"

It did sound even more ridiculous when he said it like that. "I don't know. I don't know what to do. None of it feels right."

They stayed on the concrete floor for long minutes. "You need a job, right?"

"Yeah."

"But you also need some cash flow to get the yarn going in the next two weeks."

"Right."

"And marrying me is out?" He sounded like he really meant it.

"I like you and all, Jonathan, but I don't think I'm quite desperate enough to marry a man for his money." Kenzie breathed the *not yet* to herself. She knew a marriage to Jonathan would be better than her first, very short-lived, marriage, but it still didn't seem like a good plan.

Her phone buzzed, and she pulled it out. Another voice mail from her landlord. Why hadn't she felt the call buzzing? The phone had certainly seen better days. It had started dropping calls a lot more recently, too. It wouldn't matter after it got turned off in the next week.

"Then let me hire you."

Kenzie let her head fall to the side until she could see him. "A real bona fide job offer?"

"With an advance. I'll help you get what you need for the show next weekend. I'll even take a few days off to help you however I can. Then you work for me. I don't know where yet, but I'm sure there's a job opening somewhere for a secretary or sales girl or..." He shrugged. "Something. The main company I've been running recently is security and bodyguards. I can't imagine that's your specialty."

"No, but it's not like I have a lot of experience in anything but the service industry anyway. I worked mostly fast food and waitressing jobs." She appreciated the offer, but didn't think she'd fit in any of the jobs he likely had available, and she didn't want him creating one just for her.

"I'm sure we can find something."

This time she felt her phone ring. She swiped at it when she saw Stephanie's name pop up. "Hello?"

"Kenzie? It's Alyssa's mom."

"Of course. Is Lorelai okay?"

Stephanie sighed. "She's running a bit of a fever. Not too bad, but she definitely doesn't feel quite right. She even said she wanted to take a nap."

Kenzie pinched the bridge of her nose. "Okay. I'll be over to pick her up in a few minutes." She pressed the end button and pushed herself up off the floor. "I've got to go get Lorelai."

Jonathan stood up next to her. "Why don't you get started here, and I'll go pick her up? I can have George keep an eye on her so we can get things moving."

It wasn't Kenzie's first choice, but it did make sense. Jonathan would have no idea what to do with the yarn. "That would be a big help."

He left her alone in the room. Kenzie dug out a couple of her drying stands. She needed to get the yarn dried out so she could dye it in the next couple of days. By the time Jonathan pulled back into the driveway, she had several racks sitting out in the sun with off-white yarn strewn all over them.

From a distance, she saw Jonathan carry her daughter into the house. Lorelai obviously trusted him. Her head was snuggled into his shoulder and her arms held on tight.

Kenzie was glad her daughter's trust had never been betrayed, at least not that she knew of. She didn't know her father and had never really asked about him. When she did, Kenzie was always able to change the subject easily.

Kenzie prayed Jonathan wouldn't be the one to break Lorelai's little girl heart.

It must not have taken long for him to get her settled, because he was soon outside with Kenzie, helping her get the yarn sorted out to get a better idea of where she was at.

"How is she?" Kenzie asked.

"Her temperature is just over a hundred, and she fell asleep on the way here."

"It's a two minute drive!"

"Apparently, whatever it is, it hit her hard. She also said her head hurt really bad."

Kenzie told Jonathan what she needed him to do, but her mind stayed focused on her daughter. Was it just a little bug? Or something worse? Did she need to go to the doctor? At least her health insurance would remain in effect until the end of the month.

Something else she needed to think about.

Her yarn business. Her house. Her landlord.

Her daughter.

Maybe it was time to rethink marrying for money.

At least then she'd never have to worry about that again.

Chapter

Eight

Jonathan found that he wasn't nearly as dexterous as he'd thought. The yarn posed no problems for Kenzie, but he had a more difficult time. He wasn't even sure why they were sorting through all of it if everything but about four packages in that first tub they'd opened was ruined. He had no idea how many skeins that was or how many she'd need.

"Hold up, Kenz." He straightened. "Do you have a list somewhere of what you need to have for this show?"

She pushed her hair off her face with the back of one wrist. "Yeah. Somewhere."

"Is all of this stuff pretty much toast?"

"Probably."

"Then why don't we assume it is. Let's go up to the house and get online so we can order the replacement...whatever you need. Yarn. Dye. Whatever. Then we can come back out here and deal with all of this."

Kenzie seemed to think that over. "But what if some of this is salvageable?"

"Then we salvage it and count it as bonus."

"I don't know, Jonathan."

"If you won't let me take care of it out of the goodness of my heart, then we'll work out a repayment plan that will let you grow your business and still pay me back."

She still hesitated, then nodded. "Okay. We're talking up to like ten grand though, by the time you count all the supplies and expedited shipping and stuff."

"Then let's go order."

Kenzie still seemed reluctant, but followed him into his office. Jonathan logged into his computer then stepped aside. "Go to whatever websites you need and put whatever you need to in your carts. I'll be back in a few minutes and can check out whenever you're ready."

She sat in his custom made office chair and scooted it in to the desk.

Jonathan left her there and went into the kitchen. It was a warm day, but that didn't seem to matter to Kenzie. He'd been watching her and made her a hot chocolate just the way she seemed to like it. As he walked toward his office, he found his grandmother.

"She looks right at home in there, doesn't she?" His grandmother stopped to watch Kenzie as she worked.

Jonathan watched Kenzie, her bottom lip stuck in her teeth, as she studied the screen. "She does."

"Marry the girl, Jonny. No matter what your mother says. You two are made for each other."

"How do you know that? Would it even be fair for me to marry her knowing how mother would treat her?"

"Your mother would come around. She's still smarting over the loss of Philip and other things you know nothing about. But she needs someone like Kenzie who will see past her crusty exterior and love the person she could be on the inside."

"That's a lot to ask of any woman."

"Agreed, but I'm pretty sure MacKenzie Ann is up to the task." His grandmother nodded toward her. "Her hot chocolate will get cold if you don't get in there."

Jonathan gave his grandmother a quick squeeze then headed into his office. "Here." He set the mug in front of Kenzie.

She looked up, clearly surprised. "You made me hot chocolate?"

He sat in the chair across the desk from her. "You seem to like it when you need some stress relief, so, yeah, I made you hot chocolate."

Kenzie picked it up and took a sip. "Perfect." She turned back to the computer. "I think I've got all of the yarn in the cart, but if you wouldn't mind ordering a little bit to get here tomorrow, then the rest can come a little slower. That way it won't cost quite as much. The cheapest route isn't an option though, because it wouldn't get here until the day before I leave."

"Just leave all of it in the same order." He had a feeling her idea of big savings weren't quite the same as his. Of course, his idea of big spending wasn't nearly the same as hers either.

Using one hand to move the mouse around, she took another sip of her drink. "I do need some dyes, too."

"Put whatever you need in the cart."

Kenzie looked at her watch. "If I order before eleven Pacific, it'll ship today."

He checked the time. "Then you should hurry. You've got half an hour."

There was a ton of clicking. "Okay." She stood, but her fidgeting told him how nervous she was about it. He wouldn't blink an eye, even if he wanted to.

When Jonathan sat down in the seat, he was actually surprised at how little the total was. He'd expected more. Not that he had any clue how much dye should cost.

"Normally, I wouldn't order such a big container of a couple of them, but they're out of the sizes I would order."

"It's no problem." He went through the process and typed in his credit card number, accidentally changing it to the default payment method then not changing it back on purpose.

"Um..."

Jonathan looked up to see Kenzie staring at her hands. "What is it?"

"You've already done so much that I hate to even ask."

"'Ask and you shall receive.'" Wasn't that the way the verse went?

"I need some new equipment. I hoped to order some after the show, but if I'm going to get all of this done in time, I need to order it now."

He nodded. "Do you need anything else from this yarn store, or is it all in the cart?"

"It's all in there."

"I can check out?" She nodded, and he finished the process. "Okay. Find what you need. Whatever websites you need it from. Get the best quality. Don't get something just because it's cheaper but won't last more than a week." He tried not to sound like he was pressuring her, but he did want her to get what she needed. "It's far easier to do a better job with the right equipment than to try to make do."

Jonathan traded spots with Kenzie and watched as she went directly to websites. She had to have been daydreaming about this for a while.

"What else do you need to make it go faster? To process more skeins at the same time or whatever?"

Kenzie clicked a few more times. "Either a bunch of burners that can be used on a stove – like four or six. It would be cheaper to use several more crock pots or even single burner hot plate type things."

"Is cheaper better? What about Amazon?" He told her to open another tab for Amazon and order whatever she could from Amazon Prime. He didn't tell her he'd pay the expedited shipping.

She shrugged. "Slow cookers take a little longer, but it's more set-it-and-forget-it than using the stock pots. It's also easier to use more crock pots because you can just plug them in wherever and set them off to the side. There's no steam to worry about. Stuff like that."

Jonathan nodded. "Let me finish your orders there, and then we can make a run to Walmart and see what we can find." They traded seats again and fifteen minutes later, he'd told George their plans and were off to town.

Kenzie waited until she was hidden safely in the shower to let the tears flow.

It was too much.

She had no house. No car. No job. Nothing to call her own, except her daughter. Jonathan had spent more money on her in two hours today than anyone else had in her entire life. She'd never be able to repay him.

Her landlord was going to sue. She hadn't told Jonathan about the call yet. Her landlord hadn't believed she had such a high-powered attorney working on her behalf. Her ex-in-laws had left a voice mail she hadn't bothered to listen to yet.

No matter that she'd told them for years that Lorelai wasn't their biological granddaughter. They'd wanted to have her declared unfit since the day their son died doing stupid stuff. They called once a year, on the anniversary of the day she'd finally found their contact information, a few weeks after he died, and let them know. They read her the riot act in a voice mail she never returned, and now never listened to, and left her alone for another year.

Grateful for the unlimited hot water provided by Jonathan's tankless water heater, she let it flow over her until she finally started to feel less like she was falling apart at the seams.

Despite what she'd said to him earlier, Kenzie was very thankful Jonathan had ordered the yarn for her and even paid for the rush shipping. It would be at his house in less than forty-eight hours. With his help, and Julia's if she could, Kenzie might actually be able to do okay at the booth in a couple weeks.

Once out of the shower, she put herself back together for a family dinner. Lorelai hadn't slept all afternoon, or so George had told her, but she was sleeping again and wouldn't be coming down for dinner. Kenzie knew her daughter would be bummed to miss evening swim practice, but it couldn't be helped.

"Good evening, Mr. and Mrs. Cranston." She gave them her best smile and wondered when they'd be going home.

Mr. Cranston at least smiled back. Mrs. Cranston continued doing something on her phone and didn't acknowledge her at all. Fabulous. Dinner was going to be spectacular.

She needed to tamp down her sarcasm, even internally. At least she was seated next to Jonathan's grandmother. The older woman wasn't as intimidating as she'd first seemed.

Conversation revolved around people Kenzie didn't know. She kept her head down and ate her meal. About halfway through, another visitor arrived, this one a surprise to Kenzie. She'd

Discovering Home

Gwendolyn walked in, said hello to Jonathan's family, and took the seat across from Kenzie.

All in fairly short shorts and her SLAC t-shirt. Mrs. Cranston looked scandalized.

"How was your trip?" Jonathan ignored his mother's pointed looks.

"Good. I really liked Adam's family, and I think they really liked me."

Mrs. Cranston jumped in. "And you're still planning to go through with this crazy idea to let Jonathan adopt your baby?"

Gwendolyn shrugged. "Why not? He's family, and I know I'm not ready to be a mother."

Kenzie knew that feeling well and couldn't help jumping in. "If you decide to keep the baby, you'll find yourself far more capable than you think you are."

Gwendolyn looked thankful for the support. "Thanks, Kenz, but I don't know."

"I take it you were a single mother from the beginning." Mrs. Cranston quite literally looked down her nose at Kenzie.

She shook her head. "I was married for most of my pregnancy." A marriage she'd rather forget, but couldn't. "He died before Lorelai was born." No need for this woman to know he wasn't Lorelai's father.

Gwendolyn's face fell. "Oh, how horrible. I'm so sorry, Kenzie. I didn't know."

Jonathan reached over and rested his hand on Kenzie's where it lay on the table, but the looks his parents gave each other told her they thought it might have been her fault. She wasn't about to go into details about how stupid he'd been.

Or about the fling that actually resulted in her daughter.

"I think you're doing a great job raising Lorelai," Jonathan told her. "She's great, and she wouldn't be that way without you as her mother."

"That's what I want." Gwendolyn poked at a piece of meat. "I want someone who's going to be a great parent to my baby, and despite your vote of confidence, I don't think that's going to be me. I need to finish college, get on my feet, and I don't think it's fair to Adam to ask him to step in as a dad from the get-go."

Kenzie didn't know Adam well, but she did know him a bit. "I think you're selling him short, Gwen."

"He says he's more than willing to be a father to this baby, but only if it's what I really want deep down inside. And I don't know that it is."

"Well, then you can find a family with two parents." Mrs. Cranston sipped her water. "Jonathan doesn't need to be involved."

Jonathan squeezed Kenzie's hand again, and then let go. "I'm ready for a family, Mother. It's not up to you how that happens." He winked at Kenzie. "Besides, how do you know I won't find my one true love soon?"

Kenzie stared at her food as she spoke. "He's already asked me to marry him, you know." Kind of. "And I'm seriously considering saying yes. That would make us the ideal family for Gwendolyn's baby, wouldn't it?"

Kenzie hated that she was considering it. She'd married one man for the supposed stability he'd bring to her life and had been sorely disappointed. Deep down, she knew Jonathan wasn't anything like her late husband, or the one who'd left her after one night and without a way to contact him.

"Do you mean that?"

She turned to Jonathan to find the hopeful look on his face almost too much to bear. "Considering it, yes. But I haven't made a decision. I don't know that I'm ready to get married again to anyone." Kenzie reached out and laid her hand on the side of his face. "But if I am, I want it to be you."

Not just for his money. But for the man he was. The man he was proving himself to be by giving to her and not asking for anything in return.

Except to give him a chance to prove himself to her. To prove he cared.

Jonathan caught her hand as she pulled it away and pressed a kiss into her palm. "Just say the word, Kenz, and I'm yours."

She believed he meant it. She'd only said it to get in a jab at his parents, but Jonathan was taking her far more seriously.

In fact, Kenzie truly believed that if she said the word, they'd be married before her yarn showed up.

But what surprised her more than anything was how desperately she wanted to say yes.

Chapter Nine

Jonathan could barely believe his ears. Kenzie was actually considering marrying him?

Or could it just be a ploy for his folks?

Should he tell her what he had in his pocket?

He'd found it on an unexpected side trip to Serenity Landing Jewelers while he waited for their pizza to be ready.

Kenzie had her mind set on So Cheeeezzy, but they didn't have any delivery drivers during the day. When he got there, the pizza wasn't ready, and the sign across the street caught his eye. He'd decided why not?

And once inside, he'd found it.

The perfect ring for Kenzie.

And a matching wedding band for her.

Just in case.

He found a band he really liked, too, but didn't buy it. That just felt too weird.

The rest of dinner passed in silence. His parents excused

themselves and went downstairs to the suite they'd commandeered from Gwendolyn. Gwendolyn headed upstairs. Jonathan's grandmother winked at him as she went to her suite on the main floor.

And that left just him and Kenzie. Despite what he'd told her, she insisted on cleaning up after dinner. He wouldn't let her do it alone, though he insisted she go check on Lorelai first.

By the time she came back downstairs in casual clothes, Jonathan was nearly done with the cleanup.

"How is she?" he asked as he tossed a pod into the dishwasher.

"Sleeping. She's still running a fever, but not too high."

Jonathan started the dishwasher then took Kenzie's hand and led her to the porch. He sat on the swing in the same spot as he had a couple nights earlier.

She sat in the middle, not close enough to suit Jonathan but not all the way on the other end either.

"What's bothering you?" he asked, not letting go of her hand.

A smile appeared on her face, but it seemed forced at best. "Nothing."

"Would you tell me if there was?"

Kenzie pushed back with one foot, setting them in motion. "You've done so much for me today."

"That doesn't answer my question. Or rather, I'm pretty sure the answer is no, you wouldn't tell me because you think I've already done enough."

They swung in silence for a minute or two. "I got another voice mail from my landlord."

He started to reach for his phone.

"It doesn't have to be taken care of right now, Jon. If you give me the contact information, I can call the lawyer in the morning. And I'll find a way to pay for it, too."

Jonathan tightened his grip on her hand, certain she would

try to pull it away. "Not to put too fine a point on it, Kenz, but you can't afford him. He already works for me, and I don't have to pay him any extra, so that's not a concern."

"And you spent nearly ten thousand dollars to help me today," she shot back. "No matter how much I want to repay you in a couple weeks, it's going to take a while."

"I've told you not to worry about it. It's my pleasure to help out. Call it a small business grant you didn't have to write a proposal for."

"And everyone's going to think it's because I'm sleeping with you." He saw her wipe away a tear, though she tried to be discreet.

"So? You're not. You and I both know that. Who cares what everyone else thinks?"

"You're Jonathan Langley-Cranston the Fourth. Everyone knows you. You're perpetual tabloid fodder, even though I believe you when you say you haven't really dated in years, except for the princesses and all. It's always there. Stories of your latest supposed conquests. I can't be a conquest, Jonathan, real or otherwise."

Her words cut. The truth tended to do that.

Kenzie let go of his hand and stood up. "But I appreciate it, and even if I'm able to repay you the money, I'll never be able to truly repay you for what you've done for us." She started for the stairs. "But I need to get started on what I can with the yarn that survived."

Jonathan sighed and got up to follow her. "I'll help however I can. I may not know anything about dyeing yarn, but I can learn, and I'm perfect for manual labor."

She glanced back over her shoulder. "Have you ever done manual labor in your life?"

"Good point. But surely I can do something."

This time she didn't reply, but when they reached the workshop, Kenzie opened all of the garage-type doors he hadn't known were on the opposite end.

"I need more natural light," she told him, almost defying him to tell her to close them.

"Works for me, but there won't be light for too much longer."

"While there is, I'm going to take advantage of it." She turned back to the room with her hands on her hips. "Is there some big trash cans or a dumpster or something?"

Jonathan looked around. "Probably."

"You don't know if you have a couple big trash cans?"

"I'm never out here." He felt the need to defend himself. "I tend to do a lot more white collar type stuff and not I-need-a-workshop-and-trash-cans stuff." He headed toward the back of the workshop where there was some storage rooms and found what he'd hoped. With a 55-gallon trash can in each hand, he walked back toward her, setting them near her buckets of destroyed yarn. "Why don't you put me to work doing something innocuous while you decide for sure what to throw away?"

Kenzie hesitated then nodded. "Fine. You can get the yarn I still have ready to dye."

That sounded easy enough.

"I'm also going to need a Sam's run before everything gets here."

"We can do that tomorrow."

She dragged a board from the pile. "And probably to the Serenity Landing Home and Garden store to replace this and a couple of other things."

With the patience of Job, she explained exactly what he needed to do. He didn't understand, and it seemed to be a lot of work that could surely be done another, easier way, but he didn't question her. His mind wandered with the tedium of it, but by the time she finished going through the tubs - almost everything went in the trash - he thought he'd done a decent amount of yarn unwinding or whatever the actual term was.

Kenzie looked adorable with her feet planted and her hands on her hips and a mildly critical look on her face. "Not bad."

Jonathan's crestfallen look was priceless.

"Not bad?"

Kenzie couldn't hold back the much-needed laughter. "It's fine. As long as you do what I tell you, this part's hard to get wrong."

"It seems tedious and boring."

"It is."

"So I'm not doing it wrong?" His upturned lip mirrored his skeptical tone.

And made her want to kiss him.

Where did that thought come from? Just because she thought marrying him might not be the worst thing ever, despite his tabloid fodder life?

"No, you're not doing it wrong. How many skeins is that?"

"Skeins?"

She rolled her eyes. "How many times have you finished one string and started another?"

"Oh. This is my fourth."

That would work. She usually only did three at a time for this particular process, but four would be okay. "Finish that one, and we'll tie it off."

The rest of the yarn had been almost a total loss. She couldn't, in good conscience, sell it after it had been wet for so long.

With one hand tugging her scrunchie out of her hair, she turned back to the workshop. It would be a fantastic place to set up a permanent shop, if she could make a few, small, changes to it.

Okay. Not so small. But it wouldn't take much, comparatively, to turn it into her dream workshop.

"What's that look?"

Kenzie felt her face heat. "Just daydreaming."

"About me?" His cocky self-confidence was back.

"Not really."

"Which means kind of?"

How had he managed to get under her skin so thoroughly so quickly? "Just thinking what I could do with an actual workshop like this, set up to my specifications."

He didn't say anything until she glanced his way. Then he held up his hands in mock surrender. "Hey. If you decided to say yes, you could outfit this however you wanted. Or build a whole new building. Whatever. I'd offer to do it anyway, but you'd turn me down."

The offer was tempting, not because of what kind of workshop she could have, but because of who Jonathan seemed to be. Rather than focusing on it, she turned back to where he'd been working and gave him instructions on what to do next.

It took another hour, but the yarn she already had on hand was ready to go. Her dyes would be here in the morning. It would take time to mix the dyes up, but her recipe books hadn't been damaged. She might even be able to get Jonathan to mix some up.

Wait.

Kenzie looked around. "Where are they?"

"Where are what?" Jonathan held the lengths of yarn in his hands.

"My jugs. I had a bunch of apple and grape juice containers. Most of them were empty and probably cleaned out."

Jonathan winced. "I wonder if they got thrown out."

Her shoulders slumped. "Great. I need them."

"What are they for?"

"To mix my dyes in. I need clean containers to mix them. At least two dozen." Her frustration quickly turned to overwhelmed tears. One thing after another. And a meeting in the morning with her landlord she didn't want to tell him about, despite his earlier words.

Before she realized what was happening, Jonathan's arms wrapped around her. "It's okay, Kenz. We can find some empty bottles. If nothing else, we'll go to Walmart and get a bunch of apple juice or water jugs or spray bottles." She didn't want to look at him, but his finger under her chin tipped her face toward his. His blue eyes were filled with compassion. "I know life has been a struggle for you, sweetheart, but no matter what, you have me now."

Sweetheart? Had he really just called her sweetheart?

"And we can get you some plastic jugs of some sort. Promise."

"What about Lorelai? She's still sick. She can't go to swim team, and I don't have a babysitter while we do all of this tomorrow."

"Trust me. I already made a call to a guy I know. His daughter will be here bright and early. She's fifteen. He's a teacher at the high school. I met him a couple years ago when he did a fundraiser for another teacher."

"Teacher?" She'd gone to school in town. "Who?"

"Travis Harders."

Relief washed over her. "I liked Mr. Harders. I met his daughter a few times. She may even be on the swim team. I thought I saw her once, but I'm not usually there and not with the bigger kids."

"Good. That's taken care of then. She'll be over about 8:30, and we can go run whatever errands you need to so that you're ready to hit the ground running when the dye gets here."

She searched his eyes, for what she didn't know. "I'll never be able to repay you for all of this. Not just the financial side of it, but believing in me."

His gentle fingers brushed against her forehead, moving the hair that had fallen out of her redone ponytail. "Has no one ever believed in you before, Kenzie?"

"Not really," she whispered. "My parents wanted to, but I didn't give them much reason to when I was younger. It took a while of living a cleaned up life to repair that relationship."

"I believe in you."

"You barely know me."

"I knew everything I needed to know in that first dance."

"You didn't even know my name, and you've been in love with a princess since then," she reminded him, her voice far huskier than she wished.

"Didn't matter. I knew then what I know now, and that's enough. Name or not."

"What could you possibly know?"

"That I wanted to do this and keep doing it forever if you'll let me."

Before she could ask what "this" was, he lowered his face to hers and took her breath away with his kiss.

Chapter Ten

Jonathan poured all of himself into the contact with Kenzie. His arms tightened around her as she gripped the front of his shirt, responding to his kiss with the same fervor.

He broke away, trailing small kisses along her jawline.

Her hands stilled. "Jonathan..." she whispered.

"I know," he murmured. "This could easily get out of hand." He kissed his way back to her lips and melded his against them once more before letting go. Taking half a step back, he left his hands on her hips. He let his forehead rest against hers. "Marry me, Kenzie. I mean it sincerely. Be my wife. Let me be Lorelai's father. I'll adopt her in a heartbeat. Be the mother of my children, my partner in life." He'd never felt anything so intensely as he felt this desire to marry her, to take care of her and Lorelai. To take away her worries and make her life easier.

She didn't answer right away, but finally stepped back. "You don't know me well enough for me to give you an answer. I don't know you well enough." She gave him a half-smile. "But it is increasingly difficult to turn you down."

He smiled back at her. "Then I guess I'll have to keep asking and hope you change your mind." Time to change the subject. "What else can we do here tonight?"

Kenzie moved away and looked around. "We can put that yarn up and then call it good. You're taking a couple days off, right?"

"I'm at your disposal for most of the week." He did have a couple of phone meetings but nothing the next day.

"Then I'll have you do some more of that tomorrow morning. The rest of the yarn won't be here yet, so I can do most of the mixing of the dyes and get what I have dyed, but you should be able to do that while I work on the dye stuff." She turned to him, wide-eyed. "Did they throw out the glass quart jars? There weren't as many and surely they didn't look like trash."

Jonathan pulled his phone out to text CJ. "I can find out, but we'll pick some up in the morning if we need to."

It didn't take long to put everything away and walk back up to the house. Jonathan stopped in the kitchen to get a snack, but Kenzie headed for the stairs.

She paused, one hand on the rail and turned to look at him, her eyes darker than he'd ever seen them. "Thank you, Jonathan. For everything."

"My pleasure, Kenz." It really had been. To be able to give freely to someone who actually wanted nothing from him, who didn't see him as a sack of dollar signs, was a breath of fresh air.

Rather than saying anything else, she turned and went up the stairs. When he'd dished up some ice cream, Jonathan headed to his room, mildly surprised by the clack of nails behind him. Mr. Benny Hercules walked out of the living room where he had probably been hiding under something and followed Jonathan upstairs. He took pity on the dog and picked him up. Once on the bed, Mr. Benny Hercules turned around a few times on the pillow and settled in.

Jonathan parked himself in his recliner and turned on SportsCenter. His mind sort of wandered as he ate his dessert. Then time for a few more minutes in his Bible before bedtime. The dog must be getting more used to him, because for the first time, he slept on Jonathan's pillow overnight. In the morning, Jonathan's first stop was to let the little dog do his business in the grass outside the front door. Second was breakfast in his office, quieting his stomach while he spent time with his Maker.

By the time he closed his Bible and logged onto his computer, he could hear little girl giggles in the kitchen. Taking his coffee cup and empty oatmeal bowl with him, he found George making scrambled eggs for what appeared to be a completely healed Lorelai.

"Mr. Jonathan!" She jumped down from her perch on a bar stool. "Morning!"

He set his dishes down and swung her up into his arms. "Good morning. Are you feeling better?"

She nodded. "Thank you for takin' care of me."

Tightening his grip, just a bit, he kissed her cheek. "My pleasure, punkin."

"Mama said I can't go to swim this morning though." She pouted as he set her back on her stool.

"Probably a good idea to stay home and take it easy." He sat on the stool next to her. "You don't want to push yourself and just get sick again."

Lorelai sighed deeply. "You soun' like Mama."

"Your mama is a smart woman." He glanced toward the stairs. "Where is she?"

"She had to run an errand, sir." George scooped the eggs out onto a plate and set it in front of Lorelai.

Jonathan took a sip of his coffee. "Did she say where?" And

what car did she take?

"No, sir. She took the sedan after making sure Lorelai could stay with me for a bit."

He could look to see where the GPS in the car was, but he didn't seriously consider it. "Did she say how long she'd be gone?"

"No, but she did leave this sitting on the counter. It looks like a shopping list."

Looking over the list, Jonathan made a decision. "You want to go to the store with me, kiddo?"

Lorelai's eyes lit up. "Yay!" She shoveled a spoonful of eggs into her mouth.

Jonathan chuckled. "You don't need to eat quite that fast. We'll go when you finish and get changed."

She still hurried and came back downstairs about ten minutes later in mismatched clothes and sparkly flip flops. In one hand she held a hairbrush. "Can you help me, Mr. Jonathan?"

What did he know about doing hair? But he'd try. He took the brush and a squirt bottle of some sort. Detangler, the label said. He lifted Lorelai back onto her stool. "I've never done girl hair, so you'll have to tell me if I'm doing it right."

"You just brush it, but not too hard. Because then it hurts."

Without any other instructions, and ignoring the smirk on George's face, Jonathan sprayed her hair and got to work.

Kenzie put the car in park and wondered how she was going to make it through the rest of the day much less the ones to follow. Even driving over the slight bump between the asphalt of the drive and the concrete of the driveway sent pain shooting through her side.

She managed to get out of the car without too much difficulty, but only through sheer determination.

The sound of a powerful engine roaring up the drive caught her attention, and she saw Jonathan drive up in a shining blue Mustang with the top down.

And a squealing little girl in the back.

He braked to a stop right next to her. "Good morning." Jonathan held up her notepad. So that's why she couldn't find it. "Cassie was running late. We went shopping for you."

Great. Hopefully he followed the list exactly.

"We also stopped over at Josh's and got your jars." He reached down next to his seat and the trunk popped open. She could see a trash bag full of the glass jars in the back seat.

Lorelai undid her own car seat buckle and climbed over the side. Kenzie started to reprimand her, but Jonathan waved her off. "We had the top down, Mama! And Mr. Jonathan did my hair this morning!"

That explained the dubious ponytail. She didn't even want to think about how long it would take to brush out after riding around in a convertible all morning.

"We only had the top down the last few minutes." Jonathan set a couple of grocery bags on the driveway. "Just since we left Josh's, and I didn't go very fast."

Thank God for small favors.

He held up a giant bag of baking soda then stopped. "Why am I getting all of this out here? Hop in. We'll empty it over at the workshop. Makes a lot more sense."

Kenzie climbed in the front seat, Lorelai sitting on her lap and the jars in the back seat.

"I think we got everything on your list," he told her, driving slowly. "I followed it as best I could."

She closed her eyes and pinched the bridge of her nose. "Most of the time substitutions are okay, but sometimes it *has* to be a certain thing."

"I hope we did okay." He had to be cringing, but she didn't dare look.

"Like actual Sharpies and blue painter's tape and blue Dawn dish soap. Alternatives won't work right."

"Good. We got those. I presume it doesn't matter too much what the plastic bottles are as long as they're easy to grip?"

"Right."

The car came to a stop. "Then let's get organized so we can hit the ground running when the dyes get here."

Lorelai's elbow to her side made Kenzie suck in her breath. Fortunately, Jonathan didn't seem to notice. He would before the day was out. Then he'd want to know where she'd been, what she'd been doing, and why she hadn't trusted him to deal with it on her behalf.

And fallen on a wet sidewalk in the process.

With the big doors open into the workshop, Kenzie could see several tables set up along the side walls as well as in the middle. When had someone done that?

"I hope this is plenty of workspace for you," Jonathan called as he carried an armload of supplies in from the car.

"It is." Far more than she'd had before, though she did recognize a couple of the tables as ones she'd scavenged from various places to use in her old workshop.

"Can I help, Mama?" Lorelai carried the giant bag of baking soda.

"For a little bit, sugar, but then we have to mix up the dyes."

Lorelai wrinkled her nose. "I don't wanna help do that. It's stinky and hot."

"Hot?" Jonathan set a load of Walmart bags down on the table.

"Not specifically hot," Kenzie explained. "But you do have to wear a fairly heavy-duty dust mask and long sleeves, so it can be warm no matter the time of year."

"Gotcha." He pointed toward the wall. "I was thinking we could set up half the slow cookers along that wall and the other half along the back. They shouldn't trip a breaker then. There are also more microwaves in the trunk."

"You got more microwaves?" She hadn't thought to order those on Amazon.

"You said two, but I went with six."

"Where'd you put them all?"

"One is in the floor in the back seat. The rest are in the trunk."

She was overwhelmed, once again, by all he was doing for her.

"I didn't want to drive all over Springfield, so I got a couple different brands and styles, but all the same size." He carried two boxes back in. "Is that okay?"

Kenzie managed a nod as she blinked the tears back. "It's fine."

"Good. Does it matter how the slow cookers are set up?"

She had to shake herself out of it. "The ones that are the same will all be on the same schedule, so to speak. Even if they're the same number of quarts, but one is deeper and another wider, they'll work a bit differently."

"And that's okay?" Jonathan frowned as he set them down. "I can run to all the stores in the area, or have someone do it, if you tell me which one you like best."

"It's fine, Jon." The shortened version of his name didn't come easily, but unless he told her to stop, she needed to do it. To retain a smidge of control over her universe, because controlling the name she called him was all she had. Kenzie hid another wince as she walked to the table where all of the bags now sat. Everything needed to be pulled out and sorted.

He'd thought of everything. She'd mentioned in passing that she'd miss having a stove timer because that gave her three - it, her phone, and an egg timer reminiscent of the 60 Minutes clock. In one bag she found ten digital timers and several packs of batteries to operate them.

As long as she stayed moving and didn't try to bend too much, especially toward her left, Kenzie thought she'd be okay.

The delivery arrived about the time she finished organizing everything the way she wanted. Jonathan had set up a couple microwaves which would heat the water faster than the large pots on the free standing burners.

She looked around with her hands on her hips. "Okay. We both need long sleeves and pants that you don't care if they get dirty. You probably won't, but you might." She gave Lorelai a look. "And that means you need to find something else until Cassie gets here. We can bring the DVD player out and you can watch a movie in the corner." Thank God for portable DVD players with regular plugs and not just ones for the car.

"Can I help Mr. George?" Lorelai put the rest of grocery bags into another one to keep them from blowing around. Kenzie would use them later.

"No. You don't need to bother him." The three of them started for the house.

"He won't mind until Cassie gets here. Honest." Jonathan bumped her with his hip and pain jolted through her whole right side. "It'll be just you and me working on the dye."

If she survived that long.

Chapter Eleven

Something was wrong with Kenzie, but Jonathan couldn't put his finger on what it was. He knew his little girl hair skills weren't up to par, but surely the lopsided ponytail wasn't *that* bad.

It only took a few minutes for him to change and most of that time was spent trying to decide which jeans he liked least. He didn't really have any old work clothes.

Lorelai and Cassie were happily ensconced in the kitchen helping George with dinner prep when Kenzie reappeared.

"Let's get this done." She wouldn't look him in the eye. Where had she been? What wasn't she telling him?

But he didn't push her. Not yet.

Once back in the workshop, he followed her instructions to the letter. Water just shy of boiling. Dye powder carefully weighed and mixed into a paste then more water added.

Between the goggles, the heavy duty gloves and masks, and the near boiling water, it was definitely a hot job.

But after several hours, the assorted plastic jugs were full of dyes crossing the entire spectrum of color. They were labeled and lined neatly on one of the tables. Fortunately, her preprinted labels were dry and only needed to be marked with a couple bits of information to differentiate, though a bunch of them looked pretty similar to Jonathan's eyes. Kenzie told him the differences, but he just wasn't discerning enough in his evaluation of "purple" to quite understand it all.

Finally, Kenzie pulled her goggles off. "I think that's all of it. You'll still want to wear something that can get dirty or an apron or both when actually dyeing, because no matter how careful you are, sometimes you get dye where it's not supposed to be."

"Duly noted." But he couldn't not say anything. "But you're not telling me something. Are you in pain?"

"I tweaked my side earlier. That's all. I'm fine."

"You'd tell me if it was something more?"

He didn't believe her nod.

Once in the house, Kenzie took some mail George handed her then went upstairs to take a shower. Cassie and Lorelai were watching a movie in the basement. Jonathan checked his phone, made a call from his office then went to clean himself up. Back in the kitchen, he found Kenzie downing what appeared to be painkillers, but he didn't question her on it.

"Sir?"

Jonathan turned to see George standing by the foyer. "Yes?"

"I need to speak with you in your office, sir."

He followed his assistant into the room and closed the door behind them. "What is it?"

"I received an alert about you." He tapped on his tablet a few times then handed it over. "Someone posted that on social media, and it got picked up."

Jonathan looked at the first picture of himself walking into

Sam's Club, holding Lorelai's hand. She was looking up at him, supreme adoration on her face. He swiped through the rest of them, about eight all together, of him with Lorelai throughout the store. She was ringing up the items at the checkout. They were filling his trunk. He was helping her buckle in. CelebGossipNewz had picked the story, such as it was, and were running with it.

He read it aloud. "Jonathan Langley-Cranston the Fourth, heir to the Langley and Cranston business and political dynasties, was seen at his local Sam's Club with much lighter hair than normal and an unidentified female, age five. J4, as he's known in party circles, has no known children, nor does he have any nieces of the right age." He had no nieces at all yet. "This has led to speculation that the one-time 'most eligible bachelor' is officially off the market. We reached out to the family publicist, but there was no comment. More details as they become available." Jonathan handed the tablet back to George. "Great. Kenzie's going to love this."

"You might be more concerned about your family."

Jonathan flopped into his desk chair. "I don't care what my family thinks."

"Of course not."

He wouldn't tell Kenzie. It would upset and worry her unnecessarily. No one would identify Lorelai. Those who could tell it was her wouldn't be talking to the media anyway.

"Does the reference to your former circle of friends bother you?"

As much as he wanted to give a flippant "no," Jonathan took some time to think about it more carefully. "I haven't hung out with that crowd in a long time, though the casual celebrity gossip watcher wouldn't know that." He hated being lumped in as a celebrity. The stigma shouldn't follow him as long as it had, but because of his family name he'd never be able to shake it. "Kenzie knows. That's the important part."

George looked like he wanted to say something else, but stopped when Jonathan's phone rang. He took his leave as Jonathan swiped across it.

"Hey, Daniel. What can I do for you?" Jonathan listened as one of his lawyers explained what he'd learned in the last few minutes. So not only had Kenzie taken matters into her own hands, but her sleaze ball landlord had ignored the letter delivered the day before via courier service. "Can we sue the life out of him?"

Daniel hesitated. "I'm not sure. I know you said I work for Kenzie now, but legally I don't know if it'll hold water. I'm your lawyer, not hers. Even if I am working on her behalf, it's at your instruction, not hers. I have nothing in writing from her authorizing me to do much of anything. With most of these types, it's enough to send a cease and desist letter, and they deal strictly with me from then on. In this case, he didn't, but I don't know that the letter is legally enforceable just yet anyway. I mean, if she was your wife or something, then maybe, but until I actually have paperwork signed by her, I don't know that he'll back off. And if she went over there against our advice, then I wonder if she'll sign it anyway."

"She wants to stand on her own two feet." Jonathan ran a hand through his hair. "I'm not sure if she'd sign it or not. I'll go talk to her and get back to you."

They hung up and Jonathan prayed for wisdom. Time to talk to Kenzie.

Kenzie had never felt so beaten down in her life.

The shower hadn't helped her side. It hadn't helped her nerves. It hadn't helped the churning in the pit of her stomach when she flipped through the mail George had handed her. Maybe forwarding it hadn't been such a good idea. At least then she could keep her head in the sand for a while longer.

Bills she shouldn't need to pay - like electricity, water, and gas for the house. Bills she already couldn't pay - like hospital bills she still owed from before her late husband's death. Stupid man went to the ER for every minor ache and pain. He'd probably been looking for drugs, though Kenzie never would have suspected him of prescription drug use at the time. They'd offered to let her settle the bills several times, for much lower than what she owed, but she never had the cash needed to take them up on it.

And then there were the other bills he'd run up.

She went downstairs to find Lorelai trying to play with Mr. Benny Hercules who had taken refuge under the couch.

"Mama!" Her daughter ran toward her, barreling into her full force.

Kenzie couldn't hold back her cry of pain.

"You okay, Mama?"

She took a step back and pressed her hand against her side. "I'm fine, sugar."

"No, you're not." Jonathan's worried face was exactly what she'd been trying to avoid. "What happened?"

There was no way out. "I fell earlier. I'll be fine."

"I don't think so." He came to stand next to her. "Tell me if this hurts."

His fingers normally sent a thrill through her, but this time all she could focus on was the pain. She nodded, unable to speak.

"You're going to urgent care. I'm afraid you might have

cracked a rib or two."

She shook her head. "No. I'm not going. I'll be fine." She'd take some more ibuprofen and not tell Jonathan she couldn't afford a trip to urgent care because he'd pay for it.

"Too bad. You're going." He wrapped an arm around her waist and urged her toward the door. "Lorelai will stay here with Cassie. She'll be fine, and I'll feel a lot better getting you checked out."

She wanted to protest about the money, but he'd just offer to marry her again.

Kenzie wondered why that was such a bad idea. Her financial world had begun to crumble down around her again. She'd kept it at bay for so long, but now, with no prospects for real income anytime soon, she wondered what they would do without Jonathan's good graces. If she turned down his proposal one too many times.

And it wasn't like she didn't find him attractive. Or still daydream about falling asleep in the arms of a man worthy of the title of husband and father to Lorelai.

Someone who was already talking about adopting his cousin's baby.

That would make Kenzie the mother of two.

How long had she wished Lorelai wouldn't grow up as an only child?

Kenzie was grateful Jonathan took the Mustang. The seats were more comfortable and it was easier to get in and out of than climbing into his big truck would be.

And when she fell too hard into the seat, the shoot of pain caused her to wince. She admitted, to herself, he might be right and that she'd waited too long to take more medicine.

They made her fill out paperwork since she'd never been to the walk-in clinic attached to the hospital. If she had to go to one, she went to the one in Serenity Landing, or maybe the one in Walmart. It wasn't nearly as expensive. But Jonathan, rightly, insisted on coming to this one. If she needed x-rays they'd just send her over here anyway.

"Put me here." Jonathan pointed at the section about who was responsible for payment.

"No." She'd spend the rest of her life paying it off, but she wasn't going to let him pay for it.

"You got hurt at my house, didn't you? Something while we were out in the workshop?"

Did he really think that? "No. I got hurt this morning. I wasn't at your house at all."

He seemed skeptical, but she stuck to her guns and put her own name down. It irked her to put his address, but she didn't have another option.

The wait seemed to take forever, but eventually she was back in a room. She'd told Jonathan she didn't want him to come with her. The whole thing took another couple hours, but eventually she left with a prescription for painkillers, instructions *not* to wrap her ribs even though it might feel better because it would make it more difficult to breathe and lead to other problems, and strict instructions to take it easy.

Yeah, right.

She was a single mother with an almost five-year-old and a business to run and a major trade show in a couple weeks with nothing ready for it.

Kenzie also didn't tell the doctor she'd probably be wrapping her ribs anyway, at least for a little while each day to help her get her work done.

Jonathan stood when she walked out. On the way to the car, she told him the diagnosis and prognosis, leaving off the part about taking it easy. Once in the car, she turned her phone back on and frowned at the phone number that had left a voice mail.

She knew who it was and what they wanted.

Kenzie squeezed her eyes shut, unwilling to give into the overwhelming feeling of despair threatening to overtake her.

It was too much.

She couldn't do it any longer.

Her soul cried out for rest, for peace.

And though she tried to put her trust, her faith, in God, Kenzie was beginning to feel more than a bit desperate for a way out of the mind numbing mess her life had become.

If Jonathan asked again, she'd say yes.

Chapter Twelve

As annoyed as he was by Kenzie's response to putting him down as financially responsible, Jonathan had to respect her decision. She didn't want his money.

And that made him want to take care of her all the more.

If only she would let him.

The text messages from Josh came back to him, and he knew it was time. "There's something I need to talk to you about, Kenz."

She didn't look his way. "What?" The defeat in her voice cut deep.

"Something happened this morning. Nothing bad," he rushed to reassure her. "Not really. I don't think. But when I took Lorelai to Sam's, someone snapped some pictures and posted them to social media. They started to spread and then a couple of gossip sites picked them up. I saw one article earlier this afternoon, and Josh sent me another one while you were in the back."

Kenzie didn't move. Just sat there with her head leaning

against her hand with her elbow propped against the window.

"None of them know who she is, but there was some speculation that she might be my daughter, and I've been hiding her from the public eye for the last few years. Something about seeing the similarity between us."

"There's a similarity?"

"I guess. I mean we're both humans, but I've never even tried to look for any similarities. Certainly there's nothing that jumps out and says 'this is my child!' I just don't see it. She's adorable," he pointed out. "But not my daughter."

"So what does that mean?"

"It means there will likely be more photographers following me than usual for a bit. I'd say stay on the property as much as possible for a while, but that's about it."

"There's not a threat to my daughter?"

"Probably not. Just a few photographers trying to get a shot of the *heir to the Langley and Cranston business and political dynasties.*" He couldn't hide the bitterness. "I'm sorry, Kenzie. I haven't had pictures of me from around here get to the outside world in ages."

"It's not your fault."

Did she really mean that? Really believe it?

"And we won't be leaving your property much for a while anyway, so it's not a big deal. Lorelai can ride with Gwendolyn to swim team in the mornings and evenings. If she takes the SUV, Lorelai will be in the back and not really visible anyway. It'll be fine."

When they reached the house, Kenzie went straight up to her room. Not surprising really. She had to be tired and sore. At least her meds had been ready before they made it home, and she had been able to get them.

The next morning, Jonathan woke to find his parents and

grandmother gone. They hadn't mentioned the pictures, but he'd been able to sense the condescension from both of them. His grandmother had a twinkle in her eye he didn't quite understand.

He spent nearly an hour on a conference call with a company he did business with in Europe. Then he had his morning quiet time and went for a short run. About the time he pulled his shorts on there was a knock on his door.

"Come in," he called.

Kenzie pushed the door open. Her face alarmed him, though he tried not to let it show. She clearly hadn't slept well, and the way she walked into his room told him how much pain she had to be in.

"Are you about ready to get started?" she asked. "There's a lot to do and the yarn should be here soon, right?"

"UPS is usually by here sometime around noon. I checked your order on the website, and it shipped yesterday. I haven't looked yet this morning, but I'm sure it's out for delivery." After pulling his shirt on, Jonathan pulled his phone out to check the app. He got a notice anytime something was being delivered to his house. In a couple of taps, he confirmed what he'd suspected. "It's supposed to be here this morning."

"Then I'm heading out to work on what's already here." She turned, but stopped and stared at his nightstand. "What's that?"

Jonathan winced. "You weren't supposed to see that."

"What is it?" she demanded again.

He walked over and picked up the square velvet box. "It's an engagement ring. I found it the other day, and thought you'd like it." Was it right to just hold the box out toward her?

She took it from him and stared at it until the silence turned uncomfortable. "I love it, but is it really appropriate for you to have?" She handed it back. "We haven't even been on a real date."

"So? I've meant what I've said the last few days, Kenz. All it takes is for you to say yes."

"Yes?" Did she sound like she was wavering?

"That's it. You say the word, and we'll head down to the courthouse. Or we'll plan the wedding of your dreams." Should he drop to a knee again? Had he actually yet? "Here, I'll do it right. Then you can say yes, no, or not yet. Your choice."

Holding the box in front of him, Jonathan knelt down and took her hand. "MacKenzie Annette Davidson, would you do me the honor of making me the happiest man alive and becoming my bride?"

She didn't look at him. Didn't get excited. Didn't do anything but clutch her stomach with her other hand before giving a single nod. "Yes."

What? "Yes?" He needed to be sure.

This time a smile crossed her face, one that reached her eyes. "Yes. I'll marry you."

A feeling of joy swept over Jonathan as he pulled the ring out of the box and slid it onto her finger. He stood and framed her face with his hands. "You've made me so incredibly happy, Kenzie Ann. I'm honored." Then he kissed her. Soft and gentle, with an underlying passion he hadn't felt in a very long time.

"Did you mean what you said about the courthouse?" she whispered when they parted, her eyes staring at her left hand where it gripped his shirt.

"Absolutely. If that's what you want." But she didn't, did she? Wouldn't she want the big fairy tale wedding? He asked her.

"Could we get married today and have a wedding later? Maybe. If we decide we want to?"

"Where Lorelai could be the flower girl?" he asked, his grin widening even more.

She nodded. "Yes."

"If that's what you want to do, that's what we'll do."

"Then let's go. I want to get married now."

"Let's get Lorelai and go."

Kenzie loved the feeling of Jonathan's second kiss, but when he released her, she shook her head. "She's at swim practice. And if we're having a real wedding later, then the important thing is the two of us."

"True, but you don't want her there?" Jonathan sounded as confused as Kenzie felt.

"I'm not sure I do. Not for a quickie courthouse wedding. I want her to be a part of planning the real one though." Hoping she didn't sound as desperate as she felt, Kenzie leaned up and kissed him.

The groan in the back of his throat told her she'd succeeded in changing the subject.

"What about a minister?" he asked when she moved back.

"Do you know a judge or someone who can do it?" Didn't his family know someone?

"The lawyer who's handling your landlord is the son of a judge." Jonathan backed away and glanced at his watch. "We might be able to get him to do it if we hurry. Daniel was telling me yesterday his folks are leaving on vacation about noon. We'd have to run down to the courthouse in Trumanville to get the license then meet them somewhere."

"Why Trumanville and not Springfield?"

"It's closer. It's also closer to Daniel's parents' house. And since it's the county seat of Pond Creek County, they issue marriage licenses."

"How do you know this?"

Jonathan shrugged. "I know county courthouses issue the licenses. Trumanville is the county seat and has the county courthouse. Hence, they issue licenses."

"Then what are we waiting for? The sooner we get moving, the sooner I'm your wife." Kenzie turned away from him, afraid he'd see the disconcerting churning inside. Was this the right thing to do?

Maybe not, but she was going to do it anyway.

And then come back and dye yarn all day.

"I'm going to go change into something a little nicer," she called over her shoulder. "Not too nice, though." The last thing she needed was him putting on his best suit while she wore jeans that were fraying on the bottom and a shirt with mismatched buttons. She found a sundress she'd all but forgotten about hanging in the closet and put it on, along with her favorite sandals, before putting on a bit of make-up.

Kenzie smoothed the fabric over her stomach as she stared at herself in the mirror. The ring glittered in the sunlight coming through the window, mocking her. What had she done to deserve such a thing?

When she walked back out, Jonathan was walking toward her with a smile on his face. "You look lovely."

She patted his chest with her right hand to avoid seeing the ring. "You cleaned up quite nicely, too." His collared button-down shirt probably cost as much as her wardrobe, but it didn't scream *"I have money, and she doesn't"* either.

"What car do you want to take?" he asked, trailing behind her. "Which one will be easiest for you to get in and out of?"

Kenzie waited for him at the top of the stairs, knowing it wouldn't be easy for her to walk down them and hoping he'd go first. "Actually, I'd love to ride in the Mustang again." That was a *fantastic* car. "But probably the SUV or something that's about butt height, honestly." She wasn't sure she could climb up into or out of any of the others easily enough.

As she'd hoped, Jonathan started down the stairs. "I'm pretty sure the SUV is a bit tall, but not too tall or too short like the others might be."

"That sounds perfect."

He moved faster. "I'll pull it up front for you."

So considerate of him. She had a feeling he was like that with everyone, at least until they took advantage of his good nature. Even as she slid up a bit onto the front seat, Kenzie had to hide her wince.

"Did you take your good medicines this morning?" Jonathan asked her with a frown. "Is that why you suddenly changed your mind?"

"No." Her forceful tone surprised both of them. "It's not. I took them last night, but this morning, I've only had some ibuprofen. I've thought a lot about what you said the last few days and realized that this is what I want, too. Not because of your parents or anyone else thinking we should or shouldn't, but because I want to be your wife." She reached over and took his hand. "I want you to be Lorelai's father."

He glanced over at her, a huge grin on his face. "I am going to be her father, aren't I?"

"You're good with that, right?"

Jonathan tightened his grip on her hand. "You bet I am. I'm very glad to be the father to that little girl. I'll adopt her tomorrow if you'll let me." His face slacked a bit. "Her paternal grandparents won't mind, will they?"

She shook her head. "No. They won't mind." Kenzie stared at their joined hands. "I should probably tell you, though, they're not her biological grandparents. I was pregnant before we got married." Her bitter laugh echoed in the vehicle. "My only one night stand gave me the best thing in my life. My husband married me, knowing it wasn't his baby."

Her new fiancé didn't reply immediately.

"I'm not proud of that part of my past, Jonathan." Her heart sank. Would he change his mind? "I've never cheated on anyone, though. Never."

"It takes a big man to marry a woman knowing she's having a baby that's not his."

Kenzie snorted. "Hardly. Pretty sure he thought we'd get some kind of welfare payments he could use. The loser died before Lorelai was born. I've told his parents repeatedly she's not their grandchild. They didn't care before he died. They never really cared after either."

Until recently. But with a new last name and a husband with the influence hers had, they'd back off. She hoped.

"Have they ever met her?"

"No." She wasn't sure she'd have let them even if they'd showed interest immediately, but they hadn't.

They drove in silence for a couple of miles. "We all have a past, Kenzie. There's plenty in mine I'm not proud of either. There's no alcohol in my house for a reason."

That confirmed her recovering alcoholic theory.

"I won't judge you for your past. I know you well enough to know you won't judge me for mine. We've both been washed clean by the blood of the Lamb. From here on out, it's you and me and that's what matters. Not who was in our pasts, but that it's just the two of us in our futures."

The two of them. Washed by the blood of the Lamb. Clean. New. Starting a relationship where the expectation was monogamy. Different, sure. But a good different.

A very good different.

Suddenly, Kenzie couldn't wait to be his wife.

Chapter
Thirteen

Jonathan stood in front of the fireplace of Daniel's childhood home. Daniel's father stood to one side. Kenzie faced Jonathan, her hands in his.

"Do you Jonathan William Langley-Cranston the Fourth take this woman to be your bride? Do you promise to love, honor, and cherish her? To keep yourself only unto her for as long as you both shall live?"

Jonathan couldn't contain his grin as he said the words Kenzie had spoken a moment earlier. "I do."

"Then by the power vested in me by the State of Missouri, I now pronounce you husband and wife." His friend's dad grinned. "Jonathan, you may kiss your bride."

Jonathan squeezed Kenzie's hands and leaned down to kiss her gently.

And to think, he could spend the rest of his life doing this.

When he moved back, Daniel's dad chuckled. "Congratulations, you two."

"Thanks." Jonathan shook his hand without letting go of Kenzie's. "We need to get going though. We have a lot of work waiting for us at home." He winked at Kenzie. "My wife owns her own yarn dyeing business, and she's behind for a big show next week."

"Yarn?" Daniel's mom piped in. "What kind?"

Kenzie said a whole bunch of words Jonathan was familiar with but couldn't figure out from the context.

"I'd love to see your work, dear. Send me a link."

Kenzie dug around in her purse for a minute. "Here's my card. It's got a link to my Etsy and Facebook pages. There's not much for sale now since I lost everything I had done during the storm last weekend."

A few minutes later, they were in the SUV. Jonathan reached over to link his fingers with Kenzie's. "So, Mrs. Langley-Cranston, do we go to the bank and get you added to the accounts or wait? I'll give you the card numbers so you can order anything you need online, but you wouldn't be able to purchase anything in person."

"I didn't marry you for the money, Jonathan."

"I know." Thank goodness. If he'd thought she was marrying for the money that would have been the end of that. "But since you are now, legally, my wife, that means you get access to all of it. If you have any lingering medical bills or student loans or anything you need to pay off, just do it. I mean, I know you're pretty careful about your debt and everything, but if there's anything you need to take care of, do it." He brought her hand up and kissed the back of it. "Anything monetary that's stressing you out, it can be easily fixed now."

"There are a few things and the last round of utility payments and stuff," she said slowly, her fingers more limp in his than they had been before.

"Just don't hit seven figures, and we'll be fine." He winked at her to let her know he was joking around.

"It's not anywhere near seven figures."

He squeezed her hand. "And even if it was seven figures, it would be okay, just need to move some stuff around."

"It's not."

They were nearly home before he spoke again. "Seriously, Kenz. I don't want you to worry about that stuff anymore. I'm not saying spoil Lorelai or anything, but if there's something you want or need, just get it, and don't worry about it."

"How much is too much to spend on something then? I mean, not that I need one, but could I just go buy a new car?"

Jonathan rubbed his thumb along her knuckles. "You could, but I'd think you would talk to me about that first." He chuckled. "Now, my sisters would just do it, but you don't strike me as the type to go spend that kind of money on anything without seriously weighing the pros and cons and figuring out how to get the best deal."

"I didn't marry you for the money," Kenzie told him again, more defensive this time.

"I know." Jonathan let it drop and let go of her hand to click the button to open the gates to his property. "I guess it's time to change and get to work on the yarn?"

Kenzie folded her hands together on her lap. "You don't have to help me. I can do it."

"I want to. It's fascinating." He grinned her direction even though she wasn't looking at him. "Besides, it's our wedding day. I'd like to spend most of it with you no matter what we end up doing."

"It is, isn't it?" Kenzie stared out her window.

"It is what?"

"Our wedding day. It doesn't really feel like it. It doesn't feel real."

Jonathan wasn't sure what to make of that - or his suddenly despondent new wife. "The piece of paper in my pocket says it's very real."

"I know it is. And I know I said this is what I wanted, and it is, but I didn't realize part of me would be so disappointed not to have the whole real wedding thing."

"We will," he promised. "Whenever you want. As soon as we can plan it or wait a year and do it on our anniversary. Your choice."

"Maybe we can talk about it after Christmas? I think I've got too much on my plate until then anyway."

"That sounds fine." He pulled the car to a stop not too far from the house. "Why don't you go change, and I'll drive you over?" She had to be in pain. He hadn't seen her take any pain killers since they left several hours earlier.

Kenzie nodded as she opened her door and shifted sideways to slide out. Jonathan hurried around to help her. She let him, but reluctantly at best it seemed. Only because she was in pain? He'd already realized there would be no traditional wedding night activities given her injuries. That did disappoint him, but he wasn't a jerk.

"Are you going to make it today?" he asked, concern coloring his voice. "Is there anyone else we can call to come help?"

"I can see if Julia can, but she's pregnant and has a son who's out of school for the summer. She can't do the actual dyeing right now. Other than that, I'm not really sure. I have some yarn dyeing friends in the area, but I wouldn't offer to help them, and they wouldn't offer to help me. Some of what we do is proprietary, and it's a boundary everyone respects. Once the dyeing itself is done, maybe a couple people could come wind and get it all into skeins, but that's it. And even some of that I wouldn't want them to with all of it, because just doing that would tell them how I do some of my stuff."

"Okay. What about other friends outside the yarn world?"

"I work - worked - full time and have a daughter. I don't have time for friends. Just my yarn friends, but they won't work." She sighed and leaned to him as they reached the steps. "They're really more of acquaintances anyway."

Jonathan kissed the side of her head. "Well, you have me now." He'd throw money at it if he had to. Hire a bunch of Gwendolyn and Adam's pool friends to come out and do the same kinds of things he could do.

She started up the steps. "Let's get moving, or it'll never get done."

What in the world had she just done?

Kenzie sank back against the door, staring at the wedding band now seated next to the engagement ring. Both were so far beyond anything she'd ever dreamed of.

But wrapping her mind around the fact she was, once again, a married woman - and to Jonathan Langley-Cranston IV no less. Now a member of a political dynasty, and with secrets she hadn't yet spilled, ones she prayed wouldn't change Jonathan's mind about her.

If she was smart, or kind, she'd march right over to his room - the one she'd be expected to share before long - and spill everything, throwing herself and her daughter on his mercy.

Instead, she gathered herself, and changed clothes, slowly. She slipped the rings off and put them on the dresser. The last thing she wanted was to wear them while working with the dye and ruin them - or while working with the yarn and ruin it.

Kenzie brushed her hair back into a ponytail, wincing when she pulled too hard on her side muscles. Jonathan waited for her in the hall, pushing off from the wall when he saw her.

"Ready to get this done?" His smile was a touch too wide to be real, even if he was as happy as she wished she was.

"It's going to be a lot of work," she warned. "A lot of it isn't *hard*, but it is work and time consuming. And it takes a lot of attention to detail."

"Then give me one task at a time, and I'll go from there."

She slid back into the SUV and wondered what he saw in her.

Because she knew the one thing neither one of them had said in all their discussions about marriage in the last few days - or even this morning, except as required by the vows.

He didn't love her, though she felt herself falling hard for him. Could she live with him, be his wife, without loving him - or without him truly loving her?

Her first marriage had been loveless because she'd been desperate, and he'd been incapable of loving anyone but himself.

She could see the look on her father's face when she'd told him about her first marriage. The look on his face for the second one likely wouldn't be too different.

When they reached the workshop a minute later, Jonathan came around to open her door while Kenzie was still collecting her thoughts.

"So what's first, boss?"

She'd never been anyone's boss before. "First, we need to get water in the plastic buckets with a bit of Dawn dish soap in them and soak the yarn we've already worked on."

"Why blue and not yellow?"

Kenzie gave a half-hearted shrug. "I'm not sure why but it works right and yellow doesn't. The scent may have something to do with it. It makes the yarn ready to accept the dye. Otherwise it won't absorb it right."

"Blue it is then."

Once all the yarn was soaking, she set Jonathan to opening all the boxes and sorting the yarn. Once he was done with that, she started him getting some more ready to self-stripe. She measured water, dye, and white vinegar into the slow cookers lining one wall. All of them would be the same semi-solid color. After turning them all on and setting the temperatures, she looked around.

Jonathan was busy getting the self-striping ready to go. Kenzie walked over to the next set of slow cookers and set up another color. The third table got yet another color.

It took about two hours. Her stomach growled reminding her that lunchtime was long past.

"Are you hungry?" Jonathan called from the other side of the workshop. "My stomach is growling."

She checked her watch. "I am, but I only have a few minutes before I need to start checking dyes."

"So what's the process?"

"They're cooking now. Soon I'll go through and check them. If the dye's been mostly absorbed, I'll wring them out some, twist them, and then do the second layer. By the time I finish getting all the second layers done, it'll be almost time to start the third layers."

"Can I help?"

"You could get me something to eat. I know it's not glamorous, but getting that other yarn ready is a huge help. It won't take near as long to dye, but the process to get it ready takes a lot longer."

"All right then. Lunch and back to work."

By the end of the day, Kenzie sat down in the office chair

Jonathan had brought from inside. The way her back and hip and feet felt, it was a very kind gesture.

"Want me to push you up to the house?" Jonathan offered. "I don't want to leave the chair out here tonight anyway."

Relief washed over her. It would be much better than walking, even if she did feel kind of ridiculous. "That would be great."

In a couple of minutes, they were headed back to the house.

"What are we going to tell Lorelai?" Jonathan asked as he pushed her slowly.

"What do you think we should tell her?" she asked back, mostly because she didn't know what she wanted the answer to be. "What do we need to tell her?"

"Well..." Jonathan seemed uncertain, something she'd seldom seen from him. "Are you planning to move into my room? Or me to yours? Or some other room together?"

Ah, the million dollar question.

"I know you're tired and sore and still in a lot of pain, so unless you just really want to - in which case I won't say no - why don't you stay in your room for a few nights until you're feeling better? I don't think I'd kick you in my sleep, but there's no guarantee I won't. Neither of us is used to sleeping with anyone else."

Was there disappointment in his voice? Kenzie didn't take the time to analyze it. "I think that sounds like a good idea." Almost as good as her plan to take a hot shower or bath and go straight to bed, so she could get to work bright and early the next morning.

⁂

By the time eight o'clock rolled around the next morning, Jonathan had done nearly a full day's work.

Chalk it up to a wedding night where he didn't even sleep in the same room as his bride and the restlessness that came from the sudden distance between himself and Kenzie.

He'd heard Gwendolyn bring Lorelai downstairs for breakfast a while earlier then leave for swim team practice. Her big meet was coming up in just a few days. He'd have to make sure they were both there for it.

If he had any clue what he was doing, he'd get started on the yarn but he didn't. Instead, he called his lawyer and set up an appointment to get things like his will changed. Kenzie would be the primary beneficiary if anything were to happen to him, with plenty set aside for Lorelai as well. The adoption paperwork was already started. He needed to talk to Kenzie about it at some point during the day.

He made a plan. It would likely take a trip to the bank, but he'd set up an account that was just Kenzie's. She could spend it however she saw fit and wouldn't have to wonder if he was looking over her shoulder, silently judging her spending habits.

A couple of phone calls later and the paperwork would be waiting for them at the bank in an hour or so. They could go by at their convenience.

He browsed the Internet waiting for Kenzie to emerge from upstairs. There were no new mentions of him and Lorelai. The gossip media had already moved on to something else.

Finally, he heard Kenzie come downstairs, and he stood to meet her.

He leaned against the wall and watched her slowly descend. "Good morning. Are you still feeling super sore and stiff?"

She finally made it to the bottom. "Very."

"Did you get any sleep?"

"Some, but not much."

Surely more than he did. "Why don't we take it easy today

then? Let's dye all that self-striping stuff you had me working on and some of those placemat thingies..."

"Sock blanks."

"Right." Like he was supposed to remember that. "Sock blanks. You said those are easy."

"They are. You could probably do those, actually."

"I'd be happy to."

"I'll do another round in the slow cookers. You do the sock blanks. You can help me do the self-striping in between."

"And I had George get a few more microwaves. That'll speed up the drying process." That part had seemed to take forever the day before because there weren't enough microwaves, even though there were more than she'd had before.

"You know you can never use them for food right?"

"I know, but you'll have them if you need them." He hesitated then went on. "I do need you to sign some papers down at the bank today. Do you want to do that now or later?"

"Let me grab a bite to eat, and then let's get it over with." She started to walk by him, but Jonathan stopped her with a hand on her arm.

"Hey."

She looked up at him, tension radiating from her.

He didn't understand the reason for it, except it being so close to her show. "Good morning." Jonathan shifted his hand to her waist. "I know we've never actually shared a room, but I still missed you last night." Would she let him kiss her?

He had to take the chance. Weaving his fingers through her hair, he kissed his wife.

Chapter Fourteen

The afternoon was going to be very long and a *fantastic* way to spend their one week anniversary. One of the other moms had tried to prepare Kenzie for the biggest meet of the summer, but she was pretty sure nothing could have, especially not as sore as she'd been the last few days.

One of the local universities held the meet in their natatorium, a word Kenzie had never heard before but was apparently just a fancy name for "building for an indoor pool." The private country clubs and such had their meet in the mornings. The public and community pools had their meet in the afternoon. Lorelai didn't have to be in the pool until 12:30, but Kenzie had it on good authority that getting there any later than noon meant lack of choice in seating.

Jonathan had driven the three of them to the natatorium, letting Lorelai's excited chatter fill the emptiness between Kenzie and her husband. The one who was moving forward with the process to adopt her daughter. The process Kenzie was okay with, in part, because it meant her daughter would always be cared for and protected by a father who would legally be considered her biological father.

The one Kenzie had kissed just once since the wedding.

And, to be fair, he had kissed her.

He'd also been far more patient and understanding and kind than any new husband should have to be.

Now he carried a cooler with water bottles and protein bars and other snacks for the three of them, and any other kids who happened to be around and hungry.

"I'm thinking the back of these bleachers in front of the wall." Jonathan pointed with his head. Several sets of bleachers were in the natatorium itself. Movable glass walls had been removed and several mobile bleachers had been set up in what was normally a hallway. "It'll be easier for you to get up and around when you need to and something for you to lean back against." The top row of the permanent bleachers had a seat back.

Kenzie nodded and followed him. Lorelai sported a brand new red, white, and blue marble-y swim suit to match her teammates, the one splurge Kenzie had convinced herself to take with the money Jonathan had given her. She'd also learned her husband paid for anything when they were together. That made her feel a bit better about virtually all of the money he'd put in her account being gone.

He hadn't said anything about when the account would be refilled or if he just expected her to tell him in six months or a year that it was gone. She'd put every penny she could spare from her yarn business into it, so she wouldn't have to ask anytime soon.

Jonathan set the cooler on the concrete step between metal rows of bleachers and nudged it down a bit with his knee. "Why don't you sit one seat in, so I can run interference for you on the end?"

Kenzie just nodded and took a seat.

Jonathan helped Lorelai get ready for warm-ups. By the time the SLAC Clipper Ships took to the water, nearly seventy members had arrived. They all crowded into three lanes while other teams warmed up in the five other lanes.

"There are *a lot* of swimmers here." Jonathan put his feet up on the seat in front of him. "This seems like it could take forever."

"Alivia said something about heat sheets that tell you when every swimmer is supposed to be swimming what race."

He pulled out his phone. "And there's an app that will supposedly keep us up on the times and places and stuff. I already bought it if you want me to upload it on your phone."

She handed her brand new phone over and let him do whatever he needed to.

It was nearly an hour before Lorelai's first race. She and several other kids, including Alyssa, were swimming a medley relay. Lorelai was swimming backstroke first while Alyssa finished with freestyle. Kenzie didn't know the other two girls.

They didn't come in last, and they didn't quit. That was pretty much the best thing Kenzie could say about the race, but this particular one included kids up to age eight, instead of the usual six-and-under. That, apparently, was typical for relays.

Next up were all the older kids doing their medley relays. It turned out Kenzie knew some of them from knowing their older siblings in school or from the few practices she'd been to.

The teenagers on all the teams were quite good. In fact, their times were lower than Lorelai and her age groups', but they went twice the distance. Would her daughter be able to do that some day?

Lorelai was in the first heat of kids to do the freestyle races, and she really impressed Kenzie. She wouldn't have thought there would be nearly as much progress when Adam, Lorelai's favorite lifeguard and Gwendolyn's boyfriend, had convinced Kenzie to sign Lorelai up for swim team.

"She's doing great," Jonathan told her when they sat back down after cheering her on.

"Much better than I thought she'd do," Kenzie admitted. "It must be the adrenaline."

This time Lorelai came straight to see them. "Did you see, Mama? I didn't come in last!"

"You did great, sweetheart."

Jonathan lifted her up to sit on his knee. "Do you want a snack?"

Lorelai nodded seriously. "Something with protein please."

Kenzie and Jonathan both hid a snicker. Lorelai had no idea what protein was, but one of the older kids had told her to have protein snacks during the meet, but not to eat too much.

So trail mix and Gatorade it was.

The hours dragged on. Lorelai spent about half her time with Kenzie and Jonathan and half her time with her friends in the "small gym" down the hallway where most of the teams - and parents, it seemed - congregated between heats. The seats in the bleachers around them seem to regularly rotate parents as they came in to watch their kids. The walkways and ramp seemed to be regularly occupied by revolving adults, too.

Other swimmers cheered on their friends. She even saw a few cheering on friends who were on other teams.

"Okay, so here's what I think I figured out." Jonathan held out his tablet. "First place gets eight points, second gets seven, and so on down to eighth place. If there are less than eight swimmers, then they redistribute the other points. The relays are worth more. Whichever team has the most points at the end must be the champion."

The dad in front of them turned around. "You've got it. Which team are your kids with?"

Jonathan seemed to hesitate, so Kenzie answered. "My daughter is on the Serenity Landing team. It's her first year."

The guy nodded. "They've always got a good team. The size of the team matters a lot though. There are great kids in all age ranges, but sheer numbers help. If you look at some of the younger and older races, there may only be five or six kids competing. The bigger teams are more likely to pick up points because they're more likely to have more of those kids."

"Makes sense," Jonathan tucked his tablet back in the swim bag. "Which team is the biggest?"

"Usually a team from Springfield is, but they had some issues with their pool this year, and it's been closed down. I think SLAC might be the team to beat. They've got a *lot* of little kids this year compared to most teams."

Kenzie grinned. "They did some pretty heavy recruiting from the lesson kids. I wouldn't have thought my daughter was ready, but she's here and doing well."

Jonathan squeezed her hand. "She's doing great."

It shouldn't bother him.

There was no reason on earth it should bother him.

But it did.

Jonathan wanted Lorelai to be his daughter.

If Kenzie's late first husband had been Lorelai's father, the process would be almost half done. Instead, it would take at least a few more weeks since notifications would have to be put in local newspapers, giving the biological father a chance to come forward.

Kenzie assured Jonathan he wouldn't.

Meantime he'd stand up and whistle as she swum her individual backstroke. He knew he'd drawn attention to himself. Eventually, someone would realize who he was, and pictures would end up on social media much like the ones from Sam's Club had.

And sooner or later, someone would figure out he was married, and the secret would be out.

Such was the life of someone in the public eye. He'd managed to mostly avoid it at home for a long time, but that time was likely over.

He should have thought of that before marrying Kenzie and starting a family, even if Lorelai wasn't his biological daughter.

Watching one of these meets from the perspective of a semi-outsider showed him the good in people. There was one little boy, he couldn't have been more than four, who was less than a quarter of the way down the lane when the rest of the swimmers were finished. By the time he *finally* made it to the other end, the entire bleachers were cheering him on.

Kenzie had warned him this would be a very long day, though she didn't know from experience. He'd come prepared for the long haul, but he hadn't truly been ready for just how long the day would actually be.

Jonathan did get a bit of a break from the metal bleacher when he took Lorelai to get a snack and bought her a made-to-order tank top. There were at least a hundred designs to pick from. One of his favorites was a T-Rex trying to do the backstroke. Lorelai helped him pick out designs for Kenzie, too. They'd give it to her later.

With the shirts in a bag and cups of Andy's Frozen Custard in hand, they headed back to their seats. Lorelai got most of hers eaten before her next race was called. Kenzie helped her adjust her swim cap before she went to the basketball court down the hall to line up in the bullpen.

Ten minutes later, they watched her come in, holding hands in a row of little girls, including three other Clipper Ships swimmers.

Jonathan checked his heat sheet then handed it to Kenzie. "She'll be in lane two." Closer to them than the other end like she had been the last race.

In just a couple minutes, Lorelai was doing her best backstroke, though she pinballed from one lane rope to the other repeatedly.

A minute after that, dripping wet, she gave Jonathan a big hug. "Did you see? 'Livia said I did good."

"You did great, honey." He hugged her back then lifted her over his knees to Kenzie.

She held on tight to her daughter. "I'm proud of you, sweetie. You beat your best time."

He'd seen the times posted on the scoreboard but didn't know what to compare them to.

The rest of the afternoon and early evening dragged on for half of forever. Lorelai did her best in her races which is all any of them could have asked. The SLAC team took first place and threw the coaches into the pool. All sixty or seventy swimmers ended up in there too, taking great joy in their win.

Moms, dads, and grandparents of all kinds took pictures of their kids in the pool and then again with the kids and the coaches with the trophy. By the time they made it out of the parking lot, it was nearly seven.

"Mama, I'm hungry." Lorelai piped up from the middle seat. "Can we get something to eat?"

Jonathan glanced over at Kenzie who looked worn out. "Are you up for it? We could go to So Cheeeezzy or that barbecue place in town."

"I wanna go there! They have cheeseburgers."

Jonathan chuckled. "They have good cheeseburgers." He reached over and rubbed Kenzie's shoulder. "Are you up for that?"

She sighed, but nodded. "Sure. It's her first district championship. It's to be celebrated."

He wasn't sure he believed her, but as they neared Serenity Landing, he pointed the SUV toward the restaurant. Kenzie seemed to do her best to put on a happy face for the talkative Lorelai.

By the time they made it back to his house, Lorelai was fast asleep in her car seat.

"I'll get her," Jonathan told Kenzie. "Leave everything here, and I'll come get it in a bit."

She just nodded and slowly moved to get out. He carried Lorelai upstairs and tucked her in then met Kenzie still only part way up the stairs herself.

"Let me help you."

Indecision warred in her eyes, but finally she nodded, holding her arm out to wrap around his shoulder. But he didn't just wrap his arm around her waist.

Instead, he lifted her easily into his arms. With her head resting on his shoulder, he carried her into her room and laid her gently on the bed.

Not exactly the way he'd pictured carrying his bride over the threshold for the first time.

"Can I get you some medicine?" He sat on the edge of the bed.

Her eyes were closed by the time she answered. "The prescription medicine is in the bathroom. Two, please."

Jonathan went in and found a couple of prescriptions. Only one was for pain meds, though. The directions on it said to take one and follow with a second only if needed. She must be feeling worse than she let on to take two.

With two pills in one hand and a disposable cup of water in the other, he went back to the bedroom and helped her sit up. "Down the hatch."

She swallowed them, but leaned heavily against Jonathan's side. "Thank you."

"Are you sure you don't want to sleep in my room tonight?" He hoped his concern came through. "So I can help you if you need it. It's a big bed with plenty of room." He glanced around the room. "Or I can sleep in here with you." This bed wasn't nearly as big. "On the couch if you want me to."

"No, but thank you. Keep your phone nearby, though? Just in case."

"Of course."

Jonathan helped her lay back down then covered her with a quilt his grandmother had left behind a few years earlier. "Sleep well, love." She didn't move, confirming his suspicion she was already asleep or awfully close. He kissed her temple, then headed to his own bathroom for a long, cold shower.

Chapter Fifteen

The first thing Kenzie was aware of when she awoke was a feeling of gentle warmth followed quickly by full body aches and a few stabs of pain.

The meet the day before came flooding back. Lorelai had done her personal best, but Kenzie had suffered. Jonathan had done his best to take care of both of them, but she was still miserable and sore.

At least the medicine let her get some sleep.

A groan escaped as she rolled over.

"Do you need some help getting up?"

Jonathan's voice surprised her, but at the same time, it didn't. She looked over to see him sitting in the chair near the window and setting his tablet on the table next to him.

He stood and walked toward her, still in pajama pants and a t-shirt. His touch was gentle as helped her into a seated position. "Do you want some more medicine?"

Kenzie shook her head. "Not the prescription stuff. Just some ibuprofen will be fine. It's in the kitchen."

If he left to get it, she could get herself to the bathroom and take care of her morning bathroom break while he was gone. She didn't want him helping her in there.

"I'll be right back."

As soon as he was out the door, she stood and made her way carefully into the other room, her toes curling against the tile to try to maintain her upright position. When she made it back to the bedroom, Jonathan was waiting with her medicine.

"Feel better?" he asked with only a hint of a smirk.

"Somewhat. I need to get a shower and get out to the workshop, though. I have less than thirty-six hours until I leave for Spring Meadow, and I'm not ready."

"I'll help you. There's very little I *have* to do in the next few days for work, so I'm basically all yours."

"What about Lorelai?"

"She slept in, then Alyssa invited her over to play. I knew you had a lot to do today, so I thought it would be okay."

Kenzie nodded and downed the medicine. "Thanks."

"I'll meet you downstairs in half an hour?"

"Sounds good."

He smiled at her - a smile she felt was for her alone. The one that made her insides melt. "If I'm not in the kitchen, I'll be in my office." He started for the door, then turned. "Can I make you something for breakfast?"

"I'll grab a granola bar, but thanks." Pancakes or bacon and eggs would really hit the spot, but she didn't want him going out of his way for her.

He just nodded and went out the door, closing it behind him. It was easy enough to get in the shower, but oh so hard to get out. The warm water sluicing over her felt better than pretty much anything ever. It had to be the best hot shower she'd ever taken.

Finally, she made herself turn the water off. The yarn wouldn't get itself ready for this show. As it was, she was going to be up half the night finishing everything. She'd managed to get a little bit done the day before, but they left for the swim meet before eleven, so most of it had been a wash as far as getting any yarn stuff done.

Something smelled far too good when she slowly made her way down the stairs. Way better than a granola bar.

In the kitchen, she found Jonathan pulling a pan out of the oven. "It smells delicious."

"I made some cinnamon rolls. They're out of a can, but there are eggs and bacon to go with them."

Sure enough two plates on the bar had just enough room left for a cinnamon roll or two. "Thank you." She slid onto one of the stools. "It looks fantastic."

Jonathan asked what she wanted to drink, then brought her glass as he came to sit next to her. "Well, we missed our one week anniversary. It didn't really seem right not to do anything for it."

She didn't look at him. "Happy anniversary."

He didn't reply for a second, almost long enough for her to look up at him. "Happy anniversary," Jonathan finally said back.

What was it that was bothering him? The lack of consummation of their marriage? Her sleeping in the other room? Not telling anyone, even Lorelai, just yet? All of the above?

He didn't say anything else about it, just asked a blessing over their food. They ate in silence, until they were nearly done when Jonathan asked what they needed to get accomplished.

Despite the breakfast fare, it was nearly noon. Kenzie went through her mental checklist and told him the general breakdown. A lot of what needed doing was taking yarn that was done and dried and putting it into cakes - three or four inch high by three or four inch wide circles - and then turning it into skeins.

Without telling her, Jonathan had bought two of everything she needed. They could both be working at the same time. Hopefully, he'd do most of the walking back and forth while she did the ones she could sit for.

"You know I'm probably going to whine like a big baby, right?" Jonathan wiped his mouth with his napkin and tossed it on his plate. "It sounds incredibly tedious."

"It is," she conceded, "but it has to be done. You don't need to help. I can handle it."

She couldn't. Kenzie knew she couldn't. But she didn't want Jonathan to feel obligated either.

"I don't want you to try to handle it on your own." Jonathan's arm stretched along the back of her chair, his thumb rubbing her shoulder. "I'm happy to help."

"I know."

He kissed the side of her head. "Then I'll clean up real quick. Do you want to head on out there, or wait for me to drive you over?"

It was only a few hundred feet, tops. "I can walk." She wasn't that wimpy.

But her side still ached and her muscles already threatened mutiny.

And yet she felt better than she had over the weekend.

By the time she reached the workshop, Jonathan had caught up to her.

"I don't want you overdoing it today," he admonished as he unlocked the door. "George and I can do most of the grunt work if we need to. Or I can see if Josh has a couple guys he can spare. He hires far more than he needs to take care of his place, pays them a good salary, but then they'll go weeks without doing much work at all. Well," he amended, "then there are weeks where they'll work a ton of overtime, too. I'm sure it balances out. If he doesn't need them, he's usually more than willing to sort of loan out their labor that he's already paying for."

"Is that why they helped with the house?" Kenzie hadn't heard a peep from the landlord since she fell. The cynical side of her wondered if he knew she was hurt, and it was his fault, so he kept his distance.

Jonathan didn't answer, just opened a garage door to let in the natural light then put his hands on his hips. "So where do we start?"

This had to be the most tedious thing ever.

Jonathan walked basically from one side of the workroom to the other and back again, winding yarn onto this thingie as he did. At least it was a hand crank and not something he had to do manually. He'd screw that up.

Once each skein worth was done, he'd put it in a labeled Ziploc bag so Kenzie would know what it was later. Some of them were pretty similar, and she didn't want to mix them up on accident.

His pedometer and biceps were both getting quite the workout.

By mid-afternoon, he'd done all of the ones he needed to do. "Now, why can't we just leave it like this again?" he asked, holding up one of the cakes. About four inches high and three inches across, the circular cake thing looked fine to him. Kind of cool even.

"Because the yarn is stretched out, and you don't want it to stay stretched out."

Right. "So now what?"

"Now we take a break."

Thank God.

He was pretty sure Kenzie needed it worse than he did, even though she'd done her work sitting on a bar stool. She had to be stiff and sore.

Jonathan pulled a small bottle of ibuprofen out of his pocket and shook it. "Ready for some more?"

Kenzie glanced at her watch. "Not yet, but thanks. Another hour before I can, and I'm doing okay for now."

"I've got them when you need them." He swung his arms back and forth, smacking his shoulders each time he "hugged" himself. "How much do we have left to do?"

"Not as much as I thought we would." She sounded impressed. "Do you want to take over here for me, and I can start organizing what's done? If it's okay with you, I'd like to take it all inside and label it in there."

"Label?"

"I have business cards with my information on one side and information about the yarn on the other. I make sure it's the right one and write in the name of the color then attach it to the finished skein." She held one up. "This is a semi-solid red. That's easy." Then she held up one of his cakes. "This one has a fancier name."

"The ones on the bags."

"Right."

"Well, I can drive the SUV down here and we can load it all up. It's your house now, too, you know." Even if she did sleep about as far away from him as possible and still be on the same property. "You can do whatever work you need to up there." He grimaced. "Except maybe actually making or working with the dyes. That should probably stay out here."

She gave him the first real smile he'd seen directed at him in days. "Yes, it probably should."

Jonathan looked around. "Why don't we load all of this up?" He wiped his forehead with his sleeve. "It doesn't bother me to keep the air going to keep it somewhat cool in here while leaving the door open, but this is all stuff we could do in the house, right?"

Kenzie nodded, and he mentally kicked himself for not thinking about it sooner. She shouldn't be out here in the heat any more than necessary.

"I'll go get the SUV, and we can load it up." He took a swig from a bottle of water then walked to the garage attached to the house. It took less than a minute to back up to the workshop.

Kenzie pointed to the different tubs she'd need. He folded the seats down when he realized how much room they'd need. How had she planned to do this in her car anyway? Or did someone else have a vehicle she planned to borrow.

"I have to admit, I'm glad for the SUV. Usually, my friend Julia goes with me, and we take hers, but she's pregnant and..." She shook her head. "Nothing, but she can't go."

"Then it's a good thing I'm going with you."

She stopped and blinked. "You are? I thought I'd just take the SUV."

"You could," Jonathan started slowly, not quite sure how they'd miscommunicated. "But I cleared my weekend completely, so I could go with you. I don't like the idea of you driving that far when you're still hurting so much. And I really don't like the idea of you unloading and reloading everything. You won't even get to take a bathroom break if you're there by yourself."

He could see her concede the point. "Then I appreciate it."

"You said it's in Spring Meadow, right?"

"Yes. Lorelai is supposed to spend the Friday and Saturday

night with my parents. They're supposed to get back in town today."

Jonathan crossed his arms over his chest and felt his brows pull together. "I wonder if it's time to consider a nanny like Josh and Stephanie have."

"I can take care of my own daughter."

He nearly stumbled backward at the force of her words. His hands went up in surrender. "Whoa. I'm not saying you can't, Kenz. I'm saying a live-in babysitter might not be such a bad idea. What if your parents get held up?" He hadn't even met his in-laws and had no idea what they'd say when they found out the wedding had already happened. "That's all. Not a full-time nanny."

Her glare subsided just a bit as she appeared to think it over. "It might not be the worst idea ever. I've never even thought about being able to afford that kind of thing."

Jonathan walked over until he could rest his hands on her hips. "You can afford to now, Kenzie. Money is one thing we have in abundance." He wanted to kiss her but backed off instead. "Let's go up to the house and finish getting all this stuff ready."

He loaded the tubs into the SUV and drove them back up to the house. There he unloaded everything while Kenzie dug through stuff in the first bucket to find what they needed.

It took nearly four hours, and a pizza break, but they were finally done about ten-thirty. Jonathan sent Kenzie upstairs to take some pain meds and get to bed.

He'd load everything up, and tomorrow they'd be on their way.

Chapter Sixteen

"Where do you want all of this?"

Kenzie turned to see Jonathan with a hand truck full of plastic tubs. She had gone inside and registered. "I'm in the third row next to last booth. I'll have to see the configuration first to know exactly how to set it up."

He followed her into the large gymnasium type room. Concrete floors, dozens of people scurrying around getting their booths set up. She found hers, not on the end like she had been the year before. That had been nice. Instead, she was closer in by one spot. Though technically the same size, it felt a lot smaller.

She started to drag one of the tables to the side, but stopped when Jonathan glared at her. Though she felt better, she was just as happy to let him do the heavy work while she pointed.

While Jonathan made a few trips to the car and back, Kenzie began to set up the booth. Black tablecloths went over the rough wooden tables. He brought in her shelving units. He'd never questioned her when the UPS man brought them a couple of days after he gave her a debit card. She'd gone on a small Amazon shopping spree, but it was all stuff either for Lorelai or the business.

"Where do you want these?" he asked, easily hoisting one off the top of the other.

"Put one on each of the side tables. I'll stack the different yarns in them."

"Do they have those cloth bucket thingies to go in them?"

"They do," she admitted, "but I won't use them for this." She opened one of the buckets with the yarn in it and began to sort them into different squares. Fingerweight on one side, worsted and other, heavier weights on the other. Semi-solids went on the top shelves, variegated in the middle, and self-striping on the bottom. She attached the self-striping samples to either end of the unit so buyers could see what they would look like when they were finished.

"Did you make these?"

Kenzie looked over to see Jonathan holding up a small animal. "No. Julia makes those. She designs them and sells the patterns. I make the yarn to go with them." She held up a plastic bag with both the instructions and the yarn. "We split the money from them."

He looked it over. "I bet my grandmother and some of her friends would love these. Does she sell them pre-made?"

"Not usually." Kenzie wiped her forehead with the back of her hand. "They're time consuming to make, and you can't really sell them for enough to make it worthwhile." She pointed to a green tub. "Open that one."

He did and pulled out a handful of bags.

"Those she makes and sells. They go a lot faster. At the ones where we have a bigger booth, she brings more of a variety of stuff. She also takes special orders at those when she can make it to them and online. She lost her job not too long ago and is doing anything she can to make money for the moment."

Jonathan turned the knitted neon peacock over in his hands. "Interesting."

Kenzie wasn't sure what to make of that. She went back to putting everything where it went.

"And what's this?" He held up a clear plastic bag that had survived the flood.

"That's fiber I dyed. It's ready to be spun into yarn."

Jonathan turned it over in his hands. "Really? I had no idea what it looked like."

"I saw a lady setting up that you'll have to go see. She has yak and silk fiber..."

"Yak? Really?"

She nodded. "It's incredible. And camel and silk. They're both fantastic. I just want to sit and hold it all day long. She mostly sells the fiber for people who want to spin it themselves."

"Do you spin yarn?" Jonathan set the bag on the table and went back to unloading the tub he was working on.

"No. I want to learn, but I never have."

"You should," he encouraged her. "You've got the time once the show's over, right?"

Kenzie wrinkled her nose at where some of the colors clashed with skeins next to them. "Not really. I have to start getting ready for the Serenity Landing show that's coming up in a few months. I'll need at least two or three times this much ready to go, and I'd rather not spend a few weeks like the last two." She emptied the last of the yarn out of her bucket. "Plus I want to come up with a few more colors."

"More colors?"

Despite her pain and stress, Kenzie had to smile at his astonished look. "Yes. I need to make more of the colors that sell well, plus it'll be fall which means I need to have Christmas stuff. So I need to make some new Christmas colors."

"Not just red and green anymore?"

She grinned. "Not quite."

After about an hour, she was finally almost happy with the way everything looked.

"Can you tell me about everything? That way if you have to run to the bathroom, I can sound semi-informed?"

Did he really want to know? Kenzie launched into her sales pitches for the different yarns, but before long Jonathan was asking questions.

Good ones.

If he could retain the information, he'd be a great help over the next two days.

"Hey, Kenzie."

She looked up to see three women approaching the booth. "Hey, guys. What's up?"

"Are you coming to dinner tonight?" Several of the locals made plans to eat together when they were at the same shows.

Kenzie shook her head. "Not tonight. I fell last week and got banged up pretty bad. I'm just going to go back to the hotel and take a hot shower."

They talked for another minute then waved as they walked off.

"Who's that?" Jonathan asked quietly.

"They run Show Me Yarn. They do some great dyeing and are based out of Billings, I think."

"Practically neighbors."

"Pretty close." Billings was only a few miles from Serenity Landing. She looked around. "I think we're done for now."

"Good. Then let's go get something to eat on our way to the hotel."

Jonathan pulled into the hotel parking lot and dropped Kenzie off at the front door. The parking lot was surprisingly full. That didn't bode well.

He grabbed the two suitcases out of the back and headed inside. Kenzie still stood at the front desk, but her shoulders were slumped.

"What's wrong?" he asked before he even reached her side.

"They don't have my reservation. I made it months ago, but something must have happened." She pulled out her phone and opened her email app. "I know I have the confirmation here somewhere."

"We'll just take a second room then," he told the clerk. "Whatever you have."

"That's just it, sir," the clerk replied. "We're full for the night. Everyone is. Not only is your conference here, but there are two others and a rodeo in town."

Jonathan's heart sunk. "What about a bed and breakfast or something?"

"Sorry, sir. I talked to someone else a few minutes ago who had already called everywhere else and stopped by here, because they hadn't been able to find anything."

It didn't require any more thought. "She can have my reservation." He pulled his wallet out. "Jonathan Langley-Cranston. I should have a room reserved for the next two nights." He set his ID on the counter.

"Of course, sir." A few clicks later, he swiped Jonathan's credit card then handed it back along with a key card. "You have room 215. It's right at the top of the stairs."

"Thank you." Jonathan put his cards away and let Kenzie take the key cards. "I'll take your bag up then head home or to Marshfield or something." It was a lot closer than driving all the way from Serenity Landing again.

Rather than taking the stairs, he walked to the elevator. Kenzie had to be tired and her feet sore already. He'd text George to pick up some mats or something to stand on. Some of the good squishy ones.

"Why don't you just sleep in the other bed?" Kenzie asked as they exited the elevator. "We're both grown-ups." She stopped in front of the door and opened it.

He let her walk in and see the answer for herself.

"Oh."

One king-sized bed. What they called a suite with a Jacuzzi tub and everything. It had been the only room they had left when he'd called earlier in the week.

She stopped in the middle of the room. Her shoulders straightened. "We're both grown-ups, and we are married. It's ridiculous for you to drive all the way back to Serenity Landing, or even another town. Are you okay with sharing?"

There was a multi-layered question Jonathan didn't know how to answer. Finally, he just said, "Sure." He let the door close behind him and set both of their suitcases on the dresser.

While she looked through the bag, he texted George who said he'd take care of getting the mats. A trip to Sam's Club or the kitchen supply store first thing in the morning most likely.

"I can't believe it," Kenzie muttered.

"What's wrong?"

"I forgot pajamas. If I was alone it would be one thing, but I'm not." Was that bitterness hidden in her voice?

"Then let's make a quick trip to the store."

"I'm not used to being able to just make a quick trip to the store to buy something I forgot."

He grinned at her. "Then let's make it an adventure."

Twenty minutes later, they walked through Walmart. Jonathan left her alone to make her pajama selection. He grabbed some snacks, though he knew there was still a cooler in the SUV.

When he made it back to the front, Kenzie stood with some sort of blue fabric wrapped around her arms. "Why don't you get a swimsuit?"

She shot him a puzzled look. "Why? I have one at home."

"Because then you can use the Jacuzzi and won't have to wait for me to leave or worry about me coming back before you're ready."

Without any more urging, she wandered into the women's section and found a modest one piece. "I'm going to go try this on."

While she did, Jonathan went to the pharmacy and found some bubble bath. Lavender was supposed to be good for relaxing, right?

By the time he made it back toward the other side of the store, she was waiting. She checked out while Jonathan went to get the car.

As soon as they made it back to the hotel, Kenzie went to the bathroom with the swim suit. Jonathan ran a hot bath for her.

While she soaked, he read a political thriller on his Kindle and did his best to ignore that soon he would be sharing a bed with his wife for the first time.

Eventually, he became so engrossed that he almost jumped when she spoke.

"Which side do you want?"

Jonathan looked over to see she already wore the pajamas. The edges of her hair were wet, but she clearly hadn't washed it.

"I don't care." He plugged his tablet in and walked toward the bed. "Whichever one you don't want."

"What side do you normally sleep on?" She looked exasperated with him.

"Uh, kind of in the middle or wherever I land when I'm tired." Had he ever actually slept with anyone before? Except his brother as kids? The thought of Philip brought a fresh stab of pain. "What about you?"

"This side is fine." She sat down with her back to him. "You don't have to go to bed now, you know. If you want to read a while longer, it won't bother me."

And there was a hint he figured he better get. "Then I'll read for a bit. What time do we need to be there?"

They discussed the morning without actually looking at each other, then Kenzie laid down.

Jonathan went back to his chair and his book. Engrossed until his eyelids would stay open no longer, he decided to sleep where he was.

Better than bothering Kenzie when she didn't really want him.

Chapter Seventeen

Kenzie didn't know what to make of her new husband.

She knew he had a reputation as a party animal, a womanizer, but she believed him when he said he wasn't that guy anymore.

Sleeping in his chair the night before, after suggesting a swim suit so she could relax, both seemed to indicate he was a decent guy.

So had the mat waiting for them in his SUV. How had George gotten it so early and then driven it all the way to Spring Meadow before 7:45?

"George knows how to get stuff done," was the only answer Jonathan would give.

But Kenzie knew she needed to thank both of them. No way would she survive two full days standing on a concrete floor. The mat, one of the thick padded ones, was quite literally a life-saver.

"Thank you." She had to say it as soon as Jonathan got back from parking the car after he'd carried the mat in.

He looked up, surprised. "For what?" His reaction even seemed genuine.

"For the mat. For sleeping in the chair to make me more comfortable. For being here." For everything. For the load off her shoulders. For the relief that came from no more debt hanging over her like the sword of Damocles.

Jonathan gave her that smile. The one just for her. "My pleasure. Is there anything we need to do to finish getting ready?"

Kenzie pulled the money box out of the bag she'd brought with her. "Not really. The swag notebooks need to be dug out of whatever box they're in." The little spiral notebooks had been a trade for yarn. Everyone liked swag and, hopefully, it would lead to future orders.

She piddled around, mostly just tweaking things. Making sure the hat was on the mannequin head right. The heel of the sock needed to be just so on the foot.

And then the doors opened. Streams of people didn't come in right away, but a few trickled in. She waved to her Show Me Yarn friends while they talked and laughed.

That was nice. She always enjoyed having Julia with her to talk to when things were slow.

Maybe she should use the time to make an effort to get to know Jonathan better.

"So where did you grow up?" A nice, easy conversation starter, right?

Jonathan's head jerked around. "What?"

Or maybe not. "Where did you grow up?"

"The Carolinas, mostly. Why?"

"Just curious." So much for conversation.

He pulled his phone out of his pocket and frowned. "What?"

"Your parents haven't picked up Lorelai yet."

As she'd feared, they hadn't arrived home on time. Instead, they'd made arrangements to pick Lorelai up at Jonathan's house by seven this morning. It was now after 8:30.

Jonathan tapped on his phone then held it to his ear. "Hey, Travis. I need a favor."

Did he know everyone?

"Right. Cassie could stay at the house for the next couple nights and keep an eye on Lorelai. I'm pretty sure they know each other from the pool." He uh huh'd a few times then said good-bye. "Cassie Harders will stay at the house." He stopped with his phone halfway to his pocket. "I'm sorry. I should have asked. Do you have a back-up plan?"

Kenzie shrugged. "Bring her with me. I've done it before." To shows like this one. Not like the big one in Serenity Landing.

The first customer walked into her booth. After selling two self-striping skeins of yarn, she turned to Jonathan who leaned against the back table.

"Didn't you have Cassie's dad in class?" he asked.

"Once."

"So you grew up in Serenity Landing?" He took a seat in one of the folding chairs she'd brought along. They weren't the most comfortable, but it beat standing.

"Born and bred," she confirmed. "What brought you to the middle of nowhere Missouri?"

He chuckled. "It's not quite the middle of nowhere."

"Your house is," she retorted.

"Fair point. *Our* house is kind of in the middle of nothing except the lake. It's not far from Serenity Landing though, and Springfield is only twenty minutes away." He slid the small cooler out from under the table and pulled out two waters.

She accepted the one he offered, but didn't open it yet. "That doesn't tell me how you got here."

He seemed to think a moment, taking several sips of his water before answering. "I wanted to get away from the coasts. A small town seemed like a huge blessing. Yes, everyone knows everyone, but after a while, it's like they forget you're someone famous. The thing like the pictures with Lorelai hasn't happened in ages. At eighteen, I was pretty much done with that life."

There was more to the story, but Kenzie sensed this wasn't the time to push for it.

"Anyway, I found a good school in Serenity Landing University. It had the degree programs I wanted. I convinced my parents to buy the estate out of my trust fund and built the house and most of the outbuildings. Stayed for grad school. Finished my second Master's degree a few months ago. Haven't decided for sure what I want to do next, but I love it here. I want to stay."

That was good, because Kenzie had no intention of going anywhere.

<hr/>

"Excuse me, what's a sock blank?"

Jonathan looked over at the woman who expected him to know the answer. "Uh, I'm not the best one to answer." He glanced over to see Kenzie in an animated discussion about one of the other yarns. "But from what I understand, it's enough yarn to make a pair of socks. You just start unraveling it as you knit." He picked up a pair of knitting needles. "I do know this is her sample that you can use to try it out."

She took the needles from him and began to do something Jonathan didn't quite understand. Knit apparently.

"Very interesting." She put the needles and sock blank down and picked up one of the packaged ones. "How much are they?"

"I believe they're all marked, ma'am." He picked up a different one and pointed to the spot on the label.

"You don't seem to know much." This woman reminded him of his grandmother.

Jonathan gave her his best smile. "I'm learning."

"That's why you're here?"

He pointed over his shoulder at Kenzie with his thumb. "I'm here because she's here. It's important to her which means it's important to me, and important for me to learn about."

"You're to be commended, young man. You clearly care for your young lady, or it wouldn't matter so much to you to learn about her interests."

Jonathan grinned. "I do care about her quite a bit." He wanted to say she was his wife, but settled for, "I'm quite proud of her."

"You should be." The woman held up a skein of yarn. "I've never seen quite this color, but it's gorgeous."

"Thank you, ma'am. I wish I could take the credit, but it's all her."

"She's a very lucky girl." The woman pointed to the bottom row. "Now, what can you tell me about these?"

"I do know those are self-striping." He picked up one of the sets of samples, cards about four inches square with yarn samples wrapped around them. "So this one..." He picked up the skein she'd been looking at then found the right sample. "...should look something like this when it's done."

"And what about this sock here?" She held up a plastic foot with a striped sock.

Jonathan was proud of himself. He actually knew the answer. "That's this set here." He picked up a bag of smaller, bright colored skeins. "Then you can pick your more neutral color." He pulled a gray off the shelf. "This one is the one she used for the toe, the heel, and the top."

"Can I answer any questions for you, ma'am?" Kenzie joined their group.

"Oh, this young man has answered all of my questions quite nicely. He's had a good teacher."

Jonathan tried to hide his smile as a blush crept up Kenzie's neck and into her cheeks. "He's been a huge help to me the last couple weeks. I lost almost everything when that monster rainstorm hit, and my roof began to leak uncontrollably while I was out."

The woman looked around. "You did all of this in the last two weeks?"

"Almost all of it," Kenzie confirmed.

"Did you have this much undyed stock in?"

"No, ma'am." Kenzie hesitated. "A benefactor heard about it and replaced everything I needed, including overnight shipping when we could."

"That's fantastic." The woman picked up two more self-striping skeins. "I think this will be all for now, but if these turn out as wonderful as I think they will, I'm sure I'll order more from you later."

"Thank you." Jonathan hung back as Kenzie picked up the tablet to ring up the order.

"Are these graduated cakes?" She picked up one of the ten or so skeins that were still in the round cakes he'd made.

"Yes." Kenzie pointed to a shawl hanging on her sample wall. "They're like that one."

The woman pulled one with several shades of blue out. "I'll take this one, too."

"Of course."

Two minutes later, Kenzie had smiled and waved as the woman left, purchases in her bag.

She turned to him her with jaw dropped. "Do you know who

that was?" she whispered.

Jonathan shrugged. "Some lady who likes yarn?"

"She's in charge of the Serenity Landing show. I haven't heard if I even have a spot yet. Notifications are supposed to go out in the next couple weeks. Only a couple slots are open each year for new vendors. Then there's a three-year probation."

Jonathan blinked. "Wow. That seems a bit excessive."

"Well, it's one of the biggest shows in the country. Only the best get to be vendors. I didn't get in the last two years." She looked around, biting her lip. "I need better pictures of my booth set up. The ones I had weren't all that great, but hopefully since she saw this one, and if she likes the yarn, I can get in anyway."

Jonathan wondered if he could grease the wheels somehow. Because she deserved to be there.

"And I don't want you to give some big donation to her favorite charity or anything. If I get in, I get in on my own."

"Of course." He reached out and put a hand on her shoulder. "I'm proud of you and all you've accomplished. I knew I thought it was all pretty cool, but I had no idea how it compared to everyone else's. I've looked around some and even talked to a few of the other vendors, and I'm very impressed with your work and your presentation."

"Thanks." She peered around him. "She's talking to the Show Me Yarn girls. I know they've been trying to get into the Serenity Landing show for a couple years, too."

Jonathan rearranged a few of the prepackaged kits since one was now sold. "What's the big deal about that show?"

"It just is. Somehow, Serenity Landing started earning the reputation of having a well-run, well-attended show. When it came out she'd lived here, pictures of that princess you dated attending a few years ago showed up on the Internet. It got more popular then. They get some of the best teachers to come, too."

"Teachers? What do they teach? Like knitting?"

"Sometimes they teach basic craft stuff like that. Julia's one of the best, but her baby's due around that time so I'm not sure if she will be teaching or not. They have one *huge* class this year that I really want to sign up for, but I'm not sure I'll be able to."

"What class is that?"

She turned her back to him, seemingly to straighten already straight skeins of yarn. "Margaret of Aquitaine Toulouse is going to be there."

Like he was supposed to know who that was. But it didn't matter. "Then we'll find a way for you to go."

Chapter Eighteen

Did he really want to make sure she was able to go? Or would he just throw money at the problem all over again? "So who is she?"

"She's this lady from the European mountains somewhere. The Alps maybe? Anyway, she teaches this spinning technique that I really want to learn how to do. I need to learn how to spin first," she admitted. "At least enough to know what I'm talking about." And now that she didn't have to work full-time in addition to doing all of the dyeing and everything else, maybe she could finally learn how to use both the spindle and the spinning wheel well enough.

"You don't know how to spin?"

"I understand the concepts. I'm capable of doing it, but not very well. Once Lorelai starts preschool, maybe I'll have some time."

Jonathan started to ask her a question, but someone came into the booth and started talking to her. While Kenzie explained some of the different yarns, Jonathan took a spot near the back of the booth to handle the money side of things.

As she talked with one potential customer after another, Kenzie found the tension of the last few days melting away. She felt far better than she thought she would, likely thanks to the use of the Jacuzzi tub the night before and the rubber mat Jonathan had found for her to stand on.

By the time the convention closed down for dinner, she'd sold about two-thirds of what she'd hoped to sell for the weekend as a whole. Sunday closed earlier and probably wouldn't be quite as busy, so this was a good thing.

In the SUV on the way back to the hotel, Jonathan asked her about it. "Do you expect to sell out of what you brought?"

"Oh, goodness no." Kenzie laughed. "I wish. But you have to bring a big variety because you never know what's going to be the big seller. If you hadn't been helping me, I would have had a much smaller inventory and probably very little self-striping. It's just too time-consuming. But I sold a bunch of the self-striping today, and that's a good thing."

He seemed relieved.

"What?" she asked

"Just if you expected to sell all of it, then we weren't off to a great start, that's all. But since you didn't expect to, then it's probably going okay, isn't it?"

"If I didn't sell anything at all tomorrow, I'd break even, at least on what I normally would have spent for a show like this. Not with all the extra money you paid for overnighting everything and stuff."

"Well, that's a start. And if you get into the Serenity Landing show, you'll be a lot more prepared, right? I mean even more than you would have been?"

"If I find out soon. I talked with one of the Show Me Yarn people. Apparently, I misunderstood the email. I need to look it up again. I guess we're both on the waiting list if someone backs out. It's not just a first-come, first-served type thing. They slot people in based on what size space they want versus what's actually available. Presentation in the pictures. Longevity. Quality. All kinds of things besides your willingness to give them money."

"How many different size booths are there?"

"I think there are four tiers. A lot of times the bigger two tiers are actually two or three different groups who've gone in together. Usually, they have different products, though."

"So you and the ladies from Billings wouldn't share a booth?"

"Probably not, though I'd do it in a hot minute if it meant getting into the show. I don't have the money or the stock to fill up one of the big booths anyway. Not even half." She could come up with the stock if she needed to, but not the money.

Or could she?

There was enough left in the account Jonathan had given her to do a big stall if she could. Maybe she'd drop an email to the coordinator and let her know she was open to any size booth.

The evening at the hotel was spent getting everything organized. It would help the next day and after she got home. It would make life easier later. She knew this from experience.

Of course, she'd never had the time off work afterward either. Maybe she could put it off until Monday and get some rest this evening, along with some more time in the Jacuzzi.

That was her plan, but as she soaked in the tub, Jonathan asked her if she wanted to go out for a late dinner. Even though she planned to put on her pajamas and snack on the food in the cooler, the growling in her stomach made her decide dinner out sounded like a better idea.

And so, instead of going straight to bed, she found herself at

Spring Meadow Family Cafe.

"If I'd known we'd have time for dinner, I would have told you to bring something nicer and taken you to the Savarino's here."

Kenzie took a sip of her water. "Don't we have one in Serenity Landing, too?"

"Kind of. It's between Serenity Landing and Springfield, in the county I guess. It's in the Serenity Landing school district though."

"Italian food, right?"

"Straight from Italy," he confirmed.

"Italian food is my favorite," she confessed. "But it has too many carbs, so I don't eat it very often."

Jonathan pointed his fork, complete with bite of steak, at her. "You can have Italian without the carbs."

Kenzie found herself grinning. "Not the kind of Italian I like. Pasta with tons of creamy orange sauce and dripping in melted cheese."

"That does sound pretty good."

Silence descended for several minutes. "So I know you aren't an only child. How many siblings do you have?"

"Five." He stopped and stared at his plate. "Four. I have to accept that Philip isn't coming home any time soon. He's not coming home at all."

Right. Good job reminding him of the pain. "What about the others?"

"I don't see them nearly as much as I'd like." He poked at his mashed potatoes. "I'm the oldest. I'm also the most settled, believe it or not. Everyone else is still in their sowing the wild oats stages. They don't want me to protect or help them, except to give them money when they've run out. After me, there was Philip about two years younger. Then a gap. Catherine, Edward, Juliette, and Marianne are only about eighteen months apart each. Marianne's out of high school now. I keep expecting one of them to move here, out of the sphere of our parents, but none ever have."

She turned that over in her mind before asking another question. Because out to dinner in a strange town was the perfect place for this conversation. "I know we're whatever it is we are, and you dated royalty and stuff, but is there anyone else in your past I need to know about?"

Jonathan wiped his mouth with his napkin then tossed it onto the table. He pulled his wallet out and put enough money on the table to cover the meal and a nice tip. "Come on. This isn't the right place for that conversation."

He saw the confusion on her face, but she took a long drink of her water then followed him out of the restaurant. A tight smile was all he could manage to give the surprised waitress.

The drive back to the hotel wasn't long enough. The drive to Serenity Landing wouldn't have been long enough. Once seated in the chair he'd slept in, he knew he had to stop avoiding it.

"There was a girl once. Well," he amended, "once upon a time, there were a lot of girls, but one I thought was special. We went to this exclusive private school, but she was only there because her aunt married the dean's son or something like that. I don't remember exactly, but she didn't have the same kind of money everyone else did."

"So like *Gilmore Girls*?"

Like what? "Um, sure. Never saw it." It was a TV show, right? "Anyway, we dated for about six months. We partied a lot. I was never into drugs, but I did drink a lot." He leaned back until he

160

could dig in his pocket. The token was a lot smoother than it used to be. All those times he rubbed it when he would rather have found a good single malt.

Jonathan flipped it over and over in his fingers. "We were at the shore, on this little island where some friends' parents had houses. We were all drinking. I was, too, but I was also sick, so I went back to the house where I was staying. The rest of my friends went out on a boat between the island and the mainland."

He stared at the pattern in the carpet. "There was an accident. No one died, but it wasn't pretty." The rest would have to wait for another day. Jonathan hadn't really dealt with the emotional fallout, much less being ready to talk about it. "I decided it was time to get sober. Summer break had just started. My parents thought I was spending the summer with a friend in Europe. I told my friends I was going to New Zealand and Australia and spending the next couple months in the Outback."

When he didn't go on, Kenzie posed a question. "You didn't do either of those?"

Jonathan leaned back in the chair and flipped the coin into the air with his thumb, catching it with a thwack in his palm. "No. I got into rehab. I used a different name. Different bank accounts. No one knows. About once a year, I have private investigators look for it. They don't know enough to find it easily, but enough they should be able to if there's anything to be found."

"What happened with the girl?"

His bitter laugh echoed in the room. "We never actually broke up before I left. When I got home, I walked in on her sleeping with Philip in my room."

"Oh, Jonathan." The sympathy in her voice was nearly too much.

He shrugged. "They weren't actually dating. She'd moved on

to another guy in my class. His family had more recent ties to both the U.N. and the presidency. You'd probably know the name if I told you. They got married eventually. Have two or three kids. Both cheat on each other regularly. I dodged more than one metaphorical bullet."

The photos from the night of the accident tried to push their way forward. He never should have gotten a hold of the pictures from the police report. All of them, not just the ones fit for public consumption.

"What are you thinking?" Kenzie's soft voice began to crack the wall he'd built around that part of his life.

He thought for a moment, and finally went with the truth. "That sometimes I really wish I still drank."

"Why?"

"I wasn't part of the accident, but I still feel responsible. I knew they were planning to go on the water, but I didn't try to stop them."

"Why not?"

He shrugged. "I was young and stupid? I thought they'd pass out first. A couple of them did, including the girl I was dating. A couple others went to jail for a while."

"I thought no one died."

"That's not the only reason people go to jail after boating accidents." He rubbed the surface of the coin. "A couple did, despite their parents' connections. A couple didn't, probably because their parents could hire the best lawyers."

He looked toward her, able to feel the pain radiating out of his eyes. "Please don't try to look it up online. It's there, but trust me when I say you don't want to know any more details than that."

"Okay," she answered simply from her seat in the other chair. "I won't look. But if you ever want to talk about it more, I'm here."

She stood, and Jonathan thought she was going to head to the bathroom to change into her swimsuit. Instead, she came to stand next to him, pressing against his head with one hand.

His temple came to rest against her shirt, and he shifted enough to wrap his arm around her waist. She hugged his head to her with one arm and rubbed the arm on the far side with her other.

"Were you responsible, Jonathan? Not whether a court would say you are or not, but do you say you were?"

His head and his heart warred with each other. Finally, he told her that. "My head knows I'm not."

"But your heart doesn't yet?"

"No. My heart still feels responsible."

"You're going to have to let it go at some point, Jon." Something about the way she said the shortened version of his name felt different this time. It was kind of nice.

"I know. I've tried. Believe me."

"Maybe you need to find someone to talk to about it. Someone qualified who you can trust to keep your confidence. Maybe you just need to truly unburden yourself."

"Maybe." He sometimes wished he could.

And if wishes were horses, beggars would ride.

⁂

Kenzie could tell Jonathan was far more drained than he should be from a simple conversation. "Why don't you go take a hot shower and go to bed? In the bed?"

He shook his head against her. "I'm not kicking you out of the bed."

"I'm not offering to sleep somewhere else." Mentally, she took a deep breath. "Share with me. We can both get some decent *sleep* that way." Just sleep.

Though if he kissed her the way he had that first day, she'd have a hard time remembering why they were only supposed to be sleeping.

His shoulders finally relaxed some, and she moved away.

He stood. "I'm going to go take that shower."

She watched his back as he dug through his bag for what looked to be a pair of shorts. Once she heard the water change sounds, Kenzie quickly changed into her pajamas and propped herself up against the headboard, Kindle in hand.

Her eyes were starting to droop by the time Jonathan emerged, clad only in those shorts. She set her glasses and Kindle on the side table, sliding under the covers rather than staring like she really wanted to. Had she even seen Jonathan shirtless, ever? Except the one time she went in his room and maybe on the front of a magazine cover?

"Good night," she whispered.

She could feel his weight as he sat on the other side of the bed. "Good night. Sleep well."

"You, too. I set my alarms for the morning so we should be good there."

He said something vaguely affirmative back, and she closed her eyes, praying she'd drift off to sleep quickly.

The covers moved as he slid underneath them, but they didn't touch. Her eyes closed and she slept.

The mechanical sound of a dog barking woke her far too soon.

"I'm pretty sure that alarm tone needs to go the way of the dodo."

As Jonathan's deep, scratchy morning voice rumbled through her, Kenzie reached for her phone to turn it off. She could, but she also became very aware of an arm wrapped around her middle.

And the solid mass of a man's chest against her back.

"Sorry." His hand sort of slid across her stomach as he flopped onto his back. "I didn't mean to roll over there."

Kenzie tried to say something, but found her mouth completely dry. It took three tries to get something out. "It's okay. I'm sure you didn't do it consciously."

"Nope."

She sat up and swung her legs over the side of the bed as she reached for her glasses.

"I don't think I realized you wear those."

With them firmly in place, she twisted to see Jonathan resting there, with his head propped on his hand. "Glasses?"

"Yeah."

"I usually use those soft contacts that you can wear for like a month at a time, but I ran out and by last night, the ones I had in were well past their due date, so I took them out." She pointed to her face. "Four eyes it is."

"I think you look smart and sexy in them."

Sexy?

Really?

No one had ever called her that.

"Thanks." What else could she say? "I'm gonna go get ready."

With that, whatever moment they'd been having thankfully ended.

When she emerged, fully clothed and make-upped, she found him mostly dressed as well. "Do you want to grab a bite to eat downstairs again?" The breakfast the previous morning had been surprisingly good for a hotel breakfast.

He tied his second shoe. "Sure, sounds good."

And so started their second full day together. Kenzie missed going to church, but didn't mention it to Jonathan. She knew he attended her church regularly, though they had seldom seen each other. She thought he attended the other service, and she usually went out the side door, straight to the kids' area to pick up Lorelai and head home.

Business was far slower than she hoped, and talking to the other vendors, it seemed that they were all down from the year before. A few were talking about not returning. They had that luxury where Kenzie hadn't before now. She could only go to shows within driving distance and even most of those were kind of iffy.

Except for what had to be said, they packed up in silence. It all went into the back of Jonathan's SUV for the drive home. He held her hand, and she didn't stop him, but she wasn't quite sure what it meant. Kenzie knew she didn't want to ask.

Once back at the house, Jonathan pulled into the garage. "Is there anything we absolutely have to get out tonight besides our bags?"

She thought it over for a minute. "I don't think so."

"Then I say we leave it for tomorrow."

"I can live with that."

"Go on in and find Lorelai. I'll get your bag."

As she opened her door, Kenzie called her thanks. She found Lorelai in the kitchen making cookies with Cassie Harders.

"Mommy!" Lorelai climbed down off her bar stool and ran to give her a hug. "I missed you!"

"I missed you too, munchkin." She bent down and picked Lorelai up, holding her close. "Did you have fun with Cassie?"

"Yeah. We went to the pool and made cinnamon rolls, and we makin' cookies."

"They look yummy."

Lorelai squirmed down. "Where's Mr. Jonathan?"

"Right here, kiddo."

She turned to see Jonathan set their bags down and swoop Lorelai up into his arms. "Did you miss me, too?"

Lorelai nodded. "I did. Mr. Benny Hercules missed you too."

Jonathan chuckled. "He did, did he?"

"He likes you. He's prolly hiding under your bed."

His eyebrow quirked. "Oh? Did he hide under there a lot?"

"Yeah. He likes it."

Kenzie headed for the stairs. She wasn't needed for the conversation, and over an hour on the road meant she needed to visit the bathroom. Jonathan must have set Lorelai down and followed her, because she could hear his footsteps on the stairs behind her.

"Hey, Kenz?"

She stopped before turning the corner toward her room. Looking back, she could see Jonathan set her bag outside his door.

"I'll bring it to your room in a few minutes, but anytime you decide you want to unpack your bag in here, you're welcome."

A weird hollow feeling filled her, though she couldn't tell what it was. Good? Or bad? She wasn't sure.

Instead, she nodded and turned the corner.

She knew she had an open invitation, but he'd never been quite so blatant about it.

If it was *just* to sleep, it might be one thing, but if there was one thing she knew, it was that sleeping in the same bed with Jonathan wouldn't stay *just* sleeping for long.

Chapter Nineteen

Jonathan set his suitcase on the small couch in his room. She hadn't exactly run into his open arms, but Kenzie hadn't run away from him either. Not quite.

He did as he'd promised and took her bag to her room when he knew she was downstairs with Lorelai. Solitude called to him, at least for now.

It had been a decade, maybe longer, since he'd spent any time in a bed with a girl, and he'd never actually *slept* with one.

Waking up with Kenzie in his arms had shown him a little bit of what he was missing while his wife slept several bedrooms away.

And so he avoided both of them. In fact, they were still asleep when he woke up the next morning. He made his way to the basement gym and hopped on the treadmill. Once he moved up to a slow jog, he grabbed the remote and turned on one of the morning news programs.

Nothing too interesting.

Until the teaser nearly made him choke on his sip of water.

Is Jonathan Langley-Cranston the Fourth still America's most eligible bachelor, or is he off the market? Stay tuned, and we'll tell you what we know.

It cut to commercial, but he already had his phone out as he hopped onto the rails of the treadmill.

He pulled up the browser then swore under his breath when the basement's spotty Wi-Fi struck again. Before he could head upstairs, the news came back on.

"There was this picture a couple weeks ago of Jonathan with a little girl at his local Sam's Club. No one seems to know who she is, though some saw a resemblance between the two."

Jonathan didn't.

"Then this picture came across the wires over the weekend." A shot of him and Kenzie standing by the elevator at the hotel, Jonathan with two bags in his hands. *"What intrigued us was this."* It cut to a close-up of Kenzie's rings. *"Not just an engagement ring, is it? Jonathan has never been linked with a married woman, and surely he wouldn't be so public about an affair so close to home."*

The other hostess laughed. *"Not when he's got the connections to meet anywhere in the world."* She turned to the audience. *"So we did some digging. Less than two weeks ago a marriage license was filed for one Jonathan William Langley-Cranston the Fourth and a MacKenzie Davidson. Some Internet sleuthing turned up a Facebook page, complete with - you guessed it - pictures of that adorable little girl."*

Jonathan clicked the power button. He'd heard enough. The story was out, and it was far too late to pull it back.

His first phone call had to be to his mother. She would still be asleep on their Hawaiian vacation, but that would work in his favor. He broke the news then hung up as she drifted back off to sleep. She'd barely remember it later, but that wasn't his problem.

By then, he was outside Kenzie's door. He knocked, but she didn't answer. He opened it, just a touch then a bit further when he saw the lights were still out.

"Kenz?" he called, walking toward her bed.

"Huh?"

"I need to talk to you."

She pushed herself up into a seated position. "What is it?"

He held out his phone with the story pulled up on it. "Someone did some digging and found our marriage license."

"What? Why?" He could see her try to wrap her still sleep-fogged mind around it.

"I guess someone posted a picture of us at the hotel. It had your rings in it. Someone zoomed in, and they started digging."

She took the phone from him and began to read. He saw her rings were where they belonged, on her finger. One of the first things he'd noticed when they started working on yarn was that they were missing, but they always seemed to be back in place later.

But it wasn't the time to ask her about it.

"I need to call my parents," she groaned. "They finally made it home last night."

Their flights back to the States had been a nightmare, but Kenzie wouldn't let him send a private jet for them.

Almost like she didn't want anything to do with his money. He had to admit it was kind of a nice change after most of the girls in his life until he met Addie.

She reached for her own phone and entered her passcode. Before she could actually call, though, it buzzed. "It's them." With a swipe, she answered. "Hi, Mom. You saw the news?"

"Why didn't you tell us?" The screech coming through the phone didn't sound mad.

"Because it was so late when you got home last night. I wanted to tell you in person today."

"Is he as cute in person as he is on the magazines?" That also came through loud and clear.

"Mom!" Kenzie turned six shades of red, but Jonathan just grinned at her. "It's not exactly like that."

"So he's not a hunk?"

Jonathan raised an eyebrow at her while Kenzie seemed to slink further down under the covers. "Mom!" She made a motion for him to go away with one hand. "He's your son-in-law, you know."

"And I can't think my daughter happened to catch the handsomest man under sixty in the nation?"

Kenzie closed her eyes and sighed. "My dad just turned sixty," she told him.

"Thanks, Mom!" he said loud enough for her to hear through the phone.

"You didn't tell me he was right there!" The woman talked in all caps and exclamation points. She probably even used lots of those ?! combinations. There was an actual name for them, but he didn't know what it was. "What does Lore think?"

"She doesn't know about the wedding yet." Jonathan wondered when they'd tell her. "But she adores Jonathan."

"And he adores her!" Jonathan told his mother-in-law.

"Of course he does." Mom almost sounded huffy. "She's adorable."

Jonathan took his phone back, trying to hide his chuckle. Kenzie still hadn't sent a friend request. He sent one then searched her friend list and sent one to both of her parents. He needed to talk to her about locking her privacy settings down a bit tighter.

It wouldn't take much for the media to start hounding her friends and family.

He was surprised they weren't already.

⁂

"He just sent me a friend request!"

Kenzie groaned. "Mom. Chill. He's just a guy." She tried to shoo him away, but he just grinned that maddening grin.

"He's a Langley-Cranston, dear. And so are you and Lore now." Kenzie hated it when her mother shortened Lorelai's name. "I guess he's totally okay with what the doctors said? Were his family?" Her mother's suddenly serious turn caught Kenzie off-guard.

And left Jonathan looking perplexed. "I gotta go, Mom. I'll call you, and we'll have both of you over soon." A couple of uh-huhs and an I love you later, she hung up.

"What the doctors said?" Jonathan asked.

Kenzie stared at the very expensive comforter. "Yeah. I should have told you about that a long time ago. Well," she tilted her head, "at least before we got married. But we haven't slept together yet, and..."

"So you're planning on sleeping with me?" That maddening grin was back, but he sobered when she didn't return his smile.

"We haven't slept together yet," she repeated, "and if after I tell you this, you decide you don't want to be married to me anymore, I'll understand. It's something you should have known, but everything was such a whirlwind..." And the pressure on her shoulders had been so immense, she'd nearly forgotten.

"What is it, Kenz?" he asked softly.

She'd hated the nickname her whole life, but from Jonathan, she kind of loved it. When he kicked them out, she'd miss that. "I know how much you want a big family," she started, then

172

stopped, unable to go on.

"Yeah. So?"

"So I can't have any more babies," she blurted out. "Lorelai's birth wasn't easy, and they told me I couldn't have any more kids."

Jonathan recoiled, but only for a second before coming back toward her. "Wow. That's big."

"I know." She picked at invisible fuzz. "And if you want to end this, I completely understand."

He turned sideways so both feet were on the floor and stared toward the window. "Gwendolyn and Adam asked me a question a few weeks ago. Would I marry someone knowing she couldn't have children?"

Her heart thudded to a stop. "What was your answer?"

The sound of his slow exhale filled the room. "That I didn't know. It would depend on a lot of other factors."

"And you should have been able to make that choice instead of finding out later." Why did she want to cry around him so often?

"Hey." The warmth of his hand covering hers comforted her. "That's what adoption's for. And, without knowing the details, maybe it's something research has changed in the last few years."

"I haven't been back since she was born," Kenzie admitted.

"Then why don't we see what the docs say." He squeezed her hand. "But I married you for better or worse. I have my own version of worse that I'm sure we'll see sometime. If this is yours, then we'll deal with it."

Tension rolled off her. "It's honestly something I don't think about very often. But I should have told you."

He leaned over and kissed her forehead. "It's all right. We'll figure it out." His hand came up to the side of her face, his thumb rubbing her cheekbone as he rested his forehead on hers. "In sickness and in health. For better or worse, remember?"

Kenzie managed a small smile. "Not too worried about the richer or poorer part?"

Jonathan chuckled. "Not so much. It could happen, but it's unlikely. At least not money. There's lots of other ways to be poor, but I pray none of them happen either."

"Like the marriage of the couple you told me about?" she asked softly, not wanting to stir the old memories, but wanting to let him know that's not the relationship she wanted to have with him.

Someday.

After she told him about the money.

"Right. They're married, but poor in the things that matter."

"I've done poor when it comes to money, and I have to say I'm glad those days are over." It felt like a confession. But not quite close enough to one to tell him the whole truth.

Pressure with his thumb tilted her head up, and his lips captured hers. The kiss started soft, tender, a promise of the emotion that would come in this relationship, sooner or later.

But something changed when Kenzie reached out to grip the loose fabric of his t-shirt.

Something pent up between them. Different emotions emerged, and Jonathan shifted to face her again. His hand slid around to the back of her neck, holding her in place.

The desire flared from a place deep inside, a place she hadn't gone in a very long time. The longing to be closer was one she'd kept under control for so long, and now, it was as though that part of her knew she didn't *have* to anymore.

She was his wife. He was her husband.

The things she found herself longing for were biblically mandated.

But how to tell Jonathan?

His words from the night before flooded back.

Anytime you decide you want to unpack your bag in here, you're welcome.

Could it be that simple? Did she really want to wait that long? "Mommy?"

Jonathan stilled, his lips on hers, a bucket of cold water splashing over both of them with a single word.

Kenzie moved back, breaking contact with the lips she could easily spend the rest of her life kissing. "Yes, sweetie?"

"I'm hungry." Lorelai climbed up on the other side of the bed and crawled over next to her. "Is it breakfast yet?"

"Let me get dressed, and I'll get you something."

Jonathan stood. "I have some work to do, but I'll help you in a few minutes."

"Thanks."

He walked to the door, but stopped before leaving. When he turned, Kenzie could see her own desire mirrored and smoldering in his eyes. "Remember what I said last night, Kenz. Whenever you're ready..."

His voice trailed off, but Kenzie knew she'd be able to think of little else for the rest of the day.

Their secret was out. Maybe it was time for them to start acting like the married couple everyone believed them to be.

Chapter Twenty

*J*onathan found it difficult to think about anything but that kiss in Kenzie's bedroom, sitting on her bed. But he had to. He'd been on the phone with one of his sisters when he'd missed the call from his mother. Her voice mail made it very clear they were on their way back to Serenity Landing. His grandmother hadn't answered.

The door to his office banged open.

A furious Gwendolyn stood there.

"How could you do this?"

Jonathan leaned back in his chair. "Do what?"

"Marry Kenzie without telling me, moron." She flounced into the room, showing more of her former self than he'd seen since she'd arrived in town. "I wanted to be there when you finally tied the knot," she pouted.

"Sorry, Gwen. No one was there." He allowed himself a smile. "It was pretty spur of the moment. You know. Like elopements are supposed to be."

"Fine. I want to see the pictures."

Jonathan tapped on his phone and held it out. "That's the only one I've got." And only because Daniel's mom took it and texted it to him.

Gwendolyn studied it, but didn't say anything. "At least I know Kenzie won't be needing the apartment when it's finished. Can Adam and I live there for a while?"

"Together?" he asked with a raised brow.

She lifted her left hand to show him a ring. "He asked last night. We're getting married in December. The baby will be here, and we'll know what we're going to do."

"Are you still thinking adoption?" he asked softly, Kenzie's confession fresh in his mind.

She didn't look up. "I can't do what Kenzie does, Jonny." Her name for him when she was little. "I'm barely grown-up enough to take care of myself. After everything Adam's been through..." Gwendolyn didn't finish, and Jonathan didn't know what she was talking about. "I can't ask him to be this baby's father. Not now. Neither one of us is ready to be a parent."

"Is that what Adam wants, too?"

Gwendolyn shrugged. "He says he'll support whatever decision I make, but no, he hasn't come right out and told me his preference."

"Make him. You don't want to go into this marriage with a decision that you'll both end up regretting, because he didn't tell you what he's really thinking."

"I'll talk to him again." She leaned forward. "But I still want to know all the deets, cousin. How did you manage to elope without anyone knowing?"

"We didn't tell anyone. That's how eloping generally goes."

"Well, I'm happy for both of you. You're perfect for each other." She stood. "Congratulations."

"Back at ya." He stood and gave her a big hug. "Tell Adam I said so, too. And you two can live in the apartment as long as you want."

He needed to talk to Kenzie. If his parents were coming for a visit, then she probably needed to at least pretend to move into his room while they were here.

With a sigh, he went to find her. It took a few minutes, but eventually he did. She was in the sitting room with her laptop out and writing a check. He leaned against the door frame with his hands shoved deep in his pockets and watched her. She opened the calculator and did some figuring then wrote another check. Her nose crinkled when she licked the envelope, and Jonathan couldn't stop his laugh.

She jumped and clutched her chest. "You scared me."

"Sorry." He walked into the room. "You could set up a desk in my office, you know. No need to hunch over a coffee table."

Kenzie stretched her back. "That would be great." Her body still had to be sore, even though he knew she felt a lot better overall.

"There is something else I need to talk to you about, though."

She groaned. "The media finding out we're married wasn't enough?"

"My parents are on their way."

Her nose wrinkled again. "How bad is it that I really don't like that news?"

"Understandable." He sat on the couch across from her. "But we really don't want to give my mother any more ammunition than necessary."

She just waited to see what else he was going to say.

He didn't want to look at her. "It means we need to at least pretend you've moved into my room while they're here."

"How do we *pretend* that?"

"Move enough of your stuff in for a few days. We can be up later than my parents, and I'll wake up before them so they don't know I'm not sleeping in there."

"And when that doesn't work?"

"Then I'll sleep in my recliner like I did at the hotel." Because he didn't think he wanted to wake up with her in his arms again. Not until she truly moved in with him.

She didn't say or do anything. No nod of agreement or shake of her head. "When will they be here?"

"Sometime this evening."

"I'll move some things in. What do we tell Lorelai, though?"

"That we got married. Move her into the room across from mine. After my parents leave, you can move into the room next to hers or move her back where she is now. Soon, we need to decide which room will be hers permanently and then redecorate for a little girl."

"You don't have to..." Kenzie started.

"I *want* to," he told her gently. "She's my daughter now or will be in a couple weeks. I want her to have the room of her dreams."

"It's going to take some getting used to." She closed her laptop. "Do you have any stamps?"

He stood and held out his hand. "In my office. I can mail those for you." She handed them over. He didn't mean to be nosy, but he read the address for the top one. "FreedomWorks? What's that?"

"It's a charity I support. They give jobs to trafficked women in India making this yarn out of strips of cloth." She shrugged. "As hard as life's been at times, it's nothing compared to what those women go through. The least I can do is give some of what I earn to help them."

"That's fantastic." He'd look into it and maybe make a donation of his own. "Now, let's get this stuff done and maybe go on a horseback ride with that daughter of ours."

⋆⋆⋆

Kenzie reminded Jonathan about her fall two weeks earlier. Though she felt about a thousand percent better, she still wasn't ready for horseback riding. And she had to move some of her things into his room.

So Jonathan took Lorelai out to show her some of the stuff she'd eventually need to know to have her own horse - though he didn't tell her that. He did tell Kenzie. She wasn't so sure that was the best plan.

While they were outside, she decided what to take. Not much. A few clothes, her toiletries, some pajamas and unmentionables. As she arranged the little bit of clothing in the closet-bigger-than-her-last-house, she heard her name coming from the hallway.

"In here!" she called.

George's voice was clearer but he didn't come into the bathroom to get to the closet. "Ma'am, there's two people here claiming to be your parents."

"Really?" She hurried out and followed him downstairs where she could check the security feed. Jonathan had told her there was an app, but it wasn't on her phone yet. "That's them," she confirmed, pressing the button to let the gate swing open.

By the time their car pulled up in front of the house, she waited for them at the bottom of the stairs.

"Oh, my lands!" her mother called, opening her door almost before the car came to a complete stop. "This is spectacular."

Kenzie hugged her, holding on longer than normal. Had she already become jaded to the grandeur of this place? "Hi, Mom. I missed you."

"I missed you, too." She let go and stepped back. "Now, where's that granddaughter of mine and my handsome new son-in-law?"

"They're down at the stables." Kenzie gave her father a big hug. "Why don't we drive your car down? I fell a couple weeks ago and am still not quite back to normal. Lorelai will be so excited to see you."

They climbed back into the car and Kenzie gave her father directions. In just two minutes, they pulled up outside the stables. Jonathan and Lorelai must have heard them coming because her daughter came running out of the door.

"Nana! Papaw!" Lorelai reached her grandfather first, and he swung her up into his arms. "There's horses!"

Kenzie waited until her daughter greeted both parents then introduced them to Jonathan. All five of them piled back into the car to drive up to the house.

"Jonathan?" Kenzie started as they walked up the stairs. "Would you show my parents around while I talk to Lorelai for a minute?"

He gave her a puzzled look, but nodded.

"What we talked about earlier," she hinted.

Comprehension crossed his face. "Of course. Catch up with us in a bit?"

Kenzie nodded then reached for Lorelai's hand. "Come on. Let's go for a walk."

"What's wrong, Mama?"

Lorelai's voice sounded scared, and that was the last thing Kenzie wanted. "Nothing, sweetie, but I did want to talk to you." They stopped at a big, decorative rock near the driveway. She picked her daughter up and stood her on it.

"You know how it's always been you and me?"

Lorelai nodded.

"And sometimes you asked me about your daddy or if I would ever get married?"

Another single nod.

She took a deep breath. Time to just do it. "Well, Mr. Jonathan and I decided to get married."

Lorelai's eyes got wide, but Kenzie could see her trying not to get too excited. Not yet. "Mr. Jonathan is gonna be my daddy? Can I be in the wedding?"

"Yes. Mr. Jonathan is going to be your daddy. There's some papers to finish filling out and a judge has to say it's okay, but in a few weeks, he'll legally be your daddy."

"Can I be in the wedding?" Lorelai demanded again.

"Well," Kenzie answered slowly. "There are different kinds of weddings. Big weddings like the ones we watched on TV with the princesses." The ones she now knew Jonathan had dated. "And there are regular weddings like the one we went to where we met Mr. Jonathan."

"I 'member."

Kenzie knew she didn't, not really, but she'd seen the pictures many times. "And then super duper small weddings, where the two people just go to the courthouse to get the papers and talk to a judge and that's it. No friends or family or anything."

"Oh." Lorelai seemed to be thinking it over. "Is that what you and Mr. Jonathan did?"

"We did," Kenzie confirmed. "We've talked about having a second wedding, a big one, with you as the flower girl and everything else, but we haven't decided for sure. The important thing is that Mr. Jonathan and I are married." She held up her hand. "I don't wear these when I'm working with my yarn, and I've been doing that a lot lately. These are the rings Mr. Jonathan gave me when we saw the judge."

Lorelai gasped. "They're pretty, Mama."

Kenzie thought so, too. "Now, why don't we go inside so we can see Nana and Papaw?"

Lorelai jumped down from the rock. "And Daddy!" she called, already running toward the house. "I have a daddy!"

With a shake of her head, Kenzie started after her. She'd only made it a few steps when something made her stop. A noise behind her, in the trees. She slowly panned the area, looking for several minutes before deciding it must have been her imagination or a woodland creature. As long as it wasn't a skunk, she was fine with that.

Lorelai climbed the stairs as Kenzie increased her pace. She wished she was as excited as her daughter, but the meager amount she'd seen on the deposit slip wasn't nearly enough. The new balance in the account was so far below what it had started at that she knew she'd never be able to replace it all before Jonathan found out.

She'd told Jonathan she hadn't married him for his money, and in many respects that was true.

It was also true she likely wouldn't have married him so quickly if he didn't have money.

So now that her mind was drifting to the places it had after the kiss that morning, what exactly did that make her?

And what, if anything, could she do about it now?

Chapter Twenty-One

"Daddy!"

The voice came through the heavy wooden door before it pushed all the way open.

The word went straight to Jonathan's heart, a word he'd waited a long time to hear.

Lorelai squeezed through as soon as the door was open far enough. She ran toward him arms in the air. "Daddy!"

Jonathan scooped her up and hugged her close.

"You're my daddy now?" Her voice was muffled by the skin of his neck where her face was buried.

"I am, sweetheart." If possible, he held her even tighter. "I'm your daddy."

"I'm glad you're my daddy."

"Me, too." He opened his eyes to see his new in-laws smiling through tears. Good. They approved. It would have been a lot harder if they didn't.

The front door closed, and Jonathan saw Kenzie standing

there. He held out an arm toward her, and she walked right into it, putting her arms around both of them.

Here, in his arms, Jonathan held everything he'd ever wanted. A wife. A child who called him daddy.

The desires of his heart.

Kenzie moved away from him sooner than he would have liked. "Did you show Mom and Dad around?"

He shifted Lorelai to his hip. "A little bit. Not a whole lot."

"Mostly just the kitchen," her mother cut in, "which is *amazing*."

"It is, isn't it? Come on." She led the way, showing them around most of the house, including the room she "used to live in" and "the master bedroom." The implication was that she lived in there now. So her parents weren't supposed to know the truth.

After a couple of hours, Kenzie's parents headed back to their house. Jonathan went back into his office to catch up on some more paperwork that had been a bit neglected while he'd helped Kenzie with her yarn. Nothing too pressing, but it still needed to be done.

And while he was at it, maybe he needed to beef up his own security. Cameras were all well and good, but if the paparazzi decided to get too nosy, they wouldn't help all that much. He sent an email to one of his guys and would get it set up. Kenzie and Lorelai both needed security for the time being. At least until they could see how this was going to shake out.

As he suspected, Kenzie wasn't very happy about it when he told her about the new arrangements.

"It's just temporary," he tried to reassure her. "Until we know how fanatical the paparazzi will be. My family's representatives have already gotten calls from pretty much everyone asking for interviews and pictures."

"We have representatives?" she asked, her voice matching the weariness on her face.

"*We* don't, but my family as a whole has people that take care of statements and stuff when necessary. I'm sorry this is necessary, but it is." He tried to be as gentle as he could. "I don't like it any more than you do. It's why I live here. It'll take a couple of days to get everything into place, so when you and Lorelai go anywhere, please be extra careful."

"I always am."

"I know. But extra, extra careful. I hope it won't be necessary, but we'll have someone come in and talk to you about the kinds of things to look out for. Cars you see more often than you should. People who just don't seem quite right. Things like that."

"You mean like random guys who talk to my daughter about their dog in the grocery store?" She raised an eyebrow his direction.

It made him laugh - something he sorely needed. "Touché. But you knew who I was, and we'd met before. Even if we hadn't, and Lorelai had just talked to me, you knew who I was."

"How do you know?" she challenged. "You think everyone knows who you are?"

"It's the sad reality of my life, Kenz. I hate it. I hope to keep that from happening to you and Lorelai, but at least for now your pictures are going to be everywhere." A notification on his phone caught his attention. "Are your Facebook settings as locked down as they can be? Do you check in places?"

"I think so and not usually." Kenzie sounded puzzled. "Why?"

"We'll have one of my technology specialists come in and go through everything with both of us. I need to have mine double checked sometimes, too. I get more careless than I should."

"Do we need to post something? Change our relationship status?"

"Sooner or later. A statement is being written. You and I will both go over it and change anything we want before it's actually released."

Kenzie pulled her feet up onto the seat and wrapped her arms around her legs. "This is something I'm going to have to get used to, isn't it?"

"Somewhat," he answered, slowly and wishing things were different. "Hopefully, it will all die down in a few days, and we can go back to living a basically anonymous life."

"Do you really think that'll happen?" She sounded more hopeless than he'd felt in a long time.

"I think it could. Look at Christopher Bayfield."

"Who?"

Jonathan let loose with a grin meant just for her. "Did you ever watch *2 Cool 4 School*?"

Kenzie gave a half-shrug. "Of course. Everyone did." She sat up straight and snapped. "That's right! Just a few months ago, everyone realized that the two guys - Alex and Chris whoever - really live here."

"Christopher still does. Alexander has lived in Ravenzario for several years now."

"And he married the queen, right?" Her eyes were bright, and her face was animated. He liked seeing her this way so much better. "Lorelai and I watched it with my mom. Were you there?"

Jonathan nodded. "Yep. I've been to..." He ticked them of on his fingers as he counted. "Addie and Charlie, Rick and Ellie, Ana and Jonah, Malachi and Jessabelle, Alexander and Christiana, and Yvette and Nicklaus. How many is that? Six royal weddings in the last few years."

She made a noise that was part snort, part whimper, and part laugh. "Please tell me they're all married, and I won't have to go to any?"

"All but William, the Crown Prince of Mevendia. My family

knows several other royal families, but I doubt we'll be asked to any of the weddings." He snapped. "The Crown Princess of San Majoria. I was at her wedding a couple years ago."

"I'd rather not be at any weddings where press passes are a thing."

He gave her another smile, a sad one this time. "I'm afraid the press is going to be a part of both of our lives for the foreseeable future. In fact, probably forever."

Kenzie gripped the steering wheel of the Mustang a little harder. She should have listened to Jonathan, even though he thought it was too soon for the paparazzi hordes to have descended on Serenity Landing. She stared straight ahead, willing the train to hurry up. On either side of them sat motorcycles with two people. The passengers had been taking pictures non-stop. The drivers took them when they were stopped.

Like now.

Half a second earlier and she would have beaten the train.

"Lorelai, honey?"

"Mama, why are they taking our picture?" The fear in her daughter's voice echoed the beating of Kenzie's heart.

"Sweetheart, is your iPad in the holder on the back of my seat?" Jonathan had put the holders in all of the cars, something Kenzie still felt was overkill, but thanked God for at the moment.

"Yes."

"Can you reach it?"

"Yeah."

"Turn the video camera on. Do you remember how?" She looked in the rear view mirror to see her daughter reaching forward. "Hit the button so it's watching you."

Lorelai tapped the screen. "I did."

"Can it see out the back window, too?"

"Yeah."

"When the train finishes, start the recording, okay?" Something told her she wanted the trip home on video. She took her phone and flipped open the new Dr. Who TARDIS phone case wallet thing Jonathan surprised her with the day before. She stuck the cover in between the seat and the headrest, letting the phone hang down. It had the front facing camera going already. Jonathan had upgraded it to the newest, biggest hard drive, so it should record for a while. She'd argued when he gave it to her, but no longer.

The end of the train lumbered by. Six miles. Six long, country miles until they reached home.

"Is it recording, Lorelai?" The train arm started to lift, and one of the motorcycles sped in front of her.

"Yes, Mama."

Kenzie put the car in gear and eased forward. Another motorcycle appeared behind her. Great. Three. And the light ahead of her was red. Why was there a light so close to the train tracks? Oh, she knew Highway 60 needed a light, but still.

She breathed a prayer of relief when the light turned green almost immediately.

All three motorcycles crowded her. One on her left, despite oncoming traffic. One in front and one behind.

Maybe they wouldn't notice she was turning down Highway ZZ in a minute.

Who was she kidding? Even if they didn't, they'd catch up in a minute.

Kenzie pushed the AutoHelp button and prayed they would answer quickly.

"*AutoHelp. What is your emergency?*"

"I'm being crowded by photographers going sixty down a country road. Can you call the police?"

"*Of course, ma'am. I show you on Highway ZZ in Greene County headed south. Is that correct?*"

"Yes." She gripped the wheel tighter with her left hand and downshifted going up a hill.

"*Is there anywhere you can pull off safely?*"

"Not really. There are only a couple of places that I could pull off, and they're empty. Like the high school." If it had been in session, maybe she would have because surely they would have let her in and kept the photogs out.

"*Okay. I have the Serenity Landing PD on the line. Can you tell them what you told me?*"

Kenzie did, but added, "I think I'm nearly out of the county, though. I'm outside city limits and going into Pond Creek County."

"*We're already coordinating with the highway patrol and sheriff's offices, ma'am.*"

They topped a hill, the longest, steepest one in the area. She could easily pick up twenty miles an hour without half trying. But was that more or less dangerous?

Tears began to streak down her cheeks as the car sped up. The motorcycles hung with it, seeming to coordinate who was in front, behind and on the side. The one to her side, whichever one it was, came close enough to reach out and touch when another car roared toward them.

This was it. This is how it was all going to end.

"Mommy, I'm scared."

"Remember our prayer, punkin. God has not given us a spirit of fear." Though that didn't keep fear from spilling from her every pore. "Ma'am?" She spoke louder. "We are recording as best we can on my phone and my daughter's iPad. Just so you know." More tears. "Could you get my husband on the line?"

"Of course. Law enforcement is being kept updated on your location." Silence for a minute. "Mr. Langley-Cranston?"

"Yes?"

"This is Gloria from AutoHelp. I have your wife on the line, sir."

"Kenz?"

Kenzie could hear the fear in his voice. Up ahead, down the hill was the turn toward home. "We're headed toward our road. Can you open the front gate?" If they made it that far. The motorcycle to the left veered closer and her tires hit the rumble strip on the nearly non-existent shoulder before the ditch.

"What's going on?"

"There are three motorcycles with paparazzi."

"The police know?"

She heard sirens in the distance. "They're coming, but I don't know how long it'll take.

"The gate will be open by the time you get here."

His voice sounded dangerous. Ominous.

"We're turning off ZZ." She slowed as far as she dared and still took the turn much faster than she normally would have. And her heart turned cold. "They're slowing down. Trying to get me to stop."

"Don't stop." Jonathan's voice was mixed with the sound of wind. He must be outside. "Lay on your horn, whatever, but don't stop."

"What if I hit them?"

"You won't," he promised. "They'll move."

He sounded far more confident than she felt. The motorcycles came to a complete stop, but left enough room, unintentionally she was sure, for her to slam on the gas and shoot into the other lane between them. She upshifted, going from near-zero to too fast in no time flat.

She slowed down as late as she could to still make the turn into the drive as the motorcycles caught back up. Her eyes widened when Jonathan came into view.

He stood in front of the Gator George drove, just to one side of the drive, more than enough room for her to pull around. But it was what he held that shocked her, though it shouldn't have.

As she passed him, he raised the shotgun to his shoulder and aimed it in the general direction of the gate. By the time she reached the house, the Gator was pulling up behind her.

Kenzie helped Lorelai out of the car seat then wrapped her in her arms. Jonathan's arms then wrapped around both of them.

"Let's get inside." His voice sounded grim and pressure from his arm urged her forward. "You're both safe now."

She wasn't sure she believed him.

Kenzie wasn't sure they'd ever be safe again.

Chapter
Twenty-Two

Jonathan handed the shotgun to George who would make sure it got put away safely. He'd seen the police pulling up - probably state troopers - as George drove the Gator behind the Mustang. Jonathan sat on the back, watching the photographers, just in case.

They'd all decided breaching the swinging gate wasn't in their best interests. Whether that was because of the police cars or because he was armed, Jonathan didn't particularly care.

And pictures of him with his shotgun would be all over the Internet in no time.

Unless the police confiscated the cameras for evidence.

He urged Kenzie, holding Lorelai, into the living room.

"Oh, that sweet thing is so scared." His grandmother took over, urging Kenzie onto the couch.

"When did you get here?" Kenzie asked, shifting Lorelai to sit next to her.

"After I heard the news this morning, I knew I needed to

come." She sat down on the other side of Jonathan's wife and daughter.

He paced.

"I'm glad you're here."

Grandmother reached over and took Lorelai's hand. "Are you all right, sweetie?"

Lorelai nodded, but stayed tucked in next to Kenzie.

"Would you like to go get some ice cream? If it's okay with your mom, of course."

Leave it to Nana to find a way to get Lorelai out of the room, so they could both destress better. Holding hands, they left the room.

"Are you okay?" he asked when they were out of earshot.

"No, I'm not okay. Three motorcycles nearly ran me and my daughter off the road. I think I might know, at least a little bit, how Princess Diana felt that night. Because, seriously, they were ridiculous. My phone and Lorelai's iPad were recording the whole time. They probably still are. Check them to see what happened."

"I will. Our attorney is on his way over. He was already coming over to talk about your former landlord. We'll add this in. I'm pretty sure there's going to be at least one lawsuit out of this and some criminal charges."

"There better be." Kenzie stood up, eyes blazing. "How do they get away with this?"

"They won't. The pictures of me standing there with a shotgun will get out, even if the cameras are confiscated. I'd bet at least one was texted before their phones were taken. I'll make a statement." He didn't want to tell her what had already made its way onto the Internet. "We won't go anywhere without security teams. We'll teach you how to use the shotgun."

"I already know," she snapped. "Just because I'm a girl doesn't mean I don't know how to shoot or field dress a deer, got it?"

Jonathan held up his hands in surrender. "I get it. I know a lot of people from this area grew up hunting and stuff. I didn't know if you knew or not, but a refresher course for both of us wouldn't hurt anyway."

"Fine."

"So security. And beefing up security around here. And a couple of experts coming in to talk about things like defensive driving. You did a great job today, but they can help us both be better prepared. Hopefully, it won't happen again, but if it does we need to be ready."

Her shoulders seemed to collapse in on themselves. "I don't want to be ready. I don't want any of this."

"I know." He walked toward her until he could wrap his arms around her and let her hold onto him.

"I don't want any of this," Kenzie repeated, her voice muffled against his chest. "I don't want people chasing me and my daughter. I don't want my most private moments to be shared." He knew she didn't see him wince. "I don't want to have to be picture ready all the time or have people talking about 'baby bump or burrito lunch.' I just want to live a quiet life with my family. Make enough money selling yarn for us to live on. That's all."

Did all include him? Or just Lorelai?

Jonathan felt himself withdraw, emotionally, though he didn't let go of her. He wanted to soak up the last little bit of Kenzie he could. Finally, he took her hand. "Let's go sit out back and watch the sunset. No one will see us there."

They sat on the swing, her hand still nestled in his, as everything from the last fifteen hours tumbled over and over in his head. He knew the decision was coming, but that didn't mean he wanted to face it.

"I know it's a lot to adjust to, and I'm afraid I haven't made it any easier." He let go of her hand and leaned forward until his elbows rested on his knees. "I'm not proud of my past, Kenz. There's a lot in it that you don't know about. A lot no one knows about. Not my parents. Not the tabloids. Not even the private investigators I've hired from time to time to see what they dig up. I told you most of it, but not everything." He was losing her. And it was his own fault.

Decisions have descendants.

Choices have consequences.

And his were about to be doozies.

Almost enough to make him wish he still drank.

"I've gotten too used to life here in Serenity Landing. The serenity part is mostly right. Seldom is there any paparazzi following me around like when I visit New York or DC or LA. It's why I don't go to those places very often anymore. I like my relatively quiet life here. There's no guarantee that no one will ever dig up my secrets, despite the great lengths I've gone to, praying they're hidden. Secrets don't always stay hidden. Skeletons fall out of closets all the time, especially in families like mine. I've tried to atone, tried to pay my penance, tried to make restitution. I'm right with God. I'm forgiven. Washed clean by the blood of the Lamb."

He stood, his hands shoved deep in his pockets. "It's been far too long since I remembered that the choices I made a long time ago still affect public perception. I don't care what they think of me. I know the truth. The people who matter know the truth. But my wife is going to be subjected to that scrutiny and pressure, and it wasn't fair for me to ask any woman to deal with any of that.

"Consider the yarn and supplies my gift to you and an investment in you and your daughter's future." He took a step toward the door then stopped, his hand on the knob. "I won't ask for an annulment, but it's probably best if the rest of the world thinks we're over. I'll help you find a secure place to live. I'll pay for everything. If you want a divorce or annulment, I'll give you whatever you want." He'd give her everything. "But, at the very least, until all of this dies down, it's best if everyone thinks we're over."

Kenzie's heart shattered into a million pieces as the door closed behind Jonathan.

Tears filled her eyes and streaked unchecked down her cheeks, under her chin, and into a single river of hot liquid until it reached the top of her shirt.

Until a couple weeks earlier, she didn't know much about Jonathan outside of the tabloid headlines while she waited to check out. And what she'd seen of him at the wedding. He'd been kind and gentle with Lorelai. Taken her breath away with every heartbeat of their dance and a half. Left her with a sweet, but all too fleeting, memory.

Had it really only been three weeks since they'd met him, and Mr. Benny Hercules, in the store?

He'd gone out of his way for her since then. Taken them in, looked after everything with her meager belongings. Stood up to his parents. Taken tender care of her daughter.

Stared down a barrel.

Wasn't that all she needed to know?

The kind of man he was now, regardless of what he may or may not have done in the past?

But that past would haunt both of them as long as they were in this relationship.

She, the penniless and widowed single mom, would be

branded a gold digger.

He would be a sucker, falling for someone only after his money. Stories of his supposed conquests would likely continue long after any marriage ceremony, though she believed he would be faithful. Probably.

How would someone like her ever know for sure what went on during business trips to the Hamptons or Vail or wherever people like Jonathan went? Would he, and his fancy friends, always be laughing at her behind her back while they sipped their fancy alcoholic beverages?

But Jonathan doesn't drink.

The realization was cold comfort.

A sob caught in her throat as weight moved the swing. Fantastic. Someone to see her utter humiliation.

"What did my grandson say to cause so much pain?"

Kenzie shook her head. "Just what needed to be said, Mrs. Langley." Nana wasn't from the Cranston side of the family was she? "Everything he said was right. Every single word was true."

Mrs. Langley snorted. "True and right don't always go together in matters of the heart, my dear. Neither does smart." Kenzie still hadn't opened her eyes, but the woman's cool hand covered hers gently. "I have a feeling it has nothing to do with my daughter's perception that you're beneath her son either."

A hiccup trembled through Kenzie's body. "It doesn't."

"How long have you known him?"

"Lorelai and I met him two years ago at a wedding. We didn't see him again until a couple weeks ago."

"And you've already fallen so hard for him and he for you."

Kenzie shook her head. "I fell for who I thought he was." Because who she thought he was would never have taken back his vows, his promise to spend the rest of his life with her and Lorelai.

"His heart is breaking, too, dear. I've never seen him like this."

"It's his own stupid fault."

"Men can be stupid. And women can, too. Neither gender has a monopoly on stupidity."

"But he's right. Everything he said is right." She'd never have a moment's peace, especially not once it got out that she didn't even know who her daughter's father was - or the consequences of Lorelai's traumatic birth. Even here in Serenity Landing, this house would never be a true home. It would be more of a prison, keeping prying eyes away from her little girl and protecting Lorelai's tender heart from the worst the world could offer.

"I'm not saying it would be easy. Nothing worthwhile ever is, but that doesn't mean it's wrong."

Kenzie didn't reply. She didn't know how. Jonathan was right in what he said, though it would have been nice to talk it out like rational adults and let her decide for herself if she was willing to put herself and her daughter through it. She didn't like having decisions made for her.

A throat cleared off to the side. "Mrs. Langley-Cranston..." Right. That was her. "...your daughter is asking for you."

"Thank you, George." She swiped at her cheeks and headed up to Lorelai's room without looking left or right and praying she wouldn't run into Jonathan.

She perched on the edge of her daughter's bed and brushed her hair back off her forehead. "Are you okay, sweetheart?"

Lorelai shrugged, but didn't say anything.

After several questions, all Lorelai knew was that her head hurt, and she didn't want anything to eat. Probably all the trauma. As Lorelai drifted to sleep, Kenzie tried not to remember the things Jonathan had said, but his words replayed in her mind like a CD on repeat.

And every time it got to the part where he said their marriage was over before it started, her heart broke again - and it made her mad. She marched out of the room and toward Jonathan's, figuring that's where he'd be.

When she knocked on the door, it swung open. "Jonathan?" she called, more tentative than she had been a moment earlier.

No answer.

Kenzie took half a step in, just in time to see Jonathan walking out of his bathroom.

In a towel.

He froze, a separate towel against his head.

"So ending things with us is fixed by a shower?" Kenzie crossed her arms over her chest.

"No. But a shower helps clear my head."

"And did it clear the cobwebs out? Or are you still being an idiot?"

He turned and went back into the bathroom, emerging again a moment later in a pair of pajama pants with a t-shirt tossed over his shoulder. "I'm not being an idiot. The tabloids would never leave you and Lorelai alone. They'll never leave me alone. Never leave us in peace." Jonathan came to stand in front of her, his hands coming to rest on her hips. "I started falling for you the moment I first held Lorelai. But there's no future for us. I won't ask you to go through that. I won't let you let yourself. You have no idea what it's like."

"So you won't ever have a wife? You'll let some jerks you can't even name, who have motorcycles and camera lenses as long as your arm, keep you from having a wife and children?"

"Not per se. But it will have to be someone who already understands what the media is like, someone who can make an informed decision."

Kenzie dropped her arms and then put a hand on his chest. "How can *you* make an informed decision? You don't know me.

Not well enough to know if I'd stand up to the test of the paparazzi or anything else life could throw at us." She felt weak, inadequate, incapable of taking care of herself and Lorelai - right now. But underneath, there was pure steel, and Kenzie knew that, too. "Did I like what happened today? Of course not, but I do know this. What we have between us is something worth fighting for. At least I think so. Lorelai certainly thinks so."

Where did this girl come from? This wasn't what she'd been thinking the whole time, but she knew, deep down, this was right. "Now, I moved a bunch of my things in here because you thought your parents were coming."

"They are," he interrupted.

"Fine. Whatever. But I'm heading to bed. You can come if you want." She marched to the bathroom, brushed her teeth, and came back out to find Jonathan staring out the window. Mr. Benny Hercules was already snuggled on the bed when Kenzie climbed in the side she'd slept on at the hotel.

The only question that remained...would this be the second night she spent with her husband or would she sleep alone?

Chapter Twenty-Three

Jonathan didn't spend the night sleeping next to his wife. He wanted to, but there were actually a few more important things he needed to take care of.

Like talking with the lawyers. Videotaping a statement to release to the press. Making plans to take Kenzie and Lorelai to the other side of the world, to a place where security was well-experienced dealing with paparazzi.

When she woke up, he'd tell her the plan and have her pack. Or they could just leave and buy everything en route.

That was a better plan.

Yes, his parents were on the way and as soon as the jet could be ready to take off again, they could be on their way to Montevaro.

He'd already talked to Charlie who made sure they'd have the access they needed to places like the mountain home, a fortress with extensive grounds and no unauthorized pictures.

Once everything was in place and his parents were nearly on

the ground at the airport, he went to wake Kenzie.

She was curled around his pillow, hugging it to her chest. Wishing it was him instead of the poor substitute?

"Kenzie," he whispered, shaking her shoulder. "I need you to wake up, sweetheart."

His wife rolled onto her back. "What is it?"

"Come on. We're getting out of here. I'm taking you and Lorelai away for a while until some of this dies down."

She sat up, adorably mussed, and desperately needing a kiss. But he knew he needed to wait.

"I need to pack," she murmured, only slightly more awake.

"Just bring whatever can't be replaced. We'll get clothes and everything else on the road."

Kenzie nodded. "I'll get Lorelai's stuff then." She went into the bathroom and walked out with a box he'd seen make-up in. "This needs to go." It went on a side table while she looked around then turned back into the bathroom. This time she emerged with a few clothes. "Favorites."

She ran a hand through her hair and pulled it up into a messy ponytail. "Can you grab a suitcase or something so I can get a couple of Lorelai's things?"

"Of course. Where are your passports?" They would need them.

"They're in that fireproof box you put in your safe when we got here."

Right. He'd just grab the whole box and hope she knew where the key was.

"The key is in that make-up box," she called as she walked out.

Or that.

By the time she and Lorelai made it downstairs, Kenzie looked a bit more put together, though her daughter was still sound asleep.

"Let me take her," Jonathan offered in a near whisper. "I'll get her in the car." He walked out the back door and down the stairs to the waiting SUV. They wouldn't be going out the main entrance.

The suitcase he'd left out now held a few of Lorelai's things. Hopefully, he'd soon know what to take and what to leave when it came time to take his new daughter on vacation.

Kenzie zipped it closed as he walked back in. "Let's go."

George walked down the stairs with Mr. Benny Hercules in his arms. "I presume your dog is going with you, sir."

"Of course." Jonathan hadn't really thought about it, but why not? Lorelai loved the little guy, and the dog was finally beginning to open up to them just a bit.

George drove while the three of them sat in the middle of the back seat. The headlights were on as they made their way down the dirt path to the other end of the property. It was too dark not to. When they neared the top of the last hill before reaching the road, though, George turned them off. This gate looked more like part of a cattle pasture. Heavy duty metal bars were moved out of the way by a member of security while George turned onto the road, heading away from the main entrance to the estate.

Once over the next hill, he turned the headlights back on.

"Did you see anyone?" Jonathan asked. He hadn't.

Neither had George.

"Where are we going?" Kenzie asked from the other side of the car seat.

"The airport. The family plane is there and after what happened earlier, my parents didn't argue with us using it to get out of Dodge."

"Are they coming?"

"No. They're going to stay until they can charter a plane." He reached across the back of Lorelai's seat to brush Kenzie's hair back with his fingertips. "I know Mom wasn't crazy about this marriage when she found out about it, but you're family now. So is Lorelai. And those photographers messed with her family. If they don't back off, they'll see a whole new level of crazy out of her. She has her daughter and her grandbaby to protect."

"She really thinks that?" He understood Kenzie's skepticism.

"You should have heard her when I talked to them a couple hours ago. She was livid. I'm pretty sure even HBO would have had to censor that speech."

That earned him half a smile. "Interesting."

The rest of the twenty-minute ride through nearly deserted streets was quiet. They didn't go through the - closed - terminal, but to a gate on the side. His family's plane waited on the tarmac, and his parents stood next to the stairs.

"I'll take Lorelai on board and lay her down." George would stay on board with her until Jonathan returned.

Kenzie helped him get Lorelai out of her seat then looked for something in her bag. Jonathan wondered if she was just buying time for him to get back, so she wouldn't have to face his parents alone.

By the time he laid Lorelai down and walked back to the bottom of the steps, he found Kenzie wrapped in his mother's arms. His mother whispered to her, and Kenzie nodded.

Jonathan gave both of his parents hugs. "We're going to get going. We want to get out of here before anyone realizes we're gone. George will take you to the house the way we left and hopefully, no one will be the wiser."

A few more words, and they were on the plane. Jonathan showed an awe-struck Kenzie where to sit and told her to get some rest. In minutes, they were speeding down the runway and headed for a secure location.

Kenzie walked down the stairs of the luxury jet and onto the tarmac in a foreign country. At least they had passports. They only did because her parents planned to take them on a cruise next year, and Kenzie had been on the ball.

"Where are we, Mama?" Once Lorelai had woken up about an hour earlier, she'd been as enthralled as Kenzie at the luxurious private plane.

"We're in another country, sweetheart."

"Montevaro," Jonathan answered. "I have friends who live here. We're going to stay at their house in the mountains."

Lorelai took Jonathan's hand and skipped beside him, the fear from the day before apparently forgotten. "Is it a big house?"

Jonathan chuckled. "It is. But first we're going to go to their actual house to see them for a little bit. One of them has a little girl about your age."

"Yay!"

Kenzie came to a halt. "Wait. We're going to their *house*?"

He actually had the audacity to wink at her when they were getting ready to go to a palace. And she still wore pajamas from the night before.

"Well, first we're going to go to another place to change clothes and brush our hair and those sorts of things. Then we're going to go to their house."

That was better, though Kenzie wasn't sure she had appropriate clothes.

"Everything's taken care of," he whispered as they climbed into a black SUV with heavily tinted windows. A few minutes later, they pulled up to heavy gates swinging open.

"Whoa!" Lorelai exclaimed. "It's big!"

"This is Lydia House," Jonathan explained as Kenzie tried to keep her own awe under control. "It's reserved for guests of the family."

The butler, whose name Kenzie would never remember, showed them to a suite where clothes waited. Apparently, they already knew Jonathan's size, because a number of clothes already waited for him. They must have guessed well about Lorelai, because the clothes almost all fit perfectly.

But Kenzie went through a whole bunch before she found some that she was comfortable in. Some were too nice. Some were too big or too small and some just didn't quite fit right.

After about an hour, they were finally ready to head to the *house*. Back in the SUV, Jonathan told them a little more. "They actually live in a house on an island."

Lorelai practically bounced. "Do we get to ride in a boat?"

"You'll have to wear a life jacket," Kenzie reminded her.

"Okay!" Even though she'd done swim team, it didn't bother her? That surprised Kenzie. It must be the excitement of all things new.

"I don't know if that'll be necessary." Jonathan smirked at her. Great. More feeling inadequate in her new life.

They pulled through a couple of heavy doors into a garage of some kind.

"This is a garrison," he explained, though he didn't tell either one of them what that meant. It looked like a small parking garage.

They were met by a young woman who introduced herself as Danica. Jonathan shook her hand and kissed her cheek. Kenzie tried not to be jealous. He hadn't ever kissed her cheek, and how long had it been since he'd kissed her at all?

"This way, please." Danica led them through a hallway and up a gangplank onto a boat big enough that Jonathan was right. They wouldn't need life jackets. It was much, much larger than she'd expected.

"Mr. Langley-Cranston, you might want to take them to the front. I'll find you there when it's time to disembark." Danica's smile told Kenzie they would want to sit near the front.

They followed Jonathan through the passages. The boat wasn't as opulent as the plane they'd arrived on, but Kenzie could imagine the family's yacht probably was. Because surely they had one.

They reached the front of boat. Jonathan told her where he thought she should sit and sat next to her, lifting Lorelai onto his lap. A minute later, they began to move. Here went nothing.

Chapter Twenty-Four

Jonathan kept a close eye on Kenzie and Lorelai. Kenzie looked apprehensive. Lorelai just looked enthralled at being on a boat.

But he knew the moment she saw the palace.

"Is that their house, Mr. Jonathan? I mean Daddy." She bounced up and down on his lap.

"That is their house," he confirmed.

"It's like a castle." The awe in Lorelai's voice made him wish he weren't so jaded, so used to the kinds of things she was just discovering.

"It is a castle." What would her reaction be?

Lorelai's eyes were huge as she turned around to look at him. "Are you friends with a *princess*?"

Jonathan couldn't stop his chuckle. "I am friends with a princess." What would it be like seeing Ana now that they were both married? "I'm also friends with a prince and a queen."

"A *queen*?" Lorelai's eyes somehow managed to get even

bigger.

"My friend Addie is Queen Adeline. She's married to Prince Charlie. Addie's little brother is Prince Richard. He's married to Princess Ellie. Then my friend Princess Ana is married to Dr. Duke Jonah. They have a little girl named Stacy. And they have a dog."

She looked around, suddenly alarmed. "Where's Mr. Benny Hercules?"

"He'll meet us later." Either at the palace if they decided to stay for a few days or at the mountain residence.

"Good."

Kenzie still hadn't said anything, but finally she blew out a breath, and Jonathan saw her square her shoulders. "It's lovely."

"Are we gonna meet the queen, Mama?"

"I don't know, sweetheart. But remember the queen we saw on TV, the one with the gray hair who's been queen for a long time?"

Lorelai nodded.

"This is a different queen. In fact, she's very young for a queen. She's the same age as Mr. Jonathan?" The title struck a bit of a nerve.

"She's your age, Daddy?"

He hugged the little girl a bit closer. "She is. We went to college together."

"Will she like me?" Lorelai suddenly seemed worried.

Jonathan wondered what was taking so long. The trip could be made in far less time. He looked around and realized they were taking the long way, making a complete circuit of the island.

"Look." He pointed up to one of the balconies where a little girl waved wildly. "I bet that's Stacy waiting for you." Sure enough when Lorelai waved back, the girl turned and ran inside.

A minute later, the boat pulled to a stop at another dock.

Danica led them through stone hallways toward the palace proper.

"The queen has a full schedule today, but she is looking forward to dinner tonight," Danica told them. "A suite has been prepared for your family this evening. A car will take you to the mountain residence tomorrow, if that's acceptable, sir."

"That sounds great."

Kenzie still hadn't said anything, but she didn't look completely comfortable. She looked around, much like Lorelai, trying to take it all in. The further they walked, the more ornate the furnishings became. Tapestries. Paintings. Rugs.

"Jonathan!" He heard Ana before he saw her.

And there she was, walking across one of the large drawing rooms with her arms open. He took her hands and kissed her cheek. "Good morning, Princess Anastasia."

Good.

He felt nothing but friendship.

"Oh, please." She rolled her eyes as she dropped his hands and turned to Kenzie. "You must be the lucky woman who finally landed this man."

Kenzie did some half-curtsy thing. "MacKenzie Langley-Cranston, ma'am."

Ana smiled, though he sensed she wanted to roll her eyes again. "Please, call me Ana. And there is no need to curtsy anyone around here. You're Americans, not Montevarians. And even we only curtsy to my sister and my father, the former king, out of respect for his lifetime of service to the country. And only the first time we see them each day." She leaned in closer. "It's kind of funny to see my sister, the queen, curtsy to our father in her pajamas."

That finally drew a smile from Kenzie. "It's a pleasure to meet you."

Ana initiated the handshake and two-cheek kisses.

Lorelai couldn't wait any longer. She tugged on the hem of Ana's jacket. "Are you really a princess?"

Ana managed to somehow turn squatting down to talk to a little girl look elegant. "I am. My name is Princess Anastasia Salome Keziah. What's your name?"

"I'm Lorelai Davidson." A frown creased her brow then she looked up at him. "Do I have a new last name, Daddy?"

He rested his hand on her head. "Not yet, punkin." It took all his willpower not to glance over at Kenzie to see what she thought about that. Just a couple more weeks, and it would be official.

"How old are you, Lorelai?"

"Almost five."

"Her birthday is in a few weeks," Kenzie explained.

How had Jonathan not realized that? He'd have to find a way to make it special.

"I have a little girl. She's a couple years older than you, though. I'm sure she would love to have a friend."

Jonathan knew he shouldn't question a mother. "I thought she was five."

Ana straightened and gave a dignified chuckle. "She was when Jonah and I got married. That was a while ago. She's almost seven now."

"Mama!" The voice carried down the hallways.

"And there she is now." Ana turned, and they all saw the little girl from the balcony running into the room. Walking behind, more sedately, was a woman in a nanny uniform.

The five of them spent about ten minutes getting to know each other before Kenzie okayed Lorelai running off to the garden with Stacy.

"Where's Jonah?" Jonathan asked his friend as they walked toward the family's private residences.

"He didn't get home until nearly dawn this morning. The life of a doctor."

"What does he specialize in?" Kenzie finally asked a question of her own.

"He's a pediatric hospitalist. He works with the children in the pediatric ward of the hospital, rather than having a regular office."

"That's got to be tough work."

Ana smiled, and Jonathan knew she never would have smiled that way for him. "It is, but he is quite good at his job. The children love him, and he loves them."

"That's fantastic."

Jonathan reached over and took Kenzie's hands, linking their fingers together. Ana and Jonah belonged together. And now that he had Kenzie, he could be happy for them in a way he never could before.

He just needed to find a time to tell Kenzie that.

Kenzie wondered what was going through her husband's mind when he took her hand. Was he trying to remind himself he was a married man, and whatever feelings he had for Ana needed to go the way of the woolly mammoth?

Or could it be that he realized the same thing she had? That there was more to this marriage than just the convenience factor. More to it than money for her. More to it than some over-protective rescuer complex for Jonathan.

She liked that idea.

Or she would if it didn't mean she had to hobnob with royalty on occasion or have paparazzi hounding their every move.

"Your statement last night was perfect, Jonathan," Ana said as she opened a door to an apartment.

Kenzie looked at him. "What statement?"

Jonathan shrugged. "I told you I was going to make a statement last night."

"Can I read it?"

Ana gave that royal chuckle again. "Oh, it must be watched." She clicked a button on a remote and a webpage appeared on the screen over the fireplace. After tapping on a keyboard, several links appeared in a search engine. She chose the one to Jonathan's personal website and clicked on the video at the top. "Here."

"Good evening. This is not a press conference, but this is my statement on the events of this evening. Earlier today, it was reported that I recently married a beautiful, young, single mother. This is true. What those of you in the sensationalized media don't realize is that, when you threaten my family, I take it very seriously." Jonathan leaned slightly forward. "This is your first and only warning. I will not take kindly to photographers on our property." He picked up his iPad from the desk. "And pictures like this one..."

Kenzie gasped. There was Lorelai standing on the rock near the driveway while she told her daughter that Jonathan was her new father.

"...that had to be taken from my property will not happen again. Photographers, other journalists, or pretty much anyone who trespasses will be prosecuted to the fullest extent of the law." He swiped sideways until a still from her cell phone video appeared. "And if you feel the need to take pictures while they're out and about and nearly run them off the road, if I get another phone call from my wife scared for her life because there's no safe place for her to get away and motorcycles surround her and my daughter, then you, too, will see this when she gets home."

He swiped again and a photo of himself, likely sent by cell phone almost immediately, appeared. He stood in front of the Gator as the Mustang drove past. His grim face and shotgun told the whole story. "I will protect my family, with force if necessary."

Another swipe showed a still from the gate cameras of the motorcycles sitting there with their occupants and cameras. "I will name names. I will bring civil lawsuits. I will press charges." He swiped again to see a member of the Missouri Highway Patrol putting handcuffs on one of the photographers. "If you're lucky, Missouri's finest will get there before I feel the need to step in further."

Video-Jonathan set the tablet down and leaned forward slightly. "Leave me alone. Leave my wife alone. Leave my daughter alone. Leave. My. Family. Alone."

With tears in her eyes, Kenzie turned to Jonathan. "Thank you," she whispered. Whatever she thought he meant by making a statement, it wasn't that. She'd expected something that said the same thing, but in pretty, flowery terms. Not laid so bare. And not so defensive of both her and Lorelai.

Jonathan's warm hands rested on her bare forearms. "Hey. You're my wife. Lorelai is my daughter. No one should mess with you, and they need to know that I'm not afraid to take them on. What's the saying about pretty daughters dating? Shoot the first date, and the word will spread. That's a bit drastic, of course, but they need to know I'm not bluffing. I will take legal action, both civil and criminal. You're an unknown quantity, but they've known for a long time that they shouldn't mess with my parents, for instance. It's time to make sure they realize they can't mess with our family either."

She let herself be drawn into his arms, rested her head against his chest and just soaked up the strength he exuded. It was nice, this being able to trust someone else to help take care of her and her daughter.

Their daughter.

He'd said Lorelai didn't have the last name yet. He'd publicly claimed her as his daughter, no matter what the biology said, no matter that the paperwork wasn't final yet.

"You'll be safe from all of that here." Ana's voice pulled Kenzie back to the present.

She let go of Jonathan and turned to face her hostess. "Thank you. I appreciate your kindness."

"It's our pleasure." She glanced at a watch that probably cost more than Kenzie's salary for a couple of years. "Addie should be here in a moment. She has a few minutes between meetings, and I know she's looking forward to seeing you, Jonathan, and meeting you, MacKenzie."

"Please call me Kenzie." If she could call the princess by a shortened first name, then the princess could do the same. The door opened and in walked the woman who had to be the actual queen.

"Jonathan!" She held her arms out much as her sister had, and Jonathan responded the same way. Taking her hands, kissing her cheek, then introducing her. Did that mean he didn't feel much of anything for either one of them anymore?

"I am so happy for both of you!" The queen took her hands, but no cheek kisses. "You are just what my old friend needs. I have a feeling the two of you are quite well-matched."

Kenzie wondered how the queen could know that, but she didn't question the reasoning.

She did question the conclusion.

She was starting to believe she and Jonathan belonged together, but did he really think so? Or had he just been putting up a good front for the camera?

Chapter Twenty-Five

Jonathan thoroughly enjoyed spending the day with various members of the Montevarian royal family. Lorelai loved spending the night in the palace. She even spent the night with Stacy in the other girl's room instead of the room closer to the one Jonathan and Kenzie shared.

Because no one else knew they didn't normally sleep in the same bed.

This time, instead of waking up spooning his wife, he woke up with her snuggled into his back and an arm wrapped around his waist.

Jonathan decided he could get used to it. Covering her hand with his own, he closed his eyes hoping for a bit more sleep.

"Sorry." Kenzie's sleep-filled voice accompanied her arm sliding away.

"It's fine." His own voice sounded husky. "It's nice."

Her presence encompassed him further. "It is kind of nice."

He wanted to roll over, to kiss her good morning, but he

didn't dare. Not yet. It wasn't time to be *more* to each other, not until he'd told her how he felt.

Once he figured it out.

"What's our plan today?"

Jonathan did roll to face her, but only to talk. "Whenever we're ready, after breakfast sometime, we'll go to the family's mountain house. It's quite private, so we shouldn't have to worry about any photographers. The ones from this country, and most of Europe, know better than to mess with the Montevarian royal family's security teams."

"And the Americans?"

He reached out and brushed some hair off her face. She looked stunning first thing in the morning. "Hopefully, their European counterparts will fill them in. If not, they're in for a rude awakening when they run into the teams."

"I don't want to spend the whole time at the house, though." Kenzie picked at the sheet in between them. "I've never been to Europe. I'd like to see more than a garden."

"Good. There's a resort nearby. It's one of the more exclusive ones, so there shouldn't be too many people there willing to share or sell pictures."

"What kinds of things do they have?"

Jonathan rolled onto his back. "I'll bring you back in the winter. They have some great skiing. This time of year, there's hiking and four-wheeling and summer bobsleds."

"What exactly is that?"

"These are like roller coasters on the bobsled track. Completely controlled. No chance of the cars coming off the track or some kind of accident like in the Olympics."

"That's a relief. What about for Lorelai, though? She's not tall enough, is she?"

Things like that had never occurred to him. It needed to, now that he was a parent. "I don't know if she is. If not, there's got to be plenty of other things we can do as a family."

Kenzie flopped onto her back. "A family. That's something I haven't really thought about in a long time."

He rolled back to his side, facing her. "That's something we haven't really talked about. A little bit, but not much. You already gave birth to one beautiful daughter. What happened so you can't have any more children?"

It didn't matter to him, not anymore. They could adopt. But he didn't like the idea that something was wrong with Kenzie.

"Lorelai's delivery wasn't easy. I won't go into all the gory details, but there was a lot of bleeding. A lot. My doctor said I would need multiple surgeries to get rid of...polyps or something that caused it. I never went back for a check-up after she was born. The money just wasn't there. Even if I had, I wouldn't have been able to have the surgeries."

"Promise me one thing?"

Her head rolled so she looked straight at him. "What?"

"Let's get a second opinion. We'll see who the best doctor in the area is. I'm sure Stephanie Wilson could tell us. Go see the best and then decide what the next course of action is."

She turned that over in her head. "Okay. I don't want to go the super invasive route though. I don't think I could handle the injections and hormones and all of that. There are more than enough kids who need parents. The women who do all of that are stronger than I am."

"And Gwendolyn's baby?" He'd only offered in jest in the beginning, but he had been seriously considering it before he met Kenzie that night. Now that he was married, the desire had deepened.

But only if she wanted it, too.

"Do we really want a baby so quickly? Just a few months into our marriage?" Her tone was thoughtful, not scared.

"Keep thinking about it?"

She nodded. "Thinking and praying." This time Kenzie pushed the hair behind her own ear. "That's something I didn't do enough in that car."

"Praying?"

"Yeah."

Jonathan thought about that. "Did you really not pray? Or did you not form conscious words? Because that doesn't mean you didn't pray."

"Good point. I'm pretty sure desperate, formless thoughts were asking for all kinds of help."

He took her hand. "One thing I know I haven't done enough of since then is be grateful that you're both okay." With his head tipped forward so their foreheads touched, he began to pray aloud with his wife, really for the first time. He thanked God for being with his girls that day, for keeping them safe, and for giving them friends who could help them hide long enough to regroup.

The breath of Kenzie's whispered amen made Jonathan open his eyes. There she was, so close, and when Kenzie opened her eyes, he wasn't imagining what he saw there. Was he?

Did she want him to kiss her as much as he wanted to?

He leaned slightly closer, and her eyes fluttered shut.

"Mama! Daddy!"

Jonathan actually groaned as he landed on his back again. They'd need to make sure the door at home had a good lock and, at some point, teach Lorelai how to knock. She'd shared a room with Kenzie her entire life, until the last few weeks. Of course she wouldn't know those things.

Kenzie sat up, with the covers still in her lap. "Sweetheart, what have we talked about, especially when you're in someone else's house?" Her tone was gentle, even as she corrected the girl.

He also needed to make sure he learned how to do that.

"Knock." Lorelai's nose scrunched. "Sorry, Mama."

"It's okay, but you need to remember, especially in someone's bedroom. It's not polite, but it could also be embarrassing for both of you if they're changing clothes or something."

Like walking in on your new dad kissing your mom, though that's all it would have been.

Kenzie pulled Lorelai onto the bed. "Now, what did you need to tell us?"

***

Kenzie was grateful for her daughter's presence. She wasn't quite ready for the kind of kiss Jonathan had been about to give her.

"Stacy said there are horses at the other house. Can Daddy teach me how to ride? Please?"

She arched a brow at Lorelai.

The most adorable wrinkled nose ever appeared. "Sorry, Mama. I won't whine. But can he?"

"Are you sure Jonathan knows how to ride?" She dropped the more formal "Mr." in front of it. It was progress. Kenzie also wasn't quite ready to call him Dad to her little girl.

Lorelai nodded, completely serious. "I know he does."

Kenzie glanced over to see Jonathan hiding a smile.

"I do know how," he told them both. "But I doubt I'm a very good teacher. I'm sure we can find someone though. Now, how's Mr. Benny Hercules?"

She knew the little dog had slept with Jonathan since the first night, but this time Lorelai and Stacy wanted him to sleep with them and Stacy's Lexi-dog.

"He's good. Someone took him and Lexi-dog outside."

Right, because there were people to do mundane things like walk dogs.

"So I can learn to ride, Daddy?"

Jonathan wisely nodded toward Kenzie. "That's a decision for your mother, but if it's okay with her, you can learn some things here and more when we get home. I would imagine we could still go riding, and you can sit with me if you want."

"Okay!" Lorelai bounced off the bed. "Let's go!"

Kenzie smiled as she ran out of the room. "She's something else."

Jonathan raked his fingers through his hair. "And she has impeccable timing."

Of course. Kenzie stared at the ring on her fourth finger, the one Jonathan still didn't wear a match for. "It's not yet the time or place," she finally said.

The silence from the other side of the bed seemed to stretch into an eternity. "I know." Jonathan's arm stretched across until his hand landed on the small of her back. "But I can't say I don't look forward to the time and place when you will be my wife in more than name."

She couldn't say she didn't either, and she really hadn't expected him to agree. He rolled away, sitting with his back to her as his feet hit the floor. After grabbing a piece of cloth from the end of the bed, he stood and walked toward the bathroom. Kenzie followed him with her eyes as he pulled the shirt over his tanned skin. Whatever else her husband was, he was definitely in good shape. Better than she was. Time to start running again before she had to go to some fancy thing where she might get photographed again.

The shower turned on in the bathroom, and Jonathan poked his still-clothed self out the door. "I'll close the door if you need in for anything."

She nodded. The highly segmented bathroom meant she could take care of her morning business without worrying about running into Jonathan in his towel again - or possibly less. Despite her earlier statement, the temptation existed.

It took about an hour, but they were on their way to the other home. This time, Jonathan drove the car, but security teams both led and followed them. It didn't take as long as Kenzie would have thought before they pulled through the imposing gate of the home.

If she'd been impressed the first time she saw Jonathan's house, and the palace had been absolutely off-the-charts, this one fell solidly in awestruck.

"No one will bother us here." Jonathan spoke quietly, so Lorelai wouldn't hear. Her daughter seemed to be nearly as enraptured here as she had been at the palace.

"This is for us to stay at, Mama?"

"For a few days, sweetheart." It looked like something out of Downton Abbey or a fairy tale.

They were introduced to a gentleman wearing a tuxedo. Did men really still wear those sorts of things to do work around the house? This guy was probably a manager of some kind, but still.

After introductions, he handed an envelope to Jonathan. "This came for you this morning, sir."

Jonathan opened it and pulled out a card.

Something fancy.

He smiled at what he read and turned back to the head guy whose name Kenzie hadn't heard. "Tell them we'd love to."

"Yes, sir. Arrangements have already been made for Miss Lorelai to have guests while you are gone. The Duchess of Carmagnonia and the Duchess of Busselonio will join her for the evening."

"Very good."

Like he knew who the duchesses were. Weren't duchesses stuffy old ladies?

Except...when Prince William married Kate, she'd become Catherine, Duchess of Cambridge. And didn't some of the kids of royalty end up with titles like Duke and Duchess?

Jonathan just squeezed her hand. She'd ask him about it later.

Once again, she and Jonathan were expected to share a room. It only made sense. Kenzie knew that. And unless she wanted others making assumptions, it was the only way.

"So who exactly are those duchesses?" she asked when they were alone in their room.

His grin maddened her. "I wondered if you knew."

"If I knew what?"

"The Duchess of Busselonio is Stacy. The Duchess of Carmagonia is Lindsey, Prince Charlie's daughter. Neither of them are princesses because they're not family by birth but by adoption and marriage."

"Oh."

"And Lindsey's from Serenity Landing, don't forget. She probably knows some of the lifeguards. Lorelai will have a blast."

Before she could ask where they would be, a knock on the door interrupted. In came a maid to tell them the closet had been well-stocked with clothes in both of their sizes, as well as plenty of outfits for Lorelai in her room across the hall.

Jonathan asked about clothes suitable for riding. The young woman, who truthfully, was likely older than Kenzie, went back into the closet and emerged a moment later with a full English riding habit for both of them.

"I think riding habits might be a bit much," Kenzie said.

A shadow crossed the woman's face.

"I mean, they're fantastic, but won't some comfortable clothes work better?"

"They're probably a lot more comfortable than you think," Jonathan told her. "The breeches are basically stretchy pants reinforced where they'll rub against the saddle. But maybe the jackets are a little overboard. Technically, riding habits are long gone for most people. They had skirts for women to ride sidesaddle with, or trousers underneath that matched so no one knew they were riding astride."

"You know your women's clothing well, sir." The maid smiled at him, her slight irritation gone.

"I was riding practically before I could walk, though I haven't done nearly as much in recent years."

Kenzie sighed. "Okay, let's go."

Chapter Twenty-Six

Jonathan helped Lorelai settle back into the saddle in front of him. She'd helped saddle both horses and wore the full riding outfit, complete with jacket, despite the moderate temperature.

"We won't go fast or far today," he told her. "But we'll have someone teach you better when we get back home. You'll be jumping before you know it."

Lorelai twisted her head to look up at him. "Like in the 'Lympics?"

"Yes, like the Olympics."

Kenzie didn't look so sure, but didn't say anything. She said she'd ridden many times, though it had also been a while. She'd seemed to know what she was doing when they saddled the horses.

They rode for an hour. Lorelai wanted to keep going, but Jonathan knew he and Kenzie would both wind up sore, and that wouldn't be a good plan.

She hadn't asked what the invitation was for, and he thought he would surprise her with it. The drive was only a couple of hours long, but it would give them time to talk some more. Something they sorely needed. Not quite like a date, but if either he drove, or they were in the back seat by themselves, with privacy glass up, it would be close enough. There would be a place for them to get ready. She'd have assistants to help her.

He hoped she'd love it.

It might be the first such event, but if this was going to work between them, it likely wouldn't be the last.

They didn't venture near the end of the property, but it was so vast. It didn't seem as though they were hemmed in and protected.

By the time they made it back to the house, it was nearly lunchtime. He went to another room so they could all take quick showers to get the horse smell off them. Lunch was served in a room boasting a table large enough for the entire SLAC swim team or close enough.

The meal went quickly, but as one of the maids picked up the dishes, Kenzie stopped her with a hand on her arm.

The maid looked surprised. "Yes, ma'am?"

"I'm sorry to bother you, but I've been admiring your collar. It's not the same as the other women I've seen today."

The girl's cheeks colored. "No, ma'am. It isn't." Her eyes widened. "But I have permission."

Kenzie looked shocked, but Jonathan reminded himself that she'd never lived the life of privilege. She didn't know how some treated their servants. "Oh, goodness. I was *admiring* it. What is it made of?"

"My mum made it from some yarn she had leftover." The woman fingered the delicate collar Jonathan had thought was lace, if he thought about it at all.

"Your mother is quite skilled with knitting needles then. But what kind of yarn is it? I work with yarn," she explained. "It's kind of my business, but I don't recognize it."

There were more kinds of yarn than what he'd already learned about?

"I don't know much about it, but Lady Margaret of Aquitaine Toulouse teaches the technique. That's all I know except I like it."

"I do, too."

"Thank you, ma'am." The woman hesitated. "Will there be anything else?"

Kenzie started. "Um, no. Thanks."

"Lady Margaret of Aquitaine Toulouse?" Jonathan asked when they were alone again a moment later.

"She's that teacher from Europe. I forget where. I think I told you she'll actually be at the Serenity Landing show this year. I'd love to take her class, but I'm not sure if I'll be able to or not."

"That's right." Jonathan didn't say anything but began to formulate a plan. George would be there soon. Jonathan would have him find out all there was to know and see if there was anything yarn-ish worth the time nearby or in Mevendia.

By the time they finished eating, Kenzie and Lorelai were both yawning. He urged them to take naps for a couple of hours. As they both rested, he pulled his phone out and left to find an office or an area he could use.

Turning it on for the first time in hours, he found about what he expected. Emails and texts and missed calls. All about his video message to the paparazzi. He only chose to return a few, including a phone call to the authorities in Serenity Landing to discuss the charges against the men on the bikes.

He also talked to the firm that handled most press matters for his family. They had watched the films and listened to the tapes.

Some of it would likely be released to the media in the next day or two. Family members were being stalked at restaurants and on the street, more so than usual. They stuck with either saying nothing or the standard "no comment" that often served them well. None of them said anything about never having met the newest members of the Langley-Cranston dynasty.

George arrived, and Jonathan gave him instructions on what he wanted to find out. In a couple of hours, George would know all there was to know, and Jonathan could decide.

By the time his girls came back downstairs, a plan was in place. Kenzie finally asked what the plans were for the next day, he just grinned and told her she'd have to wait and see.

It infuriated her, but in a cute way.

And then he spent the night sleeping far too close to the wife he didn't trust himself enough to touch.

He prayed the day he would came soon, for both their sakes.

"Where are we going?" Kenzie knew she was grumpy and in desperate need of a good cup of coffee.

"You'll see." Jonathan still wouldn't tell her anything beyond the duchesses would be arriving in an hour, and the two of them wouldn't return until the wee hours of the morning, if not nearly sunrise.

At least the two of them were alone, or nearly so. They sat in the back seat of a slightly larger than normal sedan. The partition was up. It was clear glass so they could still see out the front. Kenzie liked that. It would unnerve her too much if she couldn't.

They spent most of the drive talking about everything and nothing. Finally, Jonathan told her they had about twenty minutes before they arrived, if she wanted to do her hair and makeup. He didn't expect their pictures to wind up online, but you never knew. She'd dressed in nice jeans and knee boots with a new flowy blouse before they left, but she'd only thrown her hair into a sloppy ponytail and donned no makeup.

She finished with several minutes to spare. "Now will you tell me where we're going?

Jonathan leaned back in the corner of the car and grinned. "Nope."

"You're impossible."

"You'll find out in a few minutes."

The car turned off the highway, or whatever it was called in Europe, and into a town. It pulled to a stop in front of what looked to be a market of some kind.

"Where are we?"

"The Mevendian Wool Festival." He got out and turned to offer her a hand.

Kenzie's jaw dropped. "What? Really?"

"Yep. That Lady Margaret woman is here, but her classes were all full at the times we could be here."

He'd really thought of that for her? "Thank you, anyway." She felt nearly giddy. "This is fantastic."

Jonathan took her hand, and they walked toward the main entrance. He paid the small fee to get in.

"How long do we have?"

"We have about four hours until we have to leave for the next part of our day."

She looked around. It would take far longer than that to do this place justice, but she'd take what she could get. "What's the next thing?"

"Still not telling."

With their fingers linked together, they started down the first row of vendors. She saw several things that caught her eye and looked at all of them. Jonathan offered to buy her anything she wanted. It took a bit of encouragement, but she finally bought a few small things for gifts back home or to deconstruct for herself to see how they did it. She struck up conversations with several vendors asking about some of the different products. One had stuffed animals made of fine alpaca wool. She bought one for Lorelai and each of the duchesses.

After two hours and nearly a quarter of the marketplace covered, Jonathan asked something else. "Any chance you're ready to eat yet?"

Kenzie laughed. "Whenever you are."

He slid his arm around her waist. "Since we happen to be near the food vendors, maybe we should eat now."

"Imagine that."

They ordered food from one the carts Jonathan recommended and sat at one of the tables.

That's when Kenzie noticed them. "Have they been following us all day?" she asked quietly, nodding toward the two men in dark suits.

Jonathan stared at his food. "Yes. I was wondering when you'd notice and when you didn't, I hoped you wouldn't, but they're here just in case."

"You said you didn't think anything would happen here." Kenzie wasn't sure if she was annoyed, mad, or scared.

"I don't, but there's no way to actually know, so we have an insurance policy of sorts. You don't ever expect to lock your keys in your car, but that's why you have *AutoHelp*."

He made a good point, one Kenzie grudgingly conceded. "Will they be with us all day?"

Jonathan made a funny face. "Kind of? Where we're going this evening, they won't really be needed, but there will already be strict security."

"I see." She didn't, not really. What kind of thing were they going to?

As they threw their trash away, a young man with a camera approached them.

"Excuse me, Mr. Langley-Cranston?"

Kenzie saw the annoyance flit across his face. "Yes?"

He introduced himself as a reporter for one of the local news stations. "May I take a picture of you with your wife for our photo stream about the Yarn Festival?"

Jonathan looked at her. "Is that all right with you?"

She wanted to ask for his credentials. How did they really know he was who he said he was? The station logo was on his camera bag, but did that really mean anything? "It's okay with me, if it's all right with you." Deflect. Let Jonathan decide.

"Of course," Jonathan told the man. "One picture."

Kenzie conjured up everything she could think of. How did models and actresses pose with their significant others on the red carpet?

"Just relax and smile," Jonathan whispered, his arm around her waist.

The photographer clicked then checked his camera. "I know you said one picture, but ma'am, you look a bit uncomfortable. Would you like to try another one?"

Kenzie took the chance. "Sure." She put her arm around his waist and tried to look the part of the happy newlywed.

He checked his camera again. "Much better. Thank you both."

Jonathan shook his hand, and they parted ways. "They're not all bad," he told her. "The ones the other day were the worst of the worst. Guys like that one are usually just trying to do their jobs without guys like me punching their lights out for bothering us." He shrugged. "I prefer to avoid them all as much as possible, though."

Kenzie just wanted to forget about it and get back to exploring, so when Jonathan suggested they do just that, she went along willingly. The picture would end up with a much farther reach than just a Mevendian news website, but for now, she'd enjoy the anonymity she'd likely never experience again.

Jonathan had seen and smelled and touched about all the yarn and fiber and wool and alpaca and everything else that he wanted to for the rest of his life.

But he'd married a woman in love with all of this stuff, so he knew he'd need to learn more than he ever thought he'd need to know.

After four hours of wandering up and down the rows, they'd seen maybe half of what the festival had to offer.

"Any chance we can come back tomorrow?" Kenzie asked as they settled into the car.

The thought hadn't occurred to him. "I don't know. Maybe? We could stay the night here and come back if you don't mind staying without Lorelai."

"When do I need to decide?"

"Whenever. We have a hotel room set aside for us if we'd like to use it, but we don't have to. We can drive back tonight, though we likely won't arrive until two or three in the morning. As long as you decide before we leave the venue, it's fine."

He didn't want to go back, but he would. He'd learned a lot about his wife in those few hours. She had a good eye and knew her stuff. The vendors she'd talked with had been impressed with her knowledge and her questions. They'd even gotten a glimpse of that Lady Margaret person. She was a lot older than Jonathan had expected.

The car pulled up in front of the finest hotel in Erres, Mevendia's capital city. One of the valets opened the door and held out his hand to help Kenzie from the car. George met them inside.

"This way sir, ma'am." He started for a bank of elevators. "I trust your day was most enjoyable."

"Very," Kenzie told him. "I'm guessing my husband put you up to helping plan the day, so thank you."

She was right and knew him well already. He wanted something to happen, so he found the right people to get it done. George was often one of those people, and Kenzie knew that.

The elevator came quickly after George swiped a key card.

"Is this event here?" Kenzie asked.

"No, ma'am." George wouldn't say any more, not after Jonathan had asked him to keep it a secret.

The elevator whisked them straight to the top floor. Once inside one of the suites, Kenzie stopped in her tracks.

"What's all of this?"

Jonathan rested his hand on her lower back, hoping to calm the nerves that had to be coursing through her. "One part fashion show, one part salon, one part pampering. We're going to a black tie event tonight." Tails optional, which meant he'd be wearing them.

Because when a royal family said tails optional, you wore tails.

"But first," he went on, leading her toward the room George indicated. "We both get a massage, then your hair, makeup, and nails will be done, and you'll pick out a dress. Or you might pick out the dress and shoes first so the makeup and nails all go together." He shrugged. "What do I know?"

In one of the bedrooms, two massage tables were set up.

Kenzie turned around while he quickly shucked most of his clothes and slid under the blankets. Once his head was positioned in the head thing, Kenzie took her turn. A moment later the masseuses entered.

For the next hour, they both enjoyed the attention. At least Jonathan did. Kenzie didn't say much, and he wasn't sure if she was enjoying herself or not.

When they were left alone, now laying face up, he reached for her hand, but they were a bit too far apart. "How was that?"

"Heaven." Kenzie sighed. "We can afford to get one of those a few times a year right?"

He laughed. "Sweetheart, we can afford one a day if you want. Or more, but that's probably a bit much. However often you want one, you got it."

"I don't know what she did, but my side and back feel better than I have since I fell at my landlord's office."

Jonathan let that sink in. "What?"

"I haven't felt this good since I fell."

"At your landlord's office?" He hadn't known that before, had he?

Kenzie blew out a deep breath then let her head fall to the side so she looked at him. "I know I shouldn't have gone, but I wasn't sure about all of this and your lawyers and everything. I hoped he'd back off. I'm pretty sure the fall is on tape, because I haven't heard anything from him since."

He let it go for the moment, but he'd be calling Daniel to make sure he knew and could act accordingly.

"Now what?"

"It's time for us to get dressed again and find you something to wear tonight."

They did that, backs to each other, though Jonathan longed for the day they wouldn't.

"I love these boots." Kenzie zipped one up and held it out in front of her. "I wonder where they got them."

"They're yours, Kenz." Did she not realize that? "Anything you want from the clothes back in Montevaro or the dresses tonight that you don't want to wear this time, they're yours if you want."

The second zipper stopped halfway up as she looked at him. "Really?"

"Yes."

She finished and stood as Jonathan stopped in front of her. He rested his hands on her hips and tugged her a bit closer. "Anything you want, Kenzie. It's yours. Everything I have is yours." He gave her a soft kiss. "I'll give you the world."

Jonathan wanted to tell her he'd give her his heart. She already had it, but was she ready to know that? Was he ready to tell her?

No. The timing wasn't right. Not yet.

Soon.

Before they returned home.

Then they could go back to Serenity Landing as the family he'd longed for.

Chapter Twenty-Seven

*K*enzie suppressed a gasp as the material slithered over her skin and settled into place. She'd tried it on earlier, but it was different now.

Her hair and makeup were professionally done. Her nails had been manicured and pedicured. She stepped into the silver strappy heels and wondered if this was how Cinderella felt.

And what Jonathan would think when he saw her.

He'd been dressing in the other room and Stefan, apparently a favorite stylist of the royal family, insisted Jonathan not be allowed to see her until she was completely ready.

"Your husband is waiting, ma'am." One of the assistants Kenzie couldn't keep straight opened the door from the bedroom to the living area.

"Thank you." She grasped a bit of the fabric between her fingers to keep the dress from dragging.

"You don't need to do that, ma'am. Only if you're stepping up or down and are afraid you'll step on the hem."

She dropped it. "Okay."

"And this is for you this evening. Everything you need in case you need a touch up." She held out a silver clutch. "We'll be there if something should go wrong, but it won't."

"Thank you."

Kenzie stepped into the living area to see Jonathan standing with his hands in his pockets looking out the window.

"Hi." She felt shy, like a girl getting ready to go on her first date.

He turned and his eyes widened. "MacKenzie Langley-Cranston, you look incredible. I am going to be the envy of every man there tonight, and that is quite a feat given where we are going and who's going to be there."

Her stomach churned. "Where are we going?"

With a shake of his head and a half-grin, he held out his elbow. "May have the honor of escorting you, Mrs. Langley-Cranston?"

"Sure." The shimmery silver fabric caught her eye in the mirror. It fit her like a glove where it was supposed to without being too revealing. She hadn't even needed Spanx to get everything to look right through her middle.

The ride was mostly quiet, though Jonathan pointed out a few places of interest, like the cathedral where one of those princes had gotten married a couple years earlier. It really didn't surprise her when they rolled to a stop in front of another actual palace.

This time the young man who opened her door was dressed in some sort of costume from the region's history. She couldn't begin to guess at the time period.

Jonathan joined her, again offering her his arm. Though they were on private property, photographers lined the red carpet.

"Just smile and look like you're looking forward to this," Jonathan whispered in her ear.

"I don't know what *this* is," she whispered back.

He didn't answer but stopped her with a gentle squeeze of his elbow. They looked one direction and smiled, though neither answered the shouted questions. After a minute, they walked on then faced the other way so those on that side of the carpet could get their pictures. A minute later, they were inside Kenzie's second palace.

She wanted to gawk. To just stare at the ceilings, the floors, and everything in between, but she tried to keep herself under control. "Now will you tell me?"

Jonathan covered her hand inside his elbow with his free hand. "This is the Queen Grandmother's birthday party."

"Queen Grandmother?"

"Actually I think she's technically the Dowager Queen Grandmother. She was married to the king two kings ago. Her husband was king. When he passed, their son became king. Now, her grandson is King Antonio."

"And why are we at her birthday party?"

"She's seventy, and they were having a party, and we were invited." He shrugged. "When royalty invites you to something like this, you say yes if at all possible. Plus, I've provided security for her..." He thought something over. "Great-grandson-in-law, I guess. He stayed at the house a couple months ago. The Montevarian royal family will be here. They all love Nana Yvette as they call her. No one outside the families do," he warned.

Like she'd start calling some former queen by a colloquial nickname.

Ever.

A liveried member of the staff showed them to the ballroom where they were told guests were mingling until it was time to be seated for dinner. He showed them where they would be sitting.

Kenzie wanted to just sit anyway. Mingling was way outside

her comfort zone, especially with this crowd.

"Do you know all of these people?" she whispered as she set her clutch down on the table.

"Not all, but some. Some I actually know personally. Some I know by sight." He pointed discretely. "That man next to the woman in the emerald dress?" She nodded. "That's Robert Padovano, a member of Parliament. The woman is his wife Lizbeth. We've met once or twice in passing, but I don't actually know them."

"Jonathan!"

They both turned to see a man, who looked familiar to Kenzie, walking over. He too wore a tuxedo, but he had a royal blue sash with his.

"Duke Alexander." Jonathan inclined his head a bit as he shook the duke's hand. Was she supposed to curtsy? "May I present my wife, Mrs. MacKenzie Langley-Cranston?"

Alexander smacked Jonathan on the arm. "I lived two miles from you for years." He held out a hand to Kenzie, who shook it but didn't curtsy after all. "I'm Alexander Bayfield."

"Husband of the queen of Ravenzario," a female voice said.

Kenzie turned to see a beautiful blonde woman, obviously pregnant, join their group.

"Your Majesty." This time Jonathan actually bowed at the waist a little bit. "It's a pleasure to see you again." He introduced her again, and this time Kenzie did her best to imitate the curtsies she'd seen on television.

"Please." The woman held out her hand. "I am Christiana, and I am most assuredly not your queen. The formalities are unnecessary. We owe your husband a great debt."

"It was my pleasure, ma'am," Jonathan interjected. "We are happy to be of service any time you need it."

The queen laughed. "I do hope my brother will not be running away again anytime soon."

And with that Kenzie knew one thing was certain. Whatever else it might be, this night wouldn't be boring.

Jonathan hoped Kenzie wasn't too uncomfortable. He did his best to include her in the conversations, but she seemed most comfortable just listening and taking it all in.

He turned down the offered champagne and asked for a glass of sparkling water instead. When a moment came along where he could whisper to Kenzie, he took the chance.

"You wouldn't know it now, but three of these princesses didn't marry the men they would have chosen."

She looked up at him, eyes wide. "What?"

"I don't know the whole stories behind all of them, but Princess Jessabelle met Prince Malachi at the altar. Queen Christiana was supposed to marry someone else, but he was trying to kill her, so he was thrown in the dungeon, and she married Alexander instead. Prince Nicklaus was thought to be dead for nearly two decades. He and Princess Yvette were betrothed as infants. The Ravenzarian head of security brought him home a week before the wedding."

He slid his arm a bit further around her waist. She should know she wasn't alone in this whole sudden marriage, uncertain about things, thing.

A voice came over a loudspeaker. "Their majesties, King Antonio and Queen Alicia." Everyone clapped politely and most gave a slight bow or curtsy as the king and queen entered the room.

"Our guest of honor, the Dowager Queen Grandmother

Yvette, and her escort."

An elegant older woman entered the room on the arm of a distinguished gentleman.

The clapping grew louder.

"It's her birthday, right?" Kenzie asked him.

Jonathan nodded. "It's not today. I'm not sure when it is actually, but they're celebrating her turning seventy."

Chairs scraped against the floor as everyone took a seat. Jonathan held Kenzie's for her and scooted it in as she sat. The others at the table appeared to know each other, but each politely introduced themselves. Two earls with their wives, a duchess with her husband, and siblings - Lady Margaretha and her younger brother, Lord Teobald XIV. The fourteenth. And Jonathan had thought his "the IV" was bad.

This guy was apparently quite proud of his XIV title. And Teobald, though his sister called him Ted.

He continually tried to impress Kenzie, who was decidedly not interested. She did everything but dump his bowl of soup in his lap. Jonathan thought it might have occurred to her, though.

Finally, dinner ended and the dancing began. The first dance was shared between the former queen and her escort. The second dance included her extended family members. The third dance was open to everyone.

Lord Teobald XIV stood and held a hand out to Kenzie. "May I have the pleasure of your first dance, milady?"

Jonathan exercised every bit of self-control he had remaining.

Kenzie, however, retained more grace and poise than he could ever hope to have. "Thank you, sir, for the offer, but I believe I will decline. I will sit this one out, unless my *husband* decides he would like me to join him on the dance floor."

Jonathan took that as his signal and pushed back from the table. "It would be my honor, Mrs. Langley-Cranston." She set her hand in his, and he held it all the way to the dance floor. Once in an open space, he pulled her closer than he had the last time they danced.

"You're doing fantastic," he told her. "I know Lord whatshisname is annoying, but you've handled him far better than I would have. I probably would have punched him."

"I've handled guys like him before. None of them were sullying such a distinguished family line, though."

His arm slid around her a little further, holding her a little closer, a little tighter. "Your poise and grace amaze me, Kenzie. I find myself in awe of you and what you've accomplished pretty regularly."

"I'm not anything special," Kenzie insisted. "Just a single mom trying to make it. That's all I ever was."

"Still." Her temple was at just the right spot for him to turn his head slightly and kiss it.

They danced like that for two more dances before Prince Malachi asked to cut in. Jonathan couldn't say no and knew his wife was in good hands.

"Pardon my boldness, but would you ask me for this dance, sir?"

Jonathan turned around, surprised. His heart sank when he saw Lady Margarethe.

"Fear not, Mr. Langley-Cranston. I am not my brother."

With that, Jonathan nodded and found himself dancing with her a very respectable distance away.

"I believe my brother owes you both an apology. However, you will likely be waiting an eternity, so allow me to extend an apology of my own."

"You don't own his bad behavior, Lady Margarethe. He's responsible for his own actions."

"I am inclined to agree with you. However, as the eldest,

sometimes it falls to me to correct some of his mistakes, as much as they can be corrected." They danced for another thirty seconds before she spoke again. "I am inclined to like your wife. Not only did she not give my brother what he deserved, but she mentioned you attended the Mevendian Wool Festival today."

Jonathan nodded. "We were there for a few hours. It's so big, we only made it through about half the vendors. My wife owns her own yarn dyeing business. She would like to take one of the classes from a local woman, but the timing didn't work out. The lady's coming to our town for a festival this fall, so I'm hoping she'll be able to then."

Something crossed Lady Margarethe's face, but Jonathan couldn't define what it was. "Will you be returning tomorrow?"

"We haven't decided yet. Our daughter is back in Montevaro, and my wife isn't sure she wants to be gone that long."

This time he definitely noticed pain on Lady Margarethe's face. "I can respect that. However, I would presume you only made it through the front half of the marketplace."

"Something like that, I guess."

"If your wife would like to stay, I can give you some booth numbers where she would find some things she would enjoy."

She didn't elaborate but stepped back as the dance ended.

Jonathan found himself dancing with many other women, but none the one he wanted most to find. Where was she?

Chapter
Twenty-Eight

Finally.

Kenzie breathed a sigh of relief to be back where she belonged, in Jonathan's arms.

"You didn't wind up with Lord Arrogant did you?" he asked softly as she tucked in closer to him than she could have imagined being comfortable with.

"No. Prince Malachi, Duke Alexander, all three of the royal guys from Montevaro, Prince Nicklaus, Christopher Bayfield."

Jonathan looked around. "Christopher's here?"

"I guess. He was kinda quiet. Then Prince William, and now back to you."

"My favorite place for you to be."

She ducked her head, hoping to cover what surely was a lovely shade of pink in her face. "It's my favorite, too."

They danced for most of the song before he spoke again. "Do you know when I knew I wanted to marry you?"

"When?" When she sat drenched in his car? When her house

wouldn't work?

"The first time we danced."

Kenzie blinked twice. "What?"

"The first time we danced. I was at a wedding in Serenity Landing with Princess Ellie before she married Rick. Lorelai sat with me for the wedding. I danced with her, but the first time I held you in my arms, I knew there was something special between us."

"Didn't you date Ana after that?"

"Yes," he admitted. "But I never thought I'd see you again. I didn't know your name. I knew your daughter's first name. How would I find you? So even though I knew there was something amazing between us, I went on with my life. When I saw you at the store that night, it was like being hit by a lightning bolt."

"Really?"

"Really."

Should she confess? "I have pictures from that night." Kenzie blurted it out before she could stop herself.

"What?"

"The bride is a friend of mine and when there were pictures of you dancing with Lorelai and with me, she printed them off for me. It's one of Lorelai's favorite pictures. The bride wanted to put them on Facebook with a note like 'look who came to my wedding!' but I convinced her not to. I didn't want to be another woman linked to a Langley-Cranston."

"Yet here you are."

"Here I am." It was different now. "Now I want to be linked to a Langley-Cranston. Now I know you. Now I want to spend the rest of my life getting to know you."

Jonathan didn't give any warning. He kissed her.

Far more intense than it should have been in the middle of the dance floor. He whirled her around, and then they were out on the balcony, in the shadows.

And he kissed her again.

His fingers in her hair, thumbs caressing her jawline as she clung to the front of his jacket.

"Kenzie," he whispered as he trailed kisses down her jaw and toward her neck. "There's never been anyone for me but you. I was just far too stupid to realize I hadn't met the right woman yet."

His lips captured hers again and Kenzie found herself melting against him, their hearts beating in matching staccato rhythm.

Clapping from the ballroom startled Kenzie, and she pulled back from him, looking around.

"It's time to sing to the birthday girl," Jonathan whispered.

"Oh." Right. She leaned up and kissed him gently. "We should go find our seats."

They started for the door when she whirled to face him. "Do I look okay?" she whispered. "Or do I look like I've just been making out with my husband?"

Jonathan looked her up and down with a critical eye. "I think you're okay. Your hair is fine. I think your lipstick is long gone." He wiped his lips with his thumb. "I'm not wearing it, am I?"

Kenzie shook her head, but smoothed out his lapels where she'd grabbed tight. "You're fine."

A minute later, they were back in their seats, though Lord Annoying was blessedly absent.

The cake was wheeled out into the center of the room, and everyone sang. The Dowager Queen had help from her gentleman friend blowing out the candles.

"Who is she again?" Kenzie asked Jonathan.

"Grandmother of the current king," he told her, quietly enough no one else would overhear. "I'm not sure who's with her."

That made her the great-grandmother of Prince Malachi and Princess Yvette who Kenzie had met earlier. Didn't Prince Malachi and his wife have a baby? That would make her a great-great-grandmother. Holy wow. Her grandparents had died when she was a kid. Did she know anyone who knew their great-grandparents?

"Did you enjoy the view from the balcony?" Lady Margarethe asked. "I saw you walking back in," she offered by way of explanation.

Kenzie didn't take her eyes off Jonathan. "My husband was kind enough to point out some things I'd never noticed." Did she dare? "I look forward to learning more about them. Later."

His eyes smoldered with understanding.

"Where are you staying?"

Jonathan answered, though he still looked at Kenzie.

"There's lovely views from all sides of the top floor. I am certain you will have ample opportunity to view what our fine countryside has to offer."

"I'm sure there will be," Jonathan answered, finally breaking eye contact. He nodded toward the other woman. "Lady Margarethe was telling me we should visit the festival again tomorrow. She was going to recommend some booths she thought you would enjoy."

That meant leaving Lorelai all night and most of the next day.

But it also meant she and Jonathan would be alone in that luxurious suite.

And at the moment there was nothing she wanted more than to spend the night in her husband's arms.

"I think that sounds like a great idea," she finally told him. "I'd love to visit the rest of the vendors."

Jonathan picked up her hand and kissed the back of it. "Your wish is my command. I'll make sure the arrangements are made for Lorelai."

Kenzie swallowed as he winked at her. Tonight was the night. It was time.

Only one question remained.

Would she be able to work up the nerve to tell him she loved him before things went any further?

Because she did.

With all her heart, she did.

Jonathan held Kenzie's hand the whole way back to the hotel, and wondered if there was some way he was misinterpreting the signals he'd picked up after their kiss on the balcony.

When she slid a little closer and rested her head on his shoulder, he decided he probably hadn't.

But intentions in the heat of the moment and reality several hours later weren't always the same thing.

He shouldn't get his hopes up.

Too late.

He wanted to spend the night with his wife in his arms, in his bed, and do far more than just sleep like they had several times already.

As they walked through the lobby to the elevators, Jonathan felt he did a remarkable job at looking calm. The elevator whisked them to the top floor, and a minute later they stood in their suite.

All remnants of the earlier salon were gone. Through the windows, the city glittered below.

"It's a beautiful view," he said, flipping the lock bar behind him.

Kenzie stopped in front of the windows. "It is."

Jonathan walked toward her, stopping not at her side, but behind her and slid his arms around her waist. Tension radiated off of her in nearly-palpable waves. "Whatever we insinuated earlier, Kenz, it's okay." He couldn't stop himself from dropping a kiss where her shoulder met her neck. "I promise."

Not what he wanted, but what he wanted deferred to what she needed.

"It's not that."

He didn't need much encouragement and placed another kiss slightly further up her neck. Her head tipped to the other side, giving him better access.

"Then what is it?" he murmured between kisses.

"I'm nervous. Scared."

That stopped him. "Of me? Why?"

"Not of you, but of everything." He waited for her to go on. "It's been a long time."

"It's been a long time for me, too." He tightened his arms around her. "I wish it had been far longer." They'd talked about him regretting his teen years in general, but not that he specifically regretted ever being with anyone but her.

"If it weren't for Lorelai..." Her voice trailed off, but he understood her meaning.

"I know." They stood there for another minute. "There's still no pressure."

He loosened his hold as she turned in his arms. "And I thank you for that, but..." She didn't say anything else, but leaned up on her tiptoes and brushed a kiss against his mouth.

A jolt of lightning shot through Jonathan, and he tightened his arms around her again, but didn't let himself go in for another kiss.

"But I want to spend tonight with you." Her arms wrapped around his neck. "I want to spend every night with you."

He kissed her with an intensity that surprised even him. His heart and soul were now wrapped up in the woman before him. She was his, and he was hers.

And it was time to make it official.

Somehow, without breaking contact with her lips, he picked her up and walked toward the room they would share as truly man and wife for the first time.

He set her on her feet next to the bed.

"Will you love me tonight?" she whispered. "Like there was never anyone else?"

"There never was," he vowed. "Never anyone for me but you."

He kissed her again, and two became one in a dance as old as time itself.

And when they slept, after more soft kisses and whispered declarations he wasn't sure she'd heard, Jonathan felt content in a way he'd never known.

So this was love.

He could get used to this.

But when he woke to sunlight streaming through the open curtains, he was alone.

Jonathan sucked in a breath and prayed the night before hadn't been too much for Kenzie. The little they'd packed for the side trip had been placed in the dresser. He pulled on the pajama pants he found there and went to find his wife, praying she was still in the suite.

"I love you, too, sweetheart." Her voice drifted over from the area by the window.

And when he saw Kenzie, he couldn't contain his grin. She'd put his t-shirt from before the massage on. The light gray shirt was long enough, but still gave him a good view of her long legs. Deciding there was nothing to worry about with regard to Kenzie's feelings, he walked up behind her and slid his arms around her waist like he had the night before.

But this time he didn't hesitate kissing her neck - or the spot behind her ear he'd already learned she loved. He didn't stop, even when she swatted at his arm.

"I know, sweetheart. We miss you, too. We'll be back later this afternoon, okay? *Daddy* is taking me to a yarn show so I can learn some things for my own business."

Jonathan smiled against her neck at the use of the name.

"We should be back by dinner or so. I love you." Another second, and she hung up. "How am I supposed to concentrate on talking to my daughter with you doing that?"

"You're not. You're supposed to hurry back, so I'm not all alone in there."

She didn't turn around but did turn her head enough he could kiss her. The kiss didn't go straight to intense as it had the night before, but it got there, and they both forgot anything but each other.

Jonathan was pretty sure he'd found what he wanted to spend the rest of his life doing. Loving the woman God made for him, taking care of her and Lorelai and any other children God had in store.

And as they walked around the festival, he had to remind himself repeatedly of the discussion they'd had in the car. Too much PDA would be bad until things settled down, so they would be less likely to get their picture taken by random passers-by. But all he wanted to do was be close to her.

Instead, he absorbed as much as he could, so he could help her when they returned to Serenity Landing.

And counted the hours until they could be alone again.

Chapter Twenty-Nine

Kenzie understood why she and Jonathan were mostly keeping their distance from each other, but that didn't mean she liked it.

They held hands, though even that connection seemed more intimate than it had before. It didn't mean she didn't want to walk closer to him, to rest her head on his shoulder while they stood and surveyed a vendor, or even kiss him from time to time.

The vendors Lady Margarethe had recommended fascinated Kenzie. The woman must be more familiar with yarns and fibers than she let on, because they were perfect for what Kenzie needed.

And once they were in the car on their way to Montevaro, she snuggled into her husband's side and slept most of the way back.

"We're here." His voice woke Kenzie up.

She sat up and stretched. "That was a nice nap. Thank you for letting me sleep." A kiss to his cheek was all she allowed herself.

"Nope." Jonathan's voice stopped her. "I need more than that."

Several soft kisses, and one long one, later, they emerged from the car and went into the house.

"Mama! Daddy!" Lorelai ran through the foyer and into Kenzie's arms. "I missed you."

Jonathan spoke for both of them. "We missed you, too, punkin. Did you have fun while we were gone?"

Lorelai nodded and reached for Jonathan. Kenzie handed her off. "I played with Stacy and Lindsey and got to ride a horse by myself!"

Worry flashed through Kenzie, but she tamped it down. They wouldn't have let her do anything dangerous, would they?

"Did you get to jump any fences?" Jonathan asked.

"No." Lorelai heaved a sigh. "I just went in a circle while the nice man held the rope. Stacy and Lindsey know how to ride all by themselves."

"Someday you'll be able to," Jonathan promised her.

"Lyssie knows how to ride horses, too. I miss Lyssie." Of course she missed her best friend.

"We'll go home soon," Kenzie promised. "And you'll get to see Lyssie again."

"Can we go to the pool?"

"Probably." She knew her daughter missed swimming daily and was glad Adam had talked her into letting her join the swim team.

And with that Lorelai was happy again.

They spent the rest of the day with Ana, Dr. Jonah, Stacy, and Lindsey. She spent the night alone with her husband, and the next day was much the same.

There were reports of them being seen in Europe, but nothing more than standard red carpet gossip. Kenzie wasn't sure how she felt about that, but it was better than being chased down the road by motorcycles.

Instead of spending the next night in her husband's arms

again, they spent it on the family jet, headed back to Serenity Landing. All three of them slept most of the way. Hopefully, that would help with the jet lag.

When they arrived at the house, early in the morning, Jonathan's grandmother had left, but his parents had stayed. The day was actually pleasant until after dinner. Then Kenzie found herself alone with her mother-in-law.

"It seems the two of you became much closer while you were away," she started.

Kenzie stared out the window where Jonathan pushed Lorelai on her new swing set. It was more of a playground, far beyond anything Kenzie would have picked out, but Jonathan's father had seemed almost giddy to show Lorelai.

"We spent some quality time together," Kenzie admitted. "All three of us did. Plus Jonathan made arrangements for us to go to a festival he knew I would enjoy. The birthday party for the former queen of Mevendia was a lot of fun, too." She wouldn't trade dancing with Jonathan that night for all the money in the world.

"I told you the other day no one messes with my family."

"Yes, you did."

She turned to look at Kenzie. "If you don't love Jonathan, if you're not prepared to deal with rumors of infidelity and everything else that comes with the spotlight for the rest of your life, leave now." Her eyes were cold as ice.

Kenzie's mouth opened and closed twice, but no sound came out.

"If you walk away, I will put a million dollars in an account for you and another million for your daughter. But leave before my son gets more hurt than he's already going to."

Kenzie stood her ground. "I have no intention of going anywhere. As for the rumors, I'll have to learn to ignore them, and let them roll off my back."

The older woman studied her for an intense minute then nodded. "Very well." She turned back to the window. "We will be leaving this evening."

"I hope you have a safe trip wherever you're going. And thank you."

"For what?"

"For having my back this week. I saw your comment to the press." It pained Kenzie to admit it after the offer a moment earlier. "I appreciate it more than you'll know." The woman had told the press to back off and leave her new granddaughter alone.

"I protect my family." She seemed to think over her next words. "But if push ever comes to shove, I choose Jonathan. Period. I've already lost one son, I won't lose another."

"You won't have to," Kenzie promised. "I would sooner hurt myself than I would Jonathan."

"Good."

They watched Jonathan, his father, and Lorelai playing outside and Kenzie wondered if she'd ever feel like she fit into this family.

Or if she'd always feel like an outsider everywhere but in her husband's arms.

Jonathan had seen his wife talking to his mother through the window. Neither of them ended up thrown through it, so it couldn't have gone too badly.

His parents left for the airport an hour later, just as Kenzie helped Lorelai take a bath. Soon after, Jonathan read her a bedtime story and tucked her in.

He found Kenzie curled up on the couch, Kindle in hand. "Good book?"

She shrugged. "It's good, but I've read it before."

"Then scoot over." He sat in the corner of the couch, and she curled up next to him. "Are you glad to be home?"

Kenzie nestled her head on his shoulder as he ran his thumb up and down her arm. "I still have a hard time thinking of this house as home. It's getting there, but not yet."

His thoughts wandered to the last few nights. "You're sleeping in my room tonight?" His voice turned husky, but he wanted to make sure. He needed to know.

Kenzie didn't look up. "If you want me to."

Jonathan tipped her face up. "The only place I ever want you to sleep from now until eternity is next to me."

Her mouth curved into a slight smile. "I like the sound of that." She leaned up and kissed him. "In fact, I think I might be ready to head that way."

Jonathan didn't need to be told twice.

And the next morning, they set about moving her into his room. All of her clothes, shoes, toiletries, including the purchases from Europe were moved. Lorelai's things were moved into her new room across the hall. Gwendolyn talked with them for a few minutes before heading off to work. She dropped Lorelai off with Alyssa for a couple hours.

Jonathan leaned against the door frame looking into Lorelai's new room. "What do you think she'd like in here?"

"What do you mean?" Kenzie looked up from where she placed the last stack of clothes in the dresser.

"I mean, would she want a four-poster bed with the canopy and all the princess-y stuff or what?" He wished he knew his daughter well enough to surprise them both, but he didn't. Not yet.

257

"This is fine, Jonathan, really. It's far nicer than anything she's ever had before, and she doesn't need a room designed to her every whim. Her whims change often."

"I know she doesn't *need* it, but money's not an object, Kenz." Something flashed across her face and in her eyes. Did it bother her to be called by the nickname? He realized he didn't know. "I want to be able to give her a room she wants."

"I know." She turned around and leaned against the dresser. "It just stings a bit that I was never able to give her those things myself. I wouldn't have been able to anytime in the near future without you."

Maybe that's what it was. "Then you give it to her. You've got the money now, even if it was from me initially. Buy it out of your profits from the show a couple weeks ago."

"I already spent a lot of the show money buying stuff to get ready for the next show. That's the way it works. And I'm not sure I feel right about using what's in that account for a room she'll like for two months then want to change."

"Then let me do it. Or do it out of the joint accounts."

Kenzie stared at the floor. "Why is this so important to you? Why can't she just be happy with what's already in here? I promise you she'll be ecstatic with any room she doesn't have to share with her mother."

Jonathan decided to let it go for the time being. "As long as I'm allowed to be ecstatic I get to share a room with her mother."

"Definitely."

But Kenzie seemed distracted when he kissed her. She said something about wanting to cook dinner and headed downstairs.

"What is it?" He followed her, not willing to give up that easily.

"Just having a hard time coming to terms with all of this, that's all." She made it to the kitchen and turned. "I'm glad I'm here. I'm glad I have you. I'm glad Lorelai has you. But it still takes some getting used to, that's all."

He took her hand and led her to the couch, sitting down and silently urging her to do the same. She sat next to him. "I know it's different. I know it'll take a while, but please talk to me, give me a chance to help you through whatever it is you need to get used to."

She shrugged. "Just having money. That's all. I'm not used to being able to just buy whatever I want." Kenzie turned her head into him. "I'm sure I'll be able to become accustomed to it. I do know I'll never be able to repay you."

"I don't want you to repay me."

"I know."

They sat there for nearly an hour. Gradually, the tension in Kenzie relaxed, and they talked for a long time. They talked about hopes and dreams and what they wanted out of life. Kenzie promised again to make an appointment with the best doctor around.

Lorelai came home, and Kenzie took her upstairs to take a quick shower after swimming most of the day at Alyssa's house.

A phone call told him it was time to pick Mr. Benny Hercules up from the groomer. When they returned home, Jonathan set the dog down outside the SUV. As he ran off to relieve himself, a slip of paper dropped out of the vehicle and began to blow across the driveway. He stopped it with his foot and picked it up.

Turning it over, he realized it was a deposit slip. The deposit amount seemed to match about what Kenzie had brought in from the yarn show in Spring Meadows, but the new balance stopped him in his tracks.

With his mouth set in a grim line, he let the dog in the house.

It was time to find his wife and learn the truth.

Chapter Thirty

MacKenzie?" Jonathan's voice carried through their room.

"What?" she called from the bathroom where she was organizing her assorted toiletries.

He appeared in the doorway, holding up a slip of paper between two fingers. "What's this?"

She shrugged. "I have no idea."

"It blew out of the SUV. It's a deposit slip from right after the yarn show. It's from the account I set up for you."

And that explained his mood. "What about it?"

"I told you the money was yours to do with as you wanted, but I'm a little surprised to see it so low so quickly."

She turned back to the counter top. "I didn't hear a question in there."

"What did you spend so much money on?"

"I thought it was mine to do with as I pleased, and I didn't have to answer to you about it. Don't worry. I won't be asking for more. I never intended to."

"I still want to know how you spent mid-six figures so quickly. Did you put it in a college fund for Lorelai? An account for you that I wouldn't know about in case things went south?"

Kenzie shook her head, desperately willing the tears to stay where they belonged.

"Did you marry me for my money?"

"No!" Her denial sounded too fast and too forced even to her own ears.

His glare met her eyes in the mirror.

"Yes," she whispered.

Jonathan's face remained impassive, though she could see the fledgling shreds of real trust between them shatter in his eyes.

"Kind of."

He didn't say anything but crossed his arms over his chest.

Kenzie turned around and leaned against the counter top, bracing herself against it with her hands. She couldn't meet his eyes. "The day you asked me to marry you again, I'd gotten a bunch of bills. Medical bills from my first husband. Credit cards he'd run up in my name. Electric bills I was behind on. A landlord threatening to sue me. A yarn business you'd basically just bought out. My phone was a week from being turned off. I was in so much pain, and you offered me a way out."

"I would have given you the money." He waved the hand holding that paper carelessly in the air. "I've got plenty to spare."

"I couldn't just take your money. If we were married at least it was kind of both of ours, and I wouldn't feel so indebted to you." It hadn't worked that way.

"Is that why..." He didn't say it, but the implications in his tone were quite clear.

"No," she answered, praying the Biblical wisdom about a soft answer was correct. "I expected it would happen sooner rather than later, but that's not why."

"So you married me for my money then slept with me. How does that make you any better than a..."

"Stop!" The tears finally forced their way past her closed eyelids. "I know what you must think of me. It's nothing I haven't thought myself. Or haven't stopped myself from thinking, especially at the beginning, but I can't stand to hear you actually say it." A sob shook her shoulders as she reached for the container of toiletries. "Lorelai and I will be out of your home by nightfall. I'll let you know where you can send the divorce papers. I won't ask for anything."

Kenzie tried to brush past him, but his grip on her arm stopped her in her tracks.

She looked up at him through her tears to see the still impassive face. Then he kissed her. Hard. Demanding. Nothing like the Jonathan she'd fallen in love with.

"No," Kenzie cried pushing against him as hard as she could. "Let me go."

"You've already said you're no better than..."

She stood up straight, staring him in the eye. "Maybe I'm not. But until this minute I never believed you were the kind of man to take advantage of a woman for any reason."

It was like something lost its grip on his mind, and he dropped her arm like a hot potato. Stricken was the best word for the look on his face.

Jonathan stumbled back until the wall stopped him. He just stared at her, her broken heart reflected in his eyes. Without another word, he headed for the door, stopping before he left.

"You don't need to go. I won't be back."

The sound of the door closing reverberated behind him. Kenzie crumpled to the ground, tears and sobs shaking her. A minute later, something warm and wet touched her hand.

Mr. Benny Hercules must have hidden under the bed at some

point and decided, since they were now both castoffs, she was safe. Kenzie pulled the little dog close and cuddled with him until her tears were spent, and she fell asleep on the floor curled around the little dog.

Jonathan downshifted into a curve on his way to the Springfield airport. He just prayed there was a flight leaving soon.

For anywhere.

Most of the flights out of Springfield went to larger hubs, such as Atlanta or Chicago. From there he could catch a flight anywhere, like back to San Majoria and his hut on the beach where he'd sought solitude for several months earlier in the year.

Where he could go days without seeing anyone unless he wanted to.

He pulled into short term parking and left the receipt in the visor for George to use when he picked the car up that night or the next morning.

Once inside, Jonathan checked the departures board to find a flight headed to Atlanta leaving in less than an hour. With his loyalty cards on all the airlines, he was able to skip the lines both at the ticket counter and the TSA. Not quite as convenient as using a family jet, but better than standing in lines.

These flights had no first class, though, and he found himself in an aisle seat next to a mother and a little girl who, despite being physically opposite, reminded him of Lorelai. She chatted non-stop, clearly nervous and trying to draw Jonathan into conversation. Her mother tried to get her to stop, but finally Jonathan gave in and found himself playing Barbies with the little girl.

He noticed a couple people taking pictures and figured they'd be all over social media fifteen minutes after they landed. So much for escaping.

But the longer he talked to the little girl, and her mother, the more he found his heart beginning to soften. The woman confided in him that they had just buried her grandmother-in-law, the little girl's great-grandmother who she'd adored. The girl's father was serving in the Middle East, and they didn't know when he'd even find out about the woman who raised him. Something about his unit being out of contact for the last week.

The trip had been paid for with miles offered by generous friends and family members who pooled them to provide the flights and hotel since there wasn't room in her grandmother-in-law's home for everyone coming from out of town. About half an hour before landing, he excused himself to visit the restroom though that was just an excuse. He took all of the cash out of his wallet and folded it, putting it in the pocket of his jeans. He'd find a way to stick it in the girl's backpack or the mom's bag somehow.

As they taxied toward the terminal, he pulled his wallet out again and handed her a business card. "If you're in a spot again, and there's any way I can help you, please give me a call."

The words he'd said to Kenzie came back to haunt him. When he pulled the mother's bag down from the overhead bin, he managed to stick the money into a pocket and zip it back up without her noticing. Fortunately, the bag was distinctive enough he didn't worry about getting the wrong one.

Since he had nothing with him, Jonathan carried the suitcase for them, motioning them ahead so he could ask the stewardess a question before deplaning.

He caught up with them again before they reached the end of the jet way. The little girl gave him a hug, and he shook hands with the mom.

Fortunately, the counter was experiencing a quiet moment and he didn't have to wait in line to get a return ticket for half an hour later.

This time, he was seated alone in a window seat. He stared over the landscape for the nearly two hour flight back. When the flight landed, he turned his phone back on and texted George.

Kenzie hadn't left.

Not yet.

In fact, he discovered George hadn't seen her since Jonathan walked out.

Fortunately, Lorelai was spending the day with Alyssa and appeared to have missed all of the drama. Jonathan pulled through the gates in a much different mood than when he left.

He searched the house, but didn't call out. The last thing he wanted was for Kenzie to bolt or hide.

Finally, he returned to his room, and what he saw broke his heart.

Kenzie lay on the floor where she'd been standing when he left, curled around Mr. Benny Hercules. Streaks on her cheek told him the tears had been plentiful.

Gently, carefully, he moved Mr. Benny Hercules and set him on the nearby recliner. As tenderly as he knew how, he picked Kenzie up and laid her on the bed, kneeling next to it.

Her eyes fluttered open, but before they could register recognition, he spoke.

"I'm so sorry, Kenz." Tears filled his eyes. "I'm so, so sorry. I was way out of line."

Confusion, fear, and anger warred for dominance in her expression. "What?"

The anger seemed to be dissipating, giving Jonathan a glimmer of hope. "I was wrong in how I reacted. I shouldn't have said the things I said or thought the things I didn't say. Can you ever forgive me?"

Kenzie pushed herself into a sitting position. "What changed, Jonathan? Why should I believe you?"

The doubt in her voice cut, but he deserved it. "I ran. I flew to Atlanta and planned to go on to somewhere else far away, but I sat with this little girl. She was almost the total opposite of Lorelai, but she reminded me of her anyway. I talked with her mom and realized that I have no idea what life was like for you. You've told me some, but I can't imagine what it's like wondering if you'll have enough to feed your child and have enough left over to eat something yourself. For me to judge the decisions you made coming out of that place of desperation is just wrong."

He gripped her hand. "Money doesn't mean my life has always been easy. You know that. But I said something to you about not judging my life because you'd never lived it. I should have given you the same courtesy. I'm so sorry I didn't."

"Jonathan..." Her eyes had softened as she looked at him.

His index finger covered her lips. "I need to finish. I love you, MacKenzie Annette Langley-Cranston. And I think that's why it hurt so much to think you married me only for my money. I know that's not true. I knew it hours ago. I lashed out, and I shouldn't have. It'll take time for me to prove to you I'll never behave like that again, but I'll take as much time as you need." He rested his forehead against hers. "I love you, Kenz. You and Lorelai are the one thing I've longed for forever. You're *my* family. Not my family of origin, but *my family*." He couldn't say it too many times. "And I love you."

Kenzie sat quiet for a moment. "I fell in love with you, too, Jonathan, but the things you said earlier... Even though it wasn't anything I hadn't thought myself already, they hurt."

Jonathan hardly daring to believe what she'd said. "You love me, honestly?"

Kenzie nodded. "I did. I do. But not the Jonathan that lashed out a few hours ago. I detest him."

It hurt, but she was right. "I do, too. And I hope that Jonathan never comes back. I'm ashamed of him and the way he acted." He looked straight into her eyes. "But I need you to know something. I love you, Kenzie. I don't know how you can love me after what I said, but I promise I'll spend my lifetime trying to make it up to you."

He closed his eyes as she rested her hand on the side of his face, leaning into her touch. "I do love you. And I'm pretty sure the last few hours were an anomaly, because it's not the Jonathan I've gotten to know. That's not the Jonathan who would so freely give me what I needed to survive, even if I didn't feel like I could take it."

"That's who I really am. And I really love you. I'll spend my life proving it," he vowed again.

"I know you will."

But he still sensed hesitation, and for good reason. So he kissed her, softly, then stood. "What do you say we go get Lorelai and go out for dinner?"

"I think that sounds like a great idea, but it's a bit late, isn't it?"

"Then how about dessert? We can take Mr. Benny Hercules for his first puppy cone at Andy's."

"Lorelai will love that."

"Let's go pick her up then."

With his hand wrapped around Kenzie's, he picked up Mr. Benny Hercules, and they headed downstairs. Fifteen minutes later, Lorelai was in the car, and they drove to town.

Lorelai held Mr. Benny Hercules's leash as they walked up to the counter.

Once they had their order, including a puppy cone for the dog, they found an empty bench.

"Will he eat it?" Kenzie asked her daughter.

Jonathan picked Mr. Benny Hercules up and set him on the bench by Lorelai. She held the cone out, and he sniffed it, but didn't take a lick.

"Here, let me try." Jonathan put a bit on his finger then put it on the dog's nose. The dog licked it off then decided to try the treat Lorelai held. The girl giggled as Mr. Benny Hercules enthusiastically licked the cone empty in about a minute. He then settled into a ball on the bench next to her while Lorelai ate her kid-sized sundae.

This.

This was what he'd longed for his whole life. Just simple, normal life. It didn't matter that Kenzie had needed his money, because he didn't believe for one minute that she would have married him if there hadn't been more to it than money from the very beginning. Well, he had. For a bit more than a minute, but only long enough for him to calm down and see things more rationally.

As he watched Kenzie's head nearly touch Lorelai's while they shared a quiet moment, he prayed the contentment that had settled over him would last.

By the time they got back to the house, it was nearly bedtime. Lorelai was out like a light, despite the late night sugar rush.

Jonathan finished a bit of work he'd put off during his flight to Atlanta then found Kenzie in their room, already in pajamas and turning down the bed.

He leaned against the door frame with his hands deep in his pockets, just watching her.

She glanced over. "What?"

"Do you want me to sleep somewhere else for the next few

nights?"

Kenzie stopped what she was doing and crossed her arms over her chest. "Why would I want that?"

He scuffed his foot along the carpet, staring at it like a kid. "Because of earlier. I know what I implied, what I actually said, was uncalled for and cruel. I wouldn't blame you if you didn't want me sleeping in here for a few days."

She thought for a moment before she said anything. "What you said hurt me. A lot. But you apologized, and I do believe you, but truly trusting you is going to take a while. So, while I won't stop you from sleeping somewhere else, I won't ask you to *sleep* anywhere else."

Jonathan caught her emphasis and understood, even agreed with her. "Okay then." Ten minutes later, they were under the same covers, both rolled onto their sides looking at each other. "Tell me something I don't know about you," Jonathan started.

With that began a conversation that didn't end for days, not really. It took breaks and pauses for things like sleep and meals. He learned far more about her than he had ever known before. Like how much it had hurt her when she realized she was pregnant and couldn't tell the father, because he deserved to know.

He told her more about his past, about how even though he'd been clean and sober and limited his interactions with girlfriends, he hadn't been right with God. He told her how he and Charlie had talked in Europe, and he wanted to start a family devotional time. His own had been sorely lacking of late, and Kenzie admitted hers had been, too.

Then came the day he'd been waiting for his whole life.

The day he officially became a father.

Chapter Thirty-One

The weight lifted off Kenzie's shoulders as they walked out of the courtroom.

It was legal.

Jonathan was Lorelai's legal father, and no one could ever take that away.

Lorelai hung on tightly to Jonathan's hand as she skipped through the hallway of the historic building. "You're my daddy! You're my daddy!"

Jonathan chuckled and picked her up. "And you're my girl. You have a new name, too."

Lorelai's face wrinkled as she concentrated. "Lorelai Langley-Cranston."

"It sounds good." Kenzie's mom hugged Kenzie tight.

"You done good, kiddo," her dad whispered when he hugged her. "He's the real deal."

Kenzie hugged him back. Jonathan was now legally required to provide for Lorelai until she was an adult. If something ever happened to Kenzie, she didn't need to worry about what would become of her daughter, and her parents wouldn't be burdened with raising Lorelai in their retirement.

Stephanie and Josh had joined them for the celebration. "I remember when I adopted Alyssa. It was the best day."

More hugs all around.

"Okay, how about just the new family?" One of Stephanie's writer friends, Anise, had been hired to take pictures of the momentous occasion.

Jonathan held Lorelai and wrapped his arm around Kenzie's waist. Kenzie thanked God they had already gone through tough times and come out the other side even stronger. What else could life throw at them?

Before long, they were in the middle of the field between the house and the dock along the lake. They had already taken some pictures down there with just the three of them and some with Kenzie's parents. Jonathan's parents had sent their regrets that they wouldn't be able to come. He told her they really had tried, but they both had meetings they couldn't get out of attending, and Jonathan hadn't wanted to postpone the final hearing.

Kenzie hadn't wanted to either.

Anise was very good at what she did. Before Kenzie knew it, she and Jonathan were standing with Lorelai between them, Jonathan's arm wrapped around both of them, and all three of them grinning from ear to ear. Contentment stole over her and surrounded her soul like a warm blanket.

This.

This was what she had craved for so long.

Not just a man in her life, but a good man. One who didn't judge her for her past, who put her needs and longings and the desires of her heart above his.

And in the process, they had both found what they'd longed

for. Kenzie didn't want to do it alone. Jonathan longed for a family.

After an hour of picture taking, they went back to the house for lunch and cake. Lorelai normally ran around with Alyssa whenever they were together, but this day she didn't want to leave her daddy's side. Kenzie couldn't blame her. She was stuck pretty close to Jonathan's side as well.

The rest of the day and the next few were much the same, with Lorelai basking in the glow of her new father's love.

But then Jonathan told Kenzie he was taking her out for dinner, and she should dress up.

Fortunately, she had kept most of the clothes from Montevaro and had several options. She chose not to go quite as dressy as she had for the former queen's birthday party, but there wasn't much in Springfield that would require that kind of attire.

Instead, the definition of little black dress would have to suffice. The lace overlay on the bodice hugged her curves in the right places and the skirt came nearly to her knees, but was what Lorelai would call a twirly skirt. If she spun just right, it would lift nearly straight out.

Combined with a pair of heels nicer than anything she'd ever owned, and Kenzie actually felt like she belonged in Jonathan's Mercedes. Like she wouldn't stand out in a bad way next to him in his suit, the one he looked fantastic in.

"How many cars do you actually have?" she asked as they drove toward Serenity Landing.

"Uh..." The question seemed to stump Jonathan. "I'm not really sure?"

Kenzie grinned. "Is that a question?"

"No. But I'm not sure." He held up one finger as his lips moved, then another, then a third. "At least six or seven."

"Why do you need that many cars?" Just a few weeks ago,

Kenzie would have been happy with just one that worked reliably well.

"I don't. But I like cars, and I like having different cars for different purposes. I wouldn't have wanted to drive this one to pick you and Lorelai up that night. It could have gotten swept off that road, too. Plus I can afford it."

Kenzie nodded. "Makes sense I guess." And she wouldn't need to ask him to buy a car for a long time. Not if she could use any of them.

"I give a ton of money to charity." His defensive tone struck Kenzie.

"I know you do." She'd seen the receipt for his donation to FreedomWorks. It meant a lot to her that he was helping the same women she chose to. His dollars would help far more, and she hoped he'd let her help decide where their charity dollars should go more often.

"Sorry." He reached over and took her hand. "Most of the time when someone asks something like that, it's because they're condemning me for having far more than I need, and think I'm not doing enough to help others. Believe me, I do plenty to help others, and I'm always on the lookout for other worthy causes." He squeezed her hand lightly. "Like the one you told me about."

"I saw that. Thank you. I'm glad you thought it a worthy cause."

He lifted her hand, and warmth flooded through her as he kissed the back of it. "I'm sorry I snapped at you."

"Thank you for apologizing. I appreciate it."

See? They'd made it through a major crisis and were coping easily with smaller, even imagined, slights. They would be fine.

Jonathan pulled the car into the parking lot of a nice restaurant Kenzie had never even thought about visiting. A valet opened her door while another went around and gave Jonathan a ticket.

Who knew they had valet parking in Serenity Landing?

With Jonathan's hand on her lower back, Kenzie entered the building.

"Welcome to Savorino's Italian Ristorante, Mr. and Mrs. Langley-Cranston. Happy anniversary."

Jonathan had to admit he enjoyed the surprised look on Kenzie's face when the maître d' greeted them by name and mentioned the reason for their dinner out.

"Anniversary?" Kenzie whispered after they were seated at a secluded table near a window overlooking a wooded area.

"One month," Jonathan confirmed. "It's our one month-iversary, and I thought I'd take you out to dinner."

"Happy anniversary, then." She leaned over and gave him a light kiss. "I've never been here before."

"It's one of my favorite Italian restaurants, at least outside of Italy. There are some pretty fabulous ones there."

Kenzie rolled her eyes. "I'm sure there are."

"I'll take you both sometime."

"That sounds fabulous."

He wanted to take her and Lorelai around the world to all the places he loved. To let them see the wonders God had created and enjoy the food, the people, and the cultures. Everywhere.

They would. Not right away, but eventually, they would vacation together all over the globe.

Dinner came and tasted as wonderful as always. Kenzie certainly seemed to enjoy it. Once they finished, he wiped his mouth on the napkin and pushed away from the table. Standing,

Jonathan held out a hand. "May I have this dance?"

Kenzie blushed, the way he loved, slid her hand in his, and followed him to the dance floor.

Jonathan's arm slipped around her waist as he pulled her close, resting his chin next to her temple.

"This is just the beginning, Kenz. You and me, we have a lifetime of anniversaries to spend together."

"I look forward to every one of them." She pulled back a bit and looked up at him. "Just promise me something?"

"What's that?"

"If you're going to make a big deal out of a birthday or Christmas or anniversary or something, let me know. One thing I really don't want is to have you go all out and for me to just give you something small."

"It's not the size of a gift that counts, you know." Jonathan wasn't sure he understood.

"I know. But I really don't want to end up in a situation where you get me a..." She seemed to struggle to think of something. "...a car and fantastic trip to Bali for an anniversary, and I give you general admission tickets to a baseball game and a homemade coupon for a back rub or something."

He managed to hide a wince. "You know I'd love both of those, right?" He rarely sat in general admission, but he'd sit anywhere with Kenzie.

"I know. But then your mother would ask, and I'd end up feeling the size of a gnat."

"Okay." He kissed the side of her head. "I'll do my best, but know that no matter what I get you or you get me, I'll love it." Jonathan held her a bit tighter. "And I haven't told you yet how beautiful you look tonight. I'm the luckiest guy around.

She rested her forehead against him. "Thanks." But she seemed embarrassed.

"What is it?" Hopefully not something he'd said or done.

"Nothing. Just still getting used to this."

"To what?"

Kenzie looked up, her dark eyes staring straight into his. "To having someone love me. Someone who thinks I'm beautiful not just when I'm all dressed up, but when I'm in old clothes and up to my elbows in dye." She looked down. "Someone, besides my parents and Lorelai, who loves me with no strings attached."

"No strings," he murmured and pulled her back against him. "Never strings. I love you for you, Kenz, not what you can do or what you have."

"I know," she whispered and tightened her grip on him.

Jonathan wanted to kiss her but decided he'd better wait until later, not in public.

He took a deep breath then kissed her softly, not like he really wanted to, and danced a few more dances with her before going back to their table. Kenzie turned down dessert, so he paid the check and headed outside.

"Remember," he whispered as they waited for the car to be brought back up, "we just had that conversation a few minutes ago."

She glanced up at him, a confused look on her face. "What conversation?"

He chuckled as a different car appeared in front of them, this one a brand new Mercedes convertible.

"Whose car is this?" Kenzie asked as the valet headed toward them.

Jonathan took the keys from the man and held them out to Kenzie. "Yours."

She blinked a couple of times. "Really?"

"Yep." He jangled the keys. "And there are keys on here for anything else you might need. To the house, the workshop, the front gate in case of power outage. You want to drive?"

"Yes!" Kenzie threw herself at him.

Jonathan laughed as he caught her. "You like it?"

"I do," she whispered. "I've never had a new car before. Well," she amended, "I've never had a reliable car either."

"You do now." He hoped she wasn't bothered by the fact he'd given her gifts, and she hadn't gotten him anything. He was pretty sure the whole thing had caught her off-guard, and it wouldn't have occurred to her to get him a one month-iversary present.

A few minutes later, they were flying down the open road with the top down. Kenzie was surprisingly unconcerned about her hair, and his statement to the paparazzi appeared to have worked. There were a few discreet picture takers that he'd seen, but he was pretty sure Kenzie hadn't. He'd need to mention them to her so she wasn't surprised when the pictures appeared online.

Eventually, they came to a stop waiting to turn onto Highway ZZ near the high school. "I do have something for you at home," she told him. "I didn't know when to give it to you, but today's probably good." She ran her hands over the steering wheel. "It's not nearly this nice, but I hope you like it."

"I'm sure I'll love it." He leaned over and stole a quick kiss as the light turned green.

Twenty minutes later, he stood in their shared room as Kenzie dug through one of the drawers. "Where is it?" she muttered, then, "There it is!"

She turned around, a look of uncertainty on her face as she held out a small gift bag. "I hope you like it."

Jonathan took it then reached in to pull out a jeweler's box. "What is it?" he asked as he popped it open. He had to stifle a gasp.

The wedding band he'd looked at when he bought Kenzie's

rings. The one he'd felt weird buying for himself.

"This is perfect, Kenz." He pulled it out of its spot in the satin liner.

"Let me?" she asked, taking it from him. Kenzie held his left hand in hers and slid the band onto his ring finger. "With this ring, I thee wed and with all my worldly goods, I thee endow."

She stood on her tiptoes and kissed him.

"This is the one I looked at, you know," Jonathan told her, sliding his hands around her waist and pulling her close.

"I know." She rested her hands on his chest. "I was looking and picked this one out. The sales guy saw my rings and recognized them. He told me it was the one you'd looked at. I wasn't sure you'd like it. I knew I did, but that confirmed it was the right choice."

Jonathan kissed her again, and this time she kissed him back with the fervor he'd hoped for. For the first time since his stupid accusations and his plan to run away and never see her or his new daughter again, he was able to pour all of his emotions, his longing for a family, his desire to belong, into a kiss.

And more.

And when he fell asleep with his wife in his arms, Jonathan thanked God for restoring what had been broken. They'd made it through tough times together already. Surely nothing could come between them now.

Four days after their anniversary dinner, Kenzie was upstairs giving Lorelai a bath while he got some work done. After a bit, Jonathan heard little girl giggles coming from the kitchen along with the deeper tones of George's voice as Jonathan headed for the stairs to find his wife.

His phone buzzed to tell him someone had opened the front gate. He pulled it out of his pocket and frowned when it told him whose code had been used.

He debated calling the cops. If someone was playing a cruel joke, it would be good to know there was back-up on the way. Jonathan went back and forth with himself before deciding to meet the challenge, whatever it was, head on.

Whatever happened, bringing it inside to meet his wife and daughter wasn't an option.

With the door closed firmly behind him, he stood at the top of the steps watching the car pull up in front. He started down the steps, but when the driver got out and stood up, he stumbled the rest of the way.

It was all he could do to gasp. "Philip?"

Chapter
Thirty-Two

Ten minutes after she sent a freshly-bathed Lorelai downstairs, Kenzie pulled out her phone to see who the top doc in Springfield was, and included the issues her doctor had told her about in her search.

Instead of the top doc, she found several articles about her prior doctor. Things like lying to women and unnecessary surgeries. Insurance and Medicaid fraud. Could all of it have been a lie? Was it possible she was just fine? She had to tell Jonathan.

As she read, she heard car doors slamming, but didn't recognize the car and couldn't see the front door from the window where she sat.

Kenzie walked down the stairs as enthusiastic voices floated up. She stopped before entering the foyer, because she didn't want to ruin whatever this was with an interruption. Jonathan held onto another man in bear hug, their voices drowning each other out.

A woman stood off to the side, smiling first at the men and

then at Kenzie when she noticed her.

Jonathan finally stepped away from the man, but his hands remained on the other's shoulders. "I can't believe you're really here. Somewhere deep inside, I never wanted to believe..." Kenzie could tell when he saw her. "There's someone I want you to meet. Kenz, this is Philip, my brother."

The missing one? The other man turned around. Kenzie's stomach dropped to the floor, and her heart stopped beating. "PJ?" she whispered.

"Mac?" He sounded as confused as she felt. "What are you doing here?"

"You're PJ? But you're Philip Langley-Cranston?"

No.

No.

No.

This could not be happening.

"I went by PJ sometimes a while ago," Philip offered. "But that doesn't explain why you're here. Not that I'm not glad to see you."

Please. He probably barely remembered her. But she remembered him. Too well.

"What's going on here?" Jonathan stepped toward her. "Phil, this is Kenzie. My wife."

Philip chuckled. "You married this obnoxious man? Congratulations to both of you."

Kenzie could feel Jonathan's eyes on her, though she couldn't take her eyes from Philip.

"What?" Philip patted himself down. "You look more like you've seen a ghost than an old friend."

"Friend? We were never friends, Philip. We ran in *some* of the same party circles." She never did drugs. Ever. "That's all."

He had the good sense to cringe. "You're right. Except for

that once. And I owe you a huge apology for that."

"That once," Kenzie repeated.

"Once?" Jonathan looked between the two of them. "You mean you two..." He pointed at them.

Then she saw the realization crash over him.

"You mean you two...one time?"

Kenzie nodded, hot tears spilling down her cheeks.

"And that means..." Jonathan's question trailed off.

"Yes," she whispered, her heart cracking in two.

He turned to Philip. "Get out." His voice held barely contained fury. "Get out of my house and don't come back."

"What?" Philip was genuinely confused by his brother's complete turnaround. "I didn't expect the fatted calf, but I did expect my brother to welcome me home."

Jonathan stepped further between them, blocking her view of Philip. "Welcome home. Get out of my house, and don't come back. We'll do lunch sometime."

"Mommy?" The voice from the other room caught everyone's attention.

"Get out, Phil." Jonathan's voice was low and held the beginnings of a threat.

"Mommy, can I have ice cream?"

Kenzie needed to get Lorelai out of here. Prevent her from ever coming in. Keep Philip from seeing her.

"Mommy?"

Too late. Her little girl walked in. "Come here, sweetheart."

As though she sensed the tension, Lorelai hugged Kenzie around the waist. Kenzie's hand rested on her hair as Jonathan turned to look at them, his face pinched and white.

"How old is she?" Philip's strangled voice cut through what remained of Kenzie's rebuilt heart.

"Almost five," Kenzie answered. "Her birthday is next week."

"Is she..." To his credit, Philip let the question trail off.

Jonathan turned back to Philip, once more blocking him from Kenzie's view. "And now do you see why I want you out of my house and away from my family?"

"Your...family..." Philip spoke slowly. "And I don't want to interfere with that. I *would* like to be a doting uncle, though."

Kenzie could see the woman who'd come with Philip, his wife judging by the rings on their fingers. Realization swept across her face.

"George!" Jonathan called.

"Yes, sir?" His assistant appeared, then gasped, his face lighting up. "Mr. Philip. May I say how good it is to see you, sir? I know Mr. Jonathan never gave up hope you were alive out there somewhere."

"Can you take Lorelai for some ice cream? Maybe a trip to town for Andy's Frozen Custard?"

How well he knew her daughter.

George didn't miss a beat. "That was always your favorite, too, wasn't it, Mr. Philip? Perhaps I can bring you some back?"

Philip shook his head. "No, thank you, George. It's good to see you, too."

"Come along, Miss Lorelai." He held his hand out toward Lorelai. She adored him. "It's not often your father would send me on such an errand so close to dinner time. I recommend we enjoy it to the fullest."

Lorelai still looked uncertain, but Kenzie nodded. "Go on. It won't hurt you to spoil your dinner this once."

When they were gone, Jonathan spoke again. "Why don't we go to the living room?"

Kenzie took a seat on the couch, near the corner where Jonathan usually sat and where she'd been curled up against him so many times recently. There was plenty of room for him to sit there and still not have to actually touch her if he didn't want to.

Instead, he chose the wingback chair near the fireplace.

Philip and his wife sat together, hands clasped, on the love seat.

"So now what?" Philip asked. "I'm not going to try to break up your family, Jon. Even if Kenzie should have told me a long time ago."

Kenzie wanted to fight back, to remind him he'd walked away from her, and she'd never seen him again. But she didn't have the will to do so. She sank back into the couch and hoped they'd forget she was even there.

Was it only yesterday, only a few hours ago, that she was so optimistic about everything? She should have known it was too good to be true.

And it was too late to offer Jonathan an annulment. To take her daughter and flee. Take the money his mother had offered her and set up a new life somewhere far away.

But if she could, Jonathan could still adopt Gwendolyn's baby and have a family without the constant reminders of raising his brother's daughter.

And too late to do anything but send a prayer whispering heavenward that she didn't already carry the spark of life inside her.

Because to give birth to Jonathan's child when he loathed her would be too much to bear.

There was too much swirling around in Jonathan's brain to make sense of any of Philip's words.

Philip was alive.

And married.

Kenzie and Philip knew each other.

Philip was Lorelai's biological father.

That made Jonathan her uncle, not her father.

No matter what the judge had said the week before.

Philip, who had slept with Jonathan's girlfriend all those years earlier, was the biological father of the little girl Jonathan was coming to love more than life itself.

Philip, who had slept with Jonathan's girlfriend, had also slept with Jonathan's wife.

But it all came back to one thing: Philip was alive.

"Where have you been?" Best to start there, with something more innocuous than *you're the father of my daughter.* "Where did you go?"

Philip leaned forward and rubbed his hands together. "I knew I needed to get clean. I also knew if anyone knew where I was, it would turn into a circus. So I left the car running, climbed into a car with a friend who drove me to the same rehab place you went."

Jonathan's eyes went wide. "How did you know about that?"

His brother shrugged. "I overheard you talking to a private investigator a few years ago. I figured if no one knew you went, it would be a good place for me to go, too. I got clean. I went someplace completely new, got a fresh start, and kept a low profile. I mostly worked for cash or in exchange for room and board, so I wouldn't pop up on anyone's radar."

"Mom and Dad were here until yesterday. They're going to flip."

"I know, and that's why I didn't come until they left. I'm not ready to see them yet, and I knew you could help both of us. I didn't expect any of..." He waved a hand toward the front. "...this."

The implications cut Jonathan again. "How could you? Kenzie never told you she was pregnant."

He glanced at Kenzie, sitting on the couch, where she had been earlier when he'd been next to her. She slouched, arms crossed over her chest, but didn't look at any of them. Didn't even try to defend herself.

"Why don't we talk about something a bit less intense while we all come to grips with all of this?" Philip's wife inserted herself for the first time. If Philip had introduced her, Jonathan didn't catch her name.

Right. Deescalate the situation before it got out of hand. "So how did you two meet?"

Philip and his wife told the story together, interrupting each other until even Jonathan was smiling at the series of unfortunate events that led them into each other's lives.

About the time they finished, he glanced over only to realize Kenzie had left at some point.

"I think it's time for us to go back to the hotel," Philip said. "I think you and your wife need some time alone to sort through this."

Jonathan stood to walk them out. He gave his brother another big hug. "I'm glad you're back, Phil. I know I told you to leave, but I'm really glad you're alive."

"I'm sorry there was no other way," Philip told him, clapping his back. "I thought it was best if no one knew."

"I understand." After another big hug, they left.

Jonathan closed the door behind them and went upstairs, hoping he could find Kenzie and get to the bottom of this. She wasn't in his room, or Lorelai's, or the room she'd been living in. She wasn't upstairs at all. He tried the basement and finally found her sitting on the back porch, not in the swing they'd shared several times, but on the level below it and in a chair.

Before the door fully closed behind him, he spoke. "So you slept with my brother."

"Guess so." Kenzie sniffled and wiped her nose.

"Never told him you were pregnant?"

"I never saw him again. I didn't know his last name. How was I supposed to tell him?" The words were far more confrontational than her tone. Her tone just sounded defeated.

"I guess we'll never know."

"Guess not."

He stood with his feet slightly apart and arms crossed over his chest. The silence stretched between them, becoming more uncomfortable by the second.

A car door slammed, and he could hear Lorelai's voice. Kenzie stood and pushed past him to get to the door.

"Need to take care of *your* daughter?" he asked.

"Someone has to, and since I'm the only one she can count on..."

"Since she doesn't have a biological father, you mean."

He knew his words would hurt. They were supposed to hurt her like he'd been hurt.

She didn't respond, but went inside. Jonathan took the seat next to the one she'd vacated and stared out over the landscape. He sat there until after the sun went down. When he finally went inside, he found George cleaning up the kitchen.

His assistant decided to fill him in whether he wanted to know or not. "Mrs. Langley-Cranston didn't eat much, sir, but the frozen custard didn't seem to bother Miss Lorelai. And your brother is alive! That, sir, is quite the answer to prayer."

"Don't say anything, George. He's not ready to tell my parents."

"Of course not. But you might want to check on the lady. Something's not right with her this evening."

"I'll see if I can find her."

"She's in your room. Laying down last I saw."

Jonathan thanked him and went upstairs, undecided as to what he would do - or where he would sleep. He found Kenzie already in bed. In his bed. And asleep or pretending to be. Mr. Benny Hercules moved toward him, a dark shape against the light color of the new bedding they'd bought in Europe.

He whimpered and whined, and Jonathan knew the dog needed to go out. Picking him up, Jonathan took him outside and then went back upstairs.

Kenzie rolled over to face him when he set the dog down.

"I didn't know he was your brother. I never even knew his real name until today."

Chapter Thirty-Three

The same defeat Kenzie had been feeling seemed to settle over Jonathan. "I know. I think I'm learning something new about myself." It came out in his voice.

"What's that?" She tried not to be too optimistic. He'd already hurt her deeply twice in their short marriage.

"I need to be a lot slower to speak when something hits me at the core. I tend to lash out at the one person who matters most to me in this world, and I'm sorry. Again." He ran a hand through his hair. "Next time, and I hope there won't be one, but if there is, smack some sense into me. Or remind me of this conversation. If it even looks like I'm going to start saying something before I've had a chance to think it through, just look at me and say my brother's name."

Kenzie sat up on the bed. "You mean that?"

"I do." He took her hand, sandwiching it between his larger ones.

She believed he was sincere, but it would take time for her

wounded heart to completely heal.

"I'm going to make arrangements to take a week off work all together." She knew he'd done some work while they were overseas, though not a full day's worth. "Maybe we can work on some of your yarn stuff for the Serenity Landing show. I know it's not for a while yet, but I'm sure you need to get started on it, so you don't have to do it all in a week and a half like last time."

"That would be good. I'll need a lot more yarn this time anyway. The convention's much bigger." She stood, and Jonathan stood with her.

He wrapped his arms around her, and she leaned into him.

"Do you want to do our devotional for today?" he asked, rubbing a hand up and down her back.

She liked it when he did that. With her head against his chest, she tried to soak up his strength, because she knew she was stronger with him than she was alone.

And a cord of three strands was not easily broken.

"Yeah," she answered. "Let's do that." They sat on the small couch, and he picked up the devotional book they'd been using. "And then we need to talk about the elephant in the room."

Jonathan let out a deep sigh. "Yes, we do. But I think spending some time with God together is a good place to start."

Kenzie leaned her head against Jonathan's arm while he read the scripture passage. They spent about twenty minutes talking about the scripture, and then Jonathan took her hand, linking his fingers with hers as she closed her eyes.

"Father, you knew everything that would happen today before the foundation of the earth. First, thank you for my brother, for his safe homecoming. And thank you for a wife who is far more than I deserve, kinder and more generous, far more understanding and forgiving than I could ever have asked for. Be with us, guide us, and give us wisdom as we make the decisions that need to be made."

They sat there together, each praying on their own for a moment before Jonathan whispered an amen. Kenzie followed suit.

"So..." She felt Jonathan take a deep breath and blow it out slowly. "My brother."

"Is alive." Kenzie knew that was the most important part. But she figured she should start. "To be honest, I'm surprised he remembers me. I probably wouldn't have remembered him if not for Lorelai. We didn't know each other well at all. I think I met him four times, and I knew he wasn't from here."

"He wasn't here very often. He came and stayed from time to time, but he didn't live here full time. I never knew he went by PJ."

"I know this can't be easy for you to talk about or think about, but I honestly didn't know him well. We both have pasts, obviously, but if not for Lorelai, he would have been barely more than a blip, and maybe not even that."

He seemed to think about that for a minute. "On an intellectual level, I know that your...*relationship* with Philip is about the same as my relationship with..." He searched his mind. "Ellie. Probably even less, except for the physical side of it. It wasn't a relationship."

"Exactly."

"But now we do have to deal with this reality where this one night stand you barely remember resulted in the best thing to happen to either of us. And your daughter, who I've adopted to be my daughter, is the biological child of my not-dead brother."

"So how do we handle it?"

"What do you think? She's your daughter."

Kenzie didn't know how to respond to that.

"I mean, I know she's legally my daughter, too, but the reality is you know her far better than I do. If this was ten years from now, then maybe I'd have a much better idea how we should all handle this, but it's not." His thumb rubbed along her hand. "What are your thoughts?"

There were so many of them, and she had no idea what kind of coherent order to put them in. "The selfish part of me doesn't want him anywhere near Lorelai," she blurted out. "I know that's not fair, and I don't know your brother from Adam, but that's what I think."

"I understand that. I'm inclined to think the same thing. I don't know this new Philip any better than you do."

Kenzie whispered another prayer, though she really hadn't stopped at all. "I think locking him out of our lives would end up backfiring."

"I agree."

"So, I guess we sit down with him and his wife, and we talk about our expectations. Clearly, we won't be asking for child support or anything. You adopted Lorelai legally, and his name is out of it all together regardless because I didn't know it."

"I guess it's ideal that I adopted her already. I do think we should find a way to make him a part of her life as the doting uncle and hope he leaves it at that."

It was Kenzie's turn to take a deep breath. "Yeah. That's the ideal." And maybe this time, things would go the way they were supposed to.

⁂

Jonathan sat on the couch and held Kenzie's hand while Philip and his wife, Dawn, sat on the love seat.

"Lorelai's over at her friend's house for the day," Jonathan explained. "She's spending the night tonight. We all need some time."

Philip glanced at his wife then nodded. "We've talked it over, and we're willing to accept whatever the two of you decide. The only way we'd fight you on anything is if you're completely unreasonable, and I know you, Jon. I don't think you will be."

"I hope you won't think we are." His heart thudded in his chest. Despite Philip's words, there was no guarantee. "I've already adopted Lorelai."

Philip nodded. "I expected as much or that you would soon."

"For many reasons that have nothing to do with you specifically, we're glad your name was kept out of it. Lorelai's never really had a father, and we'd like for me to be the only one she ever has."

"I can understand that." Philip looked over at his wife. "And I'm good with that. I'm happy to keep my name out of it." They exchanged another glance. "The one thing I would ask is - after you get to know us and are comfortable with it - if anything ever happens to the two of you, that you would consider us as guardians for Lorelai."

Jonathan looked down at Kenzie who was staring at the floor. "How about this? We'll think it over, talk about it, pray about it, and get to know the new you."

"That's all we ask."

Dawn turned her face into Philip's shoulder and seemed to be trying to get herself under control. If he knew Kenzie at all, she'd be looking for a chance to get Dawn off to the side and make sure she was really okay with all of this.

Or maybe that would be too hard for her. This woman, technically, was Lorelai's stepmother. That would be hard even for Kenzie.

But Dawn seemed to find some inner strength and turned

back to the conversation, but she clung to Philip's hand even stronger than before.

"I don't mean to intrude." Kenzie spoke again before he could. "But is there something more going on here?"

Jonathan looked between his brother and sister-in-law and waited for their response.

They exchanged a look of their own.

Philip let go of his wife's hand and wrapped an arm around her shoulders, pulling her to him. "We can't have children. We don't want to take your daughter from you," he rushed on. "Honest. But it's hit us pretty hard. That's all."

Jonathan's heart broke for his brother and sister-in-law. He remembered conversations from when they were younger, much younger, and how Philip wanted the same things he did out of life, including a big family.

"We're okay," Dawn told them. "We really are. I've known for a long time that I probably wouldn't be able to have children, and Philip knew that early in our relationship. We talked about the possibility that he could someday find out that he had a child out there somewhere, but we never could have imagined this situation."

"None of us could have," Philip finished. "So we want to be the best Uncle Phil and Auntie Dawn we can be. And, if I can qualify because of my history, we'll adopt a whole bunch of cousins for her."

A thought occurred to Jonathan, though he'd need to talk to Kenzie about it before mentioning it to his brother. And Gwendolyn. They'd all need to talk to her about it. Fortunately, their cousin had been spending most of her time working or with Adam and didn't know any of this was going on.

He stood. "Can you excuse us for a moment?"

Kenzie wore a puzzled look, but followed him into the other

room. "What?" she whispered.

"I know we haven't taken you to a doctor or anything, and we have no idea what's going to happen there."

She opened her mouth, but he covered her lips with a finger.

"We can figure it out later, but what if Philip and Dawn adopted Gwendolyn's baby? I've known for a while that Gwendolyn's going to ask us to adopt. I've been looking forward to it, but I've also felt a little check in my spirit. One I've mostly been ignoring, but maybe this is why."

Kenzie nodded. "Let's talk to Gwendolyn first, though. If she's not okay with it, it's a totally moot point."

"They used to be pretty close when we were kids," he told her. "But he's changed so much and then changed so much again that I don't know what she'll think."

"Then we'll talk to her as soon as we can."

He gave her a quick kiss and took her hand again, walking back into the living room. Once they sat down, he addressed the other couple. "So we're in agreement. I'm Lorelai's father. You two are going to be the best aunt and uncle she could hope for. She's got a fantastic set of grandparents in Kenzie's mom and dad. She has..." He rolled his eyes. "Grandparents who are improving in our parents."

"But?" Philip prompted.

"When are you planning to tell everyone you're alive?" Jonathan leaned forward and rested his elbows on his knees, clasping his hands together. "When the world found out I got married, the paparazzi swarmed all over this place. They're in town still, at least some of them are, though not nearly as bad as the first day."

"The day you ran them off with a shotgun?" Philip asked with a grin. "You looked like a bad..." He stopped himself before finishing. "Sorry. Still slips out sometimes."

Kenzie slipped her hand around Jonathan's upper arm. "He did look pretty fierce, didn't he?"

"We saw some of the news coverage, but didn't actually see your face, Mac. Kenzie, I mean. There were some mentions of me, and that's when I knew it was time to come home."

"Will you do one of the news programs?" Jonathan needed to know. "They all ran specials and ran them again last year. I'd been expecting to hear about another one soon."

"I don't know," Philip told them. "We haven't talked about it much. It killed me watching that last year, but I wasn't ready yet. I wasn't completely sure in my ability to stay sober."

Jonathan thought about the coin in his pocket, the one rubbed nearly smooth. "I understand," he told his brother. He stood and walked toward Philip with his arms open wide.

Philip gladly gave him a hug.

This time Jonathan was able to say without reservation, "Welcome home."

Kenzie breathed a sigh of relief when they brought Lorelai home early. She hadn't been told she might be spending the night with Alyssa, so it didn't disappoint her too badly. She did miss going to SLAC with Alyssa and Alivia which was bad enough.

When Jonathan introduced her to Uncle Philip and Aunt Dawn, Lorelai gave them hugs and then went to color them a picture.

That was it, though Philip hugged her a bit longer than most new uncles would have.

And that's how the next four days went. The five of them, sometimes with Gwendolyn and Adam, spent time together, getting to know each other. Kenzie and Jonathan talked to Gwendolyn about the possibility of Philip and Dawn adopting her baby. She promised to think about it and to get to know the new Philip.

They talked about a little bit of everything, though it tended to stay more superficial when they were together in a group. Jonathan told her about some of the deeper conversations he had with Philip when it was just the two of them.

How Philip's heart broke that he couldn't give his wife what she longed for most, even though he wasn't the one who had the biological issue. He knew well that his past could prevent them from adopting, even in a private adoption through someone he knew. The background check wouldn't be the problem, he'd pass that. But the home study, though they were looking for land or a house in Serenity Landing or nearby, could be an issue. Not the home itself, but his history with drugs and alcohol could prevent them from passing. He'd completed rehab, had letters of recommendation from professionals he'd worked with during and after his inpatient treatment.

But there were no guarantees.

It could go either way.

And then Jonathan surprised her.

"What if we sold some of our land to Philip and Dawn?" he asked, tugging his shirt off and tossing it on the chair before sitting on the bed.

Unease settled over Kenzie. "Our land?" She needed more time to process.

"Yeah. We've got a lot of land here. There's plenty with road access that they could build a ways away, closer to where we left for the airport that night, and we wouldn't see them any more than we see Josh and Stephanie's house."

Kenzie sat on her side of the bed, facing away from Jonathan, using the pretense of putting lotion on to keep from looking at him.

"Would you be okay with that?" This time his soft voice caused her to turn.

She swung her legs up and tucked them under the covers. "I don't know. This, what we've been doing the last couple of days, is one thing. And I know he's your brother, and having them stay here gives him a chance to know Lorelai better."

"But it's too close." He settled onto the bed, with the covers pulled up to his waist and his head propped on his hand. "I get that. Without all of this stuff, it might be too close."

She allowed herself an internal sigh of relief.

"And he has the money to do whatever he wants with, once everyone knows he's alive anyway," Jonathan went on. "He still has plenty in his trust funds."

"That's good." She reached over and turned off the lamp.

He reached out with his free hand and laid it on her shoulder. "Are you really okay with all of this, Kenz?"

Kenzie laid her head on her pillow and tugged the covers up around her shoulders. "I have to be. I don't have a choice. He's your brother, and despite the adoption being final, he could decide to cause problems. Personally, I'd rather he disappear into the void he's been in for the last nearly six years." Jonathan started to say something, but she shook her head. "No. I get it. But if he was a random guy and not my brother-in-law, that's what I'd want."

"If he wasn't my brother, that's what I'd want too."

That relieved her some. "Then we'll figure it out. Maybe they'll decide on their own to move somewhere not too far, but not to close."

"Like Mars?"

That made Kenzie laugh. "Sure. Mars works."

"We'll keep praying about it, and pray for clear answers."

Kenzie did something she hadn't done since Philip showed up. She leaned over and kissed him like she meant it.

The next day, Philip and Dawn were gone for hours, searching for the right place to call home. After an early dinner, Kenzie went with Jonathan and Lorelai to SLAC. She spent most of her time watching the two of them play together in the kiddie end of the pool. Josh showed up with Alyssa about an hour before they closed. The two little girls played happily together while the adults talked about the upcoming birthday party.

The two girls ran up, gaining admonitions from all three parents about running at the pool.

Alyssa started. "Can Lorrie spend the night? Please?"

"Please, Mama," Lorelai chimed in.

Josh glanced at his watch. "Mom and I are leaving in a couple hours. If it's okay with Lorelai's parents and with Alivia, it's fine with me."

Kenzie glanced at Jonathan, who shrugged. Alivia was a responsible adult. It would be fine. "If it's okay with Alivia, but no whining if she says no."

The girls held hands as they headed for the other side of the pool to ask.

"Are you sure it's okay?" Kenzie asked. "Alivia's your nanny, not ours."

Josh just smiled. "It's fine. Alyssa loves having Lorelai around. It gives her someone besides her little sister to play with."

With the nod from Alivia, Kenzie and Jonathan headed home to pack a bag for Lorelai. Josh would stop by with the girls to pick it up on their way home.

"You know," Jonathan said as they pulled into the drive. "With no Lorelai and no Philip and Dawn, you and I could get all dressed up and go out."

"We could," Kenzie conceded, "but couldn't we just order pizza and watch a movie in the basement. It's been a long few days, and I'm not up for being on the lookout for cameras everywhere." Especially not when she was almost certain her doctor had lied. She still needed to tell Jonathan what she'd discovered.

Jonathan agreed. An hour and a half later, she was curled up next to him in one of the big chairs as they watched the first of the new *Star Trek* movies. She hadn't seen it when it came out, but used to watch the original television show with her dad.

The phone buzzed. She was tempted to ignore it, but instead just couldn't find it fast enough. Jonathan's buzzed a second later. He showed her the screen.

Alivia.

That couldn't be good. Was Lorelai sick again?

Jonathan answered, his face going white as he listened to the other end of the phone. "We're on our way."

Kenzie's heart sank. "What is it?"

They were already out of the movie room when he told her.

"Lorelai's missing."

Chapter Thirty-Four

*K*enzie's heart stopped and sped up faster than it ever had, all at the same time. She gripped Jonathan's hand as he sped down the road to the Jamison Estate. About the time he got up to speed, he slammed on the brakes to turn into their open gate.

Jonathan didn't speed up the drive. He went slowly, both of them scanning the woods, though Alivia said they'd been out back.

He drove around to the back. Kenzie was out of the car before it came to a complete stop, bolting for the grass where the flashlights could be seen. She swiped up on her phone and turned her own flashlight on.

"Lorelai!" she yelled when she got to the edge of the field.

Alivia was closer than the others and turned, holding tight to Alyssa's hand. "I'm so sorry, Mrs. Langley-Cranston. I was *right here*. I turned around to help Alyssa with her shoe because she had a lightning bug in her hands, and when I turned back around

Lorelai was gone."

"Did you call the police yet?" Jonathan asked.

Alivia shook her head. "No. Mr. Wilson was going to call the chief on his way back. I called everyone here and had them start looking for her."

"How long has she been gone?" Kenzie stopped trying to fight the tears as felt his hand on her back.

The nanny checked her phone. "Twenty minutes? At first, I thought she was playing hide and seek, but when she didn't come back, I called CJ first and had him bring his sisters, looking from that direction. Then I called you."

Right. Because CJ lived in another house on the property, closer to the line between the Jamison Estate and Jonathan's property.

Sirens sounded from the north. Good. Help was on the way.

"Mr. Wilson will back in a few minutes. He knows the property a lot better than I do, but Reginald is out here."

Who? Right. The butler or their version of George or whatever.

"He knows this place like the back of his hand." Alivia swiped at her cheek. "It was only a minute, I swear."

"We know." Jonathan's reassurance probably didn't go far in making Alivia feel better. It didn't help Kenzie at all.

A snuffling sound caught her attention. Kenzie reached out her arms and lifted Alyssa into them. "It's all right, sweetheart. Lorelai was just hiding and wandered farther than she meant to. We'll find her soon, I promise."

Alyssa's arms wound around Kenzie's neck as she sobbed. Kenzie prayed her words were accurate.

Two police cars, probably county deputies, pulled up next to Jonathan's car, lights still on. They didn't hurry nearly as much as Kenzie hoped they would.

"Who can tell us what happened?" one asked.

Jonathan was able to speak the most coherently, so he repeated the story Alivia told them. He finished with, "Money is no object. Bring in whoever you can. Dogs, helicopters, whatever is necessary."

The deputy nodded. "The sheriff was already in bed when Mr. Wilson called. He's on his way."

A thought hit Kenzie. "Can I post a request for help on Facebook?"

The two deputies glanced at each other. "Not just yet, ma'am," one of them answered. "The sheriff will tell you when to post."

Kenzie pulled her phone out anyway, shifting Alyssa to one side. "Fine. I won't." She did post a prayer request, saying she couldn't give details, but please pray - God knew - and more information would be forthcoming later. Before she turned her phone off, one friend had already commented. "I'm calling my parents, though."

"I'm calling some friends in the area," Jonathan told them as he took his own phone out of his pocket. "They've got connections and equipment if we need it. They'd rather start to mobilize and be called off than not be ready when the call comes."

The deputies talked to Alivia, grilling the poor girl for what seemed like forever, but probably wasn't that long. Kenzie itched to be out there looking, but at least a dozen people were already scouring the field near where Lorelai was last seen. Every employee Josh had was out there, except Alivia.

And then everything started to happen at once. More official vehicles showed up. A helicopter hovered overhead with a searchlight pointing downward. The sheriff, a man Kenzie barely recognized from his election mailers, talked on his phone and to the assorted people that came up to him, pointing this way and that. Everyone did what he told them to, and quickly.

Josh and Stephanie pulled up, having canceled their flight out of town. Stephanie took Alyssa in the house. Kenzie wrapped her arms around herself and walked a few feet away, yelling Lorelai's name.

"We're going to find her." Jonathan's hands rested on her shoulders. "Soon."

"I know." But that wouldn't stop her.

"I need to call my brother, though. He deserves to know."

"Please don't let him come." His appearance would just take attention away from what really mattered.

"I'll try."

She needed to *do* something. She walked toward a dark area where no one was currently searching. With her flashlight on, Kenzie called for her daughter over and over.

Tears streamed down her cheeks as she pushed through thigh-high grasses. How easy would it be to miss her little girl if Lorelai had decided to lie down because she was tired.

Dear God, please let her be okay. Please help me find my baby.

Jonathan stared at his phone and did something he'd sworn he'd never do.

Called the media.

He'd met the news director at one of the local stations while they were searching for his brother. The man had given him a card, and Jonathan had put the information in his phone.

Just in case.

He'd also included his cell phone number.

"This is Bill," a sleep-filled voice answered.

"This is Jonathan Langley-Cranston. We met a couple years

ago."

"Of course." Bill sounded more awake.

"I need your help. It can't go out officially yet, but we need to be ready when it can."

"When what can?"

"How quickly can you get to the Jamison Estate?"

"Uh…" He had to be doing mental math. "Just me? No news crews?"

"For now."

"Twenty minutes? Maybe faster."

"The gate's open. We're in the back."

"I'll see you as soon as I can." Background noise told Jonathan he'd already started getting ready.

"Who was that?" Josh asked.

Jonathan told him.

"I never thought you'd call the media, not after what happened with Kenzie a few weeks ago."

"Me either, but something in my gut…" He stopped and looked around to make sure his wife wouldn't hear him. "…says this is going to be a very long night that may not end with daybreak."

"I'm inclined to agree. Whatever you need, it's yours. I'll be your spokesperson if you need me to." The grim tone in Josh's voice matched Jonathan's feeling inside.

And they were both right.

When dawn broke, there was still no sign of Lorelai.

Finally, the news was starting to spread and official search parties were being formed. They would go over everything inch by inch in the daylight.

Jonathan held Kenzie's hand as they stood next to the sheriff. In front of a bank of cameras and microphones, the man Jonathan had voted for began to speak.

"Thank you for being here today. I'm Sheriff Turner of Pond Creek County, Missouri. Most of you know me, but I see a few unfamiliar faces. A contact information sheet will be provided later this morning. We're here because last night, at approximately 9:45pm Lorelai Langley-Cranston, formerly Lorelai Davidson, wandered away from her caregiver into a field. She had been catching fireflies with Alyssa Wilson, who lives at this residence, and they were with the Wilsons' nanny. The nanny was helping Alyssa tie her shoe when Lorelai wandered off."

Murmurs shot through the reporters, and Kenzie gripped his hand even tighter.

"We've spent the night searching as best we were able. There is no reason to suspect foul play of any kind, and we fully anticipate finding her safe in the next few hours. Information is being handed out and posted on our Facebook and Twitter feeds telling volunteers where to go. Good pants or jeans and sturdy shoes are a must. Everything else will be provided for you. I can take a few questions."

"Is there any negligence by the nanny or the Wilsons?" one reporter called.

Hadn't he already answered that?

"We've conducted interviews with the nanny, the Wilsons, and Lorelai's parents. There is no reason to suspect any negligence at this time."

Another reporter managed to make her voice heard over the others. "Is it possible someone kidnapped her for ransom? The Langley-Cranston family could pay it. Or she could have been mistaken for the Wilsons' daughter of the same age. Are you investigating that?"

"We've been in contact with the FBI, but we have no reason to think so."

A third reporter, this one from Bill's station. "What about the timing? Why is it just now going out on social media?"

"We asked the family not to post anything until daybreak. There were plenty of searchers already here. The entire staffs of both the Jamison Estate and the Langley-Cranston's were here, along with numerous members of law enforcement and other communities. Until it was light out, we didn't want searchers unfamiliar with the terrain trying to navigate it."

"Jonathan!" One of the men called to him. "Is this all too similar to your brother's disappearance?"

Jonathan took a step toward the microphones. "Yes and no. Two people I love deeply went missing without a trace. This time, there is no suspicion of foul play and a relatively finite area where she could be. She probably fell asleep where she couldn't see or hear the searchers and will be found any moment now."

He believed that. He had to. And more news crews were pulling up as the press conference wrapped up. More national crews were arriving. He saw another familiar face. One of the reporters who had done fair, honest pieces on Philip. It was going to be time and soon. That's who he'd prefer to talk to.

The sheriff spoke again. "We're headed back out. Thank you for your time. There will be another press conference this afternoon. Details will be handed out as soon as it's scheduled."

They walked off and around the house. The media wasn't allowed back there. Thank goodness. Jonathan pulled out his phone and saw the text that had come in a moment earlier.

"My parents have landed," he told Kenzie. "I told them to go to the house. They need to have that reunion before anything else."

She nodded, though he wasn't sure how she could see straight. Her eyes were swollen from the tears, and she hadn't slept a wink. None of them had.

"It's going to come out today, Kenz. I hate that it's going to take away from this, but it has to be told. And we probably need to tell the sheriff everything because if it comes out later, Philip will be a suspect."

"He had nothing to do with it."

"I know that. You know that. But it's still something we need to consider."

She gave a single nod, which seemed almost beyond her ability to do. "Let's talk to him."

"Sheriff Turner!" he called. "As soon as you have a minute, we need to have a word in private."

Chapter Thirty Five

Kenzie dreaded this conversation, necessary though it was. They'd asked her about Lorelai's biological father the night before. She hadn't lied, but she hadn't been completely up front about it either.

The sheriff from a neighboring county took over instructing the volunteers, and Sheriff Turner went inside the main house with them.

"I take it this is important?" he asked.

"It is," Jonathan promised. She didn't have the nerve to say any of it. "My brother, the one who went missing a couple years ago?"

The man nodded. He'd helped coordinate that search too.

"He's alive."

Sheriff Turner hid his surprise well.

"He knew he needed to go to rehab, but needed anonymity to do it. He's been clean ever since. A couple of days ago, he and his wife showed up."

"Okay. Good. I'm glad he's alive. I've often wondered if it might be something like that." He shifted his feet. "Go on. There's got to be more."

"They've been staying at our house, but..." Jonathan looked at Kenzie who shifted to stare at the sheriff's work boots. "There's a chance he's Lorelai's biological father. We haven't done any testing, but he and Kenzie had a fling about the right time."

She knew Philip was Lorelai's father, but Jonathan hadn't lied.

"He has no plans to contest the adoption. He agreed to sign a document to that effect, because it was already finalized when he showed up. Kenzie didn't know his last name. We'd really like to keep it out of anything official, and we know he had nothing to do with this, but we felt you should know anyway. The last thing we want to do is keep what may be pertinent information from you."

"And you're sure he was at your house?"

Jonathan nodded. "I have surveillance cameras all over the outside. I haven't checked them personally, but one of my employees has looked at the copies of the recordings."

Right. Because the cops had confiscated the actual recordings to make sure they were where they said they were.

"They show him coming home about nine and not leaving at all as of about two hours ago."

"I can't keep his reappearance a secret, but I won't say anything about the suspicions if we can prove he never left the house."

"Your men have the videos. They probably already saw him coming home but didn't know who it was."

The sheriff nodded. "Fine. We'll look at it again, just to verify, and go from there."

"Can you let us break the news to the media?"

The sheriff seemed a bit irritated but nodded. "Now, can we get back to looking for your daughter?"

"Of course. Where do you want us looking?"

He sent them off with a couple of deputies from a few counties over. They headed in the direction of their house, hoping she would have just been trying to get home.

A long, thin line of matching orange vests walked through the field. All of them searched the ground carefully and called her name.

Kenzie knew the deputies on either side of her would be picking up her slack. As much as she tried to focus on the ground, her vision was blurred. Between the continually threatening tears and utter exhaustion, she couldn't focus no matter how hard she tried.

She drank water when it was handed to her, stayed in line with the deputies, did what she was told to do, all while praying desperately and ignoring her perpetually buzzing phone. If someone knew something, an official would let her know.

But finally, she couldn't pick her foot up far enough to clear the rock, and she fell to the ground.

On her hands and knees, she sobbed as her heart shattered again.

Gentle, kind hands, helped her to her feet and to a four-wheeler. Kenzie clung to the back of whoever sat in front of her, over the dips and bumps, until they reached the house.

Her mother-in-law waited there, gathered Kenzie in her arms, then helped her inside. As soon as she sat on the couch, she slumped to the side, pulling her feet up, and let herself fall into sleep. She couldn't help it.

Lorelai. Running through fields. Disappearing before her very eyes. Then back again. Her face turning evil, taunting, as she darted into the trees.

Philip yelling in Kenzie's face.

Jonathan taking off the wedding band she'd bought him and

flinging it at her, threatening to take her daughter away.

She sat up with a jolt, her breath sucked from her.

"Feeling any better?" The sympathy in the voice made her turn.

Her mother-in-law stood at the wet bar with a coffee cup in her hand.

"Jonathan told me how you take it." She turned, stirring the liquid with the skinny stirrer straw. "Are you feeling any better?"

Grateful, Kenzie reached for the cup and took her first sip. "No. Not really. Bad dreams the whole time."

"You didn't look peaceful." She sat down close to Kenzie and rested a hand on her shoulder. "We're praying, sweetheart. It's something I haven't done nearly enough of, but since getting to your house earlier today, I've realized it's something I need to do a lot more. And not just while I'm angry either."

"I'm happy for you guys, I really am."

"But it's hard to be happy for us when your little girl is missing." She finished the sentence for Kenzie, who nodded her agreement.

The door opened to let Jonathan in. "Nothing yet." He sank to the chair across from her. "They need more volunteers. The ones from this morning need a break, and there will be another shift later. We need enough volunteers for that, too."

"What about Philip?" his mom asked. "He wants to be here."

Kenzie shared a look with her husband. His mom didn't know the truth about Philip's relationship with Lorelai.

"I don't think it's a good idea." Jonathan ran a hand through his hair. "Having Philip show up alive will just detract from trying to find Lorelai."

His mother nodded. "I know, but we're all going to have to be ready to face the media when this is all over."

Jonathan's shoulders slumped a bit further. "Yeah. I know."

Kenzie knew it was inevitable, but that didn't mean she had to look forward to it.

Jonathan didn't like the look of defeat on Kenzie's face, didn't like that the search still continued. Lorelai was out there, somewhere, safe, just waiting to be found.

A text from Philip said he wanted to be out searching and wondered what the best way to do that was. Jonathan understood his concern. If it ever got out that he was Lorelai's biological father, and he mysteriously found her, things could turn south in the ever-important court of public opinion.

Jonathan would talk to Sheriff Turner and go from there. He told Kenzie what he was thinking, but she had an idea of her own.

"Why don't you get one of the news crews you'd be willing to talk to first and have them go with him, videotaping everything so there are no questions?"

Jonathan nodded and went to find the sheriff to discuss it with him. Then he made two phone calls, one to the local news editor and one to the national reporter he sort of trusted.

They were both admitted to the house and shown into Josh's office. "I have a proposition for both of you. I can't tell you what it is until you agree to some terms, though."

The two of them, who had likely never met, shared a look. "Why would we do that?" the local guy asked.

Jonathan crossed his arms over his chest. "Because I promise it'll be worth your time and a scoop your bosses will love. You, a cameraman, and that's it. You can't release what you find out until we say it's okay. That won't be long after my daughter is found, but no one else will have it, and you'll have video footage exclusive to the two of you." That they happened to be from the same network surely worked in his favor.

"Are you going to make us sign something?" the network lady asked.

"No, but if you don't abide by the verbal agreement, you'll regret it." He had to give them something, though. "If you get there and don't understand my reasoning or the rationale behind asking you to keep it under wraps until after Lorelai is found, feel free to let it out. But you'll never get a sit-down interview with any of us ever again."

"Duly noted. Can I call my producer?" the national reporter asked.

"No. Get another crew out here to do the press conferences or," he nodded at Bill, "get his local sister network to let you use their feed, but trust me on this. Or I can get someone else, if you don't want it."

That did the trick.

Jonathan gave them instructions to go to his house, and someone would be waiting for them. They weren't to tell anyone where they were going or why. He'd have to face questions about it at the next press conference, but he didn't care.

Two off-duty sheriffs' deputies from a neighboring county had already been sent to the house to start conducting a very small search from that side. Just in case she'd made it that far already. It was less than a mile as the crow flies, but as a little girl wanders, the journey would be much farther.

Jonathan started for the door to Josh's office but stumbled before he reached it.

Bill caught him. "Have you gotten any rest?"

Jonathan shook his head. "How can I rest when my little girl is missing in the woods?"

"You need to. Just like your wife has been."

He looked up, a frown pulling his mouth downward. "How did you know that?"

Bill shrugged. "Word got around that she collapsed from exhaustion and stress and was resting. I presume she's okay, or we would have heard."

Jonathan just nodded, knowing the other man was right but hating to admit it. He promised Bill he'd get some rest then watched the two of them whisper to each other for several minutes before leaving through the front door.

He stumbled his way downstairs to where Kenzie and his mother waited. After giving them a quick update, Jonathan settled onto the couch where Kenzie had been and fell asleep.

When he woke, it was nearly dark again. He knew instantly nothing had been found. They would have woken him if there was reason to.

Twilight gave way to dark and dark eventually gave way to dawn.

And still nothing.

Jonathan held Kenzie as sobs shook her body. "Where is she?" The whisper cut through his already shattered heart.

"She's out there." He rubbed a hand up and down her back. "She's found a place to hole up or is staying just beyond the searchers as she tries to get home."

"But the rain..."

Thunderstorms seemed to be heading straight toward Serenity Lake. "We'll pray they don't hit here. Maybe a little rain so she can get a drink, but not the storms that would scare her."

"She'll be all wet."

"There are little caves and shelter all over the place out there. It does make searching go a lot slower, but makes it much more likely that she's found a place to hide."

"I know."

He'd held her in his arms most of the night as they sat on the couch in the Wilson's basement and dozed. Local law enforcement were out looking, but Jonathan and Kenzie had been given strict instructions to stay put and not give officials two more people out in the dark.

"You need to see this."

Jonathan looked up as Josh turned on the television. "What is it?"

"I got a call saying it was coming on." His friend didn't elaborate. But as soon as the morning program came back on, the two people on the split-screen told him what he needed to know.

Isadora and her father.

"Mr. Newman, you've come forward to talk about Jonathan Langley-Cranston and how you don't think he's been fairly portrayed in the media in the last day or so. But first, let's refresh our viewers with your story." A short clip played about the boating accident. "Your daughter is there with you, clearly dealing with the after effects of the accident. So what brings you forward now?"

Mr. Newman shifted, clearly uncomfortable. "There's been a lot of talk on the news about how irresponsible Jonathan Langley-Cranston must be to let his new daughter wander off."

"And you don't agree?"

Mr. Newman shook his head. "He took responsibility when he didn't have to. My daughter was hurt in that accident over a decade ago. The people in the boat were friends of Mr. Langley-Cranston, but he wasn't there. It was well-established that he'd gone home long before the board ride started."

"The way I remember it, he knew they were going to go out on the boat when he left the party where they'd all been drinking."

"I never learned if he did or not. All I know is a month later, all of our medical bills were mysteriously being paid and wheelchairs showed up when we needed them, things like that, all due to Mr.

Langley-Cranston."

Kenzie looked up at him, more tears in her eyes. "Is that true?"

Chapter Thirty-Six

Kenzie looked up into her husband's eyes, currently the color of a stormy sea.

He nodded, but didn't speak, still watching the television. She turned her attention there.

"And you believe Mr. Langley-Cranston is responsible for those payments?" the reporter asked.

Mr. Newman nodded. "I've asked around over the years. All of the young people involved denied it was them, and I believed them. I never received a response from Mr. Langley-Cranston. I also noticed a bit of a timing discrepancy for the payments a few times."

"Payments? He's paying you off?" the reporter pressed.

"Nothing like that. My daughter has ongoing bills related to the accident. Occasionally, the payments come in a bit later. When looking into it, they were all times when Mr. Langley-Cranston had something major going on in his life, such as when his brother first went missing. Now that he's getting such a hard time in the media, I want the world to know he is a good man."

"Isadora, have you ever met him?"

The girl gripped the arm of her wheelchair, as nervous as her father. "No. I want to. Without his help, I wouldn't be where I am today. We wouldn't have been able to do all of the physical therapy or have the state of the art wheels."

"Didn't you get a fairly significant settlement from the families involved, Mr. Newman?"

He shifted in his seat again. "I can't speak to the settlement. I can say it would have paid for all of those same bills, but it wouldn't have allowed my wife to quit her job and stay home to help Izzy like she needed to. We would likely have lost our house and business. So, while the settlement would have made sure Izzy survived, Mr. Langley-Cranston has allowed her to thrive."

The split screen turned into a single screen of the reporter. "There you have it. Now, we're heading to our reporter on the scene outside of Serenity Landing to tell us the latest on the search for little Lorelai Langley-Cranston."

Josh clicked the television off. "Good for you, Jonathan."

It was the girl from the accident that sent Jonathan on his way to rehab.

"No asking if it's true?" Jonathan moved away from Kenzie, leaving one arm around her shoulders.

"No. I know you well enough to know you took care of that girl."

"None of it matters if we don't find Lorelai soon." Kenzie could hear the worry in his voice. "I haven't watched any of the coverage, but it doesn't surprise me to hear the media isn't being nice."

She sank back down to the couch where she'd passed the night. "We have to find her soon."

It didn't matter what the media thought about them. Only her daughter mattered.

"My brother and the news crews are headed back out in a few minutes. The teams are meeting at the church to be bussed over in about half an hour. We'll find her this morning. I have this feeling in my gut."

Kenzie had a feeling in her gut, too. But it was more of a churning in her gut than confidence Lorelai would be found safely. "I'm ready to go back out. I want to be out there looking. When she asks me if I did everything I could, I don't want to tell her I stayed inside."

"We'll talk to Sheriff Turner and try to get him to let us back out there."

The door opened, and the sheriff walked in. "Let's go. In my SUV."

Kenzie looked at Jonathan whose face showed the same worry hers had to hold. But they hurried, hand in hand, to follow the sheriff to his vehicle. Seconds after they were in the back seat, the SUV took off, sirens blaring. Cameras in front of the house turned to follow them, though she was pretty sure they wouldn't be able to tell who was in the vehicle through the dark tint of the windows.

Down the drive and to the left when they got to the road.

"What aren't you telling us?" Jonathan asked, but the sheriff didn't respond. Less than thirty seconds later, they turned onto Jonathan's property.

Kenzie's breath caught in her throat. "Is she here?"

Still no answer. They didn't stop at the house, but went further, along a rough road leading toward the lake.

There.

Ahead.

She couldn't make out how many people there were, but a small crowd headed toward them.

Kenzie heard herself gasp and couldn't stop the tears. They

neared the group, and the vehicle slowed.

She didn't wait for it to come to a complete stop. Kenzie jumped out, running the rest of the way to where Philip held her daughter.

"Lorelai!"

"Mama!" Her voice didn't sound normal, but she could hear it. As she neared, Lorelai reached for her. Kenzie took her baby into her arms. "Are you okay, sweetheart?"

"Tired. Thirsty."

"We gave her some water," one of the off-duty law enforcement members told her. "The ambulance is on the way."

Kenzie buried her head in Lorelai's shoulder as she held her daughter tighter than ever. Strong arms came around her and pulled her close.

"Daddy!" Lorelai's muffled voice was one of the best things she'd ever heard.

"I'm here, sweetheart." He kissed both of their heads. "I'm here." He seemed to look up. "Can we turn the cameras off, please?"

Cameras. Right. Because they'd been following Philip as he searched.

Another sound reached her ears. Another siren.

"Back in the SUV," Jonathan told her. The sheriff drove them back to the house where the ambulance met them.

The whole time, Kenzie and Lorelai clung to each other. Her little girl kept whispering, "I missed you, Mommy. I called and called, and you didn't come."

"I'm so sorry. I tried to find you, but I couldn't. There are so many other people looking for you, trying to find you. They started at Alyssa's house, and they were walking super slow so they wouldn't miss you."

"I just wanted the firefly, Mama, but then I couldn't see

anything." Lorelai trembled. "I couldn't find Lyssa or 'Livia."

Kenzie wanted to know more, to know the whole story, but the paramedics were there, starting an IV and asking Lorelai questions.

In the answers, Kenzie learned more. Her daughter had found the stream she'd been to with Jonathan several times. She knew Daddy had told her not to drink it, but she was so thirsty so she did. Then she followed it, knowing it would lead her to the lake, and she could get home from there. If she could find her daddy's boat.

Right. The boat and the dock. They hadn't been out there but once since they moved in and not out on the lake at all. Kenzie had all she could do not to collapse in front of Lorelai.

Jonathan helped her into the front seat and promised he'd be right behind and meet them at the hospital.

Kenzie buckled her seat belt and looked back to see her daughter being loaded into the rear. She leaned against the door as the sirens started again, and they moved away from the house and toward the hospital.

Her daughter was safe.

⁕

Jonathan leaned forward in the Pond Creek County Sheriff's vehicle, willing it and the ambulance just ahead to go faster. At least he wasn't in his own vehicle.

He answered the phone when George called.

"I'm bringing your car, sir," George told him before Jonathan could speak. "I also have Miss Lorelai's dog."

Her favorite stuffed animal. The one named Hercules. At least he knew where that part of Mr. Benny Hercules's name came from.

"Thanks, George."

"Mr. Philip and his wife will remain here until they are given leave to come to the hospital."

"I'll text him," Jonathan promised. And ask him to stay away. Hopefully, she wouldn't be held for long.

News crews surely caught them in the sheriff's vehicle leaving Josh's house. There had been a few crews along the road as the ambulance and squad car flew past. They wouldn't have *known*, but surely they guessed.

He hung up with George and texted his brother. Philip said he'd talked to their parents already. Jonathan was grateful to not have to deal with them himself right now.

There would be enough time later.

In just a few hours, Jonathan sat next to Lorelai's hospital bed where his wife was curled up with their daughter. She'd begged her mother not to leave her alone. And so Jonathan had lifted the even-tinier-than-usual little girl into his arms while Kenzie situated herself on the bed, and then he laid her down on Kenzie's lap.

They were snuggled together and sound asleep despite the midday sun peeking around the not-quite-room-darkening curtains.

A soft knock sounded a second before the door opened. Gwendolyn and Adam tiptoed in. They were on the short list of people cleared to visit. The two news crews had tried to get in, but he told them he'd provide them with a few pictures. Otherwise, only family members were allowed. Both sets of grandparents had already been and gone. Philip and Dawn still waited.

"How are all of you doing?" Gwendolyn asked in a stage whisper.

Jonathan hid a yawn behind his hand. "Exhausted. Ready to get home and get the media behind us."

"They'll want interviews about your brother."

"I know." He hesitated then went on. "Have you thought any more about what we talked about?"

Gwendolyn nodded. "I have. Adam and I talked it over. After the last couple of days, we're pretty sure we're comfortable with it, but aren't quite ready to make a decision." She rested a hand protectively over her stomach. "Does Philip know you talked to us about him and Dawn adopting the baby?"

"I don't think so. I'm not even sure they know you're pregnant."

Adam slid his arm around Gwendolyn's waist. "I think we both just want to make sure he's really stable, that's all."

"That's completely understandable." Jonathan didn't bother to hide another yawn.

"We'll head out." Gwendolyn handed him a gift bag. "Let Lorelai know that's from us when she wakes up?"

"Of course." He stood and gave both his cousin and her fiancé a hug before they left.

After texting a bit with his brother, Jonathan leaned his head back and dozed off.

It was nearly dark the next evening when he pulled past crowds of television reporters and through the gate leading to their home.

He parked behind the house, just to make sure no cameras could see them through the trees. Lorelai came willingly to his arms, with hers locked tight around his neck.

Inside, he set her on the couch while Kenzie dropped her things onto the chair.

"Thank you, Daddy." Lorelai clung to both her stuffed dog and the stuffed kitten Gwendolyn and Adam had brought her.

Philip and Dawn walked in before Jonathan could reply. Lorelai didn't offer her uncle a hug, or anything but a small smile. Kenzie, on the other hand, hugged both of them tight.

One small part of Jonathan wanted to be jealous, but the rest of him quickly squashed that thought. She was as grateful as he was they'd found Lorelai when they did.

"She was on her way home," Kenzie told them as they settled into seats around the room. Lorelai chose Jonathan's lap. "She found the boat dock and knew the road from there would take her home. I'm glad you were there to find her. That's a long walk anyway, even without being lost for a day and a half first."

Philip nodded as Jonathan tugged his little girl closer. "She was barely trudging along when we found her, but she put one foot in front of the other over and over again as we ran her way."

It didn't surprise him. His girl was tough as nails, just like her mama, and he told them so.

"Daddy?" Lorelai didn't look up at him.

"What is it, punkin?" He never thought he'd use that nickname until a few weeks earlier.

"I'm tired. Can I sleep with you and Mama tonight?"

And that was his cue. Jonathan stood up with her in his arms. Another round of hugs later, and he followed a weary Kenzie up the stairs. Kenzie gave Lorelai a quick shower before settling her with Jonathan on the chair. She was nearly asleep when Kenzie finished her shower, and Jonathan laid her down on the bed.

Mr. Benny Hercules curled up next to Lorelai, licking her cheek a couple of times before settling his head down. Kenzie lay on her side, tucking her daughter close while Jonathan hurried through a shower of his own.

He had to use his phone to light the way as he climbed into his own side of the bed. Kenzie had told him she'd be awake when he got there, but she hadn't been able to keep that promise. He reached out and brushed her damp hair back off her forehead.

"I have something to tell you," Kenzie murmured, though she couldn't be very awake.

"What's that?" Jonathan reached over and linked his fingers with hers without moving her hand from around their daughter.

"My doctor was prosecuted for unnecessary procedures and a bunch of other stuff." She shifted, but her eyes didn't open.

"What's that mean?"

"It means I'm pregnant. I wanted to tell you it was possible for a while, but every time I tried, something got in the way." Her voice trailed off as she fell asleep.

Jonathan tried to absorb the news. They would need to have a long talk in the morning. After a gentle kiss to Lorelai's forehead, he got comfortable enough he'd be able to go to sleep. He'd never imagined his bed quite this full - or his heart.

Mr. Benny Hercules rolled so his back tucked next to Lorelai, and his feet brushed Jonathan's chest. To think, finding that little dog had led to finding his family in the pet aisles of Walmart.

In discovering that scared bit of fur, he'd also discovered his family.

He'd done more than that.

Jonathan William Langley-Cranston IV, with all of his wealth and privilege, had finally found the desires of his heart, of his soul.

He'd discovered home.

.

Dear Reader,

Thank you for joining Jonathan, Kenzie, and Lorelai in *Discovering Home*! I appreciate you and hope you enjoyed it! This is the first book in the Serenity Landing Second Chances series! Next up is Christopher, Duke Alexander of Ravenzario's twin brother. After that comes Crown Prince Richard of Mevendia! YAY! I can't wait to get to those stories!

(And yes, I know. The adoption happened a bit fast. It's theoretically possible to do so that quickly in the State of Missouri, but it usually takes longer. Part of it is getting a lawyer to be on the ball when it comes to scheduling with the court, and I figured Jonathan's lawyers jumped when he asked them to. I'm also counting on a small county court having a less busy docket than a bigger one... ;) So I went with it :D.)

In just a few pages, you'll find the first chapter of *Glimpsing Hope*! Check it out! It's available now!

In just a few more pages, you'll find chapter 1 of *Grace to Save*, the first book in the Serenity Landing Tuesdays of Grace series! It's the story of Travis Harders and his daughter, Cassie. Travis is the theater teacher at Serenity Landing High School and both have shown up from time to time in other books (including Cassie in this one). It's a story that's very near and dear to my heart, to the core of who I am.

It's a story of prodigals, and redemption, and mercy, and oh-so-much grace.

You can find it available now on Amazon.

I see a meme floating around Facebook from time to time that tells readers what they can do to help their favorite authors. Buying their next book or giving a copy away is kind of a no-brainer, but the biggest thing you can do is write a review. If you enjoyed *Discovering Home* would you consider doing just that?

I would LOVE to hear from you! My email address is books@candidpublications.com. To stay up-to-date on releases, you can sign up for my newsletter - www.carolmoncado.com/newsletter (there's fun stuff - like a super special novella that will be coming FREE before the beginning of my next royalty series next year!! You'll also get notices of sales, including special preorder pricing! And I won't spam!) or there's always "What's in the Works" or "What I'm Working On Now" on my website :). You can find my website and blog at www.carolmoncado.com. I blog about once a month at www.InspyRomance.com. And, of course, there's Facebook and my Facebook profile, Author Carol Moncado. If you recently liked my Facebook *page* (Carol Moncado Books)...I hope you'll "follow" the profile as well. Facebook recently changed the rules again which means very few people (often 1-5% of "likes") will see anything I post there. Following the profile will show you my book updates, updates about books from authors I love, funny cat (or dog or dinosaur!) memes, inspirational quotes, and all sorts of fun stuff!! I hope to see you there soon!

Thanks again!

Acknowledgments

They say writing is a solitary endeavor and it absolutely can be. Sitting in front of the computer for hours on end, talking to imaginary people.

And having them talk back ;).

But the reality is no one walks alone. Since I began this writing journey nearly six years ago, I can't begin to name all of those who've helped me along the way. My husband, Matt, who has always, *always* believed in me. All of the rest of my family and in-loves who never once looked at me like I was nuts for wanting to be a writer. Jan Christiansen (my "other mother") has always believed in me and Stacy Christiansen Spangler who has been my dearest friend for longer than I can remember.

Ginger Solomon, author of *One Choice*, has been invaluable with her proofreading services.

Then there's my writer friends. My NovelSista, Jessica Keller Koschnitzky, sister of my heart. She is part of my BritCrit gals. Joanna Politano (who has talked me down off more virtual ledges than anyone), Jen Cvelvar (the best case of misidentification *ever*, not to mention best conference roomie), Kristy Cambron (who is more beautiful inside and out than any one person should be allowed to be), and Stacey Zink (who never, ever fails to have a fabulous encouraging word) are BritCritters, too. We do a lot more living than we do critting, and I wouldn't have it any other way. All five of them are beyond gifted as writers, and I thank God they're in my life. There's my MozArks ACFW peeps who laugh with me, critique, and encourage to no end. Then there's the InspyRomance crew, the CIA, my Spicy peeps (you know who you are!), and all of the others who've helped me along on this journey.

And Tamela Hancock Murray - my agent extraordinaire, who despite the lack of "anything in it for her" has supported me in this crazy indie journey.

I've said it before, but I could go on for days about beloved mentors like Janice Thompson who has poured her time and energy into this newbie, going above and beyond for me. People like one of my spiciest friends, Pepper Basham, who inspires me daily, or Julie Lessman, who has prayed me to this point. All of these and so many more are not only mentors, but *friends* - I am beyond blessed! Cheryl Wyatt, who has believed in me more than I could have imagined.

I said I could go on for days, and I could keep going. On and on. I know I've forgotten many people and I hate that. But you, dear reader, would quickly get bored.

So THANK YOU to all of those who have helped me along the way. I couldn't have done this without you and you have my eternal gratitude. To the HUNDREDS of you (I'm gobsmacked!) who pre-ordered and encouraged me without knowing it as that little number continued to climb, you have my eternal gratitude. I hope you stick around for the next one!

And, of course, last but never, *ever*, least, to Jesus Christ, without whom none of this would be possible - or worth it.

Glimpsing Hope

Serenity Landing Second Chances 2

Available Now

May 2017

"I 'll pay for them to fly commercial." Christopher Bayfield crossed his arms over his chest and stared down the duke. He could do that because the duke was also his twin brother. No one else would understand why he wanted to avoid this flight.

Alexander tugged on the bottom of his tuxedo jacket and frowned into the mirror. "Someday I'll figure out how to make this look right with the sash on the first try."

"It's your own fault for marrying a queen, Ander, but don't think you're getting out of this. I'll pay for them to fly back, first class."

Alexander turned away from the mirror to face Christopher. "Christiana, your pregnant sister-in-law, asked you to fly them back on the family plane. You're really going to turn her down?"

"If you won't let me pay for them to go back first class, I'll rent a plane for them."

"You get to tell the queen you don't want to do the one thing she asked you to do for the woman who saved her life, and the life of your niece or nephew."

Christopher hated it when his brother was right. "Then they can take the plane home, and I'll rent one of my own. Or buy my own first class ticket."

"Don't be ridiculous, Topher." Alexander limped to the door of Christopher's room, his leg still recovering from the recent shoot out with the man who tried to kill his wife. Alexander had come to Christopher's room to guilt trip him into doing this. Help fixing his tie was just an excuse. "Just ride home in the plane with them. Sit at the table and work the whole time or take the couch and sleep. I'm not saying you have to become busom buddies with the gal, just make sure she and her son don't die in a horrid plane crash on the way back. Once you land, put them in the car Jonathan will provide and go on your merry way."

Before his brother could open the door, someone knocked. Alexander opened it, and in walked the queen.

Christopher was tempted to bow, but knew that was just his inner snark. It wasn't Christiana's fault her uncle was nuts, had set up Julia to make it look like she was having an affair with Alexander, and then tried to kill Christiana when it all went wrong. The uncle had already killed Christiana's family and beloved nanny many years earlier. Christiana had only survived because she was sick and hadn't been in the car.

"Is there something wrong, Christopher?" The queen came to stand in front of him. "You look quite perturbed."

He quirked a brow at her. "You don't know me that well."

"No, but I know what your identical twin looks like when he's perturbed." The smile on her face told Christopher all he really needed to know. He would do whatever she asked. She made his brother so incredibly happy and was giving Alexander the family he'd longed for.

The family Christopher doubted he'd ever have. Not with his history.

He could do the doting uncle thing, though. Prince Harry pulled it off. Christopher wasn't a prince, but surely he could do the same. Bring cool presents. Take them to polo matches. Except he'd never played polo in his life.

"Is there a problem with the flight?"

His sister-in-law was intuitive, too. Or Alexander had warned her this might be an issue. "No. No problem."

Alexander mouthed a thank you.

"It is too bad you will not be able to stay for the ball." Christiana glanced at her husband. "You would look almost as dashing as Alexander. There will be plenty of eligible young women for you to dance with."

Christopher reached for her hand and bowed low over it, kissing the back. "There's only one woman I would want to dance with, Your Majesty, but I fear my brother will keep her all to himself." He knew how to be gallant when he wanted to be.

His brother stepped closer until Christopher moved back. "I'm pretty sure she's going to spend most of the evening sitting out. She's still not back to normal yet, and neither am I."

"Julia and Alex are ready to go home when you are," she told him. "But it is time for us to leave. Tony is waiting." The head of security was attending the ball as a guest this time.

Christopher watched as they walked away. Alexander rested his hand on his wife's lower back. Christiana leaned toward him, just a bit. They had been through so much to get to this point.

He envied them.

Not enough to get entangled again.

But he did envy his brother the happiness anyone could see.

Just a glimpse of the hope he could, even should, have had for himself.

It would never be more than a glimpse.

With a sigh, he grabbed his bag and headed down the hall. The sooner they left, the sooner this whole thing would be over.

Julia Quisenberry had very little patience left.

"Mom, are we really flying home in our own plane?" Alex asked for the thousandth time.

"Not quite." The car had nearly arrived at the airport. "Mr. Bayfield is letting us fly home with him when he goes back to Serenity Landing."

"Duke Alexander is flying to Serenity Landing?"

"No, sweetheart. His brother, Christopher, is flying to Serenity Landing. The queen asked him to fly us back with him." She'd explained it to him more than once.

"Oh. Yeah." He would have said something else, but the car glided to a stop next to a building on the airport property.

A man waited there to open the door. "This way please."

The small room held only one other person.

Christopher Bayfield.

He was doing an excellent job of ignoring them. Just like she'd figured.

After a few minutes talking with an official of some sort, Julia and Alex found seats across the room from Christopher. She kept her seven-year-old son occupied with a new coloring book and crayons. The queen had given them a travel gift basket, complete with iPads for both of them. Alex's was preloaded with games and apps he'd enjoy. She'd break it out mid-flight when he grew antsy.

Ten minutes later, a woman in a stewardess uniform came into the room and spoke with Christopher for a moment. She left, and he began to pack up his things. "We take off in fifteen minutes. You'll need to be on board in five."

He didn't actually look at them as he spoke. If he said five more words to her before the plane landed, Julia would be shocked. She didn't know why exactly he seemed to despise her so much. All of the things she supposedly did were fabricated. He knew that. Everyone knew that. Except for running into him and Alexander at the hospital in Serenity Landing, where someone took the picture that started the whole mess, none of this was her fault.

"Pack up your things," she told Alex quietly.

Her son stared at Christopher as he slung the messenger bag over his shoulder and walked out of the building. Alex didn't say anything, though, and in a minute, they followed in Christopher's footsteps.

With Alex's hand tucked securely in her own, they crossed a few feet of tarmac to the steps of the only plane in the vicinity. She urged him in front of her, knowing his eyes would be as wide as hers. Once on board, the interior was as nice as she would have expected based on the television shows and movies where they had planes like this.

It still took all of her self-control not to gawk.

"Over here, ma'am." The stewardess stood next to a couch with seat belts protruding from the crack.

Julia stowed her carry-on bags in the cabinet next to the couch and then helped Alex tighten the seat belt. The stewardess brought them each a bottle of water and asked them to remain seated with their seat belts on until the captain said they could remove off.

Alex looked through a guest packet of information about this particular kind of plane. Julia stared at the back of Christopher's head.

He sat at a table with room for four. His paperwork was already spread out much as it had been in the waiting room. The stewardess spoke quietly to him once again. He nodded, and she took a seat near the door to the cockpit. Once she was buckled in, the plane began to taxi slowly toward the runway.

Alex didn't say it, but she knew he was disappointed he couldn't see better. The back of the couch was too high for him to see much out the window behind them. The window across the plane was too far away to gawk like she wished he could.

After sitting still for a couple of minutes, the engine revved, and g-forces pressed them slightly toward the back of the plane. It wasn't as bad as she would have expected it to be since they sat sideways.

Christopher barely seemed to notice. His pen scratched on the paper in front of him, writing something long-hand.

It didn't take but a few seconds for the wheels to leave the runway as they soared into the air.

The first two hours of the flight were uneventful. Alex dozed as he lay on the couch. Julia read a book on her new iPad. The queen had thoughtfully loaded it with books she thought Julia would enjoy. Or rather, she'd probably had an employee do it.

"Mama?"

Julia set the iPad down, a frown already in place. Alex rarely called her that. "What is it, sweetie?"

"My tummy doesn't feel good."

Great. She looked around to see the stewardess in her seat reading a book. "Ma'am?"

The woman looked up, setting her book to the side. "How can I help you?" By the time she finished the question, she was at their side.

"Do you have a trash bag?" Julia didn't trust Alex's stomach when he said it didn't feel good.

"Of course." In less than a minute, there was a bag in a small can for Alex to use if he felt the need. "Now, how about some crackers or Sprite?"

Julia shook her head. "Not just yet. I'm afraid it'll all come back up."

The stewardess looked concerned. "Has he been sick?"

"No, but it always seems like there's a bug going around, doesn't it?"

After nodding her agreement, the woman went back to her seat.

Christopher glanced at them, at the same moment Julia happened to look at him. Their eyes locked, but all she could see in them was his disapproval. Of her. Of her son. Of her entire life.

Probably of her baby, too.

With one hand protectively covering her abdomen, Julia encouraged Alex to lean against her and brushed his hair back with the fingertips of her other hand.

Ten minutes later, it happened.

***

Christopher didn't look, but dug frantically through his bag searching for his earbuds before he needed the trash bag the stewardess had already slipped to him.

Just in case.

Because she knew he was a sympathetic puker.

He could handle just about anything, but not that. It was one of many reasons he was okay with never having kids, even if his friends told him it was different when the kid puking belonged to you. He didn't buy it.

With his earbuds firmly in place, the next order of business had to be music. Rather than the rock and roll he might choose another time, he went with some old school Michael W. Smith for now. With Go West Young Man filling his ears, he was able to concentrate on the paperwork before him.

Alexander had been running their family's wedding facility in Ravenzario for years. Christopher had taken over some of it since Ander married the queen. They were in the throes of planning a wedding that would never happen, for Princess Yvette of Mevendia and the deceased Prince Nicklaus of Ravenzario. It needed to be perfect, even if the planning was futile. Ander would help some when he wasn't busy doing all of his Duke-ish stuff, but most of it would fall on Topher. He'd be back every two weeks for the next six weeks and then spend the last couple weeks there.

He didn't know what the backup plan could possibly be. Christiana's younger brother had been killed in the same car accident that took her parents' lives as well as the life of her nanny. But Nicklaus had been betrothed to Princess Yvette of Mevendia since they were small children and the wedding had to be planned regardless of the prince's death.

Ander was keeping a big secret from him about it, though. Topher couldn't figure out what it was, but eventually it would come out.

Meanwhile, Topher finished writing out some contingency plans for the media. His secretary would type it up for him later. He hated typing, preferring pen on paper for this kind of thing. Maybe he should call Mady and see if he could get some acting work again. Then he wouldn't be doing this kind of work anyway.

After another hour of work on several different projects, he debated changing seats to one of the captain's chairs where he could stretch out better. He looked up and motioned to Serena.

She put her book down and walked over.

"How's the kid?" he asked quietly.

Serena glanced toward the couch. "Sleeping. He threw up three times, but it seems to have settled down for now."

"Good."

"How are you?"

"Thank you for the warning. I appreciate it."

She smirked at him. "I know how you react."

Topher grimaced. She'd cleaned up after him more than once. "Thanks. I'm going to move to the other chairs. Would you stow my bag for me?"

Serena took it from him and went to the back to store it in a closet. Topher moved to a seat on the same side of the plane as the couch, but sort of separated by a shelving unit that also held refreshments. He put his seatbelt on more out of habit than anything and stretched his legs out before deciding to grab a pillow and blanket from the cabinet next to him.

A nice long nap and this flight would be nearly over.

Instead of restful sleep, his dreams were filled with Julia and her son. He couldn't remember the dreams when he woke up, but he knew they hadn't been pleasant. Was there some sort of fight between them? But why would there be? Once they climbed in the car Jonathan would send, he'd never see them again.

"Mister?"

Topher looked up to see the kid standing there. "Can I help you?"

"My mom's asleep, but I need to go to the bathroom. Where is it?"

Shouldn't he be asking Serena? Topher looked to her seat, but she wasn't in it. A glance at his watch told him she was likely getting something to eat. It was about that time for her.

"It's in the back. It's the only door with a little slot that tells you if someone's in there or not."

The kid stared at him for a minute then turned away.

Serena walked by a second later. "You could have been nicer to him. He didn't ask to be here."

"And I didn't ask for them to be here." But he never would have told Ander and Christiana no, even if he had tried to convince them of alternatives. He'd known they wouldn't agree, but had to try.

He wouldn't go back to sleep. Instead, he pulled out a paperback and started to read. It was a political thriller by a local guy his dad recommended. Jeremiah something. Topher didn't bother to look at the front cover to remember the last name.

About the time he flipped to the last page, the plane started to descend. He glanced outside and saw lights of a small town. Not Springfield, not yet.

He used the plane's Wi-Fi to send a message to Jonathan to make sure the car would be there. Ander had arranged for Julia and her son to have security for a few weeks until they were sure the whole mess had blown over. Topher had thought about getting some for his property, though probably not for himself. He still hadn't gotten used to word being out about his past life, and his stint as one of America's twin teen heartthrobs on 2 Cool 4 School. Sometimes he dreamed about going back to acting. Maybe someday.

Twenty minutes later, the wheels thumped down, and Topher breathed a sigh of relief. It was over.

He stayed in his seat until Julia and Alex were off the plane and on their way. His bags had already been loaded into his SUV sitting nearby.

On the drive home, he used an earbud and microphone to dictate an email to his assistant outlining what he needed her to do the next day.

With his car parked in front of the house, Topher headed inside and collapsed, still fully clothed, onto his bed. It had been a long few weeks, and he needed sleep.

Lots of sleep.

If only the pretty woman with the dirty blonde hair and sick son would stay out of his dreams, it would all be okay.

Christopher Bayfield enjoys his single life. Unencumbered by relationships, he works and travels whenever he wants. He can even drop everything to do something he's been dreaming of for a while – return to acting in a Happily Ever After TV Network movie. But before he can leave a knock on the door changes his life.

Julia Quisenberry never planned to have one child out of wedlock, much less be pregnant with number two, but this was what her life had become. Unemployed and barely making ends meet with her knitting patterns and teaching, she's almost desperate enough to take a handout from her best friend.

A phone call from Christopher changes Julia's plans. He offers her a job and a lifeline, in more ways than one. So when the paparazzi threaten all he holds dear, she'll do anything to help him out – even marry him. Can they overcome the obstacles in their path to find a glimpse of hope for their own happily ever after?

Author's note: The first chapter of Glimpsing Hope *picks up at the end of* Winning the Queen's Heart *and before the events of* Protecting the Prince. *The second chapter begins in the universe's "present day" – after the events of* Discovering Home.

Previews may not be in their final form and are subject to change.

Grace to Save
Serenity Landing Tuesdays of Grace

September 11, 2001

A ringing jolted Travis Harders from a deep sleep. He cursed as the phone knocked to the floor with a clatter. "This better be good," he snapped when he got the handset in place.

A glance at the clock nearly made him groan.

4:07.

"You'll be hearing from the police soon."

He rubbed the sleep out of his eyes with the heel of one hand and tried to process the statement. The words didn't really register as the guy, whoever he was, kept talking until Travis interrupted. "What? Who is this?"

"Mark's dad." Right. Travis's best friend. "You remember us? The ones who treated you like family? Let you live with us?"

Travis's stomach sank. Mark's family had practically adopted him when he moved from southwest Missouri to the Big Apple. They had filled the gap in his life left by parents who disapproved of Travis's choice to move to New York. Mark's parents let him spend holidays and birthdays with them, with Travis making only the obligatory phone calls back home.

But none of that explained why Mark's dad would be calling the police.

"Who is it?" a sleepy Jennifer asked.

Travis covered the mouthpiece and whispered to his girlfriend, "No one." His feet hit the cool floor, and he headed for the other room. At least he had a place to escape to. Being an out-of-work-actor-turned-barista didn't pay much, but he'd lucked into a fabulous apartment. Closing the French door behind him, he tried to focus on the voice yelling from the other end of the line.

But he only caught "my daughter" and "spring break" and "drugged."

If possible, Travis's stomach clenched further as that night flooded back to him. Memories of bringing her back to this very apartment when she was in no condition to go home without risking the wrath of her parents. But after what happened between them...it was only right for him to be on the receiving end of her dad's anger. "I don't know what she told you sir, but..."

"I know all I need to know," he bellowed.

Even though he was in the other room, Travis lowered the volume on the handset. "I take full responsibility for..."

"You're right, you do!" He let loose a string of obscenities. "You'll spend years in prison! Drugging a girl! Sleeping with her!"

"What?" His whole world spun. Travis regretted every minute of that night after they got back to the apartment, but he hadn't drugged her. He didn't even know where to get those kinds of drugs. They weren't in love, never had been, but to place the blame solely on him? The next morning, they'd talked about it enough to know she hadn't blamed him.

What changed? Feeling sucker punched, Travis hung up on

the man. What he said didn't matter. Travis would find out when he was on trial for something he didn't do. On autopilot, he dressed for his five a.m. shift. Coffees of the World wasn't the best job, but it had flexible hours and had led to finding this sublet. There was no shortage of interesting characters to populate his imagination. Like the skinny brunette with the shoulder length bob who worked for Morgan Stanley and always ordered a short nonfat mocha, decaf, no foam, no sugar, no whip. She could be the heroine in one of his screenplays even if he never knew her name.

He kissed Jennifer's hair and told her he'd call after work. Five flights of stairs later, the sounds of the city waking up greeted him as he walked toward the train that would take him to the Trade Center. Standing at the top of the subway steps, he changed his mind. Travis headed for his car parked a couple streets over and called in.

Two hours later, he stopped in McLean for gas about seven thirty, filling up the tank of his Toyota Corolla hatchback. Three hours after that, he could still drive for a while longer before he'd need to stop again. He contemplated leaving the state, but decided not to, instead turning northward before leaving Allegany County.

He'd gone through more emotions than he knew he had, none of them good. Anger. Fear. Frustration. Blame. Worry. Intimidation. In western New York, things were more peaceful than they ever were in downtown Manhattan, but his insides were in utter turmoil at the thought of an arrest and trial.

His favorite heavy metal CD blared from the speakers. During the lull between songs, Travis could hear his cell phone vibrating on the passenger seat where he'd tossed it. After an hour and a half of the stupid thing ringing nearly nonstop, he finally snatched it up.

"What?" Travis growled.

"Are you okay?" Though he only talked to her twice a year, there was no mistaking his mother's voice.

Or the panic in it.

The tremor set him on edge. "Yeah. Why?"

"Thank you, Jesus," she whispered, though Travis couldn't figure out what she was thanking Him for. "Where are you? You got out okay? Were you working? There was no answer at your apartment."

Why was Mom calling just to ask if he was okay? Why was she frantic? "I'm in western New York State. Out for a drive. Get out of where?" Could Mark's dad have called already?

"You don't know?" Frenzy changed to disbelief.

"Know what?" Travis held the phone against his shoulder as he downshifted into a turn.

He could hear the tears over the static-filled line. "Two planes, Trav. They hit the Towers. Both of the buildings are on fire."

His heart thudded to a stop. "What?" Hadn't a bomber hit the Empire State Building in WWII? But two planes? On a brilliantly clear day? No weather in sight. "How bad is it?" he croaked.

"They're saying it's a terror attack. The Pentagon is on fire. There's another plane out there somewhere. Big jets, Travis. I saw the second one hit. The explosion. Papers flying everywhere. The people..." Her voice broke. "You really weren't there?" she confirmed.

"No, Mom. I'm not anywhere near there." But he needed to find a place to stop. A television. He had to see for himself. Tens of thousands of people would be dead and dying. Did he know any of them?

"There are people jumping, falling, out of the upper stories. I can't imagine." He could almost see her pacing around the kitchen alternately running her hands through her hair and wringing them together. "They're jumping from a hundred stories up. What could be so bad to make that the better option?" Her voice caught. "I don't know how I can watch this, Trav, but I can't turn away. All I can do is pray."

Pray. Right. A face flashed before Travis. The uptight former-football-player-turned-businessman from the 102nd floor of the North Tower with his caramel macchiato and corny joke of the day. Was he one of those jumping?

She gasped then whispered. "Dear God, no. No!" Her scream made him move the phone even as his stomach sank.

He pulled into a café parking lot near Danville. "What?"

"The tower. It's gone. Just gone. The south one, I think." Her voice trailed off in prayer.

The shock he'd felt after the phone call from Mark's dad paled compared to what he felt now. "Mom, I gotta go." Jen. His friends. His coworkers. He needed to make calls of his own. Find out if they were okay. And Mark. His best friend had been a firefighter for a year. He'd be down there. Inside one of the Towers. Travis hadn't talked to him since that night, the March before, but part of him, the part that still believed there was a God in heaven, whispered a prayer that Mark was somewhere safe as faces of customers and friends flashed through Travis's mind.

The blonde. The cute, petite one who ordered a crunchy, cinnamon pastry and half caf, double tall, easy hazelnut, non-fat, no foam with whip extra hot latte on Tuesdays. She flirted shamelessly, though he knew she was recently and happily engaged to some guy in Tower Seven. Her family lived near his in Serenity Landing, Missouri, and she worked at the Marriot World Trade Center in the shadow of the Towers. Could it have survived the collapse? Was Joanna now buried underneath the rubble?

"Be safe, Travis. Do you have somewhere you can go? They're

evacuating Manhattan."

"I'll be okay." He hesitated. "I love you, Mom. You, Dad, Jay. I love all of you. I'll call when I can, but I have to try to find out about my friends, about my girlfriend. I'll talk to you soon."

His mom's "I love you," came through the line as he clicked his phone off.

He started his first call as he walked into the café. Call after call failed as he stood with others, watching the screen in horror as the second tower crashed down. His problems. Mark's dad. Mark's sister. All of it fled as the enormity of what was happening sunk in.

The whole world had changed.

December 18, 2001

"It's a girl."

Abi Connealy collapsed back onto the bed, tears streaming down her cheeks as a newborn squawk filled the delivery room.

A girl.

A million thoughts flew through her mind, few of them happy, as a nurse laid the baby on her chest. So small. So scrunched up and red. Dark hair. Abi couldn't see her eyes as she wrapped her arms around the tiny bundle. "Hi, baby," she whispered. "I'm so glad you're here."

"How are you?"

Abi looked up at Brenda Wardman. Her brother's girlfriend had been a rock the last few months. She didn't need to clarify, because Abi knew what she meant. "I don't know." The voice mail she'd left her parents on the way to the hospital remained unanswered unless Brenda knew something she didn't.

Her fingers brushed over the cheek of the tiny girl. "She's

perfect, Bren." Another tear fell, this one landing on her new daughter's face as Abi closed her eyes.

The nurse took the baby to the warmer and did whatever it was nurses did, but Abi didn't see any of it. Her eyes remained closed, and she clasped Brenda's hand as more hot tears streaked into her ears. Just under twenty-four hours of labor meant she didn't have the energy to wipe them away. She knew she didn't have the will to do so even if she could have.

"Do you know what you're going to do?"

Abi wanted to yell at her friend for bringing up the most difficult decision of her life just moments after the birth of her daughter. But since Abi hadn't made up her mind beforehand, Brenda needed to know to help make the arrangements.

Except Abi didn't know.

Not for sure. She knew what the smart decision was, though her head and her heart didn't agree. But she had to put her baby first. "I'll have them call."

"It's going to be fine," Brenda tried to reassure her, but Abi heard the doubt in her friend's voice.

Right.

Fine.

Once the social worker arrived, she'd never be fine again.

Somehow, Abi managed to doze for several hours during the afternoon, but after listening to the message from her parents, the one that told her all she needed to know without really saying anything, her eyes refused to close. Instead, she stared at the bracelet encircling her wrist, rotating it around time and time again.

A knock sounded half a second before the door pushed open. "Hi, there, Abi. Someone's looking for her mama." The nurse compared the baby's bracelet to Abi's before lifting the blanketed bundle out of the clear bassinet. "The card says you're giving her formula?"

There was no judgment in the woman's voice, but Abi felt her own condemnation eating away at her. All she could do was nod.

After a few minutes of helping them get situated, the nurse started to leave, but stopped before walking out the door. "The emotions are normal, honey. They get everyone at one point or another."

Abi nodded but didn't take her eyes off the little cheeks sucking in and out. She memorized the sounds, the smells, the essence of the tiny bundle in her arms. Or tried to. Even as she did, she knew it would never work. In the morning, a social worker would come and Abi would sign the papers put in front of her.

And she'd never see her daughter again.

But when the social worker sat in the chair by the window, asking the questions, one tripped Abi up.

"Do you know who her father is?"

The night was burned in Abi's memory banks. Part of it anyway. When she hesitated too long, the worker prompted her again. Abi nodded. "Yes. I know who the father is."

"Then we'll need his signature, too."

"He doesn't know," she whispered. "I haven't talked to him since. I was going to, but then 9/11..." Her voice trailed off.

"Was he in the Towers?" the social worker asked as gently as she could.

Abi shook her head. "I don't he was. I mean, I know he wasn't one of the three thousand, but I don't know if he was there or not." She'd called his apartment from a pay phone a few weeks later. When he answered, she hung up.

"If you know who he is, we have to have him sign away his parental rights, sweetie."

Something she hadn't considered when she made this plan.

The nurse walked in, once again pushing the bassinet. Her face fell when she saw the social worker. "I'm sorry. I didn't realize you were..."

With a swipe of the overused Kleenex, Abi wiped her face. "I wasn't sure, but now I can't anyway."

The social worker left a couple of fliers and walked out with a sympathetic smile. The nurse awkwardly helped Abi get situated to feed her daughter one more time.

"Do you have a name you like?" The woman sat on the edge of the bed holding Abi's empty water bottle.

"Cassandra."

"That's beautiful."

"It was my grandmother's name. She died this past summer." The grandmother who would have adored meeting her great-granddaughter, who would have taken Abi and the baby in when she needed somewhere to turn. Had given Abi hope she'd do just that before succumbing to a sudden, massive stroke.

Abi didn't have anyone else like that in her life. Brenda would if she could, but there was no way. Abi had no other family. No one else in her life who would support her no matter what.

Darkness descended, but Abi refused to send little Cassie back to the nursery. She didn't know what she planned to do about adoption, but she wouldn't give up another minute with her baby.

Yet another round of tears leaked down her face as Abi cuddled the tiny bundle against her chest. With all but one light turned out, the desperate whisper ripped from her throat. "God? Are you there?" She'd never prayed before, but this seemed like the time to start if there ever was one. "I don't know what to do."

Baby Cassandra yawned and blinked her eyes open, staring up at her mother. The light caught them just right and struck Abi with the bright blue.

Then it hit her.

The one place she could take her daughter where she'd be safe. And loved.

December 23, 2001

Two days before Christmas, Abi sat in a coffee shop on Long Island and waited. Calling him had taken every ounce of courage she had. Leaving the voicemail took more.

Sitting there, Abi didn't know if she could go through with it. The stroller with her little girl sat to her right. On the other side of it, Brenda sat with her back to the door. Diners nearby sipped on gourmet coffee, but Abi focused on the stationary in front of her. She arrived early so she could write the note, but the paper remained nearly blank.

When she'd arrived at her parents' Long Island home after leaving the hospital, a note reiterated her father's threat. Since then, Abi had planned what to say, but realized she'd never make it through even the shortest speech. She'd planned the words to write, but now the time had come to put pen to paper, and she only managed his name. A glance at her watch told her she didn't have much time. If she didn't write it now, she'd have to make the speech. No way could she do that.

She picked up the Mont Blanc knock-off she'd received for graduation from her grandmother and scribbled a few lines. Her heart squeezed as she reread the note. She couldn't be a student and a mom. But this? Abi had her suitcase packed. She wouldn't return to her parents' home but would crash at Brenda's for a few days while her friend went out of town. Brenda knew most of what happened, but not everything. Abi's fingers furrowed through her hair, and she turned to stare out the window. There he stood. His six-foot frame seemed shorter with his shoulders slumped and hands shoved deep in the pockets of his coat. He looked at his watch and trudged across the street.

The bell over the door jangled. Abi crossed through the unfinished sentence, scribbled a last sentiment and her name, and shoved the note in her purse as he sat down across from her.

"Hi." At the sound of his voice, the knots in her gut tightened.

Abi looked up, knowing he'd see the remnants of her tears. She twisted the napkin in her hands and tried not the think about the weight she'd gained. And if he'd notice.

"Thanks for coming. I wanted to try to explain, but..." Abi shrugged. "After 9/11, after Mark..." The thoughts of her brother nearly overwhelmed her already overwrought emotions. "Daddy isn't going to pursue anything. I tried to tell him you weren't guilty, but he didn't believe me at first. He found your name in my journal on 9/11-before it was '9/11.' I'd left it lying out by accident." This time the shrug was a mere halfhearted lift of one shoulder.

"Mark?" he interrupted. "I read the list of firefighters a bunch of times to make sure he wasn't there."

"He wasn't on the lists. He was killed at a fire on 9/11. Not at the Trade Center. Another fire where they didn't have enough manpower because of everything else. They think he died right around the time the first tower fell."

Were those tears in his eyes? He and Mark hadn't spoken in months. "I'm so sorry."

Cassandra let out a cry. The disguised Brenda made a shushing sound, but Abi didn't look. She couldn't. It was too much. She had to get out. "Can you excuse me for a minute?"

She didn't wait for a reply but motioned toward the back, leaving before he had a chance to stop her. Brenda went out the front door. Abi dug the paper out and waved the barista over.

"Can you give this to that guy?"

The woman nodded. Abi fled to the other side of the street and collapsed in Brenda's arms.

Travis read the note three times before it began to sink in.

Dear Travis,

She had to have written it earlier. There hadn't been time since she excused herself.

I hate doing this to you, especially like this. I tried to handle it on my own. I thought I could, but this semester was so hard. Even more than just everything on 9/11 and Mark. I can't do it. I can't be a college student and a mom.

It took several minutes for that to really register.

A mom?

He read on, his disbelief growing with each word.

The baby in the stroller is yours. From that night. I hate that I haven't told you sooner, but I didn't know how. I couldn't tell my parents what happened, not all of it. They would blame you, and it wasn't your fault. I know this is the coward's way out, but I can't tell you to your face. Everything you need for a couple of days is in the diaper bag and the duffel on the bottom of the stroller. So is her birth certificate.

Her name is Cassandra. She's only a few days old. Please take good care of her for me. I won't be home for a while so you can't reach me. My parents left for vacation out of the country, so they wouldn't be here when she was born.

I wish things had worked out the way we planned. The way we talked about all those times. I wish

Whatever she wished, she didn't finish the thought before scribbling through it. About like their relationship had been. A wish that was never finished. He went back to the letter.

Tell Cassandra I love her.

I'm sorry.

Abi

He read it two more times, starting to come to grips with what it meant.

And then the baby began to fuss.

Taking a deep, steadying breath to fortify himself, he turned to the blanket tented over the handle of the car seat. Lifting up one corner, he saw pink. Fuzzy bunnies on the toes of a sleeper. A tiny foot kicking those bunnies in the air. He looked further and saw the bluest eyes he'd ever seen staring back at him, almost as though she knew who he was.

Her father.

Her daddy.

The one responsible for her from here on out.

And in that moment, he fell helplessly in love.

December 25, 2001

Christmas night, the little gray Toyota turned off I-44, south towards Serenity Landing, as the wailing in the backseat reached a new level.

"I'm sorry, Cassandra. We're almost there. I'll get you something to eat in a ten minutes, I promise." Jennifer kicked him out the moment he tried to explain his arrival at the apartment with a baby. Instead, he'd boxed up all his worldly belongings along with the things Abi had left for the baby and packed it in his car. They headed for the only place he knew he could get the help he needed until he had a better handle on things.

Over twelve hundred miles. Stopping every two or three hours to feed his daughter or change her diaper. Sometimes more often than that. Always taking much longer than it should. Failing to take into account how many things would be closed on Christmas Day, he ran out of the bottled water when he needed to make one more meal for his daughter. He pressed the pedal a little closer to the floor in an effort to reach Serenity Landing a little faster.

The newborn squalling had quieted a bit when Travis finally pulled to a stop in front of the house where he'd grown up. In the front window, a Christmas tree stood, multi-colored lights twinkling. In the window next to it, he could see Mom and Dad sitting at the dining room table, though he knew they wouldn't be able to see him. His brother walked in with a platter, piled high with a turkey way too big for the three of them. They'd be eating leftovers for a month.

Another squeak came from the back. "Okay, baby. We're here."

Somehow, Travis managed to get the diaper bag and the baby seat out of the car and headed toward the door, snow crunching under his boots with each step. The smell of oak burning in the fireplace both comforted him and heightened his anxiety. What if they turned him away? Then what?

Should he knock?

He hadn't been home in two and a half years. Did he just walk in?

Even with his hands full, Travis managed to press the doorbell. He took a deep breath and blew it out slowly, finishing as the door opened.

Mom stood there, her jaw hanging down for a second before her hands covered her mouth. "Travis!"

He tried to smile but failed miserably. "Hi, Mom." In the space of a heartbeat, he saw what he needed to in her eyes.

Forgiveness. Acceptance. Love. Grace. With a prayer tossed heavenward, he tried again to smile, this time successfully. "There's someone I want you to meet."

Grace to Save

Travis Harders has been a single dad since the day he learned he had a daughter with his only one-night stand. Fifteen years later, he and Cassie are getting along just fine and he's even fallen in love. The last thing he expects to find on his doorstep one Tuesday morning is Cassie's mom - the one person he thought he'd never see again - and she's asking the impossible.

Circumstances, including her firefighter brother's death on 9/11, forced Abi Connealy into a decision she's spent years regretting and her daughter grew up without her. But now, a family crisis compels her to do the one thing she swore she never would: find the daughter she'd abandoned just a few days after birth.

Shocked when Travis doesn't send her packing, Abi prays to a God she doesn't believe in that her relationship with her daughter will be restored. Travis plans to propose to his girlfriend, but their relationship hits the rocks as he and Abi both struggle with the long-dormant feelings that never had the chance to develop.

When Cassie demonstrates incredible grace toward the grandfather who refuses to acknowledge her existence, Abi begins to learn the love of a Savior - a Savior who has more than enough Grace to Save.

When she's not writing about her imaginary friends, USA Today Bestselling Author Carol Moncado prefers binge watching pretty much anything to working out. She believes peanut butter M&Ms are the perfect food and Dr. Pepper should come in an IV. When not hanging out with her hubby, four kids, and two dogs who weigh less than most hard cover books, she's probably reading in her Southwest Missouri home.

Summers find her at the local aquatic center with her four fisher kids. Fall finds her doing the band mom thing. Winters find her snuggled into a blanket in front of a fire with the dogs. Spring finds her sneezing and recovering from the rest of the year.

She used to teach American Government at a community college, but her indie career, with nearly two dozen titles released in the first 2.5 years, has allowed her to write full time. She's a founding member and former President of MozArks ACFW, blogger at InspyRomance, and is represented by Tamela Hancock Murray of the Steve Laube Agency.

CANDID Romance

Finding Mr. Write
Finally Mr. Write
Falling for Mr. Write

Montevaro Monarchy

Good Enough for a Princess
Along Came a Prince
More than a Princess

Brides of Belles Montagnes

Hand-Me-Down Princess
Winning the Queen's Heart
Protecting the Prince (Novella)
Prince from her Past

Serenity Landing Lifeguards

The Lifeguard, the New Guy, & Frozen Custard
(previously titled: The Lifeguards, the Swim Team, & Frozen Custard)
The Lifeguard, the Abandoned Heiress, & Frozen Custard
(previously in the *Whispers of Love* collection)

Other Novellas

Gifts of Love
(previously available as part of the *Snowflakes & Mistletoe*
collection)
Manuscripts & Mistletoe
Ballots, Bargains, & the Bakery
(previously available in the *Table for Two* collection)

Made in United States
Orlando, FL
14 May 2022

17852859R00219